## PRAISE FOR

# PATRICK
# SENÉCAL

## ONE MILLION COPIES SOLD!

"Unstoppably addictive."

*Quill and Quire*

"A master at unsettling our emotions and taking us very
far into the pit of madness."

*Le Soleil*

"An author that no other equals in his ability not only to
keep the readers riveted, but also to plunge them into
an unsettled state."

*L'Oeil Régional*

# SEVEN DAYS

## PATRICK SENÉCAL

TRANSLATED BY HOWARD SCOTT & PHYLLIS ARONOFF

PUBLISHED BY SIMON & SCHUSTER
New York   London   Toronto   Sydney   New Delhi

SIMON &
SCHUSTER
CANADA

Simon & Schuster Canada
A Division of Simon & Schuster, Inc.
166 King Street East, Suite 300
Toronto, Ontario M5A 1J3

This Simon & Schuster Canada edition January 2019

SIMON & SCHUSTER CANADA and colophon are trademarks of Simon & Schuster, Inc.

For information about special discounts for bulk purchases, please contact Simon & Schuster Special Sales at 1-800-268-3216 or CustomerService@simonandschuster.ca.

*Interior design by Carly Loman*

Manufactured in the United States of America

10  9  8  7  6  5  4  3  2  1

Library and Archives Canada Cataloguing in Publication
Senécal, Patrick, 1967–
[Sept jours du talion. English]
Seven days / Patrick Senécal.
Translation of: Les sept jours du talion.
Issued in print and electronic formats.
ISBN 978-1-982102-61-6 (softcover).—ISBN 978-1-982102-63-0 (ebook)
I. Title. II. Title: Sept jours du talion. English
PS8587.E544S4613 2019 C843'.54 C2018-902307-4
C2018-902308-2

ISBN 978-1-9821-0261-6
ISBN 978-1-9821-0263-0 (ebook)

*To Nathan and Romy,*
*my loves,*
*my hope,*
*my life*

I must be cruel, only to be kind.

William Shakespeare, *Hamlet*,
Act III, Scene 4

# PART 1

W HEN HE SAW THE MONSTER GET OUT OF THE CAR, BRUNO HAMEL HEARD the growling of the dog for the first time.

Thirty meters ahead of him, the police car had been stopped at the back entrance of the courthouse for a good minute already, and its occupants still had not made an appearance. Bruno had even been wondering whether they had noticed his presence, when the two police officers finally got out and opened the rear door and the monster appeared, wearing handcuffs.

Bruno saw him in the flesh for the first time. With the exception of his combed hair and freshly cut beard, he looked just like the images on television.

That was when Bruno heard the dog growling in the distance. He hardly paid attention to it. His eyes were riveted on the monster's face. He had always been wary of stereotypes: he felt that the most twisted people often looked the most innocuous. But for once, the monster really did look like a louse, like a stereotypical Hollywood "bad guy," and that bothered Bruno, though he couldn't have said why.

The police officers led the monster to the door, where some twenty

4 | PATRICK SENÉCAL

people were expressing their hatred and disgust by shouting insults at the prisoner. The monster curled his lip in an arrogant smile, but his fear was perceptible behind the tough exterior. Soon the smile would be replaced by a terrified expression. At that thought, Bruno had to make an effort not to get out of the car and shoot the monster point-blank with the pistol tucked in his belt. He forced himself to stay calm and not to move. It would be a waste to express his hatred now. He had to save it for later. A bit later.

Accompanied by the two police officers, the monster disappeared into the building, and the little group of demonstrators quieted down.

Bruno heard the dog growling again. He looked around, expecting to see it approaching, but he didn't see any animal.

One of the two police officers came back out, walked through the now quiet group of demonstrators, and got into his car. The vehicle backed up and disappeared around the side of the courthouse, into the parking lot. Bruno, whose car was still running, followed it at a distance. The police car parked near a door, beside two other patrol cars. Ten seconds later, the officer entered the building.

Bruno parked some twenty meters away and turned off his engine.

"You didn't tell me it was a cop car."

Bruno turned to the teenager sitting beside him. The kid shook his head with annoyance and repeated, "If I'd known, I'm not sure I would have said yes."

Bruno took out his wallet and counted out ten hundred-dollar bills. The boy, who hadn't been expecting such a big bonus, stared greedily at the money. He must have been sixteen or seventeen years old; he had a shaven head and a pin in his lower lip and he was quite good-looking. He went to take the money, but Bruno stuffed it in his coat pocket.

"When it's done," he said.

The skinhead nodded and opened his door.

"Not right away!"

The kid closed the door nervously. Bruno looked at his watch: ten to ten.

He lowered his sun visor, leaned his head back, and for the first time since the beginning of the nightmare, thought about the past ten days.

T HE DARKNESS HAD CHOSEN AN ESPECIALLY SUNNY AFTERNOON TO MAKE ITS
appearance. October 7 was like a summer day, and Bruno was in
his yard raking the leaves, which had fallen early this year. He
had no surgeries after noon and wasn't needed at the hospital: it was a
half-day holiday. He had started by spending an hour at his computer,
organizing photos. It was a passion for him, and as soon as he had a
minute free from his work and family, he'd be in front of his monitor,
inaccessible to one and all. But it was such a beautiful day that he had
finally gone outside to do a little leisurely yard work. While finishing
his third beer of the afternoon (might as well take advantage of the fact
that Sylvie wasn't there to preach at him!), he raked the leaves into a
huge pile to surprise Jasmine. She would be ecstatic. She'd throw herself into the leaves, insisting that her father do the same. And Bruno
would gladly obey.

Because he was crazy about his daughter.

It was twenty after three, kids were walking along the street, and the
pile of leaves was just about done. Bruno saw Louise Bédard pass and
wave to him. She'd gone to pick up her son Frédéric at school as she did

every day; the little boy was afraid to come home alone. The nine-year-old waved timidly to the doctor, and Bruno responded with a smile, touched, as always, by the sight of the disfiguring scars the child had had for three years now and which Bruno could not get used to. As he watched him and his mother disappear toward their house on the corner, he thought for the thousandth time how lucky he was. Very lucky.

An hour before the darkness descended on him, Bruno Hamel thanked providence for giving him a life with no real hardship.

After all the children in the neighborhood had passed, he started to wonder. But when he went to the school, he still wasn't worried. She might have stayed behind for extra help or some activity. But they told him Jasmine had left at least forty minutes ago. He still wasn't really worried when he got back home, expecting to find his daughter playing in the leaves with her mother. Sylvie was there, but not Jasmine. Sylvie made a few phone calls, but the little girl wasn't at any of her friends' houses.

After that, he finally started to become worried. Enough to call the police.

When they came, the police officers tried to be reassuring: seven-year-olds often made a little detour on their way home from school. "Disappearances of children are rarer than lottery winners in Drummondville!" one joked. Bruno knew that wasn't exactly true: at least once a year, he'd see an article in the local paper about the disappearance of a child. The police officers agreed to do a search although they weren't really alarmed.

They first went back to the school with Bruno, while Sylvie stayed at the house to welcome her daughter, who, of course, would return home in the meantime.

At the school, while one officer questioned the yard monitor, Bruno saw the other one walking back and forth in the field next to the school. He kept telling himself that in an hour the three of them would be home laughing about this, but he kept his eyes on the policeman, who was making a thorough search of some bushes.

Suddenly the officer stopped short, staring down at the ground. He took off his hat and slowly ran his hand through his hair . . . and Bruno's legs instantly went numb.

Walking over to the policeman, he kept telling himself it wasn't anything, that the cop had discovered a book, a cap, something unrelated to his daughter. He came closer, and despite the distressed expression on the officer's face, he was still denying it. Even when he was close enough to see a bare leg sticking out of the bushes, he kept telling himself that it was another child, another little girl, not his, not Jasmine, because it was simply impossible—this was something that happened to other children and other parents, in the papers and on television, but not to them.

He recognized her right away, and yet it wasn't her. It was *no longer* her. The first thing that broke his heart was her nakedness. She was still wearing her blue dress, but it was too tattered to cover the little body he had washed a thousand times in the bathtub . . . but that was now so . . . *defiled*! Every time Jasmine hurt herself and came into the house crying, Bruno felt the pain in his soul. But this time, there were so many bruises, so much blood . . . and yet she wasn't crying! Why wasn't she crying, she must hurt so much!

When he saw the blue hair ribbon around her neck, the ribbon Sylvie had put in her hair in the morning, warning her not to lose it, he knew she was dead.

Jasmine, his only daughter, with whom he should have been playing and laughing right now, was dead.

Then he saw her face. He had never seen it like that. And the expression . . . empty, but there was a look of horror deep in her eyes. How could there be such an emotion in the eyes of a child? Whoever had done *that* hadn't just killed his daughter, he had destroyed her soul.

Bruno fell to his knees. He reached out and gently picked Jasmine up, as he had done when she was sick or had fallen asleep in front of the television. He held her to him, laid her face in the hollow of his shoulder, and hugged her tight without a word or a cry, with only a long, wheezing expiration. He didn't notice if her body was stiff or limp, warm or cold. He noticed only that for the first time, his daughter did not respond to his caresses, did not hug him back, did not giggle with joy against his neck. For the first time, she had no reaction. And of all the hurts, that was the worst.

Still holding her to him, he closed his eyes and saw a series of familiar scenes: Jasmine running toward him when he got home; Jasmine, all serious, helping him arrange his CDs; Jasmine shouting with joy on the elephant's back at the zoo; Jasmine tracing eyes and a mouth in her shepherd's pie; Jasmine parading around in Sylvie's dresses, pretending she was grown-up; Jasmine chasing the squirrels in the park; and above all, Jasmine laughing, laughing, laughing . . .

That was when the darkness blotted out the sun.

B RUNO OPENED HIS EYES. TEN FIFTEEN. THE HEARING IN FRONT OF THE JUDGE must have started. He looked around: there was no one in the parking lot and they weren't visible from the back entrance of the courthouse. So he told the teenager he could go.

The kid got out and quickly went over to the police car. He took a couple of instruments Bruno didn't recognize out of his coat pocket and started working on the door. On the lock, to be precise.

Bruno surveyed the surroundings again. The nearest people were a hundred meters away on the sidewalk. And there was no reason for the demonstrators at the back entrance to come here. It was a bit risky (Bruno hadn't expected the little group of people to be there), but he didn't have much choice.

He noticed how drab the other cars in the parking lot were, how gray and cracked the asphalt was, how dull the sky. But he knew things weren't really like that, that it was just the way he was seeing them.

Because he saw everything differently now; his vision had been altered.

He turned his attention back toward the boy, but he was lost in thought and didn't really see him. This new way of looking he had was a reaction, an effect of the darkness.

T HE CHANGE IN HIS VISION HAD OCCURRED ABRUPTLY, WITHOUT WARNING. BE-
fore he picked Jasmine's body up and closed his eyes, Bruno saw
things one way. When he opened his eyes a few minutes later, he
saw everything differently.

He had only a vague, almost unreal memory of the hours following
the discovery of the body. Only a few moments stood out clearly in the
fog: Sylvie's hysteria, the phone call to his mother. He also remembered
how one-dimensional Sylvie had seemed. Like the walls, the furniture,
the things in the house that he looked at, distraught.

There was a filter in front of his eyes now.

All that evening, they had sat hugging on the living room couch,
not moving, barely speaking. Sylvie couldn't stop crying. Bruno, broken
with grief and despair, held her as tight as he could but didn't shed a
single tear. The darkness within him stifled even his sobs.

Two days later, at the funeral home, there were a lot of visitors: relatives (even Bruno's mother, who was almost completely incapacitated,
had moved heaven and earth to be there), friends, colleagues, and all
the board members of Hatching, the battered women's shelter where

Sylvie worked part-time and Bruno volunteered one night a week. Bruno, deeply moved, had hugged each one of them.

"This shouldn't happen to people like you and Sylvie," Gisèle, the director of the women's shelter, had said, her face bathed in tears. "God is so cruel sometimes."

Bruno had touched her cheek, his throat too tight to say anything.

He managed to talk to some friends, making a superhuman effort to suppress his pain for a few seconds. But it was no use—it was everywhere, like a wave that formed and re-formed again and again. And beneath the despair there was the darkness, the strange blackness in his soul that prevented tears and that seemed to hide something he didn't want to face yet.

Several times that evening, particularly when he was standing in front of the closed casket, he stuck his hand in the pocket where he had put the blue ribbon Jasmine had been wearing on the last day of her short life. Bruno had kept it without telling anyone, not even Sylvie. Since then, he'd always had it with him, and he felt he wanted to keep it with him forever.

In that closed wooden box was his daughter. Lying there peacefully, as if she were asleep. Every night when she went to bed, she would say the same thing to Bruno when he left her bedroom: "Daddy, don't forget your bag, don't forget your hat, don't forget anything!" It didn't really mean anything, but she had been saying it since she was three and it had become a ritual, a private joke only the two of them understood.

Looking at the casket, Bruno thought that it was the first time Jasmine had gone to sleep without their little ritual.

*Cry! Cry already, you want to so much!*

Why wasn't he able to? Why did this strange darkness in him prevent him from pouring out his grief?

During the burial the next day, under a splendid sunny sky, Bruno felt such intense panic that he came close to throwing himself on the casket screaming. The idea that his little Jasmine would be in that hole for all eternity, rotting until she completely disintegrated, was so repugnant, so unthinkable, that he wanted to run away, but Sylvie's arm around his waist gave him the strength to stay. He put his hand in his pocket and held the blue ribbon tight.

That evening, Bruno would normally have done his volunteer shift at the women's shelter. Obviously, he didn't go, which was very unusual. For three years, he had been going to the shelter one night a week to counsel the residents and sometimes treat those who had just arrived, in tears, their bodies still swollen from beatings by their partners. Sylvie worked there three days a week. She and Bruno were well liked at Hatching and had received a large card signed by all the residents. Most of the messages were addressed to the couple ("You've helped me so much, I wish I could help you"), but some of them were more for Bruno ("I'll always remember the night I arrived at the shelter in crisis and you were so kind, so gentle to me"), and others more for Sylvie ("The three best days of the week are the ones you work here"). They had read the card standing at home cheek to cheek.

All of a sudden, Sylvie turned to Bruno. "I want you to make love to me."

There was no desire or sensuality in her words, but rather an almost pleading desperation. Bruno looked at her for a long time. How long had it been since they'd had sex? Two months? Maybe three? Things hadn't been very good in their relationship for a while; they both knew it but hadn't spoken about it. There weren't a lot of arguments or specific reproaches, just dull habit and stagnation, and fewer and fewer sparks.

Bruno understood Sylvie's request. Jasmine's death should bring them together. They had to go back to being the couple they once had been—it was now or never. And it was the only way to get through this ordeal. Yes, he understood. And he hugged her and walked slowly with her up to their bedroom on the second floor.

Despite the tenderness of their intimacy, there was no real pleasure, no passion, and they stopped after a while. Sylvie cried softly in Bruno's arms, while he reflected. It wasn't that surprising it hadn't worked, but was Jasmine's death the only reason? Silently, he pressed his body to Sylvie's with such a need for fusion and solace that he fell asleep in that position.

The next day, in the late afternoon, Bruno went to Jasmine's school. He watched the children leaving the school, and some of them recognized him and looked sad. Bruno had the impression that they were all faded and washed out, but he knew that wasn't the case. It was the filter over his eyes.

When there were no more children coming out of the school, Bruno stayed there, unmoving, staring at the door, wishing with all his might that it would open and Jasmine would come out. But it remained closed. He took the blue ribbon out of his pocket. The blood on it had dried. He rubbed it against his cheek, closed his eyes for a moment, and returned to his car with his head down.

T HE KID WAS STILL WORKING ON THE CAR LOCK, BUT BRUNO WAS LOST IN HIS memories and hardly saw him.

THE FIVE DAYS AFTER THE DARKNESS CAME HAD BEEN THE SADDEST AND MOST despairing. But they had also been filled with determination: determination to get through this, determination to regain the closeness with Sylvie, determination to be stronger than fate. Of course, Bruno was still too weakened by grief to put up a real fight, but he believed in doing so. Despite the darkness within him, he really believed in it. He and Sylvie had to climb out of this abyss, and as long and painful as it was, they would have to do it one day at a time.

But on the night of the fifth day, the telephone rang.

At the other end of the line, Bruno heard a voice that was hoarse yet soft. Everyone who had called until then had asked in an embarrassed tone how he was doing, which seemed to him an insult. This man was the first one to say something different.

"This is Detective Sergeant Mercure. Excuse me for disturbing you at such a difficult time."

Bruno didn't answer. He was curious.

"But I have a good reason: we've found your daughter's murderer."

Bruno felt something crumble inside him, tightening his stomach, making him dizzy and drying his mouth. It took him some time to understand what was happening to him. For four days he had been so absorbed by the loss of Jasmine that, as crazy as it now seemed to him, he hadn't given a thought to the fact that there was a rapist, a killer, and that he was still at large. For the first time, his feelings moved from his loss to the existence of this killer. It shook him so much that he had to sit down, with the phone still to his ear.

"Jasmine . . . Jasmine's . . . murderer," he stammered.

Mercure said he hadn't been hard to find. He had been prowling around the school for a few days and he had spoken to some of the children. Some teachers had also noticed him, so identifying him had been easy. They had questioned him last night. He had given an inconsistent and confused alibi and had contradicted himself.

After a long silence, Bruno asked, "He confessed?"

"As good as. When he realized it looked bad for him, he said, 'It looks like I'm screwed.' We're holding him, Dr. Hamel."

Bruno was silent again. He really didn't feel well.

"What happens next?"

Mercure explained that the man would appear in court the following day and would then be held at the detention center in Drummondville. About a week after that, there would be a preliminary hearing in front of a judge to determine the trial date.

"He'll be going away for a long time, you can be sure of it. Rape with extreme violence, murder, surely premeditated . . . and a little girl. He's almost certain to get twenty-five years."

"Twenty-five years?"

"That's a life sentence. He would only be eligible for parole after fifteen years."

"But . . . you mean he won't spend the rest of his life in prison?"

Bruno had surprised himself by saying that.

"Twenty-five years is a long time, Dr. Hamel. Even fifteen. To spend your entire life in prison, you have to do something really . . ."

He stopped, realizing his blunder, but Bruno had understood and he retorted curtly, "The rape and murder of my daughter isn't serious enough, is that it?"

"That's not what I meant."

There was an embarrassed silence. His mouth dry, Bruno heard himself ask, "How is he reacting? Is he . . . is he showing remorse?" He rubbed his forehead. Why was he asking these questions?

"He knows he's in for it, and it scares him. But he's acting tough and . . . no, he isn't showing remorse. When we spoke of the horror of his crime, he . . . well, he smiled. It's bravado, obviously, but . . ."

Bruno nodded, his face suddenly white. He said blankly, "Thank you."

And he hung up. He remained seated there for a while. He was trying to imagine this man who, when he was accused of the basest crimes, could just smile.

Smile.

This unnamed killer suddenly emerged from the darkness that until then had filled Bruno but that was now slowly stirring. And his sadness became a little less intense.

He finally noticed Sylvie standing in the doorway to the living room.

"They found him, didn't they?"

It was the first time she had spoken of the killer, at least to Bruno.

"Yes, they found him."

He summarized the information he'd been given. Sylvie put her hands over her mouth and cried. Bruno realized that, unlike him, she had already been thinking of Jasmine's murderer.

"He'll get twenty-five years for sure," he explained mechanically. "And parole after fifteen. Probably."

Sylvie was surprised at how detached he was, and asked if he wasn't relieved.

"I—I don't know. I . . ."

He couldn't help imagining the smile of the faceless killer.

Sylvie became very grave. She took his hands and pulled him to his feet. Her voice clear, without crying, she said, "Bruno, we have to have another child."

And after a pause, "As quickly as possible."

"You can't have any more."

"We'll adopt one."

"I—I'm not ready to replace Jasmine so quickly."

"I'm not talking about replacing her, you know that."

"No, of course not, but . . ."

She was going too fast for him, and the phone call from the police had upset him too much for him to think clearly. And the darkness was giving him a sick feeling in his stomach.

"I'll think about it, but . . . not right away."

She nodded, sniffling, and said she understood. He stroked her cheek, smiled, and said he needed to get some fresh air, alone, and might not be back for supper. She seemed a bit surprised, but didn't argue. He hugged her and went out.

He walked for a long time, all the way downtown, haunted by the phone call from the police.

Twenty-five years . . . maybe fifteen.

He had a late supper in a restaurant on Brock Street, but after a few mouthfuls, he pushed his plate aside in disgust. He tried to regain the strength of the sadness he had felt for five days, but it was hard, because it had been pushed aside by the heavy darkness weighing on it.

When Bruno got back from his long walk in the city, Sylvie was in front of the TV. She didn't ask where he had gone or what he'd done. She only said softly that he was just in time for the news. She had set the VCR to record in case he got back too late. His mother had called to see how things were. He nodded in silence. His mouth was dry. He went to the kitchen and got a beer from the fridge and came back and sat down beside Sylvie.

After the national and international political news, the news anchor said the Drummondville police had just arrested a suspect in "the horrible death of little Jasmine Jutras-Hamel." There was a clip of the Drummondville police station, with two officers escorting a young man in handcuffs.

"That's him!" breathed Sylvie.

Bruno gripped her thigh and squeezed it hard. With his free hand, he picked up the remote and turned up the volume. A voice-over stated, "Last night, the Drummondville police arrested a suspect in the case of last Friday's brutal rape and murder of little Jasmine Jutras-Hamel. The suspect is . . ."

Bruno suddenly pressed the mute button. Surprised, Sylvie asked him why he'd done that. He stared at the remote, also surprised. Why had he done it? And he heard himself answer in a voice that seemed to come from outside him, "I don't want to know anything about him. Not his name or what he does or anything else."

Sylvie asked why. Bruno stared at the screen as if he were looking for an explanation.

"Any information about him, about his personality, would make him seem too much like a human being."

Yes, that was it. That man couldn't be human, that was obvious. A human being wouldn't have done what he did. And Bruno didn't want to consider him a person. That was the only way to . . .

To do what, exactly?

He rubbed his forehead, perplexed.

Sylvie didn't say anything for a few seconds.

"Well, I want to know that information."

"You can watch the recording later."

He looked at her imploringly.

"Please."

He knew it was an absurd thing to ask, but he couldn't help it. She nodded, understanding. She said she was going to make coffee and would watch the videotape later. He thanked her and she went to the kitchen.

There was another story on the screen now. Bruno pushed stop on the VCR, rewound the tape, and with the sound still muted, watched the part with the suspect again. He was in his twenties, with long, dirty yellow-blond hair, jeans with holes in them, and a worn leather jacket. He had a few days' growth of beard, dull, lifeless eyes, and a slack jaw. A nasty-looking guy.

That guy had approached Jasmine. He had talked to her, had lured her into the bushes on some pretext. And behind a bush, he had forced her down on the ground, had torn her dress, had penetrated her and struck her again and again . . . while she had tried to scream for help, to call her mommy and daddy to come to her. Finally, he had put the blue ribbon around her little neck and strangled her. The last emotion she had felt in her short life on earth was huge, incomprehensible suffering.

In Bruno's hand, the remote crackled faintly.

All of a sudden, the young man on the television turned toward the camera and gave a quick smile, arrogant and scornful. In that fraction of a second, Bruno's heart turned to stone.

The news anchor came back on the screen, moving his lips sound-lessly. Bruno rewound the cassette again and replayed the part up to the smile. Had he been smiling like that while beating and raping Jasmine? Probably . . . and he would smile like that when he got out of prison, whether it was in fifteen or in twenty-five years . . . fifteen, probably.

Bruno got up and quickly went to the stairs, passing Sylvie, who asked where he was going.

"I'm going to bed," he answered quickly. "I'm really tired."

It was when he went to bed that Bruno would really abandon himself to his sorrow. Lying still in the bed, he would let the memories of Jasmine wash over him, and fall asleep drowning in his pain. But tonight, lying with his face buried in the pillow, he wasn't able to get in touch with his sadness. He could just barely feel it at the edge of his soul, but the darkness thickened to the point where he felt nauseated.

When Sylvie came to bed an hour later, he still wasn't asleep, al-though he had his eyes closed. And at two in the morning, he was turn-ing over in the sheets, his body covered in sweat, his mind confused. Every time he tried to fix his thoughts on Jasmine's face, every time he tried to find relief by immersing himself in sadness, he saw the killer's face with its horrible smile. And in his head, the time passed, the years passed, until the little girl had turned to dust, while the killer was get-ting out of prison, smiling.

Smiling, still smiling, still smiling . . .

What could Bruno do to make him stop smiling, to make him grimace with fear and suffering as Jasmine had?

A rush of blood, of violence and fury, suddenly swept over him with such force that he leapt out of bed and rushed from the bedroom as if he were fleeing a man who had been in the bed just seconds ago.

He went down to the kitchen for a glass of water. But he couldn't swallow it—the darkness blocked his stomach. He was seized with nausea and just had time to make it to the bathroom to throw up in the toilet. While he was vomiting, his head was filled with images of madness.

When he stood up, he felt strangely calm. He looked at himself in the mirror, at first with surprise. Then his expression became grave.

Walking slowly, he went into the living room. He turned on the TV and watched the recording of the news again. With the sound still off, he watched the images, and hit pause when the killer was smiling toward the camera. The young man was frozen on the screen, and at that moment, he became the monster.

Bruno went over to the TV, leaned down to put his face close to the screen, and stared at the monster frozen in front of him.

The darkness didn't just intrude on his sadness, but took it over completely, spreading like wildfire throughout his whole body, even filling his eyes.

When he went back to bed ten minutes later, he didn't even try to sleep. Lying on his back, he stared at the ceiling while his mind raced. At first his thoughts were scattered and chaotic, but over the hours, they became clear and coherent. All through the sleepless night, one sentence kept surfacing out of the storm of ideas in his head: the monster would appear before the judge for his preliminary hearing in one week.

In one week.

B RUNO STARTED WHEN THE BOY CAME BACK TO THE CAR AND SAID NERVOUSLY but proudly that it was done. Bruno gave him the thousand dollars.

Happy with the money in his pocket, he said to Bruno, "I don't know what you're planning to do, but it's cool that you're doing it against the cops!"

Bruno looked at him without emotion.

The boy added conspiratorially, "Don't worry, I won't say anything to anyone."

"It really doesn't matter," Bruno said.

The skinhead scurried off, and in ten seconds he had disappeared from view.

Bruno made sure there was still no one in the parking lot and got out, holding his doctor's bag. When he got to the police car, he pulled the door handle on the driver's side; the door opened without resistance. And there was no sign of tampering. The boy had done a good job.

Bruno sat down in the driver's seat and closed the door. He took his supplies out of the bag—a number of sheets no bigger than the pages of a notepad. Each one had four dark rectangles two centimeters by four stuck to it.

Very carefully, trying to avoid touching it, Bruno peeled off one of these little rectangles and applied the adhesive side to the underside of the steering wheel where the driver wouldn't be able to see it. Although Bruno had asked Martin to make them as dark as possible, they were still lighter in color than the wheel, so he didn't want to take any chances.

Bruno covered the whole underside of the steering wheel with these little rectangles. Now it would be impossible for the driver to touch the steering wheel without pressing his fingers against them. Bruno had also asked Martin to make them as thin as he could. And since they were placed close together with no breaks, there would be no unevenness, and he hoped the driver would not be able to feel them.

He hoped.

If he did feel them and decided to check the underside of the steering wheel, it would ruin everything. At that point, Bruno would take direct action . . . with his weapon. Which he hoped wouldn't happen. He was really no match for two experienced cops.

Bruno held the wheel with both hands, but let go after a second: he mustn't let his fingers stay in contact with the little rectangles for too long. But that second was enough for him to be sure you couldn't feel the little stamps. At least, he didn't think you could.

He put the sheets back in his bag and looked outside. Someone left the parking lot and disappeared in the distance. Bruno got out of the car, locking the door behind him. He quickly went back to his own Saturn, and once he was in it, he began to breathe normally again. He was covered in sweat, and he took off his coat and threw it onto the back seat.

He glanced at his watch: ten twenty-five.

Nothing to do now but wait.

He idly looked at the cars parked around him. His gaze fell on a Jaguar. So much money for a stupid heap of metal.

Bruno was well-off, but not because that was what he sought; his work paid well, that was all. If it paid less, he would have done it anyway. Bruno had never placed a lot of importance on money. He had tried to base his life on other values. He and Sylvie each had a car, but nothing luxurious. They had a nice, comfortable house, but it was not one of those twenty-room mansions, which they could have afforded. They had a cottage in the country, but it was nothing special, practically a log cabin. Jasmine went to—*had gone to*—a public school, because Bruno didn't believe in private schools. Sylvie shared his opinions and social values, and they were teaching—*had taught*—those to their daughter. Some of Bruno's colleagues found his attitude irritating and called him a bourgeois pseudo-leftist who supported all the right causes to ease his guilty conscience. Bruno just laughed at them.

But in the last few days, for the first time in his life, Bruno had understood the real power of money.

A T NINE O'CLOCK IN THE MORNING, BRUNO WAS STILL STARING AT THE BED-
room ceiling. He hadn't slept all night, but he didn't feel at all
tired. Except mentally, perhaps, because he had been thinking
hard. While Sylvie was still asleep, he got up and dressed. He noticed
a heavy feeling in his shoulders, but he figured it was the effect of lack
of sleep. He left the house without making noise. His step was resolute,
his face set.

At the bank, he took out five thousand dollars in cash. Then he drove
for forty-five minutes, until he reached Trois-Rivières, where he bought
a black wig and false beard. He left the city and went back onto the 55,
traveling north. After a couple of turns, he reached the 351 and kept
going north, passing quickly through Saint-Mathieu-du-Parc. Leaving
the village, he watched the road carefully, and after two or three minutes, he took Pioneers Road, along the shore of Lac des Souris, which
was hidden by the trees. From time to time, he passed a lane through
the trees, leading to a house, usually a summer cottage. Twice he turned
in to one of them, but quickly backed out again: wrong place.

The third time he turned off, Bruno knew it was the right place. The lane was narrow, bumpy, and surrounded by forest, and it descended steeply some hundred and fifty meters to a clearing. In the center of the clearing was a small wooden house. It looked very Swiss. Some fifty meters behind the house, Lac des Souris sparkled in the autumn sunshine.

Bruno got out of the car and looked around. It was a beautiful spot, especially with the autumn colors, but he was unmoved by it. He checked to make sure the road above couldn't be seen from the house. There were no neighbors within view; the nearest one was half a kilometer away. Then he examined the house.

About two years before, during the summer, one of Bruno's colleagues, Josh Frears, had asked him for a favor. Josh had forgotten the file of a patient he had to see that afternoon. He couldn't go pick it up himself because he had to be in surgery in fifteen minutes. Josh was about sixty years old, a widower with no children; there was no one who could bring him the file. A little embarrassed, he had asked Bruno to go pick it up for him. They weren't on particularly friendly terms (they had a good working relationship, nothing more), but Bruno was the only doctor with a few hours' space in his schedule at that time.

The reason Josh was a bit uncomfortable asking the favor was that during the summer he lived in his country house near Saint-Mathieu-du-Parc, a village in the Mauricie region, a hundred kilometers from Drummondville. Bruno wasn't thrilled at the prospect of the long drive, but the older doctor was in a jam, so he had agreed. Josh had given him instructions on how to get to the cottage.

"My keys are upstairs in my office but I don't have time to go get them," he had added. "But I keep a key hidden outside the cottage, in case of emergency."

He had told Bruno where to find the key and given him the code for the alarm system. Bruno had gone to pick up the file and he had been impressed by the place. The cottage was lovely, but the site was really breathtaking. When he returned to the hospital more than two and a half hours later, he had congratulated Josh for having such a beautiful place. The old doctor was known to be rather antisocial; he mostly kept to himself and had no close friends. But one subject he seemed keen on was his cottage, and he spent a good ten minutes talking about it with Bruno. He had bought it eight years earlier, and he spent the summers there, from May to September, alone and happy in the middle of the forest. It involved a lot of driving back and forth to the hospital, but he loved it too much to spend the summer in town. Between October and April, he only went there occasionally, because the place wasn't as interesting in the winter.

The following day, Bruno had already forgotten Saint-Mathieu-du-Parc, the cottage and everything else.

But this morning, he had remembered it again. He had also remembered that Josh went to Belgium to an international conference of cardiac surgeons every year in October. The conference was two weeks long, but Josh always stayed there on vacation the rest of the month. He'd been doing that every year for the past five years.

And this year as well.

It could not be just chance. It was a sign. A sign that what Bruno wanted to do was not only possible but also legitimate.

Bruno went to the outdoor fireplace. The hearth had a wide protective grill. He slipped his hand behind it and felt around. Did Josh remove the key at the end of the summer? He found the little magnetic box that held the key.

Perfect. He stepped onto the porch and looked at the door, the only entrance to the cottage. There didn't seem to be any extra locks for the winter. Again, perfect. Now the most important thing: had the code for the alarm system been changed? When Josh gave it to him, he had said it was easy to remember because it was the same as the address of the hospital. Impossible to forget.

It hadn't been changed in the two years.

He opened the door and went into the kitchen, which was rustic despite the modern oven and refrigerator. Bruno went to the little keypad on the wall and entered the code: 570. The alarm system was deactivated.

Bruno nodded. He couldn't have found a better place: it was a private cottage, considered to be inhabited all year round (even though the doctor rarely went there in the winter). They'd never come looking here. And Josh was in Europe until October 28.

It could not be just chance.

The only risk was that a friend of Josh's could arrive unexpectedly for some reason. Or the old doctor might have asked an acquaintance or a neighbor to come by from time to time to check that everything was okay. Bruno was prepared to take that risk.

He went into the living room, which was an extension of the kitchen. It had the same feeling, old-fashioned and modern at the same time, with antique wood furniture and an old corded telephone but a new television and a high-tech stereo. On the walls were abstract paintings. On a few shelves there were wooden knickknacks, mostly representing cats. Bruno went to the big window and looked out at the sparkling ripples on the surface of the lake. But to him, the water looked dull and gray. He muttered, "Sorry, Josh."

He went into the narrow hallway leading to the two bedrooms and the tiny bathroom. The bedroom on the left, which was used as an office, was where he'd come to pick up the file two years ago. The room was about twenty feet long by fifteen feet wide. There was a modest desk, a small metal filing cabinet, two chairs, and a closet. There were a few paintings on the walls. A window looked out on the lake.

Bruno spent a few minutes examining the room. He glimpsed his reflection in the glass of the window and studied it for a long time. If he put his mind to it and didn't back down, he would go all the way. There was still time to stop everything, to go back home, take Sylvie in his arms, and weather the storm with her.

He saw the smiling face of the monster.

He put his hand in his pocket, took out Jasmine's blue ribbon and looked closely at it.

Thirty seconds later, he got to work.

He finished in the late afternoon and went to Grand-Mère, a town some thirty kilometers away. He quickly checked out the downtown area, making a mental note of two or three places, and then he went into a modest restaurant. He started by calling Sylvie. He told her he had spent the day at the hospital.

"You've already gone back to work," she said, surprised.

He said he needed to do something, that doing nothing just made things worse. He added that he would be home late because he needed to catch up on his paperwork.

A little later, while eating a sandwich and drinking a beer, he read the "Work Wanted" section of the local newspaper. He was interested in ads saying "Handyman" or "Interior or Exterior Work." His father used to call these people "odd jobbers." There were six of these ads in the Shawinigan paper.

It was five twenty. A perfect time to reach people.

He went to a phone booth with the paper. There was no question of using his cell phone; he didn't want the police to be able to trace the numbers he had called.

He dialed the number in the first ad and asked the man who answered if he did carpentry and welding. No problem for the first, but for the second, he wasn't so sure . . . if it was simple, maybe . . . otherwise, probably not. Bruno hung up. He called the second number, a man named Beaulieu, who was not only an expert carpenter but said he was also a pretty good welder.

"All right, then, listen to me without interrupting, Mr. Beaulieu. If you aren't too concerned about the limits of legality, you could make a lot of money. Not only that, there's almost no risk. All you have to do is build something a bit unusual. If you're interested, meet me at six thirty in the park on Thirty-Fourth Street, near the slide in the playground. Just for coming to meet me and listening to what I have to say, I'll give you three thousand dollars, whether or not you accept my offer. If you accept it, you'll make a lot more."

When the man started to say something, Bruno hung up. He was surprised how easily he had played his role. He called the number in the third ad. The man also worked as a mechanic. Bruno repeated the same pitch, with one difference: he arranged to meet him at seven thirty at the pay phone in the bar Chez Lili. Like Beaulieu, the guy didn't get a chance to answer.

Bruno didn't call the other numbers. Three were enough for today.

He went back to his car. He put the black wig on his head, which was already quite bald despite his young age of thirty-eight, and put on the false beard. He put a pair of sunglasses on and looked at himself in the rearview mirror. He looked weird, but he didn't care. Safety first.

The first man didn't show. The second one didn't either, but he sent someone. Bruno had parked some fifty meters from Chez Lili, and from there he could see the pay telephone through the front window. At seven thirty-five, a police car stopped in front of the bar. Two police officers went in and headed straight for the pay phone. From his vantage point, Bruno even saw them questioning the waiter.

Bruno started the car and drove off, slowly so as not to attract attention. As he drove, he removed his disguise.

Just before leaving town, he stopped at a phone booth and called the people from the three other ads. One of them didn't seem comfortable with mechanical devices, but the two others were suitable. He recited the same spiel as before, except that he made the appointments for the following day. The first one was for nine o'clock at the slide in the playground, and the second for ten at the phone booth he was making the call from.

He got home at eight forty-five and went directly to the fridge to get a beer. Sylvie asked how it was being back at work. He answered that it had been hard, but that at least it had partly distracted him from his sadness and pain. He was surprised at how easily he lied.

"I spent the whole day alone," she said reproachfully.

He said that perhaps she should go back to the women's shelter. Spending the whole day wallowing in misery wasn't exactly healthy, was it? She thought about it and, with a sigh, shook her head.

"I don't feel ready yet."

She was so weary, so listless, so defeated. She held out her arms to him. He went to her and they hugged.

"Are you all right?" she asked.

"Why?"

"I don't know. You feel so tense."

He didn't answer. He would have liked to abandon himself completely to tenderness, but the darkness prevented him.

When he went to bed with his eyes on the ceiling and his face hard, it took him a good two hours to fall asleep.

The next morning at nine, he was parked at the playground in Grand-Mère, watching the slide from a distance. It was Thursday and the children were in school, so the park was almost deserted. But a man walked up to the slide, stopped, and waited there, looking nervously about.

Wearing his disguise, Bruno approached in turn. The weather was mild. It would be warm again. It was as though fall had forgotten to come. The man watched Bruno suspiciously.

"Gaétan Morin?"

"Yup, that's me."

Forty-five years of age, already graying, a protruding belly, but muscular arms and legs. A gray baseball cap. He was chewing on a toothpick, trying to look relaxed, but you could tell he was nervous.

"What's with the getup? Are we in a James Bond movie?"

"I told you this could go beyond the bounds of legality."

"Yeah, but . . ."

He scratched his head. He was finding this a bit too mysterious.

"I came out of curiosity."

Bruno took an envelope from his coat and gave it to Morin.

"Three thousand dollars for your trouble, as promised."

Morin looked around. Some distance away, there was a woman reading on a bench. Two people were walking and talking. From time to time, a car passed along the main street. He finally dared to open the envelope and quickly count the money. He put the money under his coat and looked around again, and then back at Bruno. His expression had suddenly changed to one of interest, as if he hadn't really believed Bruno until then. Bruno was direct: now that his curiosity was satisfied, Morin could leave if he wanted. But if he were to accept Bruno's offer, he could make a lot more.

"How much?"

Bruno nodded almost imperceptibly. Morin was the kind of guy who lived a quiet, monotonous life, dreaming of money, and from time to time pulling off some scam that wasn't too compromising. Exactly what Bruno needed. So he gave him the numbers right away: a first install-ment of thirty thousand dollars and then seven thousand a day for a certain period. What Bruno saw on Morin's face was not greed, but fear. He hadn't been expecting that much money.

"Hey, don't expect me to kill anybody!"

"You won't have to kill anybody. In fact, what I want you to build for me isn't illegal. But after you've built it, I want to be sure you'll keep your mouth shut."

Morin, relieved, looked interested again. Bruno added, "It's up to you to decide if silence is too serious a crime for you."

The toothpick between Morin's lips was twitching.

"Just what is it you want me to build?"

"You're a good mechanic, right?"

"I can do anything, sir."

Bruno took a paper from his pocket, unfolded it, and gave it to Morin. He explained that it was a rough sketch just to give him an idea. Morin looked at the sketch and the toothpick stopped moving, while his eyes grew wide.

"I realize it's quite complex. If you don't think you have the skills, tell me right away. But if you feel you can do it, I'll give you more details on-site."

"Shit! What are you going to do with *that*?"

"I'm also paying you not to ask questions."

Silence. Morin eyed him closely. Bruno was glad he'd worn the dark glasses.

"When do you want me to build it?" Morin finally asked.

"As soon as possible."

"Perfect. I can start tomorrow if you want. I have some contracts, but I can cancel them."

Morin suddenly seemed reassured and even eager, as if, now that the decision was made, he was in a hurry to start. His attitude intrigued Bruno.

"And the seven thousand a day you're going to give me for my silence . . . that'll be for how long?"

"Two weeks."

That wasn't true. It wouldn't be for that long, but Morin didn't need to know that. The handyman made a quick mental calculation and his eyes grew brighter.

"You'll start giving me that amount right after I finish building your . . . your little contraption?"

"Exactly. I'll start the next day."

"I can build it for you in two days."

He was in such a hurry, almost more of a hurry than Bruno. Was he in urgent need of money?

Josh's cottage, Morin so eager . . . everything was coming together so nicely. These were signs. Signs that Bruno was right to do what he was planning.

In the distance, a woman got up off a bench and walked away. Morin nodded, having nothing else to say. He took the toothpick from his mouth, considered it for a moment, put it back in his mouth, laughed nervously, and shrugged. Bruno asked if there was a telephone number where he could reach him personally, and Morin gave him his cell number. They agreed to meet at the same time and place the following morning. Morin nodded, hesitated again, and clumsily stuck out his hand. Bruno looked at it curiously for a moment and then shook it mechanically. He was finding it more and more difficult to carry out these everyday actions, to observe the social conventions, which seemed so distant and foreign now, so far from the darkness.

Finally, Morin turned and walked away, his steps becoming faster and more energetic. He must have been in a rush to get into his car and shout for joy.

Bruno gave a long sigh, rubbed his eyes under his glasses, and went back to his car. He left Grand-Mère without even bothering to keep the second appointment.

He was back in Drummondville at eleven, and went to his bank. He had a short conversation with his banker, who seemed puzzled and somewhat discouraged but agreed to meet with him the following afternoon. Bruno left the bank with five thousand dollars cash.

He got to the bus station just in time for the next bus to Montreal. He had his disguise with him in a travel bag.

When the bus stopped in Longueuil, Bruno got out, wearing his disguise.

He spent more than an hour downtown and then took the subway to Montreal.

At about four thirty, still wearing his disguise, he went to a used car dealer and bought a green '92 Chevrolet for the ridiculous sum of a thousand dollars, without negotiating. The whole transaction took less than ten minutes. The dealer, who had initially been suspicious of this weirdo in disguise, was so delighted he almost swallowed his cigarette.

Bruno then found a sex shop that specialized in accessories for fetishists. He made a purchase and came out carrying a bag containing a rectangular cardboard box.

A half hour later, he parked the old Chevrolet on Sainte-Catherine Street near Saint-Laurent. After thinking about it for a minute, he left the wig and beard in the car; he wouldn't need a disguise. He also left all but a thousand dollars of his cash hidden in the car, under the front passenger seat.

He went to eat in a little Vietnamese restaurant. At ten minutes to seven, he was walking along Sainte-Catherine Street. It was dark already, but there still was no autumn chill. Bruno passed a few young punks, some prostitutes, some shady-looking characters, but he didn't dare approach any of them. He was a bit nervous and he still had that new heavy feeling in his shoulders.

In a narrow, dirty alley, he saw a man having an animated conversation with a young girl. The man, who was in his thirties, was dressed in a flashy black suit with extravagant rings on his fingers. He was moving in a theatrical way as he talked. From her outfit, it was obvious the girl was a prostitute, and she was clearly being rebuked by the man. Bruno stood watching them from the street, hesitant to approach. After a minute, the girl came out of the alley looking dejected, and went back to the street.

Summoning up his courage, Bruno turned into the alley and approached the pimp, who was lighting a cigar. Bruno began speaking, quickly but with assurance. The pimp started by laughing scornfully and even motioned for Bruno to leave. Bruno was so insistent that the pimp finally became annoyed, and then got really angry. He grabbed Bruno by the collar, shoved him against the wall, and spat threats at him. Bruno managed to maintain his composure and showed the pimp a thousand dollars from his wallet. The pimp was at first incredulous, and then he let go of Bruno to count the money. Bruno continued talking, and now the pimp really listened, keeping his eyes on the wad of bills in his hands. Finally, his face cold but no longer menacing, he gave Bruno the answer he was looking for. Bruno walked quickly out of the alley and lost himself in the crowd on Sainte-Catherine Street.

For the next hour, he wandered aimlessly in the neighborhood. Once or twice, he was approached by young girls, but he didn't even look at them. While walking, he thought about the birthday party they had organized for Jasmine the month before. It had started at four thirty in the afternoon, but Bruno had arrived an hour late because of a complicated surgery. His lateness wasn't a disaster, but he had been disappointed, and so had Jasmine. He had said, "I'll never let you down again, sweetheart, I promise you. I'll be there whenever you need me." He was exaggerating, but he really was sorry and he wanted so much to make her happy. And with all the innocence of a seven-year-old, Jasmine had believed him. She had kissed him and given him a hug.

Of all Bruno's dark musings, the worst was the thought that six days earlier, Jasmine had called to him for several unbearable minutes and he hadn't come. She had died without understanding why her father hadn't kept his promise. Suddenly dizzy, he sat down on a bench, put his head back and took a few deep breaths.

At eight o'clock, Bruno returned to his car to get the rest of the money. He went to a seedy hotel nearby and went up to room 27. It was squalid and stank of drugs and sex. The pimp was there, but he wasn't alone; a giant black man was standing off to the side, his arms crossed, his expression sour.

"Okay, man," the pimp said, "you got the other two grand?"

"I want to see them first."

The pimp smiled slightly and motioned to his sidekick. The giant took an automobile license plate from his jacket and threw it on the bed.

"You're sure it's clean?" asked Bruno.

"You won't have any problem with it, man."

Then the giant took out a revolver and put it on the bed. Bruno nodded and handed the other two thousand dollars to the pimp, who counted it with a satisfied look. He gave Bruno a little lesson, explaining how to load the revolver and take off and put on the safety. Impressed, Bruno carried out each of the operations. He never would have guessed a revolver was so heavy!

"Try aiming it now."

Bruno raised the weapon and, not knowing what to aim at, pointed it toward the window.

"You see the little sight at the end of the barrel? It has to be right on your target. You aim and then you pull the trigger."

Bruno aimed at a point on the window, but the weapon shook slightly in his hand. He saw a face appear in the glass, ghostly but vaguely familiar, with long blond hair and a scruffy beard, and an unchanging mocking smile. The revolver stopped shaking in Bruno's hand, and his finger pulled the trigger. There was a click.

"You're a natural, man!" laughed the pimp.

The giant gave him a dozen bullets. Bruno put the license plate, the revolver, and the ammunition under his coat.

"Thanks," he said.

The pimp just nodded. As Bruno was leaving, he said, "I don't know what you're planning to do, man, but let me warn you, it's easier than you think."

With a little smile, he took a puff on his cigar.

Back in Drummondville, Bruno left the old Chevrolet in the parking lot of the seniors' residence where his mother, a widow, had been living for two years. Only residents or visitors with permits were allowed to park there, but he knew from experience that the police never checked and you could leave your car there without any problem, even overnight.

He put the revolver, the ammunition, and his purchase from the sex shop in the trunk and put on the new license plate. Then he walked back to the bus station, where his Saturn was waiting for him.

At eight forty, he got home. Sylvie was in the living room watching TV.

"I had an emergency surgery tonight," he explained.

"You could have called," she said accusingly.

He didn't say anything and his face remained impassive. She looked at him for a moment with a sad, perplexed expression. But Bruno was staring at the television screen because he had just seen Jasmine on it. Sylvie had been watching a video they made, and Bruno recognized it; it was from his birthday, last May. Sylvie had filmed Jasmine reading a poem she had written for him for the occasion.

"I know it's masochistic," sighed Sylvie, "but I can't help it. I've spent a good part of the day watching these videos."

There was a celebration on the television screen—bright lights, colored balloons, red and yellow party hats. But to Bruno, all the colors were dulled. Only Jasmine shone brightly, with her yellow dress, her long chestnut hair, her intelligent hazel eyes, the little beauty mark near her right ear, her mischievous smile.

She was holding a sheet of paper in her delicate hands and shifting from one foot to the other. She ended her poem in a clear, confident voice:

*Of all the papas in the world, the very best is mine!*
*Happy birthday, Papa, have a happy time!*

The guests applauded enthusiastically while Bruno, moved and proud, hugged his daughter and kissed her hair, which had smelled like honey ever since she was little.

A terrible pain seized Bruno's throat. He felt tears coming and a sob rising in his throat, yet he didn't cry. He hadn't cried once since the darkness came.

The telephone rang. After four rings, Bruno decided to get up and answer it in the kitchen so as not to disturb Sylvie.

Although every voice had sounded the same to him in the past few days, he immediately recognized the soft, hoarse tone.

"It's Detective Sergeant Mercure, Dr. Hamel. I'm calling to tell you Lem—"

"I don't want to know his name," Bruno interrupted quickly.

The detective sergeant didn't show any surprise. He explained that the preliminary hearing would take place the next Tuesday, the 18th. In five days. Bruno mentally did some quick calculations.

"Could you explain exactly what the procedure is? Where will he leave from, at what time, and so on."

"I beg your pardon?"

"I have no intention of going to the courthouse. I don't want to see him. But here, at home, I want to picture every step as it happens. Do you understand?"

Mercure said he understood. Slowly, in an almost reassuring tone, he explained that the accused would leave the detention center in a police car at around nine o'clock to go to the courthouse. The hearing was set for ten o'clock. The judge and the lawyers would speak, and then the date of the trial would be set. The whole thing should last at most a half hour, or an hour if there was a delay. After that, the accused would be taken back to the detention center, where he would stay until the trial.

"And are you still sure it was him?" asked Bruno.

"The DNA tests confirm it."

Bruno closed his eyes.

Mercure said he would continue to keep Bruno posted, and before ending the conversation, he said without sentimentality, "I hope you and your wife . . ."

"We're not married."

". . . you and your partner are finding the strength to get through this, Dr. Hamel."

Bruno didn't answer, and the police officer hung up.

Bruno went and got a beer from the fridge and took a long swig, leaning back against the counter. The kitchen was dark, with the only light coming from the fixture in the hall.

Sylvie came in and asked who had called.

"It was the police. The preliminary hearing is next Thursday."

He was barely aware that he was lying about the day. He added that the DNA tests had been positive. Sylvie put her arms around Bruno. Taken by surprise, Bruno hesitated for a moment, and then returned her hug.

"Oh, Bruno! Last night I dreamed they hanged the guy! They hanged him outside in front of a screaming crowd! Like they used to do a century ago. I was in the crowd, and I . . . I was shouting with joy!"

Bruno's face hardened, but he remained silent.

"You were with me in the dream," continued Sylvie, "and you were shouting too. It was . . . it was completely crazy."

"Why is that so crazy?"

She thought about it, blinking. Why was he asking such a rational, analytical question, while she was so emotional? A bit reluctantly, she answered, "Well . . . it's just that . . . you and I have always been against the death penalty, and . . ."

"I've always had questions about it, you know."

"Yes, but . . . but you were still opposed to it . . ."

He grimaced in annoyance. After thinking for a minute, he asked, looking into her eyes, "And now, what do you want? Do you want Jasmine's killer to die?"

Sylvie kept staring at him, taken aback by his tone, his questions, his intensity. She gave a long, painful sigh, leaned her head on his chest again, and answered in a small, breaking voice, "I wish our little Jasmine could come back to us."

They stayed entwined for a long time, but Bruno's face remained hard.

The next morning at nine, two cars left Grand-Mère, one following the other closely. The first one was a green '92 Chevrolet, and the one behind it was a pickup truck filled with tools, lumber, and metal parts. After about a half hour, they drove through Saint-Mathieu-du-Parc, continued along Pioneers Road, and turned into the lane leading to Josh's cottage. Bruno got out of the Chevy, wearing his disguise. Morin got out of the truck and looked around admiringly.

"Nice little place! Have you had it for a long time?"

"I thought I was clear . . ."

Morin shrugged apologetically. Bruno, a travel bag slung over his shoulder, led him into the house, to the guest room. The room was now completely empty and the drapes were drawn. Bruno had removed all the furniture and hidden it behind the house.

"Here it is."

After a quick look around the room, Morin gave Bruno a rather fearful look, but didn't say anything. Bruno started to explain in detail what he wanted. Morin listened attentively, making notes on the plans Bruno had given him. From time to time, his eyes widened, but he kept on writing, asking technical questions, examining the walls and ceiling, and going back to the plans.

When Bruno finished, Morin scratched his head uncertainly.

"Listen, I want to be sure that if you get into trouble because of . . ." He motioned to the plans. "You won't give my name."

Bruno swore he wouldn't, but Morin laughed.

"Come on! What guarantee do I have?"

"What about me? What guarantee do I have that you'll keep quiet?"

Morin thought for a moment and then agreed that was fair.

"And you say it will be finished for tomorrow afternoon?"

"It should be, if this is what you want."

Bruno explained that he'd be back in late afternoon. Morin was to go ahead with the work, and was not to leave before his return. He also told him not to call anyone and not to leave the house, or at least not the property. He took two wrapped sandwiches, a beer, and a chocolate bar out of his bag.

"Here's your lunch for today. Tomorrow, bring your own lunch."

At eleven thirty, Bruno was back in Drummondville. He ate lunch at the Charlemagne and went to Sainte-Croix Hospital at around one.

The hospital felt unfamiliar. He could hardly believe he'd been working there for the past seven years. The walls were so ugly, the patients so shrunken, the lighting so harsh. He managed to avoid meeting any of his colleagues in the halls.

He went to his office and got two empty medical bags. He went to the surgery department, but when he saw the two doctors that were there, he turned back and went to the pharmacy instead.

As he had expected, Martin, the pharmacist, was alone. He was surprised to see Bruno back so soon, but Bruno said he was still on leave and had just come to pick up a few things.

Martin thoughtfully asked how Bruno was doing. He was young, good-natured, and brilliant, but like everyone, he had his weaknesses. That was precisely why Bruno had chosen him. Cutting the discussion short, Bruno said he needed some nitroglycerine patches. But not ordinary ones.

"I want them very, very thin . . . so thin you can hardly feel them."

He specified the type and the exact thickness. Martin listened, puzzled, and gave a questioning chuckle. What was this order that was so special? What treatment could require this kind of thing? When Bruno said it was personal, Martin became uncomfortable. He couldn't make it without a prescription . . . After all, Bruno knew how things worked, didn't he?

"Your friend three years ago didn't have a prescription either," Bruno said.

Three years earlier, Martin had illegally sold a friend certain substances and Bruno had found out. Martin, desperate, had said he had had a lot of debts but that everything was resolved now and he would never again get involved in that kind of thing. Bruno hadn't turned him in. Because he had believed him, because Martin was a good pharmacist, and because, dammit, you don't destroy someone's life for one little mistake! So he had kept silent. Since that time, whenever Martin ran into him in the corridors, he was so friendly and nice that it was embarrassing. Bruno had never mentioned the incident to him again. He would never have dreamed of taking advantage of the situation.

Until today.

Martin reddened, but he adopted a conciliatory tone.

"Bruno, right now you're . . . you're upset by what happened . . . and that's normal. Maybe you . . . should get some rest and re—"

"Listen, Martin, if you don't make me up those nitro patches for Sunday, I'll reveal that old story."

He should have been ashamed of using blackmail like that, but he didn't feel anything. Nothing at all.

Martin went from scarlet to white. Bruno, unperturbed, said he wanted thirty of them, black.

"Black?" stammered Martin. "I . . . I'm not sure that's possible."

"As dark as possible, then. Do the best you can. And I also want some of these antibiotics and these sedatives," he said, handing Martin a list. "Give them to me with the patches. And I swear to you that the patches won't be used to kill anyone."

Martin tried to find out more, but in vain. Bruno said he wanted the drugs in two days. He told Martin to meet him on the little bridge in Woodyatt Park at ten o'clock. If he brought the police with him, Bruno would bring up the past. Martin, defeated, practically whimpered, "Shit, Bruno, what's the matter with you?"

Bruno held his gaze for a moment. He licked his lips as if he were about to say something, but changed his mind and walked away.

This time when Bruno went to the surgery department, it was deserted. He quickly chose a number of things: surgical instruments, syringes, IV bags, bandages, and disinfectants. He put everything in his two bags and left.

On his way out, unfortunately, he ran into Jean-Marc, the chief of the department, who said the appropriate things for the situation: poor Bruno, how are you managing, how's Sylvie doing, we're thinking of you, and so on. He asked if Bruno had decided when he would come back to work.

"I don't know yet," Bruno said in an emotionless voice.

"Take all the time you need," Jean-Marc said reassuringly. "We've scheduled your urgent surgeries with Benoît and Peter. There's no hurry. You and Sylvie need time together."

He seemed curious about the two bags, but he didn't ask any questions.

A half hour later, Bruno left the bank with a briefcase containing twenty thousand dollars in cash.

He went to the supermarket and bought two hundred dollars' worth of food. At the last minute, he added two cases of beer.

At four o'clock, he was back at Josh's place, wearing his disguise. He went directly to the guest room. Morin barely stopped working to say hello. Bruno looked at the work. It was taking shape. It was progressing nicely.

"Can you guarantee me that you'll finish tomorrow?"

"Yup."

Bruno brought the bags of groceries in and put everything away in the cupboards and fridge. Morin appeared in the kitchen. Although he was now more at ease with this character in his grotesque disguise, he still seemed nervous occasionally. He said he was finished for today. Since he knew the place, he would be back tomorrow at nine thirty. Before leaving, he asked, "So . . . would it be possible to have a small advance?"

His tone was close to begging, and he suddenly seemed almost like a drug addict in need of a fix. Bruno gave him an advance of five thousand dollars. The other twenty-five thousand would be for tomorrow after the job was done. Morin was so pleased, he almost flew to his truck.

Bruno opened a beer and took it to the guest room, where he drank it leaning against the wall looking at Morin's work.

At five thirty, in Drummondville, he parked the Chevy in the parking lot of the seniors' residence, where his Saturn was waiting. He left the two bags in the trunk of the Chevy.

He got home at five forty. He went directly to his office, a small book-lined room with a computer and printer. He put the briefcase containing the money in the closet.

Sylvie was in the kitchen cooking, and she was glad to see Bruno come home at a normal time.

In the dining room, which was almost too bright, they ate pasta, speaking in very low voices as if there were someone asleep. Or rather, it was Sylvie who spoke, with Bruno answering in monosyllables. He had an odd feeling, as if he weren't really in the room and his body were just a dummy going through the motions. Because his mind was very far away . . . in a little cottage a hundred kilometers away.

"I went to work this afternoon," Sylvie said, "but I left after two hours. It was . . . too hard."

She smiled apologetically. She was forcing herself to be strong, but she wasn't quite succeeding. Her face, framed by her long hair, looked gray and old.

"I wonder how you manage to work," she added.

He didn't say anything, but took a mouthful of food for the sake of appearance. She smiled again, with real pleasure this time: "Anyway, tomorrow's Saturday. We'll be able to spend the day together."

Uncomfortably, he explained that he had to work the next day. When Sylvie expressed surprise, he said she knew perfectly well he sometimes had to work on the weekend. Sylvie's jaw dropped and she put her cutlery down.

"What is it, Bruno? You're escaping your pain by working, is that it?"

For a moment, he thought of telling her the whole story, but he stopped himself. It was too risky. She might not understand. Later, yes, but it was too soon now. He just shrugged.

Sylvie replied in a quavering voice, "Listen, I know things weren't that great between us before . . . but now we have to . . . we have to try, because . . ."

"Sylvie, I . . ."

He tried to find something gentle and reassuring to say, but gave up and said impassively, "I just don't feel like talking."

"What's happening to you? In the first three or four days, you were so gentle, so caring, so *there*, and now, since the day before yesterday, you're . . . you're different, more distant, more . . ." She gave a little sigh. "And why did you go back to work so quickly?"

She held out her arms over the table and he took her hands.

"Our daughter is dead, Bruno, and I need you! Is that so hard to understand?"

She had almost been shouting, but she immediately calmed herself. She added, speaking evenly but with intensity, "And don't you need me?"

He withdrew his hands with annoyance. Couldn't she just leave him alone?

She drew back and looked at him with amazement and alarm, as if she no longer recognized him. She got up and was about to leave the room when Bruno said in an emotionless voice, "Sylvie, in a few days, you'll understand all this, you'll see . . ."

"What are you talking about?"

"Later, you'll understand. Very soon . . ."

"Understand what?"

She was almost crying with rage and despair. Bruno repeated, "You'll understand."

Sylvie left the room in tears and went upstairs.

Alone, Bruno continued eating.

Fifteen minutes later, Sylvie came back down carrying a small suitcase. Coldly, she said she was going to her friend Ariane's house.

"I need human warmth and solace."

"I understand," Bruno said.

Sylvie said he knew where to find her if he needed her.

"I'm sorry," he murmured, but his tone of voice said the opposite.

Sylvie nodded and left without another word.

For just an instant, Bruno felt his stomach contract with remorse, but the darkness came like an antibody protecting his system from viruses. He turned back into a dummy and his mind returned to Josh's cottage. He ate the pasta mechanically, not tasting anything.

H E WAS A LITTLE CHILLY. AS HE WAS PUTTING ON HIS COAT, HE GLIMPSED THE policeman walking between the cars in the parking lot.

He lay down on the passenger seat. Parking was surely allowed here, but he wanted to avoid any contact. He stayed down for two minutes and then sat up again. No cop in sight.

His watch read ten thirty. God, he could really use a beer!

He looked at his hand, perplexed. He felt like it wasn't his, like it didn't belong to him. In fact, since the darkness, he had the feeling of being in somebody else's skin, in a different body but one he knew perfectly. And in the past four days, that impression had intensified.

T HE NEXT DAY, HE GOT UP EARLY, SHOWERED, HAD A QUICK BREAKFAST, AND left, taking the briefcase full of money and his laptop.

He went and got the Chevrolet and headed for Saint-Mathieu-du-Parc, wearing his disguise. Morin was waiting at Josh's place, sitting on the front steps smoking a cigarette. It was still sunny, but a little cooler than the preceding days. Morin said he figured he should be finished about three o'clock that afternoon.

"Fine. I'll try to come back about then, but I might be a little late. Don't leave before I get back."

"Don't worry, I want to get paid!" Morin said pointedly, chewing on his toothpick.

In the car, Bruno prepared eleven rolls of seven thousand dollars each in hundred-dollar bills. That made thick rolls, but they would still be pretty easy to hide. That was why he'd set the amount at seven thousand dollars. He could have chosen ten thousand, but the rolls would have been too bulky, and therefore too hard to conceal in narrow spaces.

In Grand-Mère, he returned to the park on the main street, and after searching for fifteen minutes, hid seven thousand dollars in one of the metal bars of the rocket in the playground. Half an hour later, he found a steel fence around a textile factory. The eighth fence post was held in the ground by a cement footing. The footing had a big crack in it, and Bruno pushed the second roll in there. He noted the precise locations in a notebook. He found two more hiding places in Grand-Mère and then drove out of town.

He hid the seven other rolls in two other villages near Grand-Mère. So the seventy-seven thousand dollars were dispersed in eleven hiding places in three villages. Eleven safe places that were almost impossible to find by chance. And each time, he was careful not to draw attention to himself. Nine hiding places would have been enough, but he didn't want to take any chances. There could always be a hitch.

This took him all morning and a good part of the afternoon, so he got back to the cottage at three thirty.

Morin had finished the work and had cleaned up. Bruno examined the setup closely. While Morin explained how to use everything, he tried out the various mechanisms. Everything worked perfectly.

Josh would never have recognized his office.

In spite of the apathy that had come over him with the darkness, Bruno could not help feeling some admiration for Morin. Honest or not, he really knew what he was doing. He congratulated him in a flat voice. Morin shrugged, but he was obviously proud. He gave Bruno a little key and said, "It opens all the rings. On the chains and on the table."

The two men returned to the living room. There were four empty beer bottles on the table. Morin chuckled apologetically: "I found the beer in the fridge and I figured . . ."

Bruno gave him the remaining twenty-five thousand dollars. Morin counted the bills several times, hardly able to believe his eyes. He had never seen so much money in one place.

"And starting tomorrow, you'll be making another seven thousand dollars a day," Bruno reminded him.

He explained the method of payment: every day between nine and six, he would call Morin and tell him where the money was. If he found out that Morin had talked to anyone, the calls would stop automatically, and so would the payments.

"And if you talk, I'll know about it, believe me."

Morin said nothing. Bruno warned him that he wasn't ever to come here, for any reason. If Bruno caught the slightest glimpse of him, the agreement was null and void.

"And what if you're lying to me? What if you don't call me tomorrow?"

"Then you can come and see me."

"Or I could turn you in."

"Turn me in for what? For having you build me some equipment? I haven't done anything illegal."

"Not yet . . ."

The two men looked at each other for a moment. Morin seemed to be feeling more confident and there was a hint of irony in his expression. Bruno's face remained inscrutable under his disguise.

"Don't talk to anyone about this business, Mr. Morin, and you'll make seven thousand dollars a day for two weeks. After that . . ."

He shrugged.

"After that, you can do whatever you like."

He was about to add, "because it won't matter anymore," but he decided not to.

When he went to Morin's truck with him, Bruno saw a tool he found interesting—a sledgehammer with a long handle and a head heavy enough to smash big rocks. Bruno asked how much for the tool.

"It's not for sale. I need it."

Bruno offered him five hundred dollars and Morin handed over the sledgehammer. He almost asked a question, but changed his mind with a shrug.

The two men did not shake hands. Two minutes later, the pickup was driving off up the dirt lane.

Carrying the sledgehammer, Bruno went back to the guest bedroom and studied the sinister installation for a long time. It was precisely as he had imagined it, and yet he felt nothing. As long as this equipment was not used, it would mean nothing to him. He leaned the sledgehammer against the wall near the door and went back to the living room.

He looked out the big window, drinking a beer. Above the lake, completing its lazy descent, was the sun—a sun that Bruno saw as dull and washed out. A light breeze had come up, and on the shore hundreds of (drab) red and (faded) yellow leaves were dancing gently.

Before returning to Drummondville, he went to the village of Saint-Élie. He quickly drove around the village, but without finding what he was looking for. He went on to the next village, Charette, some twenty kilometers from Saint-Mathieu-du-Parc. He drove around for a while and finally found an isolated old duplex with a "For Rent" sign on it, with the owner's phone number. Again using a telephone booth, Bruno called the owner, and then went to see him at his house. It was several kilometers from the duplex, which suited Bruno perfectly.

Wearing his disguise but without the dark glasses, Bruno said his name was Gauthier and that he was a writer looking for a quiet place to write for a couple of months.

"Usually I rent by the year, not by the month," said the landlord, an old man.

Bruno offered double the regular rent, in cash. The old man accepted and gave Bruno the key.

"I should tell you, you probably won't see me again," the new tenant said. "When I write, I'm a hermit. I don't answer the telephone, or the door if someone comes knocking."

"Don't worry, I never bother my tenants," answered the old man with a smile.

Ten minutes later, carrying his laptop, Bruno went to the rustic little two-bedroom ground-floor apartment, which was completely empty. There was an old telephone, but the line wasn't in service. He left his laptop in the apartment and went out again.

He called the phone company from a phone booth and spoke briefly with an employee.

"Everything will be ready on Monday, right?" he insisted.

"Before noon, sir."

Then he made another call. Once again, he was assured by the person at the other end that everything would be ready on Monday.

He got home at six forty-five. There were no messages from Sylvie on the answering machine. He wondered if he should call her, and realized he didn't feel like it.

He ate a steak.

He watched television without really paying attention to any of the shows.

His mother called. She cried. He spoke to her gently, saying that he and Sylvie were doing better and he would go and see her very soon. A little later, there was a call from one of his friends. This time, Bruno said rather curtly that he didn't feel like talking.

He went to bed at ten o'clock, but he found the bed big and cold. He got up again and went to Jasmine's bedroom and lay down on her bed. He fell asleep in a few minutes.

At five to ten the next morning, he was in Woodyatt Park. He walked around the tennis courts to the path along Saint-François River and toward the little bridge. The wind was chillier than the day before and it seemed like autumn had finally come. Quite a few people were strolling along the path, which had been transformed into a multicolored carpet; some were even sitting reading on the benches, well bundled up, and children were running up and down. He had counted on all this Sunday activity. It was always easiest to go unnoticed in a crowd.

Martin was waiting on the little bridge, holding a medical bag and nervously smoking a cigarette. When he saw Bruno, his face darkened and he tossed the butt in the river. He handed Bruno a large envelope. Bruno discreetly checked the contents before putting it under his coat. Then Martin gave him the bag, which held antibiotics and sedatives. A pair of lovers crossed the bridge. Martin still said nothing; he just stared at Bruno, almost with contempt.

"I'm sorry, Martin," Bruno said, his face impassive.

Martin grinned disdainfully and then walked stiffly away.

Bruno surveyed nature all around him. He had always found autumn the most beautiful season of the year. But today, it had never seemed so drab. A little girl of about five crossed the bridge singing, a doll in her hand. Her mom followed her, watching her absentmindedly.

The lighthearted child's laughter echoed in Bruno's head. He quickly walked away.

In front of the tennis courts, he ran into his neighbor Denis with his nine-year-old son, Frédéric. Surprised and uncomfortable, Denis asked how he and Sylvie were. The discussion was almost unbearably painful for Bruno. For days, he had been feeling nothing but rage and aggression, and that made it harder to put on an act.

At one point, little Frédéric spoke up in a sad voice:

"I'm very sorry about Jasmine being dead too . . ."

Bruno looked down at the child. He stared for a moment at the disfiguring scars he'd had for the past three years. Not very long ago, Bruno had counted himself lucky every time he saw that child.

He had to bite his lip hard to keep from screaming.

"Anyway," Denis said with nauseating compassion, "if you want to talk, I'm here for you."

He added, moving closer, "I know what you're going through."

And he gave Bruno an understanding look! Bruno looked at him for a long time and then said evenly, "As far as I know, your son isn't dead, he's only disfigured."

Denis's features went rigid, while little Frédéric's eyes, at first stunned, filled with tears. He began to cry, and his father bent down to comfort him. Bruno wished he could have regretted his words, but he felt no regret. He silently watched the little scene and felt a dark jealousy. He violently envied this man for being able to comfort his little boy.

Denis looked up at Bruno, but there was no reproach in his eyes. Only a vague, intolerable understanding pity.

Bruno strode away with a sudden pain in his stomach.

In the car, he closed his eyes and rubbed his temples. One last effort . . . one or two more things to take care of and everything would be ready.

During the dinner hour, he went to parks, parking lots, and arcades where he knew he could find young people who didn't do much except hang around, talking to each other and smoking. Making sure to avoid anyone he knew, he approached nine boys in succession, choosing those who looked the toughest and shadiest.

"I have five hundred dollars for you if you'll agree to pick the lock of a car door two days from now."

Five refused his offer, offended: who did he think they were anyway, crooks? Two seemed tempted, but resisted, no doubt suspecting a trap. Another told him outright that he would have been glad to do it but he knew nothing about breaking into cars. Each time, Bruno quickly walked away.

But the ninth one, a conceited-looking skinhead, agreed, attracted by the money. His coat sported the slogan "No faith—No mercy." Bruno made an appointment with him for Tuesday at nine thirty in the morning across from the Box Office bar.

"Nine thirty? I'm gonna miss school!" the skinhead said ironically.

"I'm sure you're really upset about that."

"For five hundred bucks, I'd skip the whole year!" the kid said, taking a drag on his cigarette.

Bruno told him he would get the money when he did the job, and then he left, with the boy watching him, amused and intrigued.

He had a quick bite in a restaurant and went to park his Saturn at the seniors' residence. He was surprised to find a ticket on the Chevrolet. He crumpled it up and tossed it away before getting into the car.

He had to call Morin. There was no question of using the phone in the house or his cell phone, so he stopped at a phone booth. Morin answered on the first ring.

"It's me" was all Bruno said.

"Yeah, I recognized you."

Morin's voice was a bit excited but, above all, surprised.

"Jeeee-zus! After a while, I didn't believe it anymore and I thought you wouldn't call!"

"Here's where you can find today's seven thousand dollars."

Checking his notebook, he gave detailed directions to the hiding place.

"Wait, wait, I have to get all this down."

"Is it clear?" Bruno asked when Morin was finished.

"Very clear!" Morin said excitedly. "And it's not far from . . ."

"I'll call you tomorrow."

Bruno hung up.

A little less than an hour later, he arrived in Longueuil. He stayed there awhile and then returned to Drummondville.

He spent the rest of the afternoon searching the outskirts of the town for a safe place to leave the Chevy without anyone noticing it. At around four thirty, he finally found one. He had been driving along Golf Course Road for a few minutes and had even gone past Highway 20, beyond the city limits of Drummondville. There were woods on both sides, with a few scattered houses. He came upon a little dirt road into the woods, like the one to Josh's place but flat.

Bruno turned onto the road, and in about twenty seconds, he came to a clearing with no buildings, no remains of campfires, no garbage . . . in short, no sign of human activity. He stopped the car and got out. He could just barely see Golf Course Road. The land must belong to some-one, but it clearly wasn't used much.

What were the chances of anyone coming here in the next two days, when it was obvious that nobody ever came here? Close to zero. He would have to be really unlucky.

But it wasn't impossible. What would he do if the Chevrolet wasn't here in two days? Well, he'd steal a car, or get one any way he could.

He estimated that he was ten minutes from downtown at normal speed. That should do it.

He opened the trunk and took out one of the two medical bags. He left the disguise and the antibiotics from Martin in the trunk, but he kept the envelope of nitro patches. Then, taking the bag, he walked to Golf Course Road, where he stuck out his thumb for about ten minutes before a young man about twenty picked him up and took him to the seniors' residence, where his Saturn was parked.

Standing beside his car, his hands on his hips, he looked around, thinking hard. Had he done everything he needed to do? Had he forgotten anything? He had the feeling that, since the darkness, everything had been happening in a single endless, numbing day.

Everything was ready. Everything was in order. All the pieces were in place.

He ran his fingers through his sparse hair with a very long sigh, climbed into the Saturn, and started the engine.

All he had to do now was wait for Tuesday.

TEN FORTY IN THE MORNING. IT SHOULD BE ALMOST DONE NOW.

Three little raps on the side window made him start. A policeman was gesturing to him to lower his window. Shit! He really hadn't seen him coming!

"I'm waiting for somebody."

"This parking lot is for employees of the courthouse only, sir. Visitors have to go to the other side."

"I told you, I'm waiting for somebody. I'm waiting for the lawyer . . . Jean-Claude Bourassa."

It was the name of a lawyer Bruno knew very slightly.

"He asked me to wait here. He should be coming out any minute now."

The cop exhaled: if Mr. Bourassa wasn't there in ten minutes, Bruno would have to move. Bruno said he understood and thanked him, and the policeman left.

Ten minutes. The monster would surely come out by then.

Ten minutes was so short. It was nothing compared to the days that had passed.

Long, quiet waiting.

ALL SUNDAY EVENING, BRUNO SAT IN THE LIVING ROOM DOING NOTHING. HE just let the darkness ripple through him.

The telephone rang twice, but he didn't even answer. No more strength to pretend.

Sylvie did not call.

Bruno sat there for more than three hours. He felt nothing, except the weight on his shoulders, the weight that had never left him since the darkness came.

At nine o'clock, he told himself that the time might pass faster if he was in bed. He went upstairs and, like the night before, lay down in Jasmine's bed.

For the first time, he dreamed of his daughter. He was sitting in a field on a chair, and he was waiting. In front of him on the ground, there was a closed coffin. He knew it was his daughter's. Little dull sounds came from inside, like someone insistently knocking on a door, and a muffled child's voice kept repeating, *"Daddy! . . . Daddy!"* There was no fear or suffering in the voice, but impatience, urgency. Bruno, sitting still in his chair, answered the voice from the coffin: *"Patience, honey! It won't be long now, not long at all."*

And in the distance, at the far end of the field, a dog was running silently toward him.

The sun was blazing bright when Bruno woke up at eight in the morning. He ate breakfast, but without appetite.

What could he do until the next day? Nothing. Nothing at all. So he went and sat down in the living room and started waiting again. Soon he was barely aware that he was in his house.

The hours passed, slowly.

When no thoughts had crossed Bruno's mind for quite a while, a word lit up in his head like an alarm, as if it had been waiting crouched in the shadows for that precise moment to burst through the fog.

Morin.

Bruno jumped up, making every bone in his body creak, and looked at the time: two ten. He left the house, got in his car, and drove to a phone booth.

When Morin recognized Bruno's voice, he got very excited:

"The money was exactly where you said it would be!"

"Of course."

"Yeah, I know, it's just that . . ."

Morin stopped, embarrassed. Obviously, he was still having trouble believing what was happening.

Bruno checked his notebook again and told Morin the exact place where he could find the second bundle of money.

"That one too, it's not too far from . . ."

Bruno hung up.

Three minutes later, he was back home. The violent emergence from his cocoon had made him a bit dizzy. He returned to the living room and went back to waiting.

When the telephone rang at about four, he answered it, barely realizing what he was doing.

It was Sylvie. They greeted each other uncomfortably, especially Bruno, who still felt disoriented.

"You sound tired. What are you doing?"

"Nothing."

Silence, then Sylvie asked in a desperate voice, "Do you think we should see each other? To talk?"

"No."

There was no anger in his voice.

Sylvie smothered a sob and pleaded, "What's happening to you, Bruno? I don't recognize you anymore. Something awful is happening inside you and I don't know what it is! Talk to me! Tell me what's going on!"

Bruno closed his eyes and rubbed his forehead with his free hand, grimacing. He didn't want his waiting to be disturbed, he didn't want anyone to come and stir up the darkness inside him. Why was he being hassled with these trivial questions? He shouldn't have answered the phone. So he interrupted Sylvie, saying quickly, "Listen, Sylvie, don't call me anymore. There's no point. I'll call you. And then you'll understand."

"Stop this! You told me the same thing the other evening! What are you talking about? What . . ."

He hung up. He sat down again in the living room and didn't move any more. The telephone rang a few more times, and then there was silence.

Time passed.

Bruno noticed that his stomach hurt. He realized that it was seven o'clock and he hadn't eaten since morning. He heated some soup and made himself a salad. He felt like having a beer, and drank two, sitting at the table staring at the wall in front of him.

That night he dreamed the same dream. But this time, the knocking was so hard that the coffin lid shook, and Jasmine's voice was impatient and was starting to sound angry and frustrated: *"Daddy! . . . Daddy!"* And Bruno answered, *"Just a few more hours, honey!"* In the distance, in the field, the dog was getting closer and closer. It was a huge black Great Dane. It didn't make any sounds, but its fangs were bared and its eyes sparkled threateningly, and it was now only about twenty meters from Bruno.

*"Daddy!"*

*"Okay, honey! I'm coming now!"*

He woke up just when the dog pounced on him, its teeth bared.

When he opened his eyes, he looked at the alarm clock: eight thirty, exactly the time he'd wanted to get up.

He washed, dressed, and transferred the contents of his pockets from his pants from the day before to his jeans. For a moment, he held Jasmine's blue ribbon in his hand. The dried bloodstain was dark and brownish now.

He ate quickly and went to his office and got the bag he had brought with him the day before. After thinking for a moment, he also took the briefcase containing the remaining thousands of dollars. Walking out of the house, he contemplated it for a brief moment. Then he got into the Saturn and drove off.

He felt a very slight sense of excitement.

At precisely nine thirty, he stopped in front of the Box Office, and the young skinhead got into the car, smiling.

"I was wondering if you were really going to come or if you were putting me on the other day. It looks like you're serious about this thing."

Bruno stared at him blankly and drove off again without a word. Five minutes later, he stopped in the parking lot behind the courthouse and cut the engine.

"What the hell are we doing here?" asked the kid, who wasn't enjoying himself so much now.

"We're waiting."

The kid tried a couple of times to talk to his strange employer, but finally gave up.

At nine forty-eight, Bruno saw the monster in the flesh for the first time . . . and heard the growling of the dog.

A T TEN FIFTY-SIX, AN OFFICER CAME OUT OF THE COURTHOUSE AND GOT INTO the police car. Bruno, suddenly alert, started his engine.

The patrol car went behind the building and parked close to the rear door. The officer got out, went back through the demonstrators, who had been waiting all this time, and entered the building. Obviously, he didn't discover the patches on the wheel.

Thirty meters away, Bruno was waiting nervously.

After two minutes, the door opened again and the monster came out, escorted by the same two police officers. The three men walked to the car with the demonstrators again raining insults on them.

The monster still had that vaguely arrogant look on his face. They put him in the back seat, and the two officers got in the front . . . and Bruno held his breath. It was the moment of truth. If the car didn't start in the next ten seconds, it would mean they'd discovered the patches.

Twenty seconds passed. The demonstrators kept shouting their rage. Half a minute. It was all over, the driver had felt the patches, and the whole plan had collapsed! In a sudden panic, Bruno was even starting to open the door, his hand on the revolver under his belt, thinking fast about what to do—anything except *give up!* Suddenly, the police car backed up and headed toward the parking lot exit.

His hand shaking, Bruno drove off too.

At precisely eleven o'clock, the two cars were heading down Saint-Joseph Boulevard toward the detention center. Behind the steering wheel of his car, Bruno never took his eyes off the vehicle some twenty meters ahead.

He now felt very calm. Heavy, but calm. He was saving his emotions for later, in a couple of hours . . .

. . . when hate and joy would be joined in a most devastating marriage.

# PART 2

# DAY 1

THROUGHOUT THE PRELIMINARY HEARING, DETECTIVE SERGEANT HERVÉ MERcure never once took his eyes off Lemaire.

The trial would take place in four months. Lemaire was pleading guilty, but Mercure doubted that it would do him any good. He'd get at least twenty years. That should have satisfied Mercure, but it didn't. And this wasn't the first time he had not found an arrest totally satisfying.

He was watching Lemaire's face as he listened to his lawyer in silence. His expression was frightened yet arrogant. As Mercure had also observed during his arrest and interrogation. At one point, when Sergeant Bolduc confronted Lemaire about his muddled answers, Lemaire had even turned toward Mercure and said coldly, "What's with you, looking at me like that?"

Mercure had said nothing.

Lemaire laughed and added, "You ask too many pointless questions!"

Anthony Lemaire, twenty-eight years old, was born in Joliette, into a poor family of four children, a violent father, and an alcoholic mother. He had done badly at school and dropped out at sixteen to take the first in a series of unskilled jobs. He had tried several times to find a girlfriend, but according to his mother, as tough and arrogant as he was in everyday life, he was awkward and unsure with girls, and they always broke up with him. He ended up withdrawing and going out less and less. When he was twenty-two, his mother moved to Saint-Hyacinthe to get away from her violent husband, and Anthony had gone with her. He had found a job pumping gas, had a falling-out with his mother, and started another string of unsuccessful relationships with the opposite sex. Two years earlier, he had been charged with raping and murdering a little girl. Since they had found no trace of the perpetrator's blood or sperm or even a single hair, no DNA test was done, and he had been released for lack of evidence. He had then moved to Drummondville, where he had found another job as a gas station attendant. Since no one there knew him, he had tried to make some friends. And he had again tried to find a girlfriend. But once again, his awkwardness had earned him ridicule, and with his arrogant, superior façade, he had again become isolated, only rarely going out with a few losers for a drink or to smoke joints. He had started a few bar brawls, but nothing serious.

And there it was: the classic, even banal, portrait of your average petty criminal. But that didn't explain everything. Mercure had frequently come across guys with that profile, and they weren't all rapists and murderers.

What was there in the soul of this man?

The hearing, which had begun late, was finally over. The judge withdrew, and the accused was escorted to the prisoners' exit by the two officers.

Until Lemaire disappeared through the door, Mercure never took his eyes off him.

———

Sergeant Michel Boisvert got into the passenger's seat of the police car and turned toward Lemaire, who was sitting in the back.

"You want to know what I think?" he said scornfully. "I hope you get life! And if it was up to me, I'd send you to be tried in the States! There, they'd put you to death, and that would be just fine!"

Sergeant Bertrand Cabana sat in the driver's seat, telling his colleague to calm down. The muffled insults of the demonstrators could be heard from outside, a few meters away. Behind the partition separating the front and back seats, Lemaire, handcuffed, had an insolent little smile on his face. Cabana started the engine and notified the station by radio that they were leaving the courthouse. Holding the steering wheel with both hands, he headed toward the exit of the parking lot. There he stopped at a red light and examined his hands curiously.

"You okay?" Boisvert asked.

"It's just that . . . the steering wheel seems . . . I don't know . . ."

He touched the steering wheel again, looked at his fingers a second time, puzzled.

"As if it . . ."

He shrugged.

"You can psychoanalyze your steering wheel some other time. The light is green," Boisvert joked.

The car headed down Saint-Joseph Boulevard. There wasn't much traffic. They drove in silence for a few minutes. Boisvert was morose. It was his first encounter with a child murderer and, dammit, he hoped it was the last! He had two kids himself, five and nine years old, and if some bastard ever laid a finger on one of them . . . He was tempted to turn around and insult the scumbag again, but he thought better of it, and just muttered to himself.

Out of the corner of his eye, he saw Cabana take off his cap and rub his forehead, grimacing. Boisvert asked again if he was okay.

"Headache," Cabana answered, putting his cap back on.

Boisvert was bothered more by his stomach: escorting this bastard in the back seat made him want to puke.

Cabana took off his cap again and groaned, his face suddenly pale. This time, Boisvert repeated his question with real concern. Cabana mumbled that he really didn't feel well. The detention center wasn't much farther. Was he all right driving for three minutes, or should Boisvert take his place? The car was starting to weave as Cabana went limp and his eyelids started to flutter. Frightened, Boisvert ordered him to pull over, which Cabana just managed to do. In the back seat, Lemaire was frowning. The car finally stopped.

"Hey, Bert, what's the matter with you?"

Cabana started to mumble something, but then he collapsed on the steering wheel and stopped moving. Terrified, Boisvert started shaking. Lemaire was watching the scene, an amused smile on his lips.

Boisvert was about to radio the station when the passenger door opened and a balding man of about forty leaned inside and said, "Excuse me, Officer, I was driving behind you when I thought I noticed . . . Is there a problem?"

"You just close that door and mind your own business!" shot back the sergeant.

"I'm a doctor, maybe I can help your colleague . . ."

Boisvert finally noticed the bag the man was holding and how calm he looked, and after a fraction of a second's hesitation, he told him to go around to the driver's side. The doctor walked around the car, opened the driver's door, and put his bag on the floor at Cabana's feet. Meanwhile, Boisvert was asking the station to send an ambulance. The doctor lifted the driver's head. Cabana's eyes were closed and he offered no resistance.

"Maybe it's a heart attack, huh?" suggested Boisvert awkwardly.

"Maybe . . ."

The doctor looked at Cabana's pupils and said, "He needs air. Help me get him out of the car as quickly as possible."

Boisvert didn't even hesitate. Lemaire was handcuffed and the two back doors only opened from the outside. Three seconds later, they were laying Cabana down on a little patch of grass by the sidewalk a few meters from the car. They were in front of the Celanese factory, and there were few pedestrians. Nevertheless, a handful of curious people gathered around them, in spite of Boisvert's efforts to keep them back. Lemaire was following all this with interest through the back window of the car.

The doctor rubbed the unconscious policeman's forehead for a few seconds and then stood up, saying, "I'm going to get my bag. I left it in your car. Keep rubbing his forehead the way I was."

"Christ! I hope he's not going to die!"

Boisvert knelt and started frantically rubbing his colleague's forehead, while the doctor walked quickly toward the police car. Under the watchful gaze of the onlookers, he pleaded with his colleague to wake up.

Suddenly Cabana opened his eyes and blinked several times. Boisvert couldn't help giving a little cry of joy. He looked up to tell the doctor . . . and saw the police car speeding away.

Still on his knees, he watched stunned as the vehicle swerved onto the median and turned onto the other side of the boulevard, setting off a chorus of honking and screeching brakes.

"Hey! That guy took your car!" an onlooker said stupidly.

Boisvert jumped to his feet, pulled out his revolver, and pointed it toward the car, shouting, "Stop! Stop!" But of course he couldn't fire on a busy street! That second of hesitation was enough to allow the car to disappear.

Boisvert lowered the weapon, dismayed. Behind him, Cabana stood up and, in a hoarse voice, asked, "Hey . . . what's going on?"

———

Bruno drove along the boulevard at close to eighty kilometers an hour. At red lights, he would slow down a little to make sure he could get through, then continue at full speed. That was the advantage of being in a police car: no one bothered you. If he'd known how, he would have turned on the siren.

He had put on gloves before taking the wheel. He didn't want to get an overdose of nitroglycerine as the policeman had. He took a quick glance at his watch: nine minutes past eleven.

"Hey, what . . . what the hell are you doing?" the monster behind him asked.

Bruno didn't answer him, didn't even glance at him in the rearview mirror. He stared at the road ahead, his face unperturbed, with a single sentence echoing in his head: *It's going to work. It's going to work.*

He went past the courthouse again, past Saint-Pierre Street, and then made a sharp right onto Des Châtaigniers. The area was more residential, but he barely slowed down. Two women who were trying to cross at the corner of Des Pins backed away in terror. Finally, he got to Golf Course Road and turned left, his tires screeching. There were no traffic lights and not many stops on this road, with houses on one side and the golf course on the other. He sped up to a hundred.

Behind him, the monster was demanding explanations more and more impatiently, but Bruno maintained his silence.

He crossed the bridge over Saint-Germain River, took the overpass over Highway 20, crossed the city limits, and continued on a road bordered by woods. In less than a minute, he slowed down and turned onto the little dirt road. For a second, he was sure the green Chevy would be gone. But there it was, waiting patiently in the clearing, and he pulled up beside it.

Eleven fifteen. Bruno had done the route in record time. The police must barely have begun their search. The monster was getting upset: what the hell were they doing here in the woods? Bruno cut the engine and turned toward him. The monster calmed down and, more cautious, asked, "Who are you anyway?"

Silently, Bruno opened his bag, took out a bottle of chloroform, and splashed some on a cloth. He got out of the car and opened the back door. The monster recoiled a little and raised his handcuffed hands. Bruno, still holding the cloth, leaned inside and stared at him in silence, his face expressionless.

The monster gave a nervous little chuckle.

"Come on, say something! Who are you?"

Suddenly, Bruno pushed the cloth over the monster's nose and mouth, holding the chain of the handcuffs with his other hand. The monster struggled for a few seconds, then passed out.

Bruno grabbed him by the collar, pulled him closer, and looked at him intently for a long time. His features hardened and his eyes became black as night. His breath became noisier, hoarser, and his jaw was clenched so hard that his teeth were starting to hurt.

Not right away . . . soon.

He heard a growl, distant and indistinct. He let go of the monster and looked around, expecting a guard dog to leap for his throat.

There was no animal in sight. Unless the growling was coming from a far-off neighbor. He thought he had noticed a house not too far from here on the road.

One more reason not to hang around.

He dug around in the glove compartment and found some keys. One of them opened the monster's handcuffs. Bruno picked up his bag, took out a syringe and a vial, and prepared an injection. After rolling up one sleeve of the monster's leather jacket, he stuck the needle in his arm, ensuring a few hours of sleep.

He went and opened the trunk of the Chevy and put the sleeping body in it. Then he put on his disguise, got in behind the wheel, and drove off.

Three minutes later, he was rolling along Highway 20 toward the Mauricie region.

———

Mercure went into the Saint-Georges. The waiter greeted him with a friendly "Hello, Inspector!" and brought him a cup even before the policeman had ordered. At first, Mercure would correct people, telling them that the title "inspector" was outdated and no longer applicable, that he was in fact a detective sergeant. But it was no use: they all kept calling him "inspector." He had finally given up; people had definitely watched too much *Columbo*.

Sitting close to the big window in the front, the policeman drank his coffee and watched two little old men walking slowly in Saint-Frédéric Park across the street.

When he went to the station shortly, he would call the victim's parents to tell them the trial date. Until now, he had only spoken to the father, Bruno Hamel. Mercure recalled the voice of this man he hadn't yet met. During the first call, Hamel's voice had been weak and sad— completely normal under the circumstances. But during the second call, he'd had a totally different voice: calm, cold, hard.

Mercure would try to meet him. In fact, if he hadn't been so busy, he would already have gone to see him. The police were generally quite good at taking care of criminals and their victims, but they too often forgot another important category of people: the walking wounded. Since one of the missions of the police was prevention, they were making a serious mistake in neglecting these people. Very often, in Mercure's opinion, the line separating them from the criminals was very thin. Sometimes it just took a single thing to make one of them start growing a new skin and turn into a criminal.

This Hamel guy, for example. His voice on the telephone . . . so controlled, so distant. It was the voice not only of someone who had suffered, but of someone in the process of growing a new skin.

He finished his coffee with a sigh. Maybe he was imagining things. It wouldn't be the first time. With a vague smile, he waved to the waiter and left.

Walking into the police station at eleven forty-five, he found the squad room abuzz with activity. Officers were rushing around, sending urgent radio messages or barking orders. He hadn't even had time to take his coat off before Wagner came over. An incredible story— Mercure would never believe it.

"Did somebody shoot Her Honor the Mayor?" Mercure asked calmly.

"No kidding, Hervé! Somebody stole the car transporting Lemaire! With Lemaire inside! The guy who did it was following in a car and . . ."

He explained. Mercure shook his head, bewildered. Why would anyone do that? Wagner had an idea about that. The guy's car had been identified. The chief paused for effect and said, "It was Bruno Hamel. The father of Lemaire's victim."

Mercure didn't react for a few seconds. Then he closed his eyes and bowed his head.

He knew he should have gone to see Hamel sooner.

———

At twelve forty, the Chevy stopped in front of Josh's cottage.

Bruno went in right away, picked up the phone, and dialed a number. There was no risk in using the old phone in the cottage: why would the police be interested in calls made by Josh Frears?

There was no excitement in Morin's voice this time, no attempt to start a conversation; he was starting to understand how things worked. Bruno described another hiding place to him, also in Grand-Mère, in a tree trunk at the town limits. After a few seconds, Morin said simply, "Fine, I've got it."

Bruno hung up.

He went and got the monster and dragged his sleeping body to the room that had been Josh's office. He dropped him on the floor about a meter away from the back wall, and quickly undressed him completely. He even untied his hair, which had been tied back in a ponytail with an elastic. He opened the bedroom closet and threw the clothes in it. He returned to the naked body. Thin. Pale. A few scars.

Two chains hung from a hook in the ceiling down to the floor. Metal rings were welded to the ends of the chains. Bruno put the monster's hands through the rings and closed them. He took a few steps back and looked at the monster lying on the floor, naked, his hands shackled. Perfect. He looked like a chained dog.

Why that strange comparison? He didn't look like a dog at all.

The other ends of the chains extended diagonally from the hook in the ceiling to a hand winch by the window, where the curtains were closed. The chains were wound around the winch. Bruno did not intend to use the winch for the time being. Not right away. Nor the very special table off to one side, also made by Morin. That would also be for later.

Now it was ready. Now all this had a meaning.

He left the room, walked to the kitchen, took a beer from the fridge, and dropped into an armchair in the living room.

He looked at the beer, the living room, and the window, and for the first time since the coming of the darkness, he smiled.

———

"And it didn't occur to you that it might be a trap!" Wagner exclaimed.

It was one ten in the afternoon. Boisvert was sitting in front of Mercure's desk, his elbows on his knees, staring at the floor.

"No . . . not really, no."

"A doctor who was following you just when Cabana didn't feel well! Who got you to leave the car! Who went back to get his bag! Really, Michel!"

"Come on, Greg! This isn't a movie, it's not New York City! This is Drummondville, for crying out loud! Have you seen an ambush since you've been working here?"

"A trap," Mercure said nonchalantly, sitting behind his desk.

"Huh?"

"Ambush isn't the right term. Trap would be more accurate."

Wagner started pacing back and forth behind Boisvert. As usual when he was in a tense situation, his face was red and contorted. Grégoire Wagner was fifty-eight years old, stout and imposing, with thick, curly black hair and a black mustache; he had been commanding the Drummondville station for eight years and always looked like he was about to have a heart attack. When he got upset, as he was now, it was much worse.

"In broad daylight, on Saint-Joseph Boulevard!" he growled, rubbing his swollen neck. "In front of witnesses!"

"How's Cabana?" Mercure asked.

He was already better. He had pretty much recovered. He had had a spectacular drop in blood pressure. But how had Hamel been able to make that happen to Cabana at just that time?

"Maybe it was a coincidence," suggested Boisvert.

The look from his superior convinced Boisvert not to make any more suggestions.

"What about Hamel's wife?" asked Mercure.

They still hadn't reached her. She must have been involved. Maybe she had already joined her husband.

An officer knocked and came into the office, and told Mercure that they had found the police car in the woods along Golf Course Road. The forensics team had examined it and found nitro patches on the steering wheel.

"Nitro!" Wagner exclaimed.

There was no sign of Hamel or Lemaire, but there were tire tracks indicating that another car had been waiting for them. The site was being combed for more clues.

Mercure remembered that, a few days earlier, Hamel had asked him to explain in detail the procedure of the preliminary hearing. The detective sergeant had complied. But how could he have foreseen what Hamel was going to do?

"Greg," Mercure said, "I'd like to be in charge of this case."

"Of course you will! You handled the Lemaire case, so there's no reason you shouldn't continue."

Silence. Mercure went over his notes on a sheet of paper. He asked Boisvert, "Did he seem calm to you during his little act?"

"Extremely."

The detective sergeant sighed, far from reassured by this answer.

The intercom on the desk buzzed and a voice asked if Wagner was there. It said the forensics team had not been able to ascertain the make or color of the car. All they knew was that it was losing oil and that it had Goodyear all-season tires, two or three years old. Wagner raised his arms, discouraged: might as well stop half the cars in the province! He paced for a few seconds, shaking his head. Hamel's intentions were crystal-clear.

"We're going to find Lemaire's body in a couple of hours, mark my words!" Wagner said.

———

Sitting in the living room, Sylvie glanced anxiously at the clock for the thirtieth time since noon. Two o'clock. Where was he? She had returned home intending to have a calm, serious talk with Bruno. When it turned out that he wasn't there, she had called the hospital, but they had told her he hadn't been back to work since the tragedy. So he had lied to her! But what had he been doing the past few days? What was he doing now? She imagined him wandering the streets in a state of total confusion, unable to deal with his emotions. She had accused him of not taking care of her, but maybe she had been wrong. Maybe he was the one who needed to be taken care of.

She had been thinking for the past two hours and had made a decision. When he came home, she wouldn't ask any questions. This time she would wait for him to talk, without pushing him. And if he opened up to her, if he really communicated, she would suggest they get help, that they go see an expert. She had thought that they would get through this alone, but she had been wrong. This ordeal was too big for their relationship, which had been in trouble for a while now. With help, they would find each other again. And if they managed to get through this tragedy, they would be stronger than ever.

She wiped her eyes with the back of her hand. They would also adopt a child. It was essential. Vital. For her, but also for Bruno. For them.

The doorbell rang. She got up reluctantly. She really didn't feel like seeing some solicitous friend today. When she opened the door, she was surprised to find a man of about fifty, thin, with a long, tired face, who greeted her politely but without smiling.

"This is where Bruno Hamel lives, isn't it?"

———

They were facing each other across the little kitchen table. Between them, two almost full cups of coffee were getting cold. Sylvie was leaning on her elbows with her hands on her temples, pushing waves of her long black hair up. She looked like a boxer recovering from a KO; her eyes were red and swollen, but she had stopped crying five minutes ago. Outside, a neighbor was raking his lawn.

Mercure looked at her in silence for a long time. One thing was already clear to him: she was not an accomplice.

"What are you thinking about?" he finally asked.

Without changing position, still distraught, she answered in a weak voice, "Lately, I found him so strange . . . And all those days he spent away, I don't know where. He was upset, but not . . . not like he should have . . . I mean, in the beginning, yes, but . . . on the fourth or fifth day, something happened, he changed. There wasn't only despair in him, there was . . . something else . . . something much darker."

"Did your husband . . ."

"We're not married."

That's right, Hamel had told him that.

"Was your partner violent by nature, Ms. Jutras?"

"On the contrary, he was a pacifist."

Sylvie talked about the dozens of petitions he had signed protesting violence against women or children or political prisoners.

"Do you have a recent photo of him, where you can see his face clearly?"

Sylvie disappeared for a few minutes and came back with a photo she gave to the detective sergeant. It had been taken at his thirty-eighth birthday party, in May. It showed a man who was almost completely bald, with a rather long face and brown eyes that were small but penetrating, intelligent. He seemed a little older than thirty-eight. He was looking at the camera with his thumb up. He was smiling serenely. He looked happy.

Mercure looked at the photo for a long time, then slipped it into the inside pocket of his coat.

Suddenly the telephone rang.

They both looked at the phone hanging on the kitchen wall. Mercure asked if there was a cordless phone in the house. Yes, it must be in the living room. The policeman dashed there and came back with it five seconds later. The fourth ring was sounding.

Sylvie stood up and went to the wall phone. Mercure gave a signal, and she answered at the same time he picked up on the cordless.

"Hello?" she said in a flat voice.

"It's me."

She closed her eyes and put her hand on her cheek. Mercure was listening carefully as he recorded the time of the call in his notebook.

"God, Bruno! What . . . what's gotten into you? Did you . . . You haven't killed him, have you?"

"No, he's still alive."

The voice was calm, in control. Sylvie sighed with relief: he could still get out of this okay. Mercure, while remaining silent, gave a little nod of satisfaction.

"And he'll stay alive for seven days."

Sylvie blinked, taken aback, while the policeman frowned. She asked what he meant. She didn't understand. Still calm, Hamel explained, "I'm going to kill him next Monday, and after that, I'll turn myself in to the police."

She gave an incredulous little gasp. Mercure felt a cold shiver run down his spine. But he didn't move, and continued listening carefully.

"Do you understand now?" Hamel asked. "Do you understand what I was planning?"

Sylvie shook her head. It didn't make sense, he couldn't be serious!

"I'm very serious, Sylvie."

"But it's insane! What . . . what are you going to do with him for a week?"

Hamel didn't answer. Mercure didn't need to hear the answer; the chill within him turned to ice. Sylvie seemed to have understood too, and she blanched, her hand over her mouth.

"Listen, Sylvie, I'm calling you to tell you I'm sorry. I know I've caused you a lot of pain."

Mercure was paying close attention to the voice. Of course, from certain intonations, certain words, he could sense that Hamel was really sorry, but the detachment and hardness were so dominant, they overwhelmed everything else. With his free hand, he took out the photo of Hamel, and for the rest of the conversation, he kept his eyes on it.

"But at the same time, I wanted you to know what I intend to do because . . . if anyone can understand, it's you. I don't need you to give what I'm doing legitimacy, but Jasmine was your daughter too, so I think you . . . you can understand."

"Bruno, you . . . Think about what you're doing. This is just crazy! You can't do this, it's not like you! I love you, Bruno! It's *your* life you're destroying, not mine! I love you! And if you still love me, come home! Come home now, quickly!"

Silence.

"Do you still love me?" Sylvie asked, panic in her eyes.

For the first time, Hamel's voice faltered slightly.

"I . . . I can't love anyone now, Sylvie."

She ran her fingers through her hair, searching desperately for new arguments. Mercure tried to make out the background noises: car sounds, people talking, city sounds, anything that would give him a clue. But there was nothing.

"If it were . . . If somebody else were doing what you're doing, you would be against it!" Sylvie continued. "You'd think it was insane!"

"But that's just it, it's not happening to somebody else, it's happening to me!" Hamel replied with surprising anger. "That makes all the difference! I'm the victim of the dog! Me!"

"Of the dog?" Sylvie stammered. "What dog?"

"What?"

"What dog are you talking about, Bruno?"

"What do you mean, Sylvie?"

She shook her head, incredulous. Mercure frowned again.

"Okay, I'm going to hang up now. I was hoping . . ."

"You can't do this!" Sylvie shouted. "You can't, you've gone completely crazy! You can't do it!"

"Don't say I'm crazy!" Hamel replied. "On the contrary, I'm very clearheaded!"

He sighed and changed to an incredulous, almost pleading voice. "So you don't see it? You don't see the meaning of what I'm doing?"

"Bruno, you . . ."

"Isn't there some part of you that approves of what I'm doing, Sylvie? Even if all this upsets you, revolts you, is there not a small part of your soul, of your heart, that's satisfied with what's happening?"

She was caught off guard and didn't answer.

Totally calm again, but in a terribly dark voice, Bruno continued, "For the next seven days, each night before you go to bed, you'll be able to say to yourself that the monster who raped and killed our daughter has endured a day of suffering. Every day, you'll be able to say to yourself that he's experiencing the kind of torture he subjected Jasmine to. And every day will be worse than the one before. He will never again smile that damn little snotty smile. Do you understand? Until next Monday, you will know that somewhere, our daughter's murderer is screaming in pain. Think about that, Sylvie, and try to tell me you're completely against the idea!"

Sylvie opened and closed her mouth, confused.

"*Just say it!*" Bruno insisted.

With the telephone at his ear, Mercure was observing Sylvie. Her face was contorted as if she was in agony.

"I . . ."

She couldn't say anything more, and bit her lip, frightened by her inability to answer.

"I won't torment you anymore, Sylvie. I won't call you again. Later, I'm sure you'll under—"

"This is Detective Sergeant Mercure," interrupted the policeman softly.

Silence at the other end of the line.

"Do you hear me, Dr. Hamel?"

"Actually, I'm not surprised you're there," Bruno said evenly. "Now that you know, I have nothing to add. So I'll call you next Monday, after I've killed the monster. Then I'll tell you where I am."

"Dr. Hamel, what you're doing won't bring back your daughter."

"Do you take me for an idiot? Of course I know that. That's not the purpose."

"Do you think it will ease your pain?"

"No."

"Why, then?"

There was a pause at the other end of the line, and then, "It will alleviate my feeling of injustice and powerlessness."

"I think you're making a mistake," Mercure said.

"I think I don't give a damn."

"If you torture and kill that man, you'll be a murderer just like him."

"I'll be a murderer, but not just like him."

This answer caught Mercure off guard.

Hamel continued, "In seven days, it will be all over. Until then, there's no point trying to look for me. You won't find me. Don't bother Sylvie; as you've heard, she had nothing to do with it."

"Dr. Hamel . . ."

Mercure, sensing that the doctor was going to hang up, spoke a little more insistently, more gravely, without losing the hoarse softness of his voice.

"Dr. Hamel, you'll lose your job, you'll go to prison. Your life will be destroyed."

"It already is."

The connection was cut.

"He has a cell phone, doesn't he?" Mercure asked Sylvie.

"Wh . . . what?"

"Your partner has a cell phone, doesn't he?"

She replied yes, and he asked her for the number. He dialed it immediately, but in vain: no answer. Mercure wrote the number in his notebook and turned back to Sylvie, who seemed completely lost.

"So you think that . . . that he's going to torture him, is that right?" she asked. "For seven days?"

He didn't answer, but his silence was eloquent. It was obvious, wasn't it? Hamel certainly wasn't holding Lemaire hostage to discuss philosophy with him.

She shook her head again and put her hands on her temples. This wasn't possible, it wasn't Bruno, he could never do something like that, never! She was on the verge of tears again.

Mercure tried to imagine Hamel these past few days, and it fascinated him. Because he hadn't just waited for Lemaire at the courthouse door to put a bullet in his head in a fit of rage that had made him lose all judgment. No. For more than a week, Bruno Hamel had coldly prepared a meticulously detailed plan. For more than a week, he had known very well that he was going to kidnap Lemaire, take him to an isolated spot, and torture him. He had planned how long he would keep him. He had planned to kill him in the end, and then give himself up to the police. Everything he had done these past few days was directed toward that goal. He had found a safe place without attracting anyone's attention, had likely gotten hold of a car, probably outside the city, had inquired about the formalities of the preliminary hearing, had prepared the nitro patches, had found a way to unlock the door of the police car. There was nothing impulsive in any of that. On the contrary, there was intelligence, thought, calculation. And the insanity of the plan hadn't stopped him.

Mercure stroked his right cheek. Something had broken in Bruno Hamel.

An image of the tormented man came to his mind.

"Would you have any idea at all where he might be hiding?"

Holding back her tears, Sylvie thought for a moment, shrugged, and mentioned their cottage in the Eastern Townships. He also asked for the names of Bruno's parents and his close friends.

"You want to question them?"

Mercure was almost sure Hamel was hiding someplace nobody knew about, but he had to check every possible lead. Maybe one of them would have an idea. She gave a few names and telephone numbers, which Mercure wrote down. Then, as if she couldn't hold herself back anymore, Sylvie slumped down in her chair and started sobbing. Mercure watched in silence. He had rarely seen someone so physically affected by sorrow. Sylvie Jutras was devastated. She looked like a survivor of some terrible catastrophe who hadn't slept in days. And wasn't that exactly the case? She was still in mourning for the death of her daughter when a second tragedy had been added to the first one. He remained respectfully quiet and took the opportunity to skim through what he'd written in his notebook.

"Dammit! I'm fed up with bawling all the time!" she cried suddenly, hitting the table feebly.

"Is there someone who could come and spend a few days with you? I really don't think you should stay here alone."

She began to protest, but he was so insistent that she finally agreed. Another thing: would she let him put a tap on her telephone? They would automatically record all her conversations, but the only ones the police would listen to would be those with Hamel. If he called again, of course. She agreed, and Mercure said a technician would come by later in the day. He was about to ask her not to talk to anyone about this, but he couldn't bring himself to—it seemed too cruel. In any case, she wouldn't be capable of it.

When he was about to leave, she stopped him.

"The phone call he just made . . . can you trace it?"

"Since he must have used his cell phone, we could tell which cell relayed the call."

"Which cell?"

He scratched his head.

"Listen, I'm not an expert in electronics, but basically, the radio waves from cell phone calls are sent by transmitters called cells. The message is sent to the cell closest to the sender—Hamel—and then that cell communicates with the cell closest to the receiver—you."

"Are there a lot of these cells in Quebec?"

"Hundreds."

Sylvie looked discouraged, but Mercure explained that it was precisely because of that fact that they could tell where a call came from.

"The more densely populated the region, the more cells there are. If he called from Montreal, for example, the cell would give us a zone of just a few square kilometers. If he called from some remote village, there might be just one cell in about twenty square kilometers or more, so it becomes less precise. But that's already a clue."

He hesitated.

"If you find out where he is, will you tell us?"

Sylvie, taken aback, answered yes.

"You're sure about that?"

He remembered her silence, her hesitation, before, when Hamel had asked her if there wasn't a part of her that approved of his actions. But she gave the same answer, without hesitating. He asked why.

"Because I want to see him again as quickly as possible."

Mercure nodded.

She smiled bitterly.

"That wasn't the reason you were hoping for, was it?"

"I wasn't hoping for any particular reason," he replied gently. "Don't forget to call someone to keep you company."

She promised. As she was closing the door, he could see that she was trying hard not to cry.

In his car, before driving off, he looked at the house for a while. A pretty cottage, surprisingly modest considering that the owner was so rich. Warm, with brightly colored flowers, shrubs of all sizes, and a big yard covered with dead leaves. He imagined Hamel, Sylvie Jutras, and little Jasmine playing in the yard.

He examined the photograph of the doctor again. Earlier, when Hamel had called, the detective sergeant had tried to connect that voice with this face. He couldn't do it.

There was no relation, no connection between this smiling, serene face and that dark, detached voice.

———

Bruno put down the computer mike and breathed a long sigh of relief.

It had worked perfectly. That proved he'd managed to learn something in his computer course last year.

When he arrived at the duplex, he had tried the telephone and found that the phone company had kept its word and the line was connected. He had set his computer up on the kitchen counter and configured it to connect to the Internet, and everything had gone very well.

Even better, Mercure had been with Sylvie when he called. In less than an hour, the police would be on his trail. On his false trail.

There was only one dark spot in the picture: Sylvie didn't understand. She thought he was crazy. But she was still in shock. In a few days, she would change her mind, he was sure of it. Imagining the monster suffering would change her mind.

In any case, what she thought didn't matter to him anymore. And never would again.

Before leaving, he put on his disguise again, except for the dark glasses, which definitely made him look too suspicious. Outside, there was no one on the glum, deserted street. He glanced toward the window of his apartment. The light was off and the curtains drawn. He got into his car and left Charette.

When he stopped the car in front of the cottage, he checked his watch. It was three ten. It had taken him about fifteen minutes to return to Saint-Mathieu-du-Parc. It was close enough if he had other calls to make, and far enough in case there was a hitch.

The house was completely silent. Before leaving for Charette, Bruno had given the monster another injection to make sure he wouldn't miss seeing him wake up. He still had a few hours to sleep.

In a magazine rack beside the couch, he found a few medical journals. He made himself comfortable and began to read.

———

In his office, Wagner paced back and forth, loosening his necktie. Mercure, sitting in a corner with his hands folded across his belly, watched his movements with a certain weariness.

"So you think he's serious?"

"Yeah, I think he is."

Wagner swore, started pacing again, stopped, and said, "He's gone crazy obviously!"

Mercure didn't comment.

An officer came in. He said Hamel had indeed used his cell phone. And they had located the cell that had relayed the call to Drummondville. It was in Longueuil and it covered one of the biggest neighborhoods of the city, including part of downtown.

"Longueuil," Mercure murmured with astonishment.

"Good, we know where he's hiding!"

"I'm not so sure. Maybe he only stopped there to call his wife. By this time, he could be hiding somewhere in the Laurentians."

"Well, it won't cost us anything to send his description to the guys in Longueuil, will it?"

Mercure shrugged, and Wagner passed on the order by telephone. Then he started pacing again.

"You had a tap put on his wife's phone?"

"Yes, they said ten minutes ago that it had been done."

"Okay. So what's your plan?"

The detective sergeant cracked the joints in his thin neck. Soon he would go and question a few people. Tomorrow he would review the situation with his colleagues Pleau and Bolduc.

"There are still reporters waiting outside!" growled the chief. "They want something for the six o'clock news! What should I tell the vultures?"

"Everything. They'll find it all out anyway."

"I'd rather not mention the seven-day deadline. Or tell them we traced his call to Longueuil."

Wagner took a few more steps and leaned both hands on the back of his chair. Mercure didn't remember ever seeing him sitting in it.

"What do you think of all this, Hervé?"

The detective sergeant gave a sad sigh.

"I think the guy has grown a new skin."

———

Seven ten in the evening. The monster would surely wake up soon.

Bruno had eaten at around six, a tuna sandwich with a beer. He had examined the cat curios in the living room, which were kind of cute. He had even rummaged a bit in the cupboards in Josh's bedroom, across from the monster's room, and found a bottle of Scotch. He hadn't drunk any. He didn't particularly like liquor and drank it only on special occasions. He had also found a pair of binoculars, which Josh must have used for bird-watching. He even came across a few porn magazines, which he leafed through without much interest.

Now he was lying on the couch, staring at the ceiling. There was a TV, but he had no desire to turn it on. The more time passed, the more Bruno's excitement mounted—the excitement of the batter at the plate in the ninth inning when there are two men out and three on base and the hitter is certain he's going to hit a home run.

Certain.

A noise. Muttering.

Quickly Bruno went to the monster's room. He was lying on the floor with his eyes still closed, moving one arm a bit and turning his head from side to side. He gave a little moan and then was quiet. In a few minutes, he would be awake.

The ball would be pitched any second now.

Barely feeling his heart rate increase, Bruno went to the winch and started turning the crank. The chains tightened and lifted. First the monster's arms were slowly raised, then his torso. Bruno kept turning the crank until the body was completely vertical, the feet barely touching the ground. Then he locked the winch. The monster's mutterings were becoming clearer and his head was moving more.

Bruno went to the table on the left, close to the winch. It was huge, almost a meter wide and two and a half long, solid wood. There were four metal rings screwed into it, two at each end. It stood on a single post, also of wood and very thick. But between the post and the tabletop there was a complicated metal mechanism with a lever and a crank. Bruno moved the lever and pivoted the table into a completely vertical position. Then he pushed the lever toward the monster. The table was heavy, and Bruno gritted his teeth with the effort; the enormous casters under the post turned slowly until the upright tabletop was against the back of the hanging body.

Bruno backed to the door and observed the scene. The monster, completely naked, was held in a standing position by his shackled hands. He was no longer swinging, but leaning against the upright tabletop. He licked his lips and squeezed his closed eyelids tight, and finally opened his eyes. Fully awake now, his face framed by his long yellow-blond hair, he looked around wildly. Finally he saw Bruno. He mumbled a few inaudible words and looked up at the chains on his wrists. Fear washed over his face. He realized that the position he was in did not bode well for him.

"Wha . . . what's going on?"

Bruno said nothing. The monster looked at his chains again, turned his head toward the table behind his back, and glanced down at his naked crotch.

"What am I doing naked? And why am I chained up?"

He pushed against the table with his legs. His body swung forward and immediately bounced back against the table behind him.

"Fuck, man! Say something!" he cried, now angry.

Bruno's face was unperturbed, but within him, a terrible process was taking place. The rapist and killer of his little Jasmine was there in front of him. At his mercy.

The monster laughed without conviction and even started to smile his arrogant smile.

"Come on!" he said in a voice that had become uncertain. "Tell me what's going on."

At the sight of that little smile, Bruno finally opened the doors of his heart and soul to the hate he had been controlling for the past week. At first it was a trickle, but in a few seconds it turned into a river, a raging torrent that swept through his being, destroying everything in its path. And this devastating flood occurred in the most complete, most horrifying silence.

The monster must have seen glimmers of that tide reflected in Bruno's eyes, because the fear quickly returned to his features.

With surprising speed, Bruno grabbed the sledgehammer that was leaning against the wall and stepped forward. His eyes flashing with fury, his face waxen, he raised the tool sideways. And just when the monster realized what was going to happen, the sledgehammer smashed into his right knee. The blow was so violent that the heavy table behind him was knocked back a centimeter.

The crack of the kneecap shattering was immediately followed by the deafening scream of the monster, whose body had stiffened. Even before the scream ended, Bruno dropped the sledgehammer and went back and released the winch. The two chains quickly slackened and the monster collapsed onto the floor at the foot of the table. Bruno watched him writhing on the ground, screaming in pain and holding his mangled leg. There was no emotion on Bruno's face. But in his eyes, the fury was gradually subsiding, replaced by a morbid fascination.

After several long seconds, Bruno left the room, leaving the screaming monster behind. He went to Josh's bedroom and took the bottle of Scotch to the kitchen, where he filled a glass. He looked at the glass with vague amusement and downed it in a single gulp. Then he sat down in the armchair in the living room and looked out the window at the moonlit lake. He heard a muted litany of sounds coming from the other room. Once or twice, he thought he made out words like "fucking bastard," but it was mostly limited to grunts and howls.

Those sounds! Bruno was practically drunk on them! Hearing them, he felt something finally relax within him. The weight that had been with him since the coming of the darkness was still there, but he felt a kind of release, as if he had been standing on one leg for an eternity and he could finally stand on both feet again. He felt more tired than he ever had before, a comfortable, pleasant fatigue. His shoulders sagged, his arms went limp, his face softened, and he closed his eyes.

Lulled by the symphony of curses and wailing, he fell into a peaceful sleep.

# DAY 2

S0?"

Sitting at his desk, his hands folded behind his neck, Mercure was watching his two colleagues, waiting. Christian Bolduc, twenty-eight years old, a refrigerator in width and height, shrugged.

"We don't have much to go on."

Anne-Marie Pleau was dwarfed beside him, although she was quite a big woman. She was thirty-six years old, but her face, with its delicate features, was that of an adolescent girl and contrasted with her rather masculine body. She was looking at a copy of the photograph of Hamel.

"He called from Longueuil yesterday, right?" she asked.

"Yes, but I'd be surprised if he's there. If I wanted to hide with a guy I'd kidnapped, I doubt I would do it in the middle of a city. We have no indication that he's still there. He could be anywhere."

He sighed, folding his hands over his nonexistent belly. A needle in a haystack. Hamel had really planned things well. Mercure's mind kept returning to the same thing: that cold, surgical preparation.

Surgical, yes, that was the word for it. He chuckled joylessly. His two colleagues looked puzzled.

"Okay. I want you to go question these people," he said, handing them each a list. "These are friends and relatives of Hamel. I went to see his mother yesterday, a widow who lives in a seniors' residence. She's in such a state of shock that she's incoherent. She won't be any use to us. We also checked his cottage in the Eastern Townships, and of course, he's not there. Send people to question employees of service stations around Drummondville, especially the ones on Highway 20 on the way to Longueuil. Have them show them the photo of Hamel."

"Are you hoping that . . . ?"

"Not really, no."

A brief silence, then Mercure rapped the arms of his chair and said, "Okay, let's get to work!"

———

Bruno opened his eyes at twenty minutes before noon. He had slept more than fifteen hours straight in that chair without waking up once! That had never happened to him before, not even when he was a teenager and had been at a party smoking hash all night.

He had dreamed of threatening jowls and shiny fur. And there was a strange noise with the dream images, like a distant knocking. A weird, meaningless dream.

He stood up, stiff all over, still feeling that oppressive weight. Out the window, the lake beckoned with thousands of little waves. In spite of that dull look everything now had, Bruno still found it pretty.

To say he was happy would have been an exaggeration, and even indecent. Besides, he knew that happiness was no longer for him. It wasn't what he was looking for, anyway; what he wanted was a kind of satisfaction. And he felt that, the day before, he had climbed the first rung of the ladder that would take him there.

He fingered Jasmine's blue ribbon for a moment, and then put it back in his pocket.

He picked up the old telephone and called Morin and told him where the money was. Morin played along, replying in monosyllables, but Bruno could hear the satisfaction in his voice. He must think he had a good fairy watching over him.

He had just hung up when he heard an uncertain voice calling, "Is anyone there?"

Bruno looked toward the hallway, his eyes suddenly lighting up. He walked down the hall and into the room. The monster was sitting on the floor with his back against the vertical table and his injured leg stretched out in front of him. When he saw Bruno, his face showed a strange mixture of relief and fear: relief at seeing that he had not been abandoned, and fear when he recognized Bruno. He touched the thigh of his injured leg softly.

"My . . . my knee," he complained in a trembling voice. "I think it's broken."

The knee had doubled in volume and was now blue, with yellowish patches. Internal bleeding, of course. The monster was right: the kneecap must be mush. Bruno had hit a perfect home run. According to plan.

"You broke my knee!"

Bruno leaned against the wall and crossed his arms. The monster asked, then begged, for explanations, then got discouraged, and then begged again. And Bruno just stood there with his arms crossed, looking at him in a vaguely interested way.

The monster then became solemn.

"I know who you are."

Bruno didn't flinch, but he listened.

"You're Hamel, right? The father of the little girl who was raped and killed?"

Bruno took a slightly hoarse breath.

The monster said, "I'm innocent. It wasn't me. You got the wrong guy."

He tried to look angry and play the victim, but it was so false that Bruno found it insulting and lost his temper. He picked the sledgehammer up from the floor and walked toward his prisoner, raising it in the air. Every trace of assurance left the monster's face. He huddled against the table, his arms raised, and pleaded, "No! No, don't hit me! Come on, don't hit me anymore!"

Bruno stopped and looked curiously at the monster, who was panting and trembling and still pleading for mercy. Bruno suddenly realized that there was another possible form of torture, one he hadn't thought of, different from physical torture but perhaps just as effective.

He slowly lowered his weapon. The monster looked hopeful but still wary. Bruno turned around as if he were leaving the room, and even took a few steps, but then he suddenly turned around and ran toward the monster, brandishing the sledgehammer, with an exaggerated, theatrical expression. The prisoner screamed in pure terror and covered his face with both hands. Bruno lowered the sledgehammer and laughed a booming laugh, throwing his head back. But there was something strange in his laughter, a peculiar, indefinable sound.

With a last chuckle, Bruno leaned the sledgehammer against the wall and left the room under the monster's terrified gaze.

He made himself a late breakfast. Yes, fear, waiting, uncertainty . . . that could be as effective as physical torture.

While Bruno was eating his eggs and toast, the monster shouted that he could smell the food, that he was starving and wanted something to eat. Bruno stood up, his plate in his hand, and returned to the room. When he saw the plate, the monster gave a weak hopeful smile, but he started moaning when he saw Bruno calmly eating in front of him, leaning against the wall.

"Come on! Give me something to eat! My stomach hurts and I'm thirsty!"

Bruno chewed his toast in silence and took another bite. The monster began to protest. Since his broken knee prevented him from standing up, he pounded the floor like a child having a tantrum.

"I tell you it wasn't me, goddammit! And I haven't had my trial yet! Do you understand? It wasn't me!"

Bruno had a crazy impulse to remind him that he had pleaded guilty, but he held back. The monster leaned his head against the table and closed his eyes.

"Give me something," he begged. "Anything . . ."

Bruno stopped chewing and spat out the huge mouthful he had in his mouth. The sticky, shapeless mixture of egg and bread fell a few centimeters from the monster. He stared at the chewed food and made a face.

"You fucking bastard!"

The doctor threw his empty plate like a Frisbee. Instinctively, the other man covered his face, squealing, but the plate missed him by a good fifty centimeters and smashed into pieces on the back wall. The monster's eyes filled with fear, the same fear that must have been in the eyes of his little Jasmine. It was so good to see that terror in his eyes. Oh, yes, so good!

He left the room, closing the door behind him. Slowly, he tidied up the kitchen. Once he heard the sound of chains. The monster must be trying to crawl painfully to the door with his broken knee. But the chains were not long enough, Bruno knew that. After a minute, the rattling of the chains stopped and the muffled moans could be heard again.

As he was putting the butter in the fridge, the doctor had a grimace on his face that could have been likened to a smile.

He put on his coat and went out. The weather was perfect for the season: sunny, but cold enough to be invigorating. Bruno walked toward the lake, the dead leaves rustling pleasantly under his feet, surrounded by the joyous cacophony of the birds. At the shore, he stopped and contemplated the lake. But the splendid spectacle didn't occupy his mind for long. He was imagining the monster in the house, terrified, wondering what would come next, weeping uncontrollably faced with the unknown.

Bruno closed his eyes, looked up at the sky, and let the cold autumn breeze caress his face.

———

In normal times, Josée Jutras and her sister Sylvie looked alike, but now Sylvie just looked like a survivor. It was past one in the afternoon, but she was still in her dressing gown, and the red rings under her eyes convinced the detective sergeant not to ask how she'd slept. She was sitting very straight in a chair, with her elbows on the arms, staring unseeing at the carpet. Mercure figured she must be thirty-five, but she looked ten years older.

"Coffee, Inspector?" asked Josée Jutras, sitting on the couch.

Mercure looked at her. She must be older than her sister, although she gave the impression of being the younger of the two.

"No, thank you. I'm only going to stay a few minutes."

He had sat down without taking off his coat.

"I watched the ten o'clock news last night," Sylvie's sister continued. "They said something about a seven-day deadline, that Bruno was going to kill the guy on Monday and would turn himself in then. They know everything!"

She might be surprised, but Mercure wasn't. Sylvie, distressed, must have called a few people to talk yesterday, and they had called other people, and so on. And this morning, reporters from Montreal had come and asked Wagner some questions, and he, reluctantly, had confirmed everything.

"Do you know anyone in Longueuil?"

Sylvie said no. Could Bruno be hiding there?

Mercure told her that it was far from certain.

"I would like you not to mention anything about this Longueuil lead to anyone. If the reporters talked about it and your partner heard, that could cause him to panic and . . ."

The two women indicated that they understood.

"We tried to call him back on his cell phone," he added. "But he keeps it turned off."

"I tried to call him too . . . all evening."

She sniffled, but sat up straight, still looking at the floor. Mercure checked the notes in his notebook.

"That thing he said yesterday, that he was the victim of the dog now . . . did you understand what he meant?"

Again she shook her head.

"In fact, he himself didn't seem to be aware of . . . of that image," added Mercure to fill the silence, which was becoming oppressive.

No reaction. Josée finally said something. "I think my sister is most afraid of what is going to happen to Bruno when you find him. Maybe . . . maybe you could tell us about that."

Mercure scratched the top of his head. It was hard to say. If they found him now, he would be charged with kidnapping, assaulting a police officer . . .

"Assault?" Sylvie said suddenly, finally looking up.

"Well, yeah, for the nitro overdose."

"But an hour later the policeman was fine!"

"I know, but . . ."

He scratched his head again, ill at ease.

"But since there were extenuating circumstances, he would only get a few months in prison. Maybe he wouldn't go to prison at all . . ."

Sylvie didn't react; she just kept her eyes riveted on the detective sergeant, urging him to take his reasoning to its logical conclusion. Summoning up his courage, he continued, "But all that will also depend on what condition Lemaire is in."

"And what condition was poor Jasmine in? Doesn't that count?" shot back Josée.

Sylvie closed her eyes for a moment.

"It's . . . You're mixing things up, Ms. Ju—"

"And what if he isn't found before he kills Lemaire?" Sylvie interrupted. "What will happen to him?"

"We will find him."

"You won't find him, and you know it," she replied evenly. "You have hardly any leads. He had a reason for keeping him for seven days. It's too short for you to have time to trace things back to him."

Mercure was taken aback. Sylvie repeated insistently, "How much, if he kills him?"

This time, the policeman couldn't help sighing.

"I suppose he'd get the same sentence as the murderer himself!" Josée said nastily.

Mercure looked the woman straight in the eye.

"It's very likely . . ."

Josée gasped in horror. Sylvie did not react, but all the blood drained from her already pale face and her nostrils quivered.

"It would be first-degree murder," Mercure explained pathetically. "Unless it were proven that he wasn't responsible, which does not seem to be the case."

Josée shook her head, offended. Sylvie, pensive, murmured, "He knows it."

"I beg your pardon?"

"He knows he'll go to prison. And he doesn't care."

Mercure nodded gravely. But Josée continued to object: to spend years in prison for eliminating the murderer of his daughter! Where was the justice in that?

"Ms. Jutras, you have to understand that—"

"Do you have children, Inspector?"

The discussion had taken an unpleasant and inappropriate turn. He was not obligated to answer, but since he still wanted to be polite, he answered tersely, "No."

"That's it! If you lost the person you loved most in the world as my sister did, you . . ."

"My wife died five years ago."

An icy silence followed this statement. Josée turned scarlet, opened her mouth, closed it again, and looked down at her hands.

"I . . . I'm . . . I'm sorry, Inspector."

Mercure lowered his head, rubbing his hands together and telling himself he was an idiot. What was he doing bringing that up? He had always been able to keep his cool!

"Really," Josée said. "I'm sorry I—"

"It's okay," Mercure interrupted brusquely.

He finally looked up. Sylvie was staring at him intently. In her eyes he read surprise mixed with curiosity.

"In any case," he said quickly, "I'm sure we'll find him before he does anything irreparable."

With those words, he averted his eyes from Sylvie's.

He stood up. He had regained his calm, reassuring manner. He asked if, before leaving, he could take a look around the house. Especially the master bedroom and Hamel's office, if he had one. Josée seemed surprised by the request, but Sylvie agreed without hesitation.

Mercure went upstairs alone, and first went into the bedroom. Tasteful, simple decor, nothing garish, nothing ostentatiously rich. A few paintings on the walls, reproductions of classic works. On the desk, photos of Hamel and Sylvie. And little Jasmine. One of them showed Hamel with his daughter. Mercure picked it up and looked at it for a while. The little girl was kissing her father, who looked very happy.

He left the bedroom and went into the room Hamel used as an office. There was a desk, a filing cabinet, and a few more family photos. Lots of books, mostly medical books but also a few novels, completely unknown to Mercure. And a few comic books too, including *Calvin and Hobbes* and *Get Fuzzy*, as well as *Mafalda*, which Mercure wasn't familiar with. He picked one up, read a little, and smiled. A comic book with a social and political message.

On the desk was a computer, quite a new one, judging by the design. There were shelves with a pile of computer books, dozens of floppy disks and CDs, and other computer gear Mercure wasn't familiar with.

There were two posters on the walls. One was a funny drawing by someone named Mordillo. It showed a street of houses that were all identical, gray and drab, except for one, which was painted in vivid colors. In front of the house, a person was being arrested by two police officers. Mercure chuckled silently. At the bottom of the poster were the words "Amnesty International."

The other one was much less funny. It was a strange drawing, vaguely childlike, mainly black, white, and gray, with a little blue. Mercure examined it for quite a while. In the entangled lines and twisted shapes, you could recognize distorted, terrified faces, a woman screaming, holding a caricature of a child, an incongruous electric lightbulb, the head of a nightmarish neighing horse, and especially, the peculiar, troubling head of a bull. Mercure knew nothing about painting, but he felt perfectly the extreme violence emanating from that disturbing and falsely naive work.

Under the painting, in a white box that took up the whole bottom part of the poster, was written in big black letters: PICASSO. And, in smaller letters: *Guernica*. Of course, he knew who Picasso was, but the title of the work meant nothing to him. He looked at it again, fascinated, and wrote down the title in his notebook.

Before going downstairs, he took a glance at the little girl's bedroom. Bright, sunny yellow walls, a single bed with a comforter that had images of horses on it. On one wall, in multicolored wooden letters, the name "Jasmine." Shelves with a rag doll, a clown doll, and a bag of marbles. An open toy chest. An enormous koala bear in one corner. A dream catcher in front of the window. Two pictures on the walls, one of a galloping horse and one of a unicorn. A poster showing five boys singing, the New Kids on the Block or the Backstreet Boys, Mercure always got them mixed up. A family photo on the desk.

Mercure left the room, his head down, his hands in the pockets of his long coat.

"There's nothing missing from his stuff?" he asked Sylvie when he got back downstairs.

"I don't think so. I don't even think he . . . he took any clothes."

"And in his office?"

"I took a quick look. I really didn't know Bruno's office well. I hardly ever went in there. It was his den, when he wanted to fool around by himself on his computer. He even took an evening class on computers last year, he liked it so much. And an advanced class too. He was really a computer nut . . . Well, he still is, it's just that . . ."

She stopped and rubbed her forehead with a painful sigh.

Mercure glanced around the living room, looking for other details related to Hamel. He saw some videocassettes and asked what they were.

"Home videos. We have a little camera and . . ."

"Can I take them?"

Sylvie looked at him for a moment before answering, "If you like, but there are eighteen . . ."

"Let's say the ones from"—he thought for a moment and shrugged—"the last couple of years."

Sylvie picked up four cassettes. As she handed them to the detective sergeant, she said, "You have a funny way of investigating."

There was no sarcasm or reproach in her tone. On the contrary, she said it gently, in almost a friendly way. Mercure smiled at her as he took the videos, and thanked her, promising he would keep her up-to-date.

"And thank you, Ms. Jutras, for keeping your sister company during this difficult time."

Josée nodded, still embarrassed because of the scene earlier.

As he was walking to the car, he saw a man with a child walking on the sidewalk. The man glanced toward Hamel's house and asked Mercure if he was with the police. The detective sergeant said yes.

"I heard about it on the news. It's . . . it's really horrendous. Poor Bruno." He held out his hand. "Denis Bédard. I live on the corner, just over there."

Mercure introduced himself and shook his hand.

"And this is my son, Frédéric."

The child, about ten, smiled shyly. Mercure greeted him, thinking to himself that the boy would have been handsome without those terrible scars on his face.

"I saw Bruno the other day in a park. He was so somber, so strange . . . So aggressive . . . full of hate . . ."

"Does it surprise you that he went that far?"

"You can never be surprised by the reactions of a parent whose child has been killed or attacked . . ."

As he said this, he glanced sadly at his son and gently put his hand on his shoulder. The boy stood there meekly, impressed by the big policeman. Mercure saw the melancholy in Bédard's face, the love in his gesture toward his son.

"Well, good luck, Inspector. I sincerely hope you find him before the seven days are up."

He looked sadly at the boy again, turned back to the policeman, and repeated, looking into his eyes, "Sincerely."

He walked away holding his son's hand, while the boy kept staring at the policeman. Mercure took one last look at his scars, obviously old but still hard to bear.

In his car, he thought as he smoothed his hair. He looked at his calendar and saw that he was supposed to go to Montreal this week. One of his three annual visits to Demers.

He wondered if he should put it off until this whole business was over. At the same time, he knew he needed those visits.

Well, he thought he did.

He looked at his watch: one thirty. A little lunch at the Charlemagne would do him good.

He drove off.

———

At two o'clock, Bruno entered the room holding a big glass of water.

The monster's eyes shone. His body, slumped against the table, straightened up; he almost stuck out his tongue in excitement. Bruno handed him the glass. The monster seized it from his hands and gulped it down. Bruno glanced at the smashed knee. It was bigger and more purple than before. He was bending over the leg when two hands grabbed his throat and squeezed hard, and a hysterical voice screamed, "Let me go! You hear me, you sick bastard? Unchain me. Let me go or I'll strangle you!"

Bruno struggled. When he was close to suffocation, he punched the swollen knee. The blow wasn't very hard, but it was enough to make the monster let go and start screaming. Wild with rage, Bruno took hold of his prisoner's skull and smashed it against the table. The monster's body went limp. Stunned, he started moaning and slowly moving his head from side to side.

After catching his breath, Bruno took advantage of his prisoner's semiconscious state to examine the leg. He felt the thigh and gently touched the knee with his fingers. For the time being, it would be okay.

But the monster was burning up with fever. Bruno stood up and went over to his two medical bags in the corner. He opened one and came back to his prisoner with a pill. He put it in the mouth of the monster, who was still half knocked out, and forced him to swallow it by making him drink the rest of the water.

The idea was not to alleviate the monster's suffering, but to prevent his condition from deteriorating too quickly. Because if he got too weak, he wouldn't be able to tolerate anything . . .

. . . and he wouldn't last a week.

The water woke the monster up completely, and Bruno stood up, on his guard. Fear returned to the monster's eyes when he saw Bruno. And Bruno again imagined the eyes of his little Jasmine, full of that powerless fear. He kicked the monster hard in the belly, causing him to double over and cough painfully. There, let him try to smile now! If he still could! A red cloud came over Bruno. He grabbed the sledgehammer and turned toward the monster. The monster, still grimacing with pain and holding his belly, looked at the tool with terror and cowered against the table. The red cloud dissipated and Bruno stood motionless.

No, not right away. Savor the wait. And the spectacle of the monster, naked, suffocating, paralyzed with terror, was already very satisfying.

For now.

He left the room, closed the door, went and got a beer, and drank it slowly, sitting in the living room.

Suddenly the monster began to scream. Not screams of suffering or fear, or specific words; just an overflowing, as if a valve had given way.

The monster screamed, screamed, screamed . . .

And Bruno drank his beer.

———

Back at the station, Mercure asked, just as a formality, if anyone had been able to reach Hamel. The answer was no.

"When Bolduc and Pleau come in, send them straight to me."

Around three o'clock, Mercure received a distressing telephone call—from Lemaire's mother. In a feeble, unsteady voice that betrayed her state of advanced inebriation, she asked if they had found her son. Mercure told her they had no leads. Mrs. Lemaire became surly and aggressive.

"You're not finding him on purpose! You're just as happy if someone tortures and kills him for you! Admit it, goddammit!"

In less than a month, this woman had just suffered the two greatest shocks of her life: the first, discovering that her son was a child rapist and murderer; the second, knowing he was in the hands of a vengeful father who was going to torture him and then kill him after seven days. So how could Mercure blame her for being upset?

Then she just broke down and cried.

"Don't forget that before being a killer my son is a human being, Inspector! A human being who is capable of love . . . and of being loved too! Who loves me, and who I love too! *Don't forget it!*"

He could have said (judging from Anthony Lemaire's file) that she hadn't been such a loving mother, that she had ignored her son for years and had basically abdicated her maternal role. Had she forgotten that? Of course, he didn't say anything like that to her. It would have been pointless, childish, and above all, unfair. Because now, this woman, regardless of whether or not she had been a bad mother, was miserable. And that was all that counted for the moment. So all he said, in an understanding tone of voice, was, "I won't forget it, madam."

He hung up, and suddenly realized he had a headache.

The two officers returned to the station around four o'clock, and rather sheepishly admitted they had come up empty-handed. Hamel's friends and colleagues were shocked, but had no idea where he could be hiding. And at the service stations, the employees had practically laughed at the cops. According to them, a customer's anonymous face was as distinct in their memories as an individual blade of grass in a lawn. "Unless," one of them had said, "he looked like Brad Pitt. Which is certainly not the case with your guy!" he had added, looking at the photo.

Mercure was not really disappointed. What else could he have expected? Pleau handed him a transparent plastic bag containing a thin little rectangle of dark paper.

"A sample of the nitro pieces stuck to the steering wheel," she said. "The forensic guys examined them. They say they're not conventional patches, that they were made to order, probably by a pharmacist. They would be surprised if a surgeon like Hamel could have made them himself."

Mercure took the bag. There might be a lead here. He wrote in his little notebook: "Hospital—pharmacists re patches."

When the two police officers were about to leave, the detective sergeant asked them if they knew Picasso.

"Sure, he was a painter," Bolduc answered spontaneously.

"Yes, I know that, but do you know his paintings at all, in particular the one called . . ." He checked his notebook. "*Guernica*, that's it. Does that mean anything to you?"

Bolduc shrugged. Pleau knew which painting it was, but had no idea what it meant.

Mercure left his office a little later to report to Wagner. The chief was in his standard pose—standing behind his chair with both hands on the back.

Wagner grumbled about the report, but he couldn't blame Mercure. He knew he had almost nothing to go on.

"Say, Greg, do you know Picasso?"

"Of course. He delivers my paper. Very nice guy."

Mercure, taken aback, did not react. Wagner got angry. "Of course I know who he is! Why are you interested in Picasso?"

"There's a painting by him that I saw in Hamel's house."

Wagner did not object. He knew his inspector's methods. In some cases, they were a complete waste of time, but they had sometimes led to surprising results.

"*Guernica*. Does that mean anything to you?"

"It's his most powerful painting. One of his most famous. And one of his most violent too. It's about the Spanish Civil War. Picasso wanted to show the horrors of war, the pain and misery men could create . . ."

Mercure stood there openmouthed.

"I'm impressed, Greg!"

"You're forgetting that my wife teaches art history," sighed the chief, his hands in his pockets. "If you only knew how many museums I've had to visit on our trips."

"Oh yes! I was also thinking . . ."

Wagner gave him a funny look, not knowing how to take that remark, but Mercure had already left.

He told his colleagues in the squad room that he would be in the screening room for a few hours. If Hamel called, they should let him know immediately. Carrying the videocassettes, he shut himself up in the small room containing two chairs, a table, a TV, and an ancient video machine.

———

At five forty-five, Bruno cooked some pasta, which he intended to eat while watching the six o'clock news on TV. Obviously, his story would make the headlines, although he did not particularly want it to. If he'd had a choice, he would have done without the publicity, but since it was inevitable, he might as well see how they were covering it.

At five fifty-five, he walked into the monster's room, carrying a glass of water and a plate of pasta. The fast had gone on long enough. If the monster didn't eat, he would become too weak.

The monster fell on the food. He grabbed the hot pasta with his bare hands, stuck his nose in it, and got his long blond hair in the sauce. Bruno watched him eat for a moment, and then thought again: *This is your daughter's rapist, her murderer, here he is, the bastard.* He had clenched his fist, ready to strike, when the monster raised his reddened chin and, with eyes full of hope and a nervous smile on his lips, mumbled, "That was nice, that was . . . very kind of you. You . . . you're being nicer to me now. Maybe . . . maybe . . . it's almost over, huh? You're going to free me? You've finally realized it wasn't me, right? Huh?"

At first, Bruno was so surprised that he didn't even hit him; then he became pensive. Letting the monster feel some hope was not a bad thing. The more he hoped, the more terrible his despair would be afterward. Yes, letting him hope was an excellent idea. So much so that Bruno made a superhuman effort to indulge him with a reassuring smile, and he became even more excited. Then Bruno left the room, glancing back one last time at his prisoner, who was absorbed in his food again.

Back in the living room, Bruno burst out laughing. Once again, he noticed the strange tone, and this time he was able to put his finger on what it was: there was no real joy in his laughter. He was laughing, he wanted to laugh, but his laughter sounded hollow.

Troubled, he went and got himself a plate of pasta, and sat down in front of the TV. He didn't turn the sound up too much, because he didn't want the monster to hear it. Since the TV was not on cable, the picture from Radio-Canada was a little snowy, but it was clear enough to see everything and hear everything. They talked about politics and international affairs for the first five minutes, and then they came to his story:

"Still no leads on the whereabouts of Bruno Hamel, the thirty-eight-year-old doctor who . . ."

Behind the news anchor, there was an inset of a photo of Bruno. Fascinated in spite of himself, Bruno took a bite of his food, his eyes riveted to the TV. They talked about his seven-day ultimatum. They showed images of the monster going into the courthouse flanked by two police officers. Bruno had already seen them several times. He smiled when he saw the monster's arrogant expression. Since the day before, he no longer looked like that. The off-camera voice of the reporter explained, "It all began on October seventh, when the Drummondville police arrested a young man and charged him with the rape and murder of young Jasmine Jutras-Hamel . . ."

Then a photo of Jasmine filled the screen. Smiling, lovely, fragile. The mouthful of pasta stuck in Bruno's throat.

"The young man in question, Anthony Lemaire, pleaded guilty one week ago, and . . ."

Bruno gave a scream and, without even realizing it, sent his plate flying off his knees as he frantically grabbed the remote control to mute the sound. On the TV, the images of the monster continued to go by, but in silence.

No personal information on the monster! He didn't want to know anything about his life, nothing! And he had just learned his name! That was already too much!

On the TV, there was a photo of Bruno and then images of Sylvie running away from the reporters, but Bruno didn't dare turn up the sound again for fear of learning more about Lem—about the monster.

Too bad, then! He just wouldn't watch the news anymore! After all, he didn't care, did he?

Well, he did now . . . now that he'd seen the first images, heard the first words. Now he wanted to know. But especially, it was the only way he had to keep up with developments. Because, of course, the police were investigating, and only the TV could provide him with information on that.

Unless he listened with the remote control in his hand, ready to mute the sound every time they were about to divulge information about the monster? Ridiculous and risky . . .

Suddenly he had an idea.

He put on his disguise and left the house.

———

On the screen of the old TV, Jasmine, dressed up as a sheep, was doing a simple dance with four other little girls in similar costumes. She was a bit awkward, but her enthusiasm was a pleasure to see. To Mercure, she was neither the best of the five little dancers, nor even the prettiest. But he was sure that to Bruno Hamel, Jasmine had been the best and most beautiful dancer in the world.

Mercure finished his club sandwich. He had been watching the first of the four cassettes for close to two hours. At the bottom of the screen, the date stamp read April 12, 2000, therefore six months earlier. He had also witnessed two birthday parties, an outing to the zoo, a camping weekend, and various other little slices of an ordinary life.

He had watched it all closely. As he would watch the other three cassettes. He was particularly interested when Hamel appeared on the screen—almost always in a good mood, spontaneous, sometimes a little tipsy, but never behaving inappropriately. And crazy about his daughter. He was a little less demonstrative with Sylvie, on the other hand. Not cold or indifferent, but . . . they seemed like an old couple. Already.

Wagner rushed into the room. He was relieved to see Mercure.

"Ah! You're still here! Perfect!"

The detective sergeant was not really surprised to see his superior at the station, even after six o'clock. It was not rare for Wagner to stay at his desk late into the evening. Since his divorce the year before, he lost himself in his work.

"It's Hamel on the telephone!"

Ten seconds later, Mercure was in the squad room, where four officers were waiting anxiously for him. The detective sergeant took the telephone Wagner handed him and noticed that the speaker was on. It irritated him a little that everyone would hear the conversation, but he knew Wagner didn't want to miss anything. With his free hand, he took out his notebook and pen and wrote the time of the call while answering in a completely natural voice, "Good evening, Dr. Hamel. This is Detective Sergeant Mercure."

"Why was I transferred to you?"

Always that cool control.

"I'm in charge of your case."

"My case . . ."

Wagner and the other police officers were listening attentively.

"I just watched the news. They're talking quite a bit about my case."

"That's surely no surprise to you."

"No, of course not. But they give a lot of information about the monster."

"About who?"

"The monster."

Silence. Hamel continued, "They gave his name on TV. I suppose they also talked about his past, gave his background and all that nonsense."

"What's your point, Dr. Hamel?"

"I don't want any more information about him to be revealed."

"I don't understand."

"I don't want to hear any personal information whatsoever about the monster on TV. Not his name, his age, or what he did for a living—nothing."

Mercure looked up at Wagner. The chief was rotating one finger close to his head, indicating that Hamel was crazy.

"Come now, we have no control over that."

"Find a way."

"Listen, Dr. Hamel . . ."

"No, you listen to me. If the TV news . . ."

"I'm telling you we don't have—"

"Stop barking, you dirty dog, and listen to me!" Hamel suddenly exclaimed.

Everyone was taken aback by the outburst. Stunned at first, Mercure quickly jotted a few words in his notebook, knitting his eyebrows. Calm again, as if he had never lost his temper, Hamel continued, "If I hear the least bit of information about my prisoner's life, I will put him through the worst time of his life."

"May I remind you that he's already going through the worst time of his life?"

Hamel was silent, no doubt caught off guard. At last he said, "I could kill him before the seventh day."

"I don't believe you."

"Do you want to take that chance?"

Mercure didn't answer. Hamel added, "And torture covers a lot. You can always do something worse."

Mercure felt an icy shiver run up his back from the base of his spine to the back of his neck, giving him gooseflesh. My God, what had happened to the man he had just seen laughing so many times in the videos? An image of the tormented man came to the policeman's mind. Hamel hadn't just grown a new skin, he had put on a carapace, a suit of armor, dark and cold.

"I'm a surgeon, Inspector; don't forget that. I can do what I like with a human body and still keep it alive."

Wagner ran his fingers through his hair and pursed his lips as if to whistle.

"Precisely. You're a doctor," Mercure replied. "What about the Hippocratic oath? You're supposed to heal people, not take their lives."

"Doctors treat humans, not monsters."

The policeman licked his lips, trying to find another tack to take, but he wasn't able to. The man's hatred was as smooth and slippery as a wall of ice.

"We can't just impose your demand on all the media."

"Just TV. Just the French-language channels."

A pause, and then: "That's it. I'll call you on Monday."

"Do you realize you're going to lose everything?"

"I've already lost everything, Inspector, I already told you that. You're repeating yourself."

"But you still have your partner. Unless you were already losing her too . . ."

Wagner tilted his head to one side as if to ask where Mercure was going with this.

"It's true, when you kissed her at your birthday party, it looked more like a mechanical kiss than a demonstration of love."

Mercure was far from convinced that this would get him anywhere. He even felt vaguely ridiculous, and judging by the looks of his colleagues, the impression was shared. But he was putting out feelers at random. He had to try something.

But all Hamel said, without a hint of emotion, was "Do something quickly. I'm planning on watching the news before I go to bed."

He hung up. Several sighs were heard in the room. Mercure hung up too, and said to an officer, "Pat, find out where he was calling from."

———

In the apartment in Charette, Bruno turned off the computer. The phone call hadn't been a bad thing: it would lead the police even further off the track. Still, he had to avoid coming here too often. It was not impossible that they would discover the false lead in Longueuil and would trace him back here. It was precisely because of that possibility that he had called from this apartment and not from Josh's place.

And what was that nonsense about him and Sylvie? Mercure must have watched their videos. Funny idea . . . In any case, it didn't make any sense. It proved that Mercure really had nothing and was grasping at straws.

He put on the wig and beard, and left. On the sidewalk, he met a man who was about to go up to the upstairs apartment. The man looked surprised to see a new tenant, and gave him a smile, mumbling a friendly good evening. He was about to add something, maybe even start up a conversation, but Bruno just said a quick hello and continued on his way.

He got into his car and drove off.

———

A heated discussion had broken out in the Drummondville police station on how they should proceed. Mercure thought they should give in to Hamel's demand. Wagner was less convinced.

"And what then? If we don't listen to him, he'll cut off three of Lemaire's fingers instead of two, is that it?"

"If we get him mad, he could lose control and kill Lemaire earlier than planned!" replied Mercure. "And even if he doesn't kill him, even if he only cuts off one extra finger—as you say!—the least we can do is try to avert any," he searched for the word a moment, "any additional reprisals against Lemaire. We have a duty to do that."

Wagner was convinced. The word "duty" had had its effect.

Boisvert, who was in the room, sighed with irritation. "I think we're going to a lot of trouble to protect a child murderer!"

The chief shot him a withering look, and Boisvert said nothing more. He just shrugged. Mercure read the words he had written in his notebook before: *Told me to stop barking, called me a dog.*

He finally looked up at his superior.

"So, Greg?"

Wagner sighed, his hands on his hips.

"Okay. We're going to need the Montreal police for that."

Relieved, Mercure said he would take care of it. He started walking to his desk but stopped. "By the way, we have another clue . . ."

"I know. He's hiding in a place where he has a TV. Therefore, there's electricity."

"That's right."

"That's a huge help," Wagner said with dark irony.

Pat hung up the phone and said Hamel had used his cell phone again.

"And the cell that retransmitted the message is the same one as yesterday, in Longueuil."

Wagner and Mercure looked at each other with surprise.

"So he really is hiding there!" exclaimed the chief. "I'll call the Longueuil station right away so that they can get to work on it. They'll comb the area served by that cell, you can be sure of that."

And he disappeared into his office. Mercure looked dubious. He didn't understand how a man who had planned everything down to the tiniest detail could make the blunder of hiding in the middle of a city . . . and then could carelessly use his cell phone twice. He would be found quite quickly—in twenty-four hours at most. But that didn't fit at all with Mercure's profile of Hamel.

He shrugged and walked to his office. Even if Hamel was sure to be found soon, there was no reason to take chances. So he called the Montreal police and told them about Hamel's demands.

———

Bruno had been sitting in front of the TV for at least two hours, watching programs that, until now, had never interested him. He tried to forget the monster's name, but in vain. Anthony Lemaire. He couldn't get it out of his head. But he had to forget it, to put it as far as possible out of his mind and erase every trace of humanity associated with the monster.

He was finishing his third beer. He was not drunk, not even tipsy. It took him quite a bit more to get drunk. He just felt more relaxed. Usually, he also felt a kind of lightness, but not now. Not even alcohol could overcome the heaviness he felt. All the same, he felt okay.

He brought the beer to his lips and surprised himself by finishing it in two gulps. He hesitated before going to get another, a fourth. What reason would he give Sylvie if she were here and had asked him why he was drinking so much?

Shit! Four beers, that was nothing! Sometimes he drank more! What had gotten into him to make him think like that?

He stood up and walked to the monster's room. Before, when Bruno had come back from Charette, his prisoner had called to him loudly. Had he been shouting all the time Bruno had been gone? Bruno hadn't even bothered to go see him. But he had been quiet now for a couple of hours.

As soon as Bruno came into the room, the monster, who was leaning against the table, sat up, excited, clanking the chains on his hands.

"Is this it now? Have you come to free me?"

Bruno took a few steps forward, struck by a nauseating smell. The plate of pasta on the floor was not only empty, but spotless—the monster had licked it clean. A little farther away, about two meters from the table, the presence of a small dark pile explained the stench. Humiliated, the monster mumbled that he had not been able to hold it any longer. He went back on the offensive.

"I tell you it wasn't me! What do I have to say to make you believe me?"

Bruno looked at him solemnly, and the monster hesitated between hope and fear. His words came so quickly that they were barely understandable:

"I was set up by the cops! I didn't want to plead guilty, but they forced me! And the DNA tests were rigged! They're a bunch of bastards. Damn dirty dogs! I'm innocent! Come on! Do you really think I could rape and kill a little girl?"

His lips quivering, he tried a pathetic smile, which sent an electric shock through Bruno's soul. He went very close to the monster. The injured knee was stable. Perfect.

The monster held out his chained wrists.

"Come on . . . let me go . . ."

Without a word, Bruno opened his fly and pulled out his penis. The monster was taken aback at first, and then he suddenly thought he understood.

"Oh, you want me to . . . to . . ."

Bruno didn't answer. Impassive, he held his member in his right hand, a half a meter from the monster's face. There was revulsion on the monster's face, but he didn't dare to defy him openly.

"I . . . I can't do that, man!"

However, he reached toward the organ, his face more and more tense. And when he closed his eyes and started to painfully open his mouth, the urine splashed his face. His head jerked back so suddenly that it hit the tabletop. He tried to protect his face with his hands, shouting incoherently, but the stream of urine continued to spray him. Blinded, he managed to grab Bruno by the hips, but Bruno kicked him in the belly and he let go. Bruno continued to relieve himself on his prisoner, his eyes sparkling. *Is this how he humiliated my daughter, the son of a bitch? Well, now it's my turn to spray him, to cover him with filth, to defile him!* And Bruno, his mouth twisted in an evil grin, kept pissing on the monster's belly, his legs, and especially, his face. The monster doubled over, his hands on his belly, gasping for breath and spitting out the urine that had gone in his mouth.

When the stream finally subsided, Bruno looked at his prisoner lying on the floor in a puddle, coughing and cursing, his wet hair sticking to his face. Then he turned and walked to the door.

"Fuck you!" shouted the monster behind him. "Fuck you, you sick bastard! When the police get you, I'm going to find you and rip off your head, do you hear me? You're dead, asshole!"

In spite of the closed door, the shouting continued for a few moments.

In the living room, Bruno sat down on the couch and started watching TV again. It had done him enormous good. In every sense of the word. He had the feeling he had just climbed another rung on the ladder leading toward the satisfaction he was seeking. Yes, one rung higher, certainly.

He suddenly tried to remember the monster's name. He thought as hard as he could, but could not come up with it.

He had managed to forget it.

He stretched his legs with pleasure. He did not feel like beer at all anymore. He started taking an interest in the show on TV.

———

Mercure hung up, relieved. The boys from the Montreal police had just called. They had confirmed that the three French-language networks, SRC, TVA, and Quatre-Saisons, would follow instructions regarding Lemaire. They had grumbled a bit, of course, but had finally agreed, especially when the Montreal chief had mentioned the possibility of an injunction . . . if he were given no choice, of course.

Mercure stood up and looked out at Lindsay Street, which was lighted by street lamps and store windows but was as deserted as a country lane. Now all he had to do was go home to his too big house, have a bite, watch a little TV . . . and think about Madelaine, of course.

Again he thought about the visit he had to make to Demers this week.

He grabbed his coat. In the hallway, he heard from the squad room that a fight had been reported in a motel room. He saw the light coming from under Wagner's door. He thought for a moment of going in to see him, but then walked to the exit.

———

At ten o'clock, Bruno watched the Radio-Canada news. The images were the same and so was the journalist's voice, but there were a few differences in the text:

". . . held prisoner for two days now. The kidnapped man raped and killed the young daughter of the same Bruno Hamel on . . ."

Bruno nodded. He listened to part of the story: there was no specific information on the monster, his life or his personality. Bruno changed the channel to Télé-Métropole, where the report was just ending. This time, they just called the monster "the prisoner," and once again said nothing about him.

He turned off the TV, satisfied and even a little surprised. He had more power than he'd thought.

---

He stretched. Although he'd gotten up very late, he was dead tired. And tonight he would sleep in Josh's bed.

But first he felt like climbing another rung on the ladder of satisfaction.

When he entered the room, the smell of excrement and urine made him grimace. The monster was lying on his back, asleep. His knee was still swollen, still purplish, but it hadn't really gotten worse. The monster had moved away from the table a little, trying no doubt to avoid the puddle of urine.

Without hesitation, Bruno grabbed the sledgehammer and whistled loudly as he approached the sleeping man. The monster started, opened his eyes, and saw Bruno brandishing the weapon. His face had barely started to twist in fear when the sledgehammer crushed his left knee.

Another dull crack, another horrible scream. Bruno stepped back a few paces and his features relaxed. He contemplated the monster, who was screaming on the floor and writhing in pain, moving only the upper part of his body now that both his knees were broken. For a few minutes, Bruno watched the grotesque spectacle, which he did not find unpleasant.

*So, asshole, did Jasmine twist like that under your body while you were breaking her, destroying her? Did you look at her with the same pleasure I find in watching you suffer now?*

Bruno felt his soul climb one more rung. But as he reached that higher level, he thought he heard a weaker, more muted sound mingled with the monster's shouts. He tilted his head slightly, listening carefully. The sound was too weak for him to identify. Perhaps it was a distortion produced by the larynx as a result of so much screaming.

He tried to ignore that dissonant sound and continue enjoying the spectacle. But that secondary sound, that distortion, really bothered him, though he couldn't say why.

When he was completely sated by the scene, he left, closing the door behind him, and went into Josh's bedroom across the hall. The room was much smaller than the other one and held only a double bed and a dresser. Bruno got undressed and lay down. In the dark, he could still hear the monster moaning. No calls, no words, only constant whimpering. Bruno listened carefully. The strange, diffuse sound had disappeared. It must be something that was audible only from close up.

He fell asleep to the sound of the same concert as the night before.

# DAY 3

S ITTING NEAR THE BIG WINDOW OF THE ST. GEORGE PUB, MERCURE WAS CON-
centrating so hard on rereading his notes, looking for patterns in
Hamel's two calls, that he had hardly touched his coffee.

One constant was Hamel's calm, cold detachment. He was nothing
like the father in the happy, sociable family in the video from the day
before. Nothing like the man who put up Amnesty International posters . . . and a Picasso painting depicting the excesses of human violence
and horror.

Another constant was Hamel's lucidity. He was aware of what he
was doing, aware that he was committing a crime, aware of the consequences. So aware that he even intended, at the end, to turn himself in
to the authorities. Because, as he had said twice, he had lost everything.
Except the possibility of revenge.

Mercure let his eyes wander outside for a moment. He remembered
having himself had that feeling of infinite emptiness after Madelaine's
death. The feeling that nothing would have meaning anymore. Except
that he had reacted differently from Hamel. And that had made it possible for him to get through it.

But had he really gotten through it?

Demers, for example . . .

He shook his head. This was no time to think about that. Get back to Hamel.

Because that was the worst thing about it, the most terrible thing: Hamel did not want to get through it. He had no desire to.

"Something wrong with your coffee, Inspector?"

The waiter had come over. Mercure reassured him with a smile, took a big swallow, and turned back to the disorganized notes in his notebook.

Also, in spite of his admirable control, Hamel had lost his cool for a brief moment during each of the two calls: when he had told his partner that now he was the victim of the dog and when he had called Mercure a dog and had even told him to stop barking. Of course, that last comment could simply have been an insult; calling a cop a dog was nothing unusual. But Mercure had trouble imagining a man like Hamel calling police officers dogs or pigs. And in both cases, Hamel had not even seemed aware of the brief loss of control.

Why these references to dogs that had no relation to the conversation?

Maybe he was completely on the wrong track. It even seemed a little ridiculous to put so much emphasis on this. But since he had no leads, he didn't want to leave any stone unturned.

He put his notebook back in his coat pocket and finally finished his coffee.

———

Bruno stood on the shore, which was covered in dead leaves, contemplating Lac des Souris, his hands in his coat pockets. The sky had clouded over during the night, but not to the point that it was threatening rain.

He had gotten up quite late again this morning, still feeling the same heaviness. For the second night in a row, he had dreamed of gaping mouths full of teeth, with sounds like muffled blows. Try as he might, he could find no meaning to that dream.

This morning, he had finally realized that he hadn't brought a change of clothes. He looked for some clothes in the cottage, but didn't find any. Oh well, a week without changing wouldn't kill him. If his underwear really got dirty, he would do without. He hadn't brought a razor either, but that too was a detail. On the other hand, he promised himself a nice shower after breakfast.

He had gone into the monster's room at ten forty with a meal for him. The monster was fast asleep. Under his closed eyelids, his pupils were moving a lot, indicating troubled sleep. His face was paler than when he had arrived, almost white, and his forehead glistened with sweat. His left knee, which was more swollen than the other one, was purplish right up to the hip. The hemorrhage must be extensive. That could be serious.

So he had given the monster an injection to make him sleep another two hours. Then he had turned the crank to raise the chains until his body was in a standing position again, with the toes barely touching the floor. He had pushed the tabletop, which was still vertical, against the monster's back, and he had replaced the chains on his wrists with metal rings that were screwed to one end of the table and shackled his ankles to two rings at the other end. The monster was thus pinned to the vertical tabletop with his arms extended above his head. Bruno had then turned the tabletop back to a horizontal position and pushed it to the back wall of the room. By turning a crank extending from the apparatus, he had lowered the table to about hip height. The monster now looked like a cadaver lying on a table ready to be dissected. Then Bruno had prepared an intravenous bag and a transfusion tube. After hanging the bag from a little hook on the wall, he attached the tube to the monster's left arm. There. About a dozen hours of intravenous antibiotic should take care of the hemorrhage.

He had left the room, leaving breakfast behind.

Then he had called Morin and told him that the money for the day was in a small village close to Grand-Mère.

"That makes a little more travel for me," Morin had grumbled.

"For seven thousand dollars, I think it'll be worth your while."

"Anyway, I'd like it for the other days if the money could be hidden in Grand-Mère."

That had really surprised Bruno. So Morin hadn't realized that all the bundles of money were already hidden? Not very sharp, this guy. All the better, in fact. The less clever he was, the less Bruno had to worry about.

"The money will be where it will be, Mr. Morin. If you're not happy, you can always stop going to get it, and I'll keep it for myself."

After the phone call, he had eaten a huge breakfast. He was starving. Then he'd watched the noon news. The same report as the day before. Finally, he had gone outside, completely forgetting to shower.

He was still contemplating the lake, his new vision making him see only a vast expanse of gray, featureless water. In any case, he thought, this way of seeing things would be completely appropriate for his time in prison . . .

Prison. About fifteen years, probably. Maybe more. But he didn't care. When you don't have a life anymore, you may as well rot away in a cell.

And it was worth it.

Of course, he still didn't feel totally satisfied. That was normal. He was on the way there, certainly. He had climbed the first few rungs, but the ladder of satisfaction was tall. And he still had plenty of time to get to the top. That was precisely why he had allowed a week. So he could take his time.

The sun peeked briefly through the clouds, and its rays touched Bruno's balding head. With his eyes on the lake, he barely felt them, and a minute later, the clouds completely covered the sky again.

———

Christian Bolduc and Anne-Marie Pleau looked like a team coming back from the Olympic Games without a single medal. The day before, they had gone out with the Longueuil police. They had combed the very large neighborhood covered by the telephone cell. They had shown Hamel's photo to all the merchants, all the landlords, and all the hotel and motel clerks and apartment building janitors. Nothing. Wagner was red-faced with irritation, but Mercure kept his cool.

"Okay, go back there and continue the search. Take two more guys with you. Are the Longueuil police cooperating?"

"Yes."

"Perfect. Hamel must be in disguise. That's why no one recognizes him. Go back to the hotels and apartment buildings, and ask if they've had any complaints about strange noises in the last two days. Also, ask them if they have any tenants who never go out or who look suspicious."

"We've already asked them all that, Hervé."

"Ask again. Maybe they've noticed something new since yesterday. And if they still have nothing to tell you, ask them again tomorrow. And the next day."

Bolduc and Pleau nodded without enthusiasm.

"And don't come back here. Just call me. I want you to stay in Longueuil until you find him."

When they were alone again, Mercure and Wagner remained silent for a little while.

"If he left his cell phone on," Mercure said, "we could triangulate the signal . . ."

"What good would that do? We already know the area where he's hiding."

"But triangulation is more precise, isn't it?"

"Yes, but it's complicated to set up. It takes people with equipment, and we can't put a team on standby when we're not even sure Hamel will call again. Anyway, if he's in that area, we're sure to find him!"

Mercure shook his head doubtfully.

"That part of Longueuil is densely populated, it's very urban. I can't understand how Hamel could hide there with a hostage without attracting any attention. Maybe he goes to Longueuil to call but he's hiding somewhere else . . ."

"That seems pretty risky to me. And if that's the case, even triangulation wouldn't give us anything!" sighed the chief.

After a pause, he asked, "Did you go to the hospital before?"

Mercure said yes. He had questioned a few pharmacists. One of them, whose name was Martin Laplante, had seemed particularly nervous, and after Mercure had worked on him gently, he had finally given in. He had made the nitro patches for Hamel and provided him with various antibiotics.

"Hamel blackmailed him with some old business about drug trafficking."

"Did Laplante say anything else?"

"No. Only that he found Hamel gloomy and not himself."

"Nothing new, then."

Mercure didn't say anything. He remembered how desperate Laplante had been, convinced he was going to be considered an accomplice and also because of the trafficking business that had been uncovered. But all the detective sergeant did was thank him and leave while he watched wide-eyed.

"The chief of surgery also told me that several surgical instruments had gone missing. About the same time Hamel visited the hospital."

Wagner paced a few steps, picked up a paper clip from the desk, and asked, "You know what I'm thinking?"

"Yes."

The chief looked up, surprised.

"You're wondering what condition Lemaire is in now," continued Mercure.

Wagner nodded and looked down at his hands, bending and straightening the paper clip absentmindedly.

"And you know what? The idea doesn't really horrify me."

He made a face, threw the paper clip on the floor, and loosened his collar, asking, "And you, what are you thinking?"

"I'd planned to go to Montreal this week. I'm wondering if I shouldn't put it off."

"To see Demers?"

Mercure nodded. Wagner shook his head, making a face.

"I don't understand how you can go see that guy three times a year, Hervé."

Mercure did not reply and his superior did not insist. He knew it was a delicate subject, and in any case, he had given up trying to understand.

Mercure stood up and walked to the door. Wagner asked him what he was going to do.

"Watch some videos," he answered, completely serious.

———

When Bruno walked into the cottage at one forty in the afternoon, he heard the monster calling feebly. He had woken up. Perfect. Bruno suddenly felt excited.

He hurried out to his car again to get the bag with the purchase he had made the week before in the fetish shop in Montreal. He went back inside, took off his coat, and went to the room where the monster was still calling.

The monster was stretched out and shackled to the horizontal tabletop. He raised his head when Bruno came in. Bruno went over to him without putting down the bag. There was terror in the monster's eyes, of course, but also a strange, horrified fascination, as if he had had a disturbing revelation.

"I want . . . I want . . . to talk to you . . ."

He was trying to keep his voice calm, but pain and fear made it quaver. He was still very pale, but was not sweating anymore. He grimaced occasionally, no doubt feeling pain in his knees.

"But first, could . . . could you please give me something to eat? And something to drink?"

Bruno noticed the polite tone, which he found amusing.

"I saw that there was a . . . a full plate, there, on the floor . . . with a glass of juice. That's juice, isn't it?"

Bruno didn't move. He looked at his prisoner and waited for what would come next. The monster gave up on the meal for the time being. He hesitated, his face full of fear, and after licking his lips, said, "I . . . I'm sorry, Dr. Hamel . . ."

Bruno breathed out sharply through his nose and his whole body stiffened.

"I'm sorry for the . . . for the horrible thing I did. I . . . I'm sorry."

At those words, Bruno pulled the lever on the table and brought it back up to a vertical position. The monster gave an agonized moan.

"Dr. Hamel, I . . . I understand what you're trying to do."

Bruno pushed the table on its casters to the two chains hanging from the ceiling. The tube in the prisoner's arm was long enough to stay attached to the intravenous bag.

"The liquid you're shooting me up with, it's . . . it's some kind of medicine, huh? Because my legs are messed up, and you don't want me to die . . . ?"

Bruno stopped the table. He took a small key out of his pocket, detached the monster's right wrist from the table, and shackled it to one of the two chains hanging from the ceiling.

"You don't want me to die, because you want to . . ."

Another moan. Bruno did the same thing with the left wrist.

". . . you want to keep me alive as long as possible so you can . . ."

The sentence ended in a strangled sound. Bruno bent over and opened the rings at the bottom of the table, freeing the monster's feet. He had nothing to fear from that quarter: with his two broken knees, the monster couldn't even have pushed a balloon.

"It's really . . . really awful, what I did, I know it. If you only knew how sorry I am for it."

His breathing becoming more and more hoarse, Bruno pushed the table to the side. The monster was left hanging two centimeters from the floor, his arms stretched, his body swinging slightly. Grimacing, he continued, in a shrill, almost childlike voice.

"I need help, do you understand? Psychiatric help! It's not my fault, I can't control it, I've had such an unhappy life, I've been so . . . so humiliated . . . I was even glad I got arrested. It was time that I got . . . got treatment."

Bruno took a rectangular cardboard box from his bag, remembering what Mercure had said ten days earlier about the monster's lack of remorse, his arrogance during questioning, his little chuckle when he realized he was cornered. He was in such a hurry to open the box that his hands were shaking.

"If you . . . if you torture me, it's . . . it's . . . not going to help me! It won't help me at all. On the contrary, it will make me worse!"

The box finally opened and Bruno took out a whip, which he unrolled to its full length. Walking stiffly, he placed himself behind the monster.

"It's . . . it's . . . love I need, help and love! I . . . never got enough! Nobody loved me when I was little, nobody! Not even my parents!"

The more he went on with his psychological clichés, the more Bruno despised the monster and the more abhorrent he found him. Who did this asshole take him for? Some poor fool who wept over the people on reality shows? Did he think he was that stupid? And when he was raping Bruno's daughter, was he thinking that he lacked love? Was he feeling sorry for himself? While Jasmine was calling with all the strength in her tiny body to her father, who was not there . . . who was not there . . . *WHO WAS NOT THERE!!!!*

His first lash was that of a novice, clumsy and poorly controlled. The whip cracked feebly, barely touching the monster's back, though he still gave a short, sharp scream, more from panic than pain. As he squirmed in vain in his chains, he kept repeating that he was sorry, that he needed help . . .

"It's not my fault! I'm sick, it's not my fault!"

The second lash, while not impressive, was more successful, and a light mark appeared on the skin of the monster, who cried out again. There was a flash of joy in Bruno's dark gaze.

"It's not my fault!"

The third lash was perfect: a resounding crack, an immediate impact, and a long red streak on the left shoulder blade. This time the cry expressed real suffering. Encouraged by this success, Bruno lashed faster, with more assurance. More and more streaks appeared, blood started to flow, and the intravenous tube finally came loose. Between screams, the monster kept shouting, "It's not my fault! Not my fault!"

And Bruno, his mouth twisted in a horrible grimace, flogged the back and buttocks of his victim, who was being reduced to a mass of lacerated, bleeding flesh. Bruno was aiming to climb up another rung on the ladder of satisfaction.

Suddenly, under the agonized shouting of the tortured man, Bruno heard the strange muted sound he had heard the night before, but now it was stronger and clearer, and he thought he recognized the whimpering of an animal . . .

. . . the whimpering of a dog.

He stopped flogging for an instant, perplexed. The dog's whimpering had stopped. The monster took advantage of this respite to repeat, in a voice so mixed with sobbing that it was barely possible to make out the words, "Not . . . not my fault."

Enraged by these obscene words, Bruno began whipping him again. The monster gave another cry, and then, his voice transformed by surprising rage, he suddenly spat out, "It's not my fault, dammit! It's those little bitches, prancing around in their short dresses! They're not even ten years old, and they go around showing their asses. The little cock-teasers!"

Bruno felt as if he himself had been lashed full in the face. He leapt around to face the monster and looked at him with such fury that the monster's rage subsided instantly, replaced by panic. He mumbled an excuse, but Bruno didn't hear it; his ears were still filled with the abomination uttered by his prisoner.

Drunk with hate, he backed up a few steps and started lashing again. Five lashes struck the monster's belly and thighs; two hit his face, one slashing his forehead and nose close to one eye, the other cutting his cheek. The monster's cries were becoming weaker and weaker . . .

. . . and behind each cry, Bruno could still hear the animal whining, as if he had an invisible double who was simultaneously whipping a dog that was also invisible.

He stopped, his arm tired. Out of breath, he looked at the monster swinging at the end of his chains and dripping blood. He was only half-conscious; his head was nodding, his eyes were unfocused, and he was moaning a constant piercing moan. Bruno went to the winch and released it. The chains went slack and spun off the winch, and the monster collapsed heavily, legs first. When his broken knees hit the floor, he found the strength to squeal. Huddled on the floor in a puddle of his own blood, he started to cry.

Bruno looked at him one last time, for a few seconds. He opened the closet door, tossed in the whip, and left the room without closing the door behind him.

That had been quite satisfying. He had climbed another rung on the ladder of satisfaction. He could feel it. It had been difficult, though, and the satisfaction had been a long time coming. Why? Maybe because of that strange sound of the dog whining. What was that peculiar sound? Preoccupied by this, he went to the kitchen, opened a beer, and drank it standing up leaning on the counter.

He heard the muffled crying of the monster and decided to concentrate on that. The moaning of his prisoner always gave him a lot of pleasure and helped him relax.

He listened for a long time, and finally he forgot the whining of the dog.

———

Mercure had almost finished watching the second cassette. He hadn't learned much more than the day before, except that Hamel could be very impulsive in spite of his kindness and his altruism. Mercure had witnessed a couple of scenes where he had lost his temper. One in particular had obviously occurred during a party, where he was discussing globalization with some friends. Mercure was not surprised to discover that Hamel was against it. The discussion got pretty heated and there was quite a bit of drinking, and Hamel, at first passionate, started to get angry and then went into a rage out of all proportion, calling one of his friends a thoughtless, selfish capitalist, until finally Sylvie, ill at ease, had intervened to calm her partner down. Then the camera had discreetly stopped filming.

There were also a great many demonstrations of the love between the parents and their daughter.

Mercure pushed pause and reread the phrase he had written earlier in his notebook: *capable of sudden anger, can be very impulsive.*

He reread it several times. Impulsive anger lasts a few minutes, not a week.

He turned wearily to the two other cassettes, and thought briefly of returning them to Sylvie Jutras without watching them. But he knew he wouldn't. In spite of the boredom, he would watch them to the end. Because for Mercure, satisfaction did not only come from arresting criminals. It also came from understanding them. That is why a good third of his investigations left him with a sense of only partial success. That had been the case, for example, with Lemaire. He did not want it to happen again with the Hamel case. Whatever the outcome.

He pushed the play button on the old video player.

———

In the doorway of his ground-floor apartment, Henri Gamache, the owner of the building, sighed as he glanced at the photo of Hamel.

"You already came to see me this week," he said, handing it back to the two police officers. "You asked me the same questions and showed me the same photo, and I'm going to give you the same answer: no."

"We think he might have been wearing a disguise," Bolduc added.

"Then how am I supposed to recognize him?"

Bolduc asked if he had any new tenants. Gamache replied that he rented by the month or week, so there was a constant turnover. And in the last ten or twelve days, had there been anyone new? Reluctantly, Gamache checked his papers. There had been three new arrivals in the last two weeks: a student at Édouard-Montpetit College, a woman with a young child, and a man alone. Bolduc showed some interest in the last one: what did he look like? Gamache searched his memory: quite tall, beard, black hair.

"It could have been him in a disguise," suggested Bolduc. "Do you see him coming and going very often?"

"Do you think I have nothing to do but spy on my tenants? I'm not here during the day!"

The tenant in question was in number eight. While Bolduc and his colleague went upstairs, they called for two patrol cars to provide backup but not to go in right away. Bolduc was not really convinced. Hamel wasn't crazy enough to hide with his victim in a building like this, with so many people around. And the other tenants would have noticed something or heard noises. No, it didn't make sense.

They knocked on the door. No answer. Bolduc listened. Not a sound. He asked his Longueuil colleague to go get the extra key from the landlord. The officer came back in two minutes and they unlocked the door.

"I hope you have a warrant!" shouted Gamache from downstairs.

They entered cautiously, weapons in hand; after all, they shouldn't take any chances. But there was no one there. In the bedroom, the bed was unmade. There were some remnants of food on the kitchen counter and table. An open newspaper was lying on the living room couch. There was no trace of blood or violence. No indication of anyone being held prisoner here.

"Should we do a complete search?" asked his colleague unenthusiastically.

Bolduc sighed. What would be the point? Hamel and his victim could hardly be hidden in a drawer.

The two police officers left again, locking the door behind them. All these searches were ridiculous! Hamel and his prisoner wouldn't be hiding in an apartment building, it didn't make any sense!

"Are you going to come back again in two days, or can I hope you'll leave me in peace now?" asked Gamache ironically when they returned his key.

Bolduc just glared at him, and the two police officers left the building.

————

Sitting in an armchair with a magazine on his knees and a beer at his feet, Bruno was looking out the window, his eyes vacant. The afternoon had been long.

Around two thirty, he had returned to the monster's room. He had observed that the plate and glass were empty. In spite of his weakened condition and the pain, the monster had still crawled to his food. He was now half lying, half leaning against the wall, unable to find a comfortable position. The blood had dried on his body; he looked like an Apache warrior whose war paint was running in the rain. The two welts on his face looked nasty, but his eyes had been spared. He looked drained. But when he saw Bruno come in, he recovered a certain amount of energy and backed up as far as possible against the wall, begging Bruno not to hurt him.

Bruno had pulled up his chains again to bring him back to a hanging position, and had applied an antibiotic cream to his wounds. Not to relieve the pain, but to prevent any dangerous infections. The monster had offered no resistance. Relieved, he had kept quiet for a while, and then had started his soliloquy again, his voice rasping but surprisingly energetic: how long did he intend to torture him like this, it didn't make sense, it had to stop, he was sorry for everything . . . and he had started crying again.

Expressionless, Bruno had returned the table to the horizontal position, laid the monster on it, shackled him with the rings, and attached the intravenous tube to his arm again.

He had felt like having a beer, but for a change, he had poured himself a glass of Scotch. It was no use, though, he really didn't like the taste. So he had emptied the bottle down the sink and opened himself a beer. He had tried to read outside on the porch, but it was a little too cold. He had sat down in the living room to listen to a classical music record belonging to Josh.

He looked away from the woods and checked his watch: five twenty. In two and a half hours, he had read just five pages.

He couldn't get those whining dog sounds out of his mind. But he had to forget that and relax. TV maybe? He remembered that the TVA news started at five thirty. He switched off the music and turned on the TV, just in time for the beginning of the broadcast.

To his surprise, his story was the third item.

"No progress in the Bruno Hamel affair, the case of the thirty-eight-year-old doctor who kidnapped his daughter's murderer and . . ."

Without divulging the monster's name, they said the police still had no leads and there were only four days left until the deadline set by the doctor for killing the prisoner.

Bruno looked satisfied. The police were still floundering. It was perfect. But then he immediately told himself he was an idiot: if the police had any clues, they certainly wouldn't tell the reporters, especially since they knew Bruno was listening.

So why continue watching the news? Out of curiosity?

Again they showed the report on Lemaire's arrest, which Bruno had already seen so many times. This was a condensed version, though, and they still said nothing specific about Lemaire: they just called him "the killer."

But at one point, the journalist said, "The killer had already been arrested for a similar crime in Saint-Hyacinthe, where he was . . ."

With a scream of rage, Bruno threw his bottle of beer at the TV. Barely missing the screen, it hit the right side of the cabinet and shattered. The doctor leapt to his feet and turned off the set with a hard kick.

They hadn't taken him seriously! They'd ignored his instructions! That meant he couldn't watch the news anymore without risking finding out information about the killer. He kicked again, this time the little table in the middle of the room. He was so angry that he tripped over the fallen table twice. Each time, he kicked it again.

But he wanted to watch the news, he needed it, much more than he would have thought. He wanted to know how they were reporting the case, how people were reacting, how . . . He needed it, that was all, as ridiculous as it might seem.

Therefore he had to show them he was serious . . . that his instructions were not empty threats.

Bloody images passed through his mind: he saw himself cutting off both the monster's arms, scalping him alive, sewing his testicles over his eyes, and each of these images excited and tantalized him.

He went to get another beer and drank it down in a few gulps. He was still thinking and was unable to come up with anything. He hit the refrigerator, growling with frustration.

And suddenly, he had it.

Ten seconds later, he was in the monster's room. The monster was still shackled to the horizontal table. He lifted his head weakly. He seemed to be a little better than before, although his slashed face was still as swollen.

"You . . . you're going to hurt me again, huh?"

His voice was marked by fear, which was now constant. The voice was stronger than in the afternoon, but less clear because of the bruised lips.

Bruno searched in one of his bags and took out a small ampoule containing a transparent liquid. He prepared a syringe and returned to the monster. Most of the dried blood on his body had disappeared; it had turned into scabs and fallen to the floor. Now you could clearly see the big red welts on his belly, his torso, and his legs; they were no longer bleeding but still seemed raw.

The monster became anxious when he saw the syringe, and asked what it was. Bruno shoved the needle in his left arm and injected the substance. Panting a little, the monster started opening and closing his hands frantically and moaning. "You're going to . . . you're going to hurt me again, Dr. Hamel! You're not going to . . ."

He stopped and blinked his eyes, dazed.

"Wha . . . what's going on? Christ! What's happening to me?"

His words became slurred and his hands opened and closed with more and more difficulty, as if in slow motion. His mouth was barely moving now and the words were becoming inaudible. "Wha . . . da . . . wha's happ'n . . . ?"

He was unable to speak any more and his eyes suddenly opened wide.

Perfect. The curare had taken effect.

Carrying his two bags, Bruno went to the kitchen. He took out a series of surgical instruments and sterilized them as best he could with soap and water. He took a plate, laid a clean towel on it, and lined up the instruments.

He put on a surgical mask, a surgical cap, and latex gloves. He looked at himself in the little mirror by the door. This operation would kill two birds with one stone. It would give him satisfaction and obtain what he wanted from the reporters. Combining business with pleasure.

He returned to the room and went over to the table. The monster was petrified; none of his limbs moved, his slightly open mouth did not quiver, and his wide-open eyes stared into emptiness. Only his shallow respiration indicated that he was alive. You might think he had fainted with his eyes open.

But Bruno knew he was completely conscious, that he could see very well what was happening. Curare paralyzed the body, but it did not affect consciousness or sight . . .

. . . or sensation.

He put the plate of instruments down on the edge of the table, chose a scalpel, and raised it slowly close to the monster's face, so that the monster could see it clearly.

The prisoner's features didn't move, but there was a glimmer of panic in his frozen stare.

Slowly, the scalpel moved toward the left side of his belly, pressed against the flesh, and penetrated it. The doctor applied pressure and the blade moved upward, producing an incision about twelve centimeters long. Thin streams of blood flowed down the ribs to the table.

There was still no emotion in the monster's features, but the glimmer in his eye remained there.

In the doctor's masked face, only the eyes were visible, as sharp and cold as the scalpel. Using a retractor, he expanded the incision until it was an oval opening about fifteen centimeters wide, exposing the inside of the body.

Bruno brought his face close to the monster's and stared intently at him. The glimmer was still there in the prisoner's eyes. Without taking his gaze from his victim, with his mask almost touching the other man's nose, Bruno slowly inserted his hand into the red opening in the belly. A soft, wet noise broke the unbearable silence in the room, and the glimmer in the monster's eyes exploded, while the wheezing of his breathing grew a little louder.

*Smile*, thought the doctor. *Come now, just a little smile.*

He remained that way for several seconds, slowly moving his hand in the cavity, his face still close . . . and when he saw two big tears run down the inert face of his prisoner, his eyes narrowed until they were nothing but two blazing slits, glowing lava smoldering under black ashes.

Finally, he pulled his hand out of the large incision. His dripping fingers picked up another instrument, and under the harsh fluorescent light, the doctor silently began his operation.

# DAY 4

AT EIGHT O'CLOCK, WAGNER WAS STANDING WITH HIS ARMS CROSSED, SOL-
emnly watching Mercure enter the squad room. When Mercure
saw him, he wondered if his superior had actually slept in his office.

"TVA gave out information on Lemaire yesterday . . ."

Mercure's shoulders sagged.

"Did you hear it?"

"Yes. I was here, but I had a look at the news."

They had only said that Lemaire had already been charged with rape
and murder in Saint-Hyacinthe two years before, nothing else. Mercure
slumped into a chair with a deep sigh.

"Idiots!"

"It wasn't all that much, actually. And maybe Hamel didn't watch
TVA."

"We can always hope. We could try to call Hamel. If he heard the
news, he might be waiting for our call."

"We tried, of course."

There was a long silence, and then Mercure shrugged fatalistically:

they had to cross their fingers. He went into his office and sat for a long while, his hands folded under his chin, thinking.

Twenty minutes later, Wagner stuck his head in the door, looking agitated. They had just gotten a call from the Mister Poutine restaurant on Highway 20 toward Montreal, not far away. In front of the garbage container, one of the employees had found a package on which was written: *For the Drummondville police, from Bruno Hamel.* Mercure immediately sent one of his men to the restaurant.

"He watched the news," Mercure sighed as he sat down on his desk.

"He took the package there last night while the restaurant was closed, knowing it would be found this morning." Surprised, the chief added, "He came all the way to Drummondville for that! He's a cool customer!"

"Driving on the 20 isn't really very risky for him."

"Still, every cop in Longueuil is looking for him, and he took the risk of leaving."

After a brief silence, the chief asked, "What do you think is in the package?"

Mercure preferred not to answer.

———

The monster was waking up. Bruno went to the kitchen, picked up a plate already filled with food and a glass of juice, and walked to the hallway.

When he entered the room, the monster, still lying on the table, was awake. Bruno put the plate and glass down on the floor and went over to him. The monster looked like a zombie. It was no longer just because of his dirty hair plastered to his face, or his skin that was whiter and whiter in spite of the red welts, but also because of his limpness and inertia, even in his shackles. He turned toward Bruno. Even the fear in his eyes was weary, exhausted. He clenched his teeth for a moment, and said in a rasping voice, "You're insane, Hamel."

Not so polite anymore. Had the monster finally understood that he had nothing to gain? Bruno did not react. In a voice that was barely stronger, the other man added with difficulty, "What did you do to me last night?"

Silence. The monster lifted his head slightly.

"Answer me, dammit! What did you do to me last night? You could at least say something to me before I die!"

And as if he realized what he had just said, his face tensed with panic and he moaned, on the verge of tears, "God, I can't take it anymore! Do you understand? I can't take it anymore, Hamel!"

He sobbed.

"But I don't want to . . . I don't want to die! You can put me in prison for the rest of my life, but I don't want to die! What . . . what can I do to get you to stop? I can't take it anymore!"

While the monster moaned, Bruno activated the lever of the table and put it in the vertical position. A minute later, the prisoner was on the floor, half sitting, half lying against the wall, his limp arms on the floor, his hands still attached to the chains, which were now loose. The food was very close to him, but he ignored it. He looked like a mario-nette with its strings cut. He was still looking at Bruno, his gaze shifting between terror and despondency.

"You operated on me yesterday . . . and I felt . . . I felt everything."

He pointed to the small open slit in his abdomen, a few centimeters long.

"And you didn't even close it completely!"

With a trembling hand, he ventured to touch the incision. Strangely, it was not bleeding even though it was open. It almost looked like a closed, lipless mouth. He had an opening in his belly, and he felt nothing!

"What . . . what is it? Christ, what did you do to me! Answer me! What is this opening here?"

Bruno, who had watched him without moving, turned around and left.

He went and sat down in the living room. From the room, there were no cries, no sounds. The monster must be fascinated and terrified by that opening in his belly.

In an hour—two at most—he would have an answer.

———

Boisvert laid the package on a desk. It was about the size of a shoebox, and wrapped in white paper containing the words *For the Drummond-ville police, from Bruno Hamel*, and also the word *Danger.* The five people in the hall were looking at the package in silence, undecided. Not that the word "danger" bothered them; they all knew that word was there to dissuade whoever found it from opening the box before calling the police. But they knew that what it contained could still cause quite a shock.

"Maybe we should open it," timidly suggested Ruel, an officer in his thirties with half his face scarred by acne.

Mercure walked over to the desk and began to tear off the white paper, unhurriedly; frankly, he was in no rush to find out what was in that box.

It was, in fact, a shoebox, an ordinary shoebox, with the brand name in big bold letters. Only the traces of dried blood made it seem less banal.

Wagner loosened his collar with a nervous finger. Mercure was pre-paring himself mentally. He had been a cop for twenty-six years, but the sight of blood still got to him. Summoning up his courage, he took off the lid, holding his breath.

Inside, there was something that looked like a very long shiny sau-sage in a coil. Mercure understood almost immediately. He smothered a curse, averted his eyes, and took a deep breath.

"What?" asked Wagner impatiently. "What is it, dammit?"

He went over to the box and, in turn, recognized a section of intes-tine.

In spite of their repulsion, the other police officers could not help glancing fearfully into the box. Ruel even shouted, "Fuck! He must have cut three feet out of him!" Wagner told him to shut up. Mercure, who had his back to the table, smoothed his hair with both hands and tried, in spite of his disgust, to understand why someone would remove three feet of intestine from a man. What exactly was the effect of that?

At the same time, Ruel, who was still leaning over the box, cried out again, "There's a piece of paper too!"

Wagner ordered Ruel to pick up the paper. After hesitating, the officer reached cautiously into the box and, grimacing with disgust, took out a small bloodstained sheet of white paper. He frowned and, like a child learning to read, articulated every syllable: "Col-os-to-my."

"Huh?"

"There's just one word: colostomy."

"What does it mean?"

Ruel shrugged. None of them seemed to know. Mercure wracked his memory; the word reminded him of something, but he couldn't quite put his finger on it. In any case, he was sure it wasn't anything very nice.

"Christ! There are five of us here, and nobody knows what *colostomy* means!" fumed Wagner, raising his arms in exasperation.

"We're police officers, not doctors!" objected Boisvert.

Pat, who had been thinking, suddenly opened his mouth and raised his head. "Oh shit! It just came to me! I have an uncle who had that and . . ."

He paused and they all looked at him quizzically. Seeing Pat's nauseated look, Mercure knew that it was worse than anything he'd imagined.

———

Bruno was still in the armchair, where he had been dozing for a while (the operation of the day before had been long and his night's sleep short), when the monster's shouts rang out. Not cries of fear, this time, or of panic, but of total horror. He stood up and walked to the room.

On the floor, the plate and the glass were empty. Propped up on his hands, the monster did not even look at Bruno. He was too busy staring at the slit in his belly that had opened to reveal a brownish, sticky mass. He had obviously regained a certain level of energy, because he was repeating loudly, "Christ! What's happening to me? What's happening to me!"

The soft mass was oozing out, and a nauseating smell filled the room. The monster must finally have understood, because his eyes, still riveted on his belly, widened with repulsion.

"Damn, it can't be! *It can't be!*"

Bruno saw his face twist with effort, as if he were trying to hold back the substance, to keep it from coming out of him. This amused Bruno. He knew that any attempt at retention was pointless. The sticky mass finally came out completely and slid slowly over the monster's stomach as he moaned in disgust. Bruno's eyes shone.

*Filth for filth. You defiled my daughter, you sullied her body and her soul. Now it's your turn to be defiled, you piece of garbage, your turn to soil yourself! You're just a piece of shit, so ROT IN YOUR OWN SHIT!*

The slit opened again. The monster raised his head and gave a long cry. He finally saw Bruno, and something insane, something inhuman, flashed in his eyes.

"You're sick!" he squealed in a voice so shrill he sounded like a cartoon character. "You're sick, Hamel, sick, sick, *sick*!"

Shouting hysterically, he tried to push back the excrement that was emerging, but he only spread it over his belly, his thighs, his hands.

Without waiting for the vile evacuation to end, Bruno left the room.

———

". . . the anus is no longer used, and all the . . . the business comes out of a small opening in the abdomen."

They listened to Pat in disbelief. Ruel said, "You mean he shits from his belly?"

Mercure glared at him. Wagner paced a bit, grumbling, and then said, "Okay! Not a word of this to the reporters!"

While he was giving his instructions, Mercure, overcoming his revulsion, took the shoebox and examined every surface of it. No store name, just the brand, a common one that was sold everywhere.

He put down the box and checked the time: ten o'clock. He went to his office and got his coat, and put it on as he crossed the squad room.

"I'm going to Montreal. I'll be back at the end of the afternoon. Try to get us an injunction for the reporters."

Wagner nodded. He had understood perfectly.

Mercure's voice was unusually hard and cold. He could have called

TVA, but he wanted to tell them what he thought in person. And it would also give him a chance to visit Demers, as he should have done at the beginning of the week.

As he was about to leave, Wagner said, "I'll ask Longueuil to set up a triangulation."

Mercure nodded and left.

———

"Did you get that?" asked Bruno after describing the hiding place for the day's money.

"I got it," Morin said.

Just when Bruno was about to hang up, Morin asked, "Could you . . . uh . . . give me double today, and then I could skip a day tomorrow?"

Bruno was surprised. Morin had received some sixty thousand dollars and he already needed more? Maybe he had huge debts.

"The agreement was seven thousand a day, and that's how we'll continue."

Bruno hung up. He put on his coat and hesitated for a moment in front of the refrigerator. Wasn't it a little early for a beer? He shrugged, took one out, and went outside.

The sky was even more overcast than the day before. It would probably rain by the end of the afternoon. Bruno walked along the shore of the lake, looking absently at two ducks gliding over the water in the distance.

Last night, for the first time, he had felt no real satisfaction.

It was true that the operation was very delicate, very technical, and quite far from the usual ways of letting off steam. But still, he had used the curare precisely so that the monster would feel everything. So Bruno should certainly have experienced some kind of satisfaction.

At least, that's what he thought.

He shook his head and gave a little kick at a stone. But the kick was soft and lacked conviction. Still this damn heaviness . . . The pebble fell to the ground without even getting as far as the lake.

The sound of an animal whimpering came from the woods. Bruno turned toward it, his ears pricked. It sounded like a dog or something. But he didn't see any animal, and the sound stopped.

His imagination again!

He gulped down half his beer. He took the blue ribbon out of his pocket and examined it for a moment.

It was time for the big one, the one he had been planning from the beginning, that he had conceived the very day he had learned of the monster's arrest.

He would give him a few more hours to recuperate from his operation yesterday . . . and then this evening . . .

———

Behind the big desk, a bearded man in his forties stood up with a smile and extended his hand to the visitor coming in. Behind him, a wide window showed the skyscrapers of Montreal.

"Good day, Inspector Mercure! What brings you all the way from Drummondville!"

In spite of his pleasant manner, it was obvious that Monette was a bit nervous. He knew the reason for the visit. Mercure kept his hands in his pockets and did not sit down. He began softly.

"What were you thinking? We had an agreement. Were you trying to provoke him, or what?"

The extended hand hesitated for a moment, wondering whether to continue trying to be conciliatory, decided not to, and withdrew. The smile, on the other hand, was more stubborn.

"Have a seat, Inspector," suggested Monette, sitting down himself.

"Do you have any idea what the consequences of your actions were?"

Mercure remained standing. Monette's smile finally disappeared.

"Come now, Inspector, don't exaggerate! All we said was that Lemaire had already been charged with the same kind of crime in Saint-Hyacinthe a few years ago. Nothing more. We didn't even give his name."

"That was already too much."

"Listen, I wasn't the one who did the report . . ."

"Come on, you're the news director! And for how long now?"

"A little over a year."

"Didn't anyone explain to you that when the police ask for your co-operation, it is in your interest to listen?"

Monette sighed, embarrassed.

"Okay, we made a mistake, we apologize. We'll go back to the law of silence. But I have to say I don't agree. The public has a right to know, and—"

"Don't bore me with that right-to-know stuff!" Mercure interrupted, his voice still calm, but scornful.

"And you stop playing the offended virgin!" replied the news director, who had regained some of his assurance. "Your Hamel probably didn't see the report."

"He saw it, and he made good on his threat."

A brief silence.

"Meaning?"

"You think I'm going to reveal that to you? All you need to know is that what he did to Lemaire was really atrocious, and we have you to thank for it!"

"Was it really that awful?"

But Monette was not asking out of remorse. Mercure even detected a hint of dark satisfaction on his face, and he suddenly understood.

"It's what you wanted," he muttered, incredulous.

"What?"

"You wanted Hamel to hear the report and carry out his threat!"

"Come now, Inspector, you're going overboard."

But his nervousness had returned. Mercure took his hands out of his pockets and stepped toward the desk. He was a slight man, but suddenly he looked threatening.

"Who do you think you are, Monette? A court? A judge who decides the fate of others?"

The news director leaned back but didn't get flustered.

"And you, do you think you're God, saving the sinners and the just alike? Maybe you don't make any distinction between Hamel and Lemaire, but I do! You've taken the side of the murderer; I'm on the side of the victim!"

"And who's the victim? Right now, who's the victim of whom?"

"Stop it. You know very well that that doesn't stand up! I have a nine-year-old daughter, and if somebody killed her, I would be one of the victims! And even if I held the murderer hostage, even if I tortured him, I'd *still* be a victim!"

Monette put aside all diplomacy and inclined his head forward.

"I'm telling you, Inspector. Hamel could make Lemaire drink battery acid, I don't give a damn. And if on Monday he manages to kill that son of a bitch before you find him, our station will play the game and announce it as a tragedy. But here in my office, I'll be applauding like mad. And I don't think I'll be the only one."

Mercure grabbed him by the shirt collar, something that would really have surprised the detective sergeant's colleagues.

"You understand nothing!" he growled through clenched teeth. "Nothing at all!"

"Oh yeah?" replied Monette provocatively, without even trying to free himself.

Mercure looked at him for a moment, and then let go of him and strode to the door. Before leaving, he turned around, pointing his finger, and said, "We have an injunction now. You'll be receiving it by the end of the afternoon. Say another word about Lemaire's life on TV and I'll have you in court."

Without waiting for the news director's reaction, he left.

———

Sylvie was in the middle of a black cloud that would not dissipate. In the last few days, she had been able to come out of it once or twice. No, not really, she had been pulled out of it, dragged out for a moment. To talk, take care of details, answer questions. But those moments were brief and the cloud always re-formed around her.

She knew she could not grieve normally for Jasmine as long as the cloud remained there. But how could she help it, now that a second disaster had hit her in the face? How could she deal with two disasters at the same time?

Her sister's voice finally got through to her:

"Sylvie . . . Sylvie, come here."

Couldn't she leave her in peace? But Josée insisted, saying she had to come see something. Sylvie made a superhuman effort to come out of the cloud. She got up from her chair and walked to the kitchen. Josée was in front of the window, looking stunned. With slow, dragging steps, Sylvie went over and looked out the window with her.

In the street, there were about twenty people marching back and forth chanting inaudible words. They were waving placards, and Sylvie managed to make out what was written on them. First she felt surprise, then devastation.

She should have stayed in her cloud.

———

"How are you, Marc?"

The two men were facing each other on either side of the big glass window, each holding a telephone to his ear. Marc Demers, in his late twenties, with hair cut short and small round glasses, shrugged.

"I'm all right, sir. I still have another fifteen years to do, but I'm okay."

His voice was soft, melodious, and intelligent. And it was not just his voice that was intelligent, as Mercure had observed more than once in almost four years.

Mercure remained silent. As usual, he waited for Demers to steer the discussion. The prisoner looked down at the fingers of his free hand for a moment and said, "I haven't got a lot to say, sir. And the two last times I saw you, I didn't have much to say either. I don't know if you noticed . . ."

"That's true."

After a dozen meetings, the formality seemed a little out of place to Mercure. Once he had tried to get Demers to drop it, but Demers, unperturbed, had continued calling him "sir." So Mercure had just accepted it.

"Uh, you know, there is one thing," the convict said suddenly. "I dreamed about your wife two weeks ago."

There was no reaction on Mercure's face.

"That's not the first time."

"No, but this was different. She was dressed in a white dress and she was radiant with inner light. It was very peaceful. She looked at me silently. And that's all."

He finally looked up at the policeman and smiled slightly.

"It's a bit kitschy, don't you think?"

The remark was meant to be provocative, and Mercure knew it.

"How do you interpret it?" asked the policeman.

"I don't know. I hope you don't think your wife came to tell me she forgave me."

"Of course not."

Demers's provocation no longer shocked Mercure. He knew he did it to test him. But Mercure sensed that there was no malice in it. At the beginning there had been, but there no longer was.

"There's a theory," Mercure said, "that people in dreams are only different representations of the person dreaming."

"I know that, sir. And I see where you're going with this. My dream could be a sign that I'm beginning to forgive myself, right? After evil, indifference, then remorse, and finally, the beginning of inner peace . . . I'm on the road to redemption, right?"

It was impossible to know if he was being sarcastic. Or rather, *how* sarcastic he was being.

"It's true," Demers added. "Did you ever want to be a priest?"

Mercure looked doubtful.

"I'm not sure I'm a believer."

"Of course. You're much too interested in men to believe in God."

He glanced over at the two guards, standing motionless farther away.

"Do you intend to come and visit me like this for the next fifteen years?"

"You're not obligated to accept my visits, you know. In fact, for the first six months, you refused to have anything to do with me. I'll stop coming when you tell me to stop."

"Or when you have answers to your questions," added the prisoner, his eyes piercing behind his little glasses.

Mercure returned his gaze. Demers added, "Besides, maybe you're the one who should be talking today. You look awful."

Mercure hesitated and made a vague gesture with his free hand.

"I'm on a very special case now. Perhaps the most disturbing and complex one of my career."

He summarized the Hamel case, surprised to find himself recounting the whole thing to someone like Demers. The convict listened in silence, expressionless, with the telephone at his ear.

"What is it that bothers you about this business?" he asked when Mercure had finished.

"I don't know, I . . ."

Why was he telling Demers all this?

"It's the behavior of this guy Hamel that fascinates me and . . . disturbs me. I could very well have done to you something like what Hamel is doing, for example. But I opted for a different solution. Does that make me a better man? Am I more human than Hamel because of that? It's . . ."

He sighed and passed a hand over his forehead. Demers, vaguely amused, murmured, "More human . . ."

"I told him that if he tortured and killed Lemaire, it would make him a murderer just like Lemaire. He answered that it would make him a murderer, but not like Lemaire."

"He's wrong, sir," Demers said softly. "There are no different murderers. There are only different flaws."

"And you, Marc, what's your flaw?"

Demers gave a strange grin.

"That's your obsession, huh? It's the hope of an answer to that question that's been bringing you here three times a year for almost four years now, isn't it?"

He switched hands with the telephone and leaned his head slightly forward, suddenly very serious.

"Unfortunately—and I'm repeating this for the hundredth time—I don't know why I killed your wife. I've finally felt remorse for it, and sorrow for what I've done, but I still haven't understood why I committed a completely gratuitous murder with absolutely no motive. I went into that store intending to rob the till, I saw your wife paralyzed with terror and I fired even though she wasn't doing anything. I was totally ripped on coke, but that's no reason. I don't know what my flaw is, and that's why probably nobody will ever know why, for one brief moment of my life, I became a monster."

He leaned back a bit in his chair. Mercure said nothing, his face impassive.

"With your Hamel," added Demers, pushing his glasses up his nose, "we know his flaw—despair, devastation, loss . . ."

"Is that enough to excuse him?"

"That's not what I'm saying. Look at you—you don't come to see me in order to forgive me."

"Absolutely not."

"Of course not. You're not a fool."

Demers said this with a strange smile.

*Why am I talking to him about all this?* wondered the policeman.

"You come to try to understand," continued Demers. "That's the conscious reason. But I think there's also an unconscious reason, a reason that connects you a little to Hamel. Relatively speaking, of course."

Mercure frowned. With a half-amused, half-bitter grin, Demers explained, "Don't you think it's a kind of torture for me, seeing you three times a year? You're my bad conscience. Your presence takes me back five years in the past, forces me to face the murder I committed and its terrible consequences—your inconsolable sadness, which I sense in you in spite of your effort to keep it private."

After a short pause, he added coolly, "Under your façade of sincerity and humanism, there lies the worst torturer."

Mercure did not flinch, but he was so shaken that his vision blurred for an instant. He licked his lips and tried to make his tone ironic, but his voice quavered slightly.

"If I'm torturing you, Marc, why do you agree to see me?"

Demers had an indecipherable expression on his face, an expression that was so serious it was almost a caricature.

"For my redemption, of course, as you know very well! We all know redemption requires a certain amount of masochism."

Mercure would have liked to smile, but he could not. How could he smile at the man who had killed his wife?

Demers shrugged.

"There are all sorts of monsters. Some are monsters their whole lives, some are monsters just for a brief moment, and some are monsters without even knowing it."

And he glanced teasingly at Mercure. The policeman rubbed his eyes. This visit had taken a completely unexpected turn. But unconsciously, wasn't that why he had come? Hadn't he known deep down that Demers would give him a completely different perspective on this case? And wasn't that precisely what he had been looking for?

He had to leave, but in spite of his turmoil, he asked one last question of this man with whom he had the strangest, most ambiguous, most incomprehensible relationship.

"So Hamel has become a monster?"

Demers watched Mercure for a moment. In contrast with his suddenly serious expression, his voice remained light and melodious.

"He has become too human. There is nothing more monstrous."

———

Bruno had promised himself a shower at the end of the morning, but he forgot again.

After walking around outside for quite a while, he tried to read a novel he'd found in Josh's bedroom, but without much success. He was still unable to concentrate. Several times, he felt like going to the monster's room, but he stopped himself. He had to let him recuperate. Patience.

He drank six beers in the course of the afternoon. He had not intended to drink that much, but after his third one, when he was sitting in the living room trying to read, he again heard the whimpering of the dog from the hallway. He quickly opened the monster's door. The monster, lost in dark thoughts, just started. Then he whispered, "Could I . . . at least . . . wipe off . . ."

And he pointed feebly at the excrement stuck to his belly.

Bruno closed the door and returned to the living room. The dog's whimpering persisted, but now it was coming from outside. Furious, he went out on the porch and screamed, "Where are you, you filthy mutt? Where are you hiding?"

He was answered only by the echo of his own voice, and it gave him gooseflesh. He couldn't stand that dog's howling anymore! What did it mean? Why did he hear it? Oddly, he felt he knew the answer to that question deep down inside, but it refused to surface to his consciousness . . .

Troubled, he returned to the house. During the next two hours, he drank three more beers.

The howling of the dog stopped. Bruno even managed to read six pages, in spite of his slight drunkenness . . . or maybe *because of* it.

He glanced at his watch: five o'clock. In about two hours, he could go to the monster.

————

The rain was so fine that Mercure only turned his windshield wipers on at two- or three-minute intervals. As he drove to Drummondville, he kept thinking about his meeting with Demers. And for the first time in four years, he asked himself the question Demers had asked him: how many years would he keep going to see him?

Did he really hope to have an answer one day, an illumination that would finally make him accept Madelaine's death? The first year after his wife's death had been filled with hatred and anger. Then, suddenly, he had had enough of rage, and he had come up with the idea of going to visit Demers. And since then, he had been going to see him three times a year.

The anger and hatred had truly disappeared. But was he satisfied?

Maybe those visits had had a meaning for the first three years. But now? For a few months, he had been thinking of not going anymore, but every time, he would see his wife's body again with that hole in her head, and suddenly, the possibility of ending his meetings with Demers seemed unthinkable. So he continued.

And his mourning for Madelaine continued . . .

That idea made him frown.

His cell phone rang. It was Wagner, wanting to know when he'd be back. Mercure told him he would be there in twenty minutes and asked if there was any news. Discouraged, the chief answered that the guys in Longueuil hadn't turned up anything yet. It almost seemed like witchcraft.

"In any case, they're doing a triangulation, but it's taking longer than we thought it would. The Longueuil police didn't have the necessary equipment, so they had to go get it in Montreal. But in a couple of hours, it should be ready."

Mercure hung up. Hamel would still have to call again for them to be able to do the triangulation . . . and it was far from certain that he would.

For the rest of the trip, he no longer thought about Demers.

———

Bruno had just finished his seventh beer and his head was beginning to feel cloudy when he watched the TVA news. This time, there was no information on the monster. He sighed with satisfaction: his little demonstration had borne fruit. The reporter only repeated that the police still had no leads. And then he announced that a demonstration had taken place that day in Drummondville in relation to the case. A group of about twenty people were shown walking up and down Maple Street, in the quiet neighborhood where the doctor lived, chanting some incomprehensible words. Some were carrying placards reading "We want justice!" and "Death to child killers!" Bruno observed the scene in stunned amazement as a voice explained, "A little group of sympathizers with

Bruno Hamel's cause marched in the streets of Drummondville today. We collected statements from some of them . . ."

A man of around fifty appeared, looking sure of himself. "We approve Bruno Hamel's actions one hundred percent. I'm sure there are dozens of parents who have had a child killed by a maniac who agree with him now! They felt powerlessness! Hamel refused to accept powerlessness!"

A woman took the place of the man on the screen, and Bruno recognized Marielle Lesage, one of his neighbors.

"If a person tortures and kills a child, prison is too good for them! They should have the same thing done to them! If these murderers were turned over to the parents of their victims, I swear that would make the scum that are still running around free think twice! Bruno Hamel is not just taking revenge; he's sending a message!"

Bruno had never foreseen this kind of reaction—a demonstration in his support! In fact, he had never asked himself what impact his action might have on public opinion. These images fascinated him as much as they surprised him. On one hand, he was glad to see that certain people supported what he was doing. However, there was something he found disturbing about the demonstration, something that made him uncomfortable. And he finally understood what it was. A few weeks earlier, he would have found this kind of demonstration horrible and incomprehensible.

He clenched his fists in irritation, then gave a nasty little chuckle. Of course, he hadn't understood anything. Because nothing had happened to him yet! Jasmine was still alive and he thought he was safe from everything! It's so easy to be a right-thinking person when everything is fine in your life! It's easy to be a humanist when you've never known suffering and sorrow! But now everything was changed, and now he understood. And those demonstrators also understood, because of what he was doing.

"But this group of people does not represent everyone," continued the reporter. "Here are some comments from people watching the demonstration."

A young man of about twenty appeared on the screen.

"I could never be in favor of violence, whether or not it's motivated by revenge."

"Hamel thinks what he's doing is a solution, but he's wrong," added a woman in her forties. "I would never do anything like that."

"What do you know?" shouted Bruno, leaning toward the TV. "What do you know, you ignorant bitch!"

"Bruno Hamel should make a grand gesture," suggested an older man. "He should free his prisoner, take him in his arms and tell him he forgives him for what he did. Then they should pray together."

The doctor laughed scornfully.

A dog barked.

Bruno leapt to his feet. Even with the sound of the TV, he could clearly hear the dog growling outside, close to the house. He dashed to the door as more barking sounded.

Outside on the porch, he looked around furiously, trying not to shout as he had before. This time he wasn't dreaming—a dog *really* had barked, it wasn't in his head!

He heard a car pass on the road above, more than a hundred and fifty meters away. A few scattered drops of rain were falling from the overcast sky. A gust of wind made the dead leaves dance for a moment.

Bruno went back in, nervously rubbing his hands. He went to the refrigerator to get another beer. There was only one left. He wanted to put more in the fridge, but the two cases were empty.

Had he drunk forty-eight beers in four days?

He had also drunk a few while Morin was preparing the room. And Morin had had three or four. Still . . .

Puzzled, he went back to the living room, taking a big slug from his last bottle, and then froze in the middle of the room. On the TV screen, Sylvie was in the doorway of their house. Several microphones were being held toward her. She appeared exhausted and seemed to be speaking reluctantly. In a weak voice, she said, "No, I am not in any way associated with this demonstration. I love my partner, but I . . ." She sighed. "I cannot approve of what he is doing."

Bruno watched slack-jawed, his eyes bulging. God! She was so much thinner. She had such dark circles under her eyes. She looked so *broken*.

"Bruno has always been against any form of violence, although he had a lot of questions about it. He was a peace activist, he signed petitions, he . . ." She licked her lips nervously. "That's not him, that . . ."

"Yes, it's me!" shouted Bruno. "Stop denying it and accept it! It's me, whether you like it or not!"

"I hope that . . . that the justice system won't be too hard on him," continued Sylvie with difficulty. "That they take into account that Bruno is acting this way because he's in a state of shock . . . that the pain made him crazy . . ."

"Crazy!" Bruno laughed nastily. "Crazy!"

Sylvie could not go on. She covered her eyes with one hand and was on the verge of tears when her sister appeared behind her and took her by the shoulders to lead her back into the house.

"I haven't gone crazy!" Bruno continued to shout hoarsely. "You have no right to say that! No right at all!"

He finally realized that Sylvie had been replaced by the impassive news anchor, who was summing up the latest debate in the House of Commons. Bruno blinked, caught off guard, and started pounding the wall.

He stopped suddenly. His blows had echoed in an odd way. Like those indistinct, confused blows in his strange recurring dream.

He finally sat down again and finished his beer, brooding. Sylvie's words were hammering in his head, mixing with the alcohol. The fact that she didn't understand what he was doing was disappointing . . . but her condemning it was unacceptable. Intolerable. How could she? She was Jasmine's mother. She too had seen the murderer. She had seen him *smiling*.

After about twenty minutes, he couldn't take it anymore, and he put on his wig and false beard, got his coat, and went out.

He drove fast toward Charette, holding himself back to keep from going over the speed limit. Fifteen minutes later, he parked his car in front of the duplex and literally ran to his apartment. Without even taking off his disguise, he went to his computer, which he always left on, and typed a series of commands, and then waited, his breathing shallow, his face tense with anger. On the computer speakers, there was a ring. A second, then a third ring . . . When Sylvie's weak voice answered, Bruno bent toward the mike and said angrily, "What got into you saying that on TV?"

"Bruno! Oh, my God! Bruno, I've . . . I've tried to reach you dozens of times, why did you—"

"Why did you say that to the reporters?"

"I . . . There was that demonstration on the street, in front of the house. I found it so . . . so indecent, I had to react, to . . ."

"And calling me crazy on the air, isn't that indecent?"

"That's not what I said!"

"Yes, that's exactly what you said. Dammit, I'm not deaf!"

Her voice quavering, she begged him to stop all this and to come home. She said it wasn't too late. Bruno shook his head, furious. He saw his daughter's blue ribbon again dancing in front of his eyes. He was grasping the mike with all his strength and pressing it to his mouth.

"You don't understand, Sylvie! You don't understand at all! How could . . . how could I have loved someone who's so dumb?"

She gasped, but Bruno continued, more and more enraged.

"I'm not the one who's gone crazy. You've lost all emotion, all feeling for Jasmine!"

"That's not true! I want to mourn our daughter! I want to mourn her with you, so we can get through this together! But you, you . . . you . . . you push it away! You deny it!"

"And you, you'd be satisfied if the monster went to prison and came out again after only twenty-five years, maybe only fifteen! He would come out, all smiling, while our daughter was nothing but dust in the grave!"

"Bruno . . ."

"You're completely insensitive! I wonder if you even really loved Jasmine!"

"Lord, it's . . . You're babbling. You've completely lost your mind!"

*"Stop saying that, you bitch!"* he screamed. *"Stop it right now!"*

She started sobbing. Bruno wanted to tell her to stop blubbering, but he was suddenly completely quiet—the dog had started whimpering again.

"God! Not again!"

Still sobbing, Sylvie asked what he was talking about. Bruno spun around.

"That dog again! That damn dog!"

"Dog . . . what dog?"

"That dog won't leave me alone, it won't stop whimpering and growling. I don't want to hear it anymore. I can't take it anymore!"

Still holding the mike, he paced up and down the kitchen, looking wildly around him. Sylvie, her voice frantic, kept asking him to explain, but Bruno wasn't listening anymore. He had suddenly realized that the whimpering was coming from the speakers, mixed with Sylvie's sobbing. He pointed and screamed, "He's there! He's in there!"

"Where? What? For goodness' sake, Bruno, what . . ."

Bruno dropped the mike and slammed the computer with the flat of his hand, repeating, "He's in there! In there!"

He stopped hitting and listened. He could hear Sylvie crying . . . and the whimpering of the dog, still there.

He pounded the keyboard with his fists, hitting all the keys at the same time, screaming, *"Shut up, shut up, shut up!"* until the machine went dead.

He suddenly calmed down and stared at his dead computer, dazed. The dog was silent.

Bruno rubbed his face. God, what was happening to him? He had to get ahold of himself. This was crazy!

Had he broken the computer? He turned it on. No, everything seemed okay. He made sure everything was working properly, that each step was executed as usual, that he wasn't forgetting anything . . .

He leaned against the wall, put his hands on his head, and took several deep breaths.

It didn't make sense to get so upset. And it was careless. It was the fourth day, so it was possible—improbable, but possible—that the police would discover that Longueuil was a ruse, and would trace him to Charette. And yet, he had just burst into the apartment without taking any precautions. What if the police had been there waiting for him?

He had to be more careful. For example, he should avoid coming to this apartment. And if he had to come back, he should make sure the coast was clear.

So he opened the curtains wide and let the light in. When he went out and got into his car, he looked at the window. You could see the inside of the apartment perfectly. Excellent.

He had been driving for almost ten minutes and he felt more and more calm. But at the same time, the dryness of his throat was becoming intolerable. Christ, he needed a beer! But there wasn't any more at the cottage. Too bad, he wouldn't drink anymore, that was all! It was probably for the best anyway. If he had lost control before, wasn't it because of the seven or eight beers he'd had today?

For a few minutes, his face was impassive and he kept his eyes fixed on the road lighted by his two headlights. Then he swore. Good God! He *needed* a beer!

Going to a store, facing customers and maybe even talking to a clerk, was really risky, wasn't it?

Three hundred meters ahead, lighted by a row of streetlights, was the turnoff onto the little road to the center of the village of Saint-Mathieu-du-Parc. Normally, he would continue straight ahead to go to the cottage . . .

He clenched his teeth. Shit! He didn't need alcohol! It was just something he liked, a little pleasure! But alcohol made him too impulsive!

But wasn't there a risk that the lack of alcohol could make him even more nervous? And therefore careless?

He hit the steering wheel twice with his fist, and at the last second, he turned onto the little road to Saint-Mathieu.

When he reached the village, his nervousness increased. In the dark, Saint-Mathieu-du-Parc suddenly seemed threatening and full of traps. The rain had stopped, but the wet streets shone ominously under the streetlights. He drove through the calm streets, which were practically empty of traffic. He saw a few pedestrians, but no one paid any attention to his car.

There it was, the lighted sign of a store . . .

He stopped the car and looked around, waiting until there were no more pedestrians nearby. There was really no reason to worry—everybody thought he was in Longueuil, so no one expected to see him here in this remote hamlet. And he was disguised. He just needed to calm down. He adjusted his false beard and finally got out of the car. With a normal, confident walk, he headed toward the store entrance.

Four customers inside. And they all turned toward him, making him freeze on the spot. A real conspiracy! Two of them, an elderly man and an obese woman, even seemed a bit curious, but Bruno told himself it was the normal reaction of a villager seeing a stranger. Nothing more.

Walking more stiffly, he went directly to the fridges in the back and chose his beer. When the other customers were all gone, Bruno went to the counter with a case of twenty-four and put it down heavily. Another customer came in, greeted the woman at the cash register, and, without a glance at Bruno, walked to the magazine stand at the back.

The cashier, a woman of about fifty with orangey-red hair, looked at Bruno for a moment, maybe a little too interestedly, and then, after punching in his purchase, announced the price in a dull voice. Bruno handed her a hundred-dollar bill, which seemed to impress her.

Too many details that attracted attention, far too many!

Nervously he looked down at the floor and noticed a pile of copies of a Montreal tabloid newspaper. The main headline announced a murder, a crime of passion, but he thought he saw his name in a smaller headline at the top. He bent slightly and read: STILL NO TRACE OF DR. HAMEL! He bent more to try to make out the words of the story.

And that's when the disaster occurred.

A little tipsy after the eight beers he had drunk, he felt himself falling, and grabbed the counter to catch himself. The movement was too sudden. Was it because his balding skull was sweating? Or because he hadn't put his wig on properly? In any case, the wig slid forward and fell off. He caught it just before it hit the floor, and frantically stuck it back on his head. He felt eyes on him and turned toward the counter.

The cashier was holding his change, staring at him.

In spite of the ice suddenly running through his veins, Bruno held out his hand for his change in as natural a gesture as possible, but his fingers were trembling. The cashier did not give him the money. In an even voice, speaking slowly, she said, "I recognize you."

Bruno felt the beer turning to acid in his belly and he grimaced with nausea. He glanced toward the magazine stand. The customer was skimming through porn magazines, lost in his fantasies. Bruno looked back at the cashier at a loss for what to do. He could always make a run for the door, but that would only delay the inevitable. The police would go through Saint-Mathieu-du-Parc with a fine-tooth comb and it would be all over for him in a few hours.

Still, that would give him time to finish off the monster . . .

So Bruno was tensing his muscles to sprint when the woman leaned over the counter and, looking into his eyes, whispered in a confiding tone, "I'm with you . . ."

And she gave him a conspiratorial little smile.

Bruno forgot to breathe. He should have felt relieved, and he did to some extent, but above all, he felt as if he had received an actual electric shock. His extended hand was no longer trembling. He had become a statue standing staring at the cashier, his mouth gaping.

She looked natural again, and put the money in his hand, which he was still holding out. She said, "Thank you, good night."

Without another glance at Bruno, she went back to some papers she was filling out on the counter. But you could sense a quiet satisfaction emanating from her.

Bruno finally moved. He pocketed the money, took the case of beer, and walked to the door. His movements were uncoordinated, as if his whole body was off balance. Before pushing the door open, he took one last glance at the cashier. She was looking after the other customer, who was now buying a magazine.

On the way back, once out of the village, he suddenly understood what had just happened, and above all, what was going to happen. The cashier wouldn't talk to anybody about this incident, it would be her secret, at least until Monday, when everything would be over, and she would tell her friends with pride and a clear conscience the incredible news that secretly, modestly, she had helped the *avenger*.

Bruno braked abruptly. He got out of the car, opened the trunk, took out a beer, and gulped down half of it. He leaned against the hood and closed his eyes with a sigh.

The dark road was deserted. It had begun raining again. On both sides, the forest was dark and quiet.

The store cashier reappeared in his mind. Her knowing look, her conspiratorial smile . . .

*I'm with you . . .*

He gulped down the rest of the bottle of beer.

———

From the tape recorder on the little table in the living room came the sound of Sylvie crying, metallic and with some static.

*"Lord, it's . . . You're babbling. You've completely lost your mind!"*

*"Stop saying that, you bitch! Stop it right now!"*

Mercure was sitting in a chair near the table with his hands folded, listening with a certain discomfort to this terrible conversation. Sylvie was standing near the bookcase trying to look dignified, but her despair was palpable. Her sister Josée had tactfully gone back to the kitchen.

Less than an hour before, Mercure had been at the station viewing the last of the four cassettes of the Jutras-Hamel family. He must have had about forty-five minutes left to watch when someone came to tell him that the bug they had put on Sylvie's telephone had been activated. Sylvie was talking to Hamel. Mercure had dashed into Wagner's office to ask if the triangulation was operational.

"No, only in an hour. The boys in Longueuil just got the equipment and . . ."

Mercure had almost lost his temper, but had stopped himself and hurried over to Sylvie's house.

*"That dog again! That damn dog!"*

*"Dog . . . what dog?"*

Mercure leaned his head forward, frowning.

*"That dog won't leave me alone, it won't stop whimpering and growling. I don't want to hear it anymore. I can't take it anymore!"*

Then came the sound of angry blows, while Hamel repeated several times, *"Shut up!"* Suddenly there was a click, and then the dial tone indicated that the line had been cut.

Mercure leaned back in his armchair, stroking his cheek with the tips of his fingers.

"He was hitting something, like a keyboard . . . a computer keyboard . . ."

He took out his notebook to make a few notes.

"Anything missing from his office?"

"As I told you the other day, I didn't notice anything, but I never go into that room, so . . ."

He reread one or two of the preceding pages and asked, "You really don't have any idea what that business with the dog might mean?"

Sylvie finally sat down with a sigh. Mercure regretted harassing her this way. Obviously, she felt like going to bed . . . and waking up in a month, maybe later.

"Sorry, but I don't understand it any more than you do."

"It seems like he's getting more and more obsessive about those dog sounds. They even made him completely lose control."

Was there something they could do with this obsession? Mercure thought there was something there, but he couldn't quite put his finger on it yet. He leafed through his notebook, thinking, and then said, "The Picasso painting, upstairs, uh . . ."

*"Guernica?* It's such a violent painting."

"Precisely. You told me your partner was a pacifist, against violence."

"You can be against violence and still be fascinated by it, don't you think?"

"That's true."

And he suddenly thought of his wife and of Demers and his visits to him.

"That's exactly the case with Bruno," continued Sylvie. "The painting shows it very clearly too. It shows that man is the victim of war, but also that war is made by man. That is what's represented by that awful bull's head in the painting: civilized people can become monsters."

"Is that what Picasso was trying to show with that bull?"

"I don't know, but that's how Bruno saw it. It fascinated and terrified him at the same time."

Mercure nodded. It seemed to him that a clearer image was developing in his mind, even though it was one of unfathomable darkness.

When he was leaving, with one foot already out the door, he said, "If he calls again, phone the station, even during the night."

"He won't call again."

She had said that with a certain coldness. Holding the door open, she had such a hard look on her face that every trace of despair had disappeared from it.

"What do you mean?" asked Mercure.

"You heard him on the tape recorder . . . Nothing is possible between us anymore. However this story ends, there can't be anything between us after *that*."

"You really think so? You don't love him anymore?"

A hint of despair finally showed through her mask of ice.

"I loved Bruno Hamel. I can't love a bull . . ."

———

He got back to the cottage at six fifty-five. He put several bottles of beer in the fridge and, reeling a bit, took one with him and went and sat down in the living room, where he took a big swig. He was drunk, and now he knew it. He had to stop drinking or soon he would no longer be capable of amusing himself with the monster. An hour or two of TV would sober him up. He put his beer down on the floor and decided not to finish it. His eyes dull, he started watching a game show.

But he was still thinking about Sylvie, about what she had said. So after barely thirty minutes, he abruptly shut off the TV, plunging the living room into darkness. He'd had enough stupidity for one night. He went to his prisoner's room.

The monster, slumped on the floor, sat up slightly. He saw that his tormentor had been drinking, and fear appeared on his face . . . that constant, recurring fear.

With quick but slightly clumsy movements, Bruno turned the crank, went over to the table and opened the rings. The monster started begging again, crying, saying he couldn't take any more. Bruno didn't even look at him. All this whining was starting to get on his nerves. Anger was brewing within him, fueled by drunkenness. Why this anger? Shouldn't he have been excited?

Three minutes later, the pitiful body was lying horizontally, with the table at the height of Bruno's hips. His arms extended and shackled above his head, the monster was crying now without restraint, with not even the courage to beg any longer. Bruno went to his bag and came back to the monster, holding a scalpel with a long, very narrow blade. He looked at his victim for a moment . . .

. . . and suddenly, the anger swelled, sweeping away everything else. Rage and alcohol made him so brutal, so uncontrolled that he experienced things in a series of chaotic flashes. The monster's penis in his left hand . . . the blade cutting into the urethra, going deeper, hacking . . . blood spurting . . . apocalyptic screaming . . . How horribly Jasmine must have suffered . . . how horribly! And the flashes accelerated, the scalpel went in and out, in and out, finally cutting the glans in two.

Bruno was becoming more and more enraged, unable to climb another rung on the ladder of satisfaction, unable to take pleasure in his torture, carried away by a flood of fury he could not contain in spite of the devastation his scalpel was wreaking.

The screaming of the monster suddenly became continuous and shrill. It was no longer a human scream, it was totally animal now, it was becoming . . . it was becoming the long . . .

. . . howl of a dog.

Bruno stopped cutting and leapt back. Covered with blood, he looked in horror at the monster, who was pulling on his chains, his face convulsed with pain, and giving that long, interminable howl of a dying dog that filled the room, that filled Bruno's drunken brain . . .

Beside himself with rage, Bruno leapt forward and planted his scalpel in the monster's scrotum. The blade went through a testicle and stopped against the wooden table. The howling stopped. The monster had lost consciousness.

Silence.

Bruno remained motionless, his breathing shallow. His fury subsided, giving way to a more disturbing feeling.

Frustration.

But frustration with what?

He would have liked to go at the monster again to get rid of the frustration . . . but what was the point, since he had lost consciousness?

And Bruno felt too numb. With his fury gone, only the drunkenness remained, suddenly more tangible.

He pulled the scalpel out of the monster's scrotum and threw it limply into his bag. He walked to the door, reeling, and went straight to the bathroom. There was blood on his hands and face. He washed them with water. Dragging his feet, barely able to keep his balance, he went to Josh's bedroom and took off his dirty clothes.

His head was spinning. Nevertheless, he tried to mentally reconstruct the last few minutes. Since the coming of the darkness, he had been waiting for that moment, he had salivated at the thought of destroying that vile organ. Now he had finally done it, with a violence that should have been most satisfying . . . but the more he thought about it, the more his frustration grew.

He went back to the bathroom and urinated for a long time, holding on to the wall with both hands. When he came out into the hallway, his peripheral vision caught a presence on his right, and he turned his head sharply.

In the middle of the dark living room was a small silhouette, obviously that of a child. A little girl, judging by the long hair.

Bruno stood still, holding his breath.

He could not make out the face in the darkness. Scraps of clothing seemed to be hanging from the body. Turned toward him, the little girl remained silent and motionless.

Bruno frantically looked for the light switch in the hallway. He turned on the light and looked into the living room. The silhouette had disappeared.

He walked to the middle of the room and turned on a lamp. Nobody. Good God! He hadn't drunk that much.

Muttering, he slumped heavily into the chair, his arms dangling on either side. He stared into the emptiness, his eyes misty, cursing quietly from time to time. Because the frustration had taken root in him, deeply, inextricably, incomprehensibly.

In the silence, he thought he heard echoes of that impossible dog's howling.

# DAY 5

"TWO DAYS!"

In the middle of the squad room, Wagner pronounced the words pointedly, with frustration verging on panic, but Mercure, Ruel, and Cabana knew they should not take it personally. The chief had to vent, or else there would be an atomic explosion and everybody would suffer for it. Boisvert was sitting off to the side, pretending to work on a report on a robbery that had occurred during the night in a downtown store, but he was not missing a word of the conversation.

"But if we count today, and if Hamel only intends to kill Lemaire at the end of the day on Monday, we actually have three days left," Ruel corrected.

He had said that to boost the morale of the troops, but the chief's expression showed him that he had missed the mark. Ruel shrugged, though he still found his reasoning very relevant.

They had had the shoebox examined by experts, but nothing of interest had been found. Bolduc and Pleau had called from Longueuil a little earlier, asking if they could come back to Drummondville. But now that the triangulation was in place, Mercure had told them to stay there and be prepared.

Rubbing his neck, Wagner mumbled as if to himself, "We'll have to make Hamel call us . . ."

Mercure agreed. "Yes, we have to create an event or a situation that will provoke him to call us."

"And how would we do that?" asked Ruel skeptically.

Mercure sighed and smiled wryly. He had no idea.

"Okay. A way to make him call us!" the chief said, leaning on a desk with both hands. "Any suggestions?"

There was hesitation for a few instants, and then Cabana suggested broadcasting a false news item on TV. For example, saying that his partner had been arrested as an accomplice. Hamel would surely call to deny it. Wagner made a face. It was too obvious. Hamel wouldn't take the bait.

"And I'm not sure he'd feel obliged to help her," Mercure said, recalling the conversation recorded the day before.

They started brainstorming again. Ruel suggested, as if it was the idea of the century, that they should announce on the news that someone had just confessed to the murder of the little girl, implying that Lemaire was not guilty.

"Oh, come on! Hamel was told that the DNA tests were positive!" protested the chief. "Lemaire pleaded guilty. It was all in the news!"

"And in four days of torture, Hamel must surely have gotten him to confess to anything he wanted," added Mercure gravely.

These words threw cold water on the idea. Wagner sighed.

"We have to find a way. There must be something."

Boisvert, who had kept quiet until then, spun around in his chair to face the small group, and said, "What if we just let him die? He's a goddamn child murderer! Why are we busting our asses to find him?"

"You keep right on doing your paperwork and let the intelligent people do the thinking!" replied Wagner, who had immediately turned scarlet.

"You may be my boss, Greg, but I won't let you speak to me like that!" retorted Boisvert, standing up.

"What do you want, Michel? A little two-week holiday?"

"I want us to arrest real bad guys instead of trying to save an asshole!"

"We're not trying to save an asshole. We're trying to keep one man from killing another!"

"Whose side are you on, anyway?"

"Whose side!" yelled Wagner, choking with rage. "This isn't a hockey match, you idiot, it's a police investigation!"

"Hey! I asked you not to talk to me like that!" fumed Boisvert, walking toward his superior.

Cabana stepped between them. Boisvert and Wagner glared at each other, while the other two officers told them to calm down. Mercure, standing to one side, rubbed his eyes.

"There are already people in the streets acting like fools, but that doesn't mean we have to," Cabana said.

He was talking about the demonstration the day before in Hamel's neighborhood. In fact, that was what had made Mercure so depressed.

The two officers finally moved away from each other, casting nasty sidelong glances at each other. Wagner forced himself to stay calm.

"I'm just saying we should be doing everything we can to find him, because that's our job, that's all."

"Not just because of that," added Mercure softly.

Everyone turned toward him. Looking at his fingers, he added slowly, as if he were thinking out loud, "It's not a child murderer we're trying to save, it's . . ."

He hesitated, and then said, ". . . it's a meaning."

"A meaning? The meaning of what?"

Mercure almost answered, but he reflected for an instant and thought better of it. He shrugged and made a dissatisfied expression. Boisvert chuckled scornfully, while Cabana and Ruel exchanged weary, knowing looks. They were used to the detective sergeant's mystical flights of fancy. Wagner scratched his ear morosely, then tapped the desk in front of him.

"Okay, until we find the meaning of the universe, we could start by finding a way to get Hamel to call us again. It's a less ambitious project, but one that's more urgent!"

———

Bruno woke up at ten o'clock. God. He'd slept so much since coming to the cottage. He rubbed his painful forehead. He had a bit of a hangover, but nothing serious. Still, he lay in bed for quite a while, looking at the trees through the window. The sky was still cloudy.

The heaviness that had burdened him since the coming of the darkness seemed to have gotten worse, but maybe that was an effect of the headache. The night before, he had again dreamed of gaping jaws and dark fur, and the blows were closer than ever, and stronger.

He put on his clothes. Now they were not only creased but also covered in bloodstains. He would have to wash them. In the bathroom mirror, his reflection shocked him—he had several days' growth of beard, his sparse hair was dirty and disheveled, and his eyes were hollow and bloodshot. What was he waiting for to take a shower? He began by rubbing at the blood on his clothes with a wet towel. The dark stains remained on his shirt and pants, but they looked a little less like blood. As for the shower, he decided to eat first.

He made himself some breakfast, but ate very little. As he drank his coffee, he thought about the night before, in particular the frustration he'd felt. He thought he understood the cause: he had drunk too much. He could not get any satisfaction from the tortures he inflicted on the monster if he was doing it in a state of inebriation.

On the other hand, he hadn't been *that* drunk.

Even so, he made a decision not to have a drop of alcohol today. He promised himself. To regain control.

He rubbed his eyes. He was more messed up than he'd thought. He decided to relax for a few hours. Take a walk, for example. He put on his coat, and before going out, he went to see his prisoner.

The monster was a real wreck now. Several of the welts from the whipping, including the gash across his cheek, had become infected in spite of the ointments, and were oozing pus. His genitals were in shreds, and his body was lying in a mixture of urine, shit, and blood. His hollow-looking eyes were staring at the ceiling. The fear had disappeared, giving way to a troubling emptiness. When Bruno went over to him, he did not even turn his head.

Bruno touched his forehead; he was burning up with fever. Bruno hooked him up to the intravenous again, but did not bother with the antibiotic ointment. Even if the infection progressed, he would survive until Monday. The monster submitted with no reaction, his face completely expressionless.

Bruno thought about the dog's howling that he had heard coming from the mouth of his prisoner.

Slowly, he left the room. He really needed some air.

———

The video was almost at the end, and it was about time too, because Mercure felt like he was on the verge of visual overload. He'd had more than enough of those family scenes, parties, birthdays, and walks in the woods, especially because he had not really learned anything new about Hamel since the second cassette.

Maybe he was wasting his time.

There was little Jasmine on the screen, two years younger. She was on a swing in a park, joyfully shouting to the camera "Look, Daddy, look how high I'm swinging!" and he could hear Hamel's voice, full of delight and love: "If you go much higher, honey, you'll fly away!" There was a second child's voice and the camera turned to another kid who was also swinging. Mercure recognized him: it was the little disfigured boy he'd seen the other day when he was leaving the Hamels' house. In the video, his scars looked worse, more recent, but the child was laughing and shouting, "Look, Jasmine, I'm going to fly away too!"

Mercure glanced at his watch: almost noon. As soon as the video was over, he would go for lunch.

They'd have to find a way to get Hamel to call again.

On the screen, the little boy was leaving, shouting goodbye to Jasmine. The little girl immediately turned to the camera and said in an exaggeratedly low voice, even though the boy was now far away, "Frédéric's face still doesn't look very nice, does it, Daddy?"

Resting his chin on his hand, Mercure smiled indulgently. Hamel's voice, just as understanding, explained, "The dog bit him very, very hard, Jasmine, and he'll have marks for the rest of his life."

The weariness slowly disappeared from Mercure's face, replaced by a frown of concentration.

"And where's the dog, Daddy?"

"I already explained to you: it was bad, and they made it die."

Mercure leaned forward. On the screen, little Jasmine was staring at the camera as she played with the hem of her dress. She was not really satisfied with these answers.

"But how did they make it die?"

"They killed it, honey. Come on, let's go to the slide."

"How did they kill it?"

"Listen, Jasmine, you don't want . . . Wait a second . . ."

The camera was lowered and then turned off. The father had not felt it necessary to film this delicate conversation.

Mercure ejected the cassette from the machine with a quick movement, picked up the other three cassettes, and hurried out of the room.

———

When it started raining, Bruno went back in. His headache was gone, but he still felt morose. The sense of frustration from the day before still lingered.

He made himself some lunch but did not eat very much. He had no appetite. Was there news on TV at noon on Saturday? He found some on Radio-Canada. But when he saw they were essentially repeating the same information, he turned it off. Carrying a plate of chicken and a glass of water, he went to the monster's room.

The smell was revolting. Bruno unshackled his right wrist, but the monster left his arm in the same position, stretched above his head. Bruno put the plate and the glass down on the table, close to the prisoner's face. He still did not move. He had to eat, though, to keep up a minimum level of strength. Suddenly, he turned his head toward Bruno. When he saw Bruno, the fear returned to his eyes, but it was so shallow, so distant that it was barely perceptible. He opened his mouth and said, "I understand . . . I understand where I am . . ."

His voice was so weak. And he spoke very slowly, like an old 33-rpm record played at half speed.

"I'm in Hell."

Bruno looked at him for a moment, and then picked up the fork and started feeding him. The monster took the food passively, chewed a little, and swallowed with difficulty.

"I'm in Hell and . . . and you're the Devil . . ."

Bruno brought the glass of water to the prisoner's mouth. A swallow, a second one, and then the rest ran down his chin.

"That's it, isn't it?"

This damn frustration that wouldn't go away! Exasperated, Bruno punched the monster in the nose. There was a cracking sound, but the monster barely reacted as blood flowed from his right nostril. The doctor rubbed his knuckles and nodded. That had felt good.

For ten seconds.

Moving quickly, he re-shackled the monster's right hand and went to his bags. He would put out an eye, that should satisfy him for more than ten seconds! He stopped suddenly. Come on, cool it! The monster was still too weak, too much in shock from his mutilation of the day before. Did Bruno want to finish him off?

Irritated, he left the room.

In the living room, he picked up the phone and called Morin and told him where to find the money.

"I'll call you tomorrow."

"I know who you are."

Bruno was silent for three long seconds and then replied in a calm voice, "Really?"

"Really."

Morin's voice was slightly lilting, vaguely amused. He must be very proud of himself.

"Well, good for you. Talk to you tomo—"

"Not so fast, Dr. Hamel, I'd like to talk to you . . ."

Bruno was silent again. He was not really surprised. What was surprising was that it had taken Morin so long to catch on. But even though he had prepared himself mentally for this situation, he still felt nervous. Morin was the weak link in the whole plan.

"I don't know what we have to chat about, Mr. Morin."

"I think we have a lot of things to discuss . . ."

"Send the police and you lose fourteen thousand dollars."

There was a heavy silence, which Bruno allowed to go on.

"Do you understand what I said?" he finally asked.

"Yes," Morin answered in a strange voice.

"Good."

Bruno hung up. Morin had understood. The link would hold. He stood up and walked slowly to the kitchen. After all, just one beer wouldn't do him any harm.

Suddenly there was a ring.

Bruno turned toward the phone, as surprised as if the telephone had started talking. He answered on the second ring, and barked into the receiver, "Are you crazy, Morin?"

"Listen to me . . ."

"I told you not to call me, ever!"

"I know, but I thought of something."

"You should do less thinking! Call again, just one more time, and starting tomorrow, you won't get another cent!"

He slammed the receiver down.

Seconds passed, then minutes. But Bruno was not at all reassured.

Without putting on his coat, he hurried outside. The rain, falling harder than the day before, made a constant rustling sound in the trees. He opened the trunk of the Chevy and took out the revolver and some bullets. He went back to the house and into the living room, and clumsily loaded the pistol. He raised the weapon and examined it nervously. Then he put it down on the little living room table and waited, making a superhuman effort not to go get a beer. This was not the time to dull his reflexes with even a few slugs of alcohol. He took long, deep breaths.

He had acquired the weapon to finish off the monster on Monday. But he might have to do it sooner . . .

———

"You watched them all?"

"Every one."

"And did you find anything interesting?"

She asked this without any hope, just to be polite. They were both standing at the door of the house, she inside, he on the little porch, barely protected from the rain by the roof overhang. She was holding the bag containing the videocassettes; in spite of the bad weather, she had not invited Mercure to come in. The message was clear: she had just about had enough of police visits.

"Maybe, I don't know . . . I wanted to talk to you about it," he said, silently berating himself for harassing her. "Uh . . . your sister isn't here?"

"She went to do some shopping. I didn't have the stomach . . ."

Then, obviously reluctantly, "Come in. You're getting soaked."

"Just in the entryway then."

He took three steps into the entryway. Smoothing his wet hair, he examined Sylvie covertly: her face looked older, her skin gray, her eyes so tired.

"How are you holding up?"

"What is it you think you've found?"

He described the scene in the park between Jasmine and the little boy who had been disfigured by a dog.

"You know the story about the dog?"

"Of course. It was the biggest tragedy in the neighborhood in the last ten years . . . It's so quiet here that . . ."

She frowned, and then finally showed some interest. "You think this is connected to the dog Bruno seems to hear all the time?"

"How about if you told me about that tragedy first?"

"It was terrible. It happened three years ago, at the beginning of the summer. The Cussons, who live five houses away, had a big black Great Dane, Luky, which was very gentle with everyone. Little Frédéric Bédard, the son of some other neighbors, was five or six at the time, and he tried to pet Luky, as many children did. But this time, for no apparent reason, the dog attacked and bit him in the face two or three times."

She grimaced, shook her head and continued, "It was a miracle Frédéric even survived. I was at the Center. A few neighbors came out, including Bruno."

Mercure was becoming more and more interested.

"The rest is what he told me . . . Denis, Frédéric's father, didn't go to the hospital with his wife and son. He went and killed the dog."

"Your partner witnessed that?"

"Along with two or three other neighbors, yes. Of course, nobody did anything to stop Denis."

Mercure nodded.

"But . . . Bruno told me it was really awful . . . Extremely violent . . ."

"To the point where it could have affected him?"

"For a few days, he was really shaken."

Mercure asked her to be more specific. Sylvie thought for a moment. In spite of her weariness, she really made an effort to remember, feeling, as Mercure did, that there might be something significant in the story.

"That evening, when he told me about it, he was upset, but also . . . tormented. He was sitting in the living room, telling me what had happened for the tenth time, and he would go blank for seconds on end, as if he were seeing the whole thing again in his head . . ."

She thought some more, her fingers on her chin.

"I remember asking him what bothered him so much. He said, 'Even if it was only a dog, it was horrible . . . unbearable. But the worst thing is that in Denis's place I would probably have reacted the same way.' I told him that would have been quite normal, quite human. Then he answered very solemnly, 'I know. That's what scares me the most.'"

Mercure nodded slightly. His eyes glimmered. Fragments of images and sounds were running through his mind, trying to coalesce into a clear idea. Sylvie remained silent, struck by these memories that must have been tucked away in a corner of her brain for a long time. Finally, she said apologetically, "I'm sorry I didn't think of this story sooner, but frankly, I put it out of my mind a long time ago, and I don't see how it's related to . . . You think there's a connection?"

"I won't bother you anymore, Ms. Jutras," Mercure said softly. At least I hope not."

"You have something, don't you?"

"I don't know."

He thanked her again and walked quickly to his car, holding his coat over his head. Inside the car, he took out his notebook and wrote. He reread his notes, his pen to his lips, thinking. Then he dialed a number on his cell phone. Wagner answered.

"I'll be there in five minutes," Mercure said.

"You found a way to get Hamel to call us again?"

"Maybe . . ."

———

A little after three in the afternoon, Bruno heard the sound of an engine. Since Morin's telephone call, he had hardly budged, waiting. He had just been telling himself that Morin must not have informed the police after all and that everything could continue as before . . . and then he heard a vehicle.

Stiffly, he got up and looked out the kitchen window, ready to run to the monster's room and put a bullet in his brain. But he was surprised to see a familiar pickup truck coming down the dirt lane.

For a moment, Bruno was completely taken aback. It had never occurred to him that Morin would come himself. After a moment of hesitation, he shoved the revolver under his belt and put on his coat. Of course, there was no question of actually shooting him. But if necessary, the gun could provide a persuasive argument. After making sure it was invisible under the coat, he walked toward the door. But then he had another idea. He quickly went and got the little suitcase that contained all the money he had left, and took out a hundred dollars and put it in his wallet. Then he went out with the suitcase.

The temperature had fallen and it was still raining. Bruno stayed on the porch, protected by the little wooden roof, with the suitcase at his feet, while the truck pulled up about thirty meters from the house, beside the Chevy. Morin got out. Very relaxed, with a toothpick protruding from his smile, he stayed close to his truck and greeted Bruno.

"Ah! I'm glad to see you without your disguise. But you don't look like you're in very good shape."

"I think I was quite clear, Mr. Morin," Bruno said in a calm voice. "If you came here even once, the whole deal was off. We had an agreement."

"Yeah, well, I thought we might need to renegotiate . . ."

He looked confident and cocky, which made Bruno nervous. He even started walking toward the house, saying, "Couldn't we talk inside? It's raining, in case you didn't notice."

"We'll stay outside."

Morin stopped and smiled knowingly.

"That's right, you have a guest."

Bruno stood with his hands in his pockets and did not answer, but his heart was pounding. Morin scratched his wet head.

"I figured it out yesterday. Considering how long they've been talking about it on TV, it was about time, huh? And I also realized you must have hidden all the money ahead of time. And that gave me some ideas . . ."

"You think it was a good idea coming here?"

"We'll have to decide that together, Dr. Hamel."

A gust of wind sent a few drops of rain onto Bruno's face. Morin played with the toothpick in his mouth a few seconds, and then he said, "You'd better tell me right away where the rest of the money is hidden, don't you think?"

"It's out of the question."

"Listen . . ."

Morin looked around, then turned back to Bruno. He looked almost conspiratorial.

"That guy you're holding prisoner, I hate him as much as you do."

"That would surprise me."

"What I mean is, as far as I'm concerned, child rapists should be hung up by the balls. If you kill him on Monday, I won't lose any sleep over it. So why don't we settle this here and now? You tell me where the other two bundles of money are, and we won't bother each other anymore."

"I'm tempted to believe you, but I can't take any risks. The money I hid is my guarantee that you'll leave me in peace until Monday."

"I don't feel like busting my ass two more times to get that money."

"You call driving a few kilometers for seven thousand dollars busting your ass? Most people would crawl on their bellies for that much money."

The toothpick stopped moving in Morin's mouth and his cockiness gave way to anxiety.

"Listen, Hamel, I need that money, and fast!"

"I can give you what I have left . . ."

He picked up the little suitcase and tossed it to him. It landed on the muddy ground a meter from Morin.

"There's about a thousand dollars in there."

"No, no, that's not enough!" Morin exclaimed.

Bruno shook his head. Maybe Morin didn't have any debts. Maybe he'd lost all his money gambling and he wanted more to play again and again . . .

"Where are you losing your money, Morin? At the casino? At the track? There's a racetrack in Trois-Rivières, if I'm not mistaken."

"I don't know what you're talking about!"

His indignation was so false that Bruno knew he had guessed right. But it didn't matter; he couldn't take the risk of revealing the hiding places ahead of time. It was as simple as that.

"Sorry," he said. "We'll continue as before."

Morin's eyes flashed.

"And what if I didn't give you a choice?"

"What? By going to the police? Go ahead. But as soon as I see the slightest sign of a cop around here, I'll kill my prisoner. The police will only find a corpse, which is what I've been planning from the beginning.

I'll be arrested, but since I intended to turn myself in on Monday, that won't make any difference either. Not only will your going to the police change nothing, but you'll also be out fourteen thousand dollars."

But that didn't faze Morin at all. If anything, his assurance seemed to be gradually coming back.

"What would be even better would be if I went and got your prisoner and took him to the cops myself," he said, swelling his chest and spreading his arms to emphasize what a poor match Bruno's puny physique was for his muscles. Bruno thought fast.

"If the cops arrest me, you'll be in as much trouble as I will!"

"Come on! I was paid to build something weird, that's all! And when I finally understood what was going on, I was so shocked that my conscience as a good citizen ordered me to stop the butchery."

His smile had come back. He thought he was pretty smart now.

"You're not coming in," declared the doctor in a voice he hoped was threatening.

"Don't try to act tough, Hamel. It doesn't suit you."

"And what do you think I've been doing with my prisoner for the past five days?"

Morin chuckled.

"That doesn't count. He killed your daughter . . . So either you tell me right away where the two other payments are or I'm going in to get your friend."

Although it was not exposed to the rain, Bruno's skin was getting damp. He could feel the revolver against his belly . . . He was hesitant to pull it out.

To threaten . . . just to threaten . . .

He took a deep breath and said in an uncertain voice, "That's out of the question."

Morin nodded. He spat out his toothpick and walked heavily toward the house. Bruno quickly walked down the few steps of the porch, raised his arms awkwardly, and ordered Morin not to come in. But Morin gave him a punch in the chin, a powerful blow that sent him flying two meters back onto the wet grass. Despite his dizziness, Bruno hurriedly pulled out his revolver and, still on his back, waved it at Morin, shouting at him to stop. Morin, his foot on the first step, turned around. When he saw the revolver, there was a hint of doubt in his eyes. Then his mouth twisted into a smile of contemptuous defiance and he climbed the second step.

The revolver started to shake in Bruno's hand, and his head was spinning, preventing him from thinking coherently. Suddenly it struck him that it was all over! If Morin left with his prisoner, it would all have been for nothing, because not only would the monster not be dead but Bruno would not have had his satisfaction, he would not have climbed to the top of the ladder! He wouldn't even have come close! It would all be a failure, from start to finish! A complete waste!

No way! The monster was his and he wasn't finished with him! *The monster belonged to him!*

He fired.

The bullet missed Morin by so much that it did not even hit the house. Nevertheless, the bang made him jump off the steps. He had just enough time to turn a shocked face toward his assailant when Bruno fired a second shot, screaming with rage. This time, the bullet hit the front of the house very close to Morin's head, and he threw himself facedown in a mud puddle with his hands over his head.

Bruno stood up and walked menacingly toward him, pointing the gun. Morin had turned onto his back and was holding up his muddy hands to protect himself. Bruno, his jaw clenched, now saw Morin only as an obstacle, with no real personality, an obstacle that could spoil everything and that absolutely had to be eliminated. His finger was about to squeeze the trigger a third time . . .

. . . when suddenly, he heard a growl. He thought it was thunder, but when he heard the sound again, he recognized it as the growl of a dog that was about to attack. He looked around frantically. That dog again, again and again and again . . . !

Without thinking, he screamed and fired toward the woods.

The growling stopped.

Still pointing the gun, Bruno turned toward Morin again, but he was so dazed, it was as if he were seeing him for the first time. Still lying in the mud, Morin was wide-eyed with fear. Bruno examined the gun nervously, and after a moment, lowered it. He took a few steps back, looked around as if he did not recognize his surroundings. Wiping the rain from his face with his sleeve, he said in a weak voice, "The choice is yours, Morin."

He hobbled toward the porch and climbed stiffly up the steps, feeling heavier than ever. Behind him, Morin stood up and, after a moment's hesitation, picked up the suitcase. Without even glancing at him, Bruno opened the door of the house and went inside.

He took off his coat as if it weighed a ton. In the living room, he put the revolver down on the little table. Then, very slowly, he sat down in the armchair, laid his hands on the arms and looked at the wall in front of him.

He vaguely heard the sound of an engine starting and then gradually moving away.

He put his hands over his face and gave a long sigh.

————

"Are you ready?" asked Josée.

Standing in the middle of the living room with her suitcase at her feet, Sylvie looked around the room and then answered yes.

"And you're sure about your decision?" asked her sister.

That morning after Mercure left, Sylvie had asked Josée if she could stay at her place in Sherbrooke until it was all over.

She couldn't take it anymore. She did not feel capable of waiting for the end of this tragedy, *her* tragedy, in this house that constantly reminded her of what their life had been and, therefore, what it would never be again. She no longer felt capable of talking to the police or pushing away the reporters that were harassing her. And she would not have the strength, on Monday, to witness the outcome. It was over between her and Bruno, she knew that, so why wait? Why stay?

"Yes, I'm sure," she said.

But she then thought of something and went up to Jasmine's bedroom.

There she took a framed photo of her daughter from the dresser. She looked at it for a long time, and left the room with it in her hand.

Outside, the rain was cold. The two sisters got into Josée's car; as the vehicle moved away, Sylvie took one last look at her house.

She held the photo of her daughter against her heart and closed her eyes.

———

On TVA, they showed a few dozen people demonstrating on a busy street, defying the rain, while the reporter's voice explained, ". . . support for Bruno Hamel's cause has gone beyond the boundaries of Drummondville this afternoon. There were demonstrations reported in Victoriaville and Trois-Rivières, with close to a hundred people at each one, and even a few scattered groups in Montreal."

That was followed by interviews with two or three people who said they agreed with what Bruno was doing. Watching the report, Bruno took another slug of beer. He had sworn he would not drink during the day, but after Morin left, he had needed it too much. In any case, he'd only had two in the last few hours.

As on the day before, Bruno was not able to feel really happy at this support; he was too disturbed by these images. How could these people talk that way about something they didn't know? What was the meaning of these demonstrations?

What was the meaning of all this?

He rubbed his eyes, suddenly weary. For the first time, he considered finishing off the monster immediately.

He rejected the idea right away. What had gotten into him? He had two days left! Plus the evening, which had barely begun! Two days to work off his feelings, to find some satisfaction, to . . . to . . .

Hearing Mercure's name on television suddenly brought his attention back to the screen.

". . . Hervé Mercure, of Drummondville, who is heading up the investigation and who is on the line now. Good afternoon, Detective Sergeant Mercure."

"Good afternoon."

Bruno recognized the soft, hoarse voice. He would have liked to put a face to that voice.

"So, are there still no clues as to where Bruno Hamel is?"

"No clues."

Bruno smiled. Mercure lied well. Because of course, the police were looking for him in Longueuil right now.

". . . and that's why I wanted to take advantage of your news report to appeal to Dr. Hamel one last time to turn himself in immediately, to put an end to this insane plan."

"You think he's listening to us?"

"We have reason to believe that he watches the news, yes. So, Dr. Hamel, if you can hear me, I'm asking you to stop everything."

Bruno chuckled scornfully. Did this cop really hope to get to him with this pathetic appeal?

"That's the message you wanted to send, Inspector?"

"I also wanted to talk to him about the dog."

Bruno's whole body stiffened.

"The dog?"

"Yes. I think he'll understand what I mean."

The news anchor let him continue. Mercure's voice became lower, more solemn, but also softer.

"Dr. Hamel, I know you're haunted by the growling of a dog, that you hear it constantly around you, within you. I know that it's starting to make you . . . let's say . . . very nervous. Because you don't understand why you're haunted by that dog."

Bruno felt a little dizzy. How could Mercure possibly know that? Had he given himself away during his calls?

"But I understand, Dr. Hamel."

Bruno held his breath.

"I know what that dog is."

"You goddamn liar!" screamed Bruno, leaning forward on the couch.

"Maybe you think I'm bluffing, but I swear it's true. Your partner, Sylvie, knows it too. She's the one who put us on the track."

Bruno was panting, his face tense with anxiety. On the television, the news anchor, despite his professional detachment, seemed a bit disconcerted by the policeman's strange speech.

"Your obsession with that dog is making you lose control, Dr. Hamel. And as long as you don't know what the dog means, it will never leave you alone."

"Liar! Liar! You're nothing but a damn liar, Mercure!" Bruno started screaming again, standing up and pointing a furious finger at the television.

"Well, there it is. Detective Sergeant Mercure, I hope that your . . . ah . . . message gets across."

"Thank you for giving me this time on air."

Bruno abruptly turned off the television and started grumbling incoherently. That cop was bluffing! He wanted to get Bruno to call him again so he could try to manipulate him! Mercure knew nothing about that dog, nothing at all!

But Bruno still could not calm down.

He walked to his room to put on his disguise, and then stopped. Good God! He certainly wasn't going to go out and call! Not again! He swore and kicked the bathroom door. Echoing the noise, he heard a dog growling outside. He dashed to the door, opened it, and screamed at the forest, "Shut up! You hear me, you filthy dog? Just shut up!"

The only answer was the sound of the rain in the dark forest. He went back in and paced nervously back and forth.

*And as long as you don't know what the dog means, it will never leave you alone.*

Finally he put on his disguise and his coat. When he was about to leave, he had an idea and went and got Josh's binoculars, which he had come across not long before. He went out and got into his car, telling himself he was an idiot. But he wanted to know where those dog growls were coming from. He *absolutely* had to know.

He drove faster than usual and got to Charette in twelve minutes. He stopped the car at the end of the street the duplex was on. In the distance, he could see the window of his apartment, lit up in the rainy night. He put the binoculars to his eyes and he could see everything in the kitchen. He could clearly see the closed door, the oven, the front of the living room. He could see not only his computer, but his screen, where two mice were chasing each other: his screen saver.

There didn't seem to be anybody in the apartment. But Bruno knew that meant nothing; if the police were there, they wouldn't stand in front of the window. He watched the kitchen through the binoculars for a while longer. No movement, no shadows, nothing seemed to have moved.

He was more and more obsessed with Mercure and his dog story.

Ten seconds later, he stopped the car in front of the duplex. When he was walking to the door, someone came down the stairs from the apartment above. It was the same guy Bruno had met the other day. Bruno hunched his shoulders and stuck his hands in his pockets. But as he passed, the other tenant spoke.

"You're new here, aren't you?"

Not answering him would have seemed too suspicious. So Bruno stopped and, without facing him directly, grunted a noncommittal "Yes." The neighbor smiled, happy to chat a little. How did he like the apartment? Nice, wasn't it? The village wasn't bad either. Very small, quiet, with the river nearby. Bruno answered in monosyllables, trying to find a way to cut this painful conversation short. After twenty seconds, he finally said in a weak voice that he was in a hurry, and climbed the stairs to the landing as the man looked at him in surprise.

Bruno pressed his ear to the door of his apartment: silence. Holding his breath, he finally entered. Empty. No one had come.

Reassured, he went directly to the computer, looked for a number in his pockets, and, when he found it, typed it in on the keyboard, all the while calling himself an idiot.

———

Sitting at his desk, Mercure waited. Since the evening news was broadcast on Saturday at the same time on both networks, Radio-Canada was supposed to call him so he could deliver the same little message as he had on TVA. Hamel had been watching the news for four days, and there was no reason to think that would change tonight.

Wagner came in, looking doubtful.

"I just listened to your message on TVA. I have to say I really didn't get that business with the dog."

"It doesn't matter. If Hamel was watching, he understood it."

"And you think that will make him want to call?"

Mercure shrugged and said he hoped so. He asked if the triangulation was still in place and Wagner confirmed that it was. Mercure looked at his watch: six seventeen. Five more minutes until Radio-Canada called.

"One thing bugs me," he muttered. "The last call from Hamel led me to believe he had a computer with him. What could he be doing with it?" Silence, and then, "Maybe he uses it to call us."

"No, no, he uses his cell phone, we have proof!" replied the chief.

Mercure thought so hard he made a face without realizing it. An idea suddenly came to him.

"Unless . . ."

Mercure's telephone rang. He answered, but it was not Radio-Canada on line three. It was Hamel.

A long, rather pleasant shiver ran through Mercure's body. Good Lord, it had worked! And even faster than he'd expected! Very excited, he said he would take the call, and put the phone on speaker. Wagner understood, and he loosened his necktie.

Mercure looked at his watch and noted the time in his notebook. Then, recovering his usual calm, he pressed the button for line three.

"Good evening, Dr. Hamel."

"Tell me what you know about that dog!"

Hamel's voice no longer possessed the control he had shown in previous calls.

"So, it seems there's a dog haunting you . . ."

"Answer me, you bloody bluffer!"

"It's not a bluff, Dr. Hamel. I really believe I know what that animal is."

"Go ahead, Mercure, impress me!"

Hamel was putting on a good show, but Mercure sensed his nervousness. As if he was really hoping to learn something.

"Do you remember Luky, the Cussons' dog?"

No reaction from Hamel. Calmly, Mercure continued. "I imagine that you particularly remember Denis Bédard killing the dog. Because you were there, weren't you?"

Still silence. The memory must gradually be resurfacing in his mind. Finally, he exclaimed, with a mixture of anger and disappointment, "This is ridiculous! What's that got to do with anything?"

"You tell me."

Hamel was silent again. Mercure licked his lips. Was he on the wrong track? It really didn't matter . . . The important thing was to pinpoint the origin of the call. He could even hang up now, the triangulation must be completed. But as long as he had Hamel on the line, why not get to the bottom of this story?

"I'll help you a little," continued Mercure softly. "It seems you found his killing particularly horrible. In fact, you told your partner you would definitely have done the same thing, that it was human, and that it was precisely that that terrified you the most."

Was the doctor breathing a little more heavily?

"The violence that is dormant in every human being fascinates you, but it also repels you, doesn't it? Like that bull in Picasso's painting . . ."

"Don't play psychoanalyst, Mercure, you're way off the mark. The Cussons' dog is an old story that has nothing to do with what's happening to me."

"So what dog is haunting you?"

"I knew I shouldn't have called you! Believe me, this is the last time I'm going to fall into one of your stupid traps!"

"Don't you think you're the one who's trapped yourself ever since the beginning?"

Click. Hamel had hung up.

"Perfect!" shouted Wagner, clapping his hands. "The guys in Longueuil will find the location. They should be calling us within ten minutes!"

He smiled conspiratorially at Mercure.

"Nice work, Hervé."

Mercure smiled slightly, but less enthusiastically than his superior. The telephone rang. It was Radio-Canada, but Mercure told them the call was no longer necessary.

Seeing Mercure's pensive look, Wagner asked what he was thinking about.

"I wonder if I was on target with that dog story."

Wagner said it didn't matter, since they'd nab him in half an hour at most. He crossed the office, chuckling contentedly. "I really thought for a while that we would never find him!"

Mercure said nothing, still staring at the telephone. He was still thinking about that computer . . . but most of all, about the hunch he had had just before Hamel called and that he didn't dare share with Wagner.

———

Bruno met a few cars on the road back, but he barely saw them. In spite of himself, in spite of his anger at that stupid phone call, his thoughts were on the past . . . three years ago, to be specific.

It was June and he was repainting the porch when he heard screaming and crying. He turned around just in time to see little Frédéric Bédard run across the street . . . just in time to see that his face had been reduced to a bloody pulp.

As a doctor, he hadn't hesitated: less than a minute later, he had entered the Bédards' house and found himself in the midst of turmoil. Louise was on the telephone pleading with 911 to send an ambulance, while Denis was holding his crying son in his arms, repeating, "Who did this to you, Fred, who did this to you?"

They had put the child down on the couch, still screaming in pain. Bruno had cleaned the blood from his face and examined his injuries. He said, "It was a dog, Denis."

The father stared, incredulous. The paramedics came almost immediately and carried the child out. The mother went with them.

But not Denis. Silently, he opened a closet and took out a baseball bat. There was only one dog on the street big enough to inflict such wounds, and the two men knew it. Without even a glance at Bruno, Denis had walked to the door and left the house. Bruno had gone outside too and caught up with Denis on the street. He had put his hand on his shoulder and asked him what he was planning to do. Denis had turned around abruptly, and Bruno had quite simply not recognized his neighbor. His face was scarlet, his features so fixed and tense that they almost looked like they would crack . . . but mostly it was his eyes. Bruno had the impression that they had changed color. As if there were a filter over his eyes.

A filter . . .

And what Bruno had seen in that gaze was so frightening that he had let go of Bédard's arm and backed away a few steps.

Denis had started walking again. Other neighbors had come out of their houses and were watching him, unsure what to do. Gilles Cusson, Luky's owner, had run up to him. He was distraught.

"Denis, I . . . My God, it's horrible! I just . . . just found out what . . . And your son, is he . . . ?"

Denis had violently pushed him away and continued forward, his steps fast but so heavy. Gilles had tried to grab him, but Bruno had held him back, saying, "Leave him alone, Gilles, or he'll hit you!"

"But . . . but my dog, he . . ."

"Forget your dog."

Bruno had followed Denis. He did not intend to stop him from killing the dog, but he wanted to make sure Denis did not do anything compromising . . .

. . . and maybe he also wanted to see . . .

He was not the only one. Four other neighbors had joined them, ill at ease and yet curious. Some had timidly spoken to Denis, but he had not turned around once.

Then Luky had appeared on the lawn. He had watched his victim's father approaching, growling in a really threatening way. Bruno had never seen him like that. Luky was a really large Great Dane, but he was a gentle dog. At that moment, though, he looked like a real killer.

His eyes were like bullets and foam around his mouth indicated that he had rabies. He was crouched to attack, and his growl sounded more like that of a werewolf than a dog. Bruno wouldn't have gone near him for anything in the world. He and the other neighbors had stopped in the middle of the street, intimidated.

But Denis had not even slowed his pace. Stepping onto the lawn, he raised the bat just as Luky leapt up with a terrible howl. Luky was stopped short in midair by the bat, which shattered his jaw with a loud crack. Bruno remembered thinking to himself *Nice move, Denis!* and frankly, the sight of the dog lying on its side with its jaw broken had not inspired pity in him. Luky was making little growls that did not seem to be synchronized with the movements of his dislocated muzzle. He was about to get up when Denis hit him again on his front legs. The growls became howls, and the animal fell down on its side again.

"Go on, Denis, kill it, kill the filthy rabid animal!" screamed Pierrette, one of the onlookers.

Denis had continued beating Luky on his front and back legs, making him howl with each blow, and Bruno had realized that he did not want to kill the dog right away. He wanted it to last.

He wanted the dog to suffer.

Bruno had not felt the horror right away, but rather a vague discomfort that he could not clearly identify.

Then Gilles had run toward Denis, shouting at him to stop, but Denis blindly swung the bat to the side, hitting Gilles in the stomach. Gilles collapsed with the wind knocked out of him. Claude, another neighbor, said, "Come on, Denis . . ."

But he hadn't insisted. In fact, no one had said anything else.

———

In his car, Bruno was gripping the steering wheel harder and harder without realizing it, his dilated eyes staring at the road ahead. The car gradually slowed down.

———

Without a glance at Gilles, who was painfully trying to catch his breath, Denis had started hitting again, this time on the dog's side. The sounds had become more squishy, and Luky's yelps had turned into plaintive whimpers. There was no longer rabid rage in the dog's eyes now, only distress, while its jaw continued to open and close crookedly. There was a gush of blood from its mouth, then another. You could hear the bones breaking, the internal organs being squashed. Openings had appeared in its flank.

Gilles had stood up, sobbing, and taken refuge in his house. But neither Bruno nor any of the other neighbors had moved. They were paralyzed. Bruno had been shocked to see the dog slaughtered like this, but he had been just as shocked by Denis's face: cold, hard, and impenetrable, with empty eyes that looked on his victim with icy detachment.

Luky's whimpers had become unbearable, and Bruno had had to make an effort to keep from blocking his ears. The dying animal, now lying with its guts exposed, had managed to turn its muzzle toward its tormentor, and Denis had gone for its head. The sound of the blows had become deafening, as if someone were smashing china, and the whimpering had changed to gurgling. Then Bruno had finally felt the full horror of it. All the onlookers had felt it, including Pierrette, who had put both hands over her mouth, her eyes wide with terror. Another neighbor, Jacques, had turned and fled and, while he ran, had started vomiting.

As for Bruno, everything had gradually disappeared around him—the onlookers, the houses, the street—leaving only darkness, and in the center of it, overexposed under red light, Denis hitting Luky. What was left of Luky. Because the dog was clearly dead. Yet Denis had kept on beating it for two or three more minutes, maybe longer. The onlookers were silent, the dead dog was silent, and the street was completely silent except for the blows of the bat raining down on the shapeless, bloody carcass . . . blows that had become dull, empty, without resonance . . .

. . . and the sound of those blows had cruelly hammered Bruno's soul.

———

Bruno stopped the car on the shoulder. He had not thought about this story for a long time, and now suddenly he was so haunted by it that he had lost contact with the present. He rubbed his hands over his face. Wait . . . wait for those images to fade. But they did not fade, they remained . . .

———

Denis had finally stopped. After the last blow, he had remained bent forward, panting, with the bat still touching the broken corpse. Then he had slowly straightened up. Bruno clearly remembered thanking God that the carnage had ended. Holding the bat in his right hand, Denis had backed away without taking his eyes off Luky. He had looked at the four remaining witnesses, one by one. When his eyes fell on Bruno, the doctor had shivered. Bruno no longer saw hate or fury in Denis's eyes, but total disorientation, as if he had been asleep for centuries and had woken up in a setting he was unable to comprehend.

And for Bruno the most terrifying thing about the whole episode was that look in Denis's eyes.

Still in total silence, Denis had started walking, and everyone had stepped aside for him as if he were a leper. He had gone to the street and headed toward his house, his gait mechanical yet zigzagging, like a drunken automaton. After about a dozen steps, the bat had slipped from his hand and fallen to the asphalt with an incongruous noise. A little farther on, he had stumbled, and his left knee had even touched the ground, but he had managed to get up again and continue forward without turning around.

It was only when they saw him in the distance, going into his house, that Bruno and the other witnesses had finally looked at each other, appalled and distraught. Pierrette was crying softly, rubbing her hands together nervously.

Bruno had not glanced at the dog again. And he would have bet his last penny that the three others had carefully avoided looking at it too. They had all gone back to their houses without a word. When they had followed Denis, they had all expected to see a dog get killed. But no one had expected *that*.

Bruno had hardly slept a wink that night. And his brief moments of sleep had been haunted by the growling and whimpering of a dog and the dull, hollow sound of blows.

_____

At the steering wheel, Bruno sighed and closed his eyes.

_____

During the days that followed, Denis was not once seen leaving his house. When Bruno met any of the neighbors who had witnessed the slaughter, they said hello and chatted a bit, but no one ever mentioned *that*.

After a few days, Bruno had gotten up the courage to go and visit Denis at home. He had been alone in the house, assembling a bookcase in the living room. The stereo was playing a CD of the Guess Who with the volume turned up very loud. Ill at ease, Bruno had asked Denis how his son was doing. Without interrupting his work, Denis had answered that he was out of danger, but that he would be left with deep scars on his face. He spoke calmly and politely, but Bruno felt he was absent. And the overly loud music felt odd.

"And how's Louise?" he had asked.

"Not too bad. She still has moments of enormous anxiety, but she's so happy Frédéric is alive. She's recovering quite well."

Denis had placed a shelf on two brackets and then suddenly stopped. He had lowered his eyes and added, "Better than I am, anyway."

Burton Cummings was crooning "These Eyes," which struck Bruno as the height of absurdity. Still uncomfortable, he had asked Denis what he meant.

"You know what I hear all day, Bruno?"

Bruno shook his head.

"The echoes of the blows."

"What blows?"

"When I was hitting the dog, at the end," answered Denis in a voice that was a little more animated. "I just kept hitting it, even though I knew it was dead, because I wanted to see more blood, to hear more yelping, more frightful howls, to cause more pain! Because I would have liked to kill it another five, ten, a hundred times! And the more I hit it, the more the sound of those blows rang in my head! Especially the echoes . . ."

Bruno too remembered those sounds very well: dull and hollow. He had muttered stupidly, "There were no echoes, Denis."

"Oh yes, there were! Maybe I was the only one who heard them, but they were there! Horrible echoes, precisely because that was the only effect of my blows. And that's why I finally stopped hitting it—not because I wanted to, but because the echoes in my head had become unbearable! And they still are! Even if I put music on in the house all day long, I still hear them! They're always in my head, and I have a feeling . . ."

He had bitten his lip and added in a breaking voice, "I have a feeling they'll always be with me—the echoes of the blows. Endless hollow echoes."

———

Behind the steering wheel, Bruno opened his eyes. The car was surrounded by darkness, and the rain was drumming erratically on the hood.

How, after three years, was he able to remember every detail with such precision, such clarity?

———

A few weeks later, he had run into Denis in town with his poor disfigured son. They had made small talk; Denis had really seemed better, although he still had that filter in front of his eyes. At one point, Bruno had ventured to ask, quite seriously, "And the echoes?"

Denis had given him a knowing, bitter little smile.

"Now it's more like echoes of echoes. They're a lot less bad . . . but they're still there."

———

Bruno had not thought about it again. But sitting in the car staring at the curtain of rain in front of him, he wondered if Denis still heard those echoes.

At the time, the story had really shaken him. When he told some of his friends about it, they had laughed, saying it was only a dog, and a rabid dog at that. They were right, but that did not diminish the horror.

He had finally stopped thinking about it.

So why, three years later, at this particular time, would that story have come back to haunt him? Could it be Luky he heard whimpering and growling? Good God! But why? What was the connection?

In the rearview mirror, he saw headlights in the distance behind him. As a precaution, he drove off quickly.

No, it had nothing to do with what he was doing. Mercure was completely off base. Or he was trying to undermine Bruno psychologically. *And he had succeeded, hadn't he?*

Bruno pushed that old story out of his mind. He regretted leaving the cottage because of it. It was really stupid! He should have stuck with his first idea and stayed there!

So he concentrated on what he was soon going to do to the monster. Because tonight, he absolutely had to climb another rung.

With his free hand, he fingered the blue ribbon in his pocket.

———

"Great! Go there right away and search everywhere! I managed to get a warrant, so don't hold back! Call me as soon as you get your hands on him!"

Wagner hung up and rubbed his hands. Mercure, Cabana, and Ruel were waiting for an explanation. The chief announced that the triangulation had been successful; the signal had come from a building with twelve apartments.

"Hamel is in one of those apartments. As soon as they find him, they'll call us back. I'd say fifteen minutes at most!"

He looked at Mercure for a moment.

"You're not exactly jumping for joy, Hervé."

The Drummondville police officers were used to Mercure's emotional reserve, but Wagner thought he looked downright worried, as if something was bothering him. Mercure was sitting in a chair gently stroking his cheek and shaking his head skeptically.

"He won't be there," he said finally.

"What are you talking about?"

Mercure sighed. There, he'd said it. And just expressing his doubt out loud automatically transformed it into a certainty.

"Hamel has sent us on a wild-goose chase."

———

Bolduc, Pleau, and two more Longueuil officers were standing in the living room looking around in bewilderment. The triangulation had pinpointed this building. And this apartment was the only one that had been rented in the last two weeks and whose tenant was a single man, according to the landlord.

Bolduc remembered visiting this apartment two days before. He had not found anything then, so why would it be any different today?

"Search the other apartments!" he ordered. "Ask the guys outside to help you! Break in if the tenants aren't there! He's got to be here somewhere!" Then more softly, "We have to take him by surprise."

The three police officers went out. Perplexed, Bolduc moved from one room to another. The same remnants of food as the last time, the same unmade bed, the same book open in the living room as two days before. The same. *Too much* the same, in fact.

He had to call Mercure.

He found the telephone, but there was no dial tone. He noticed that the phone was not plugged in. However, there was another wire coming out of the telephone jack in the wall, which disappeared behind the couch. And there was a plug in the electrical outlet too, with a cord following the same path.

Bolduc pushed the furniture away with one hand, watched curiously by

Pleau and another officer, who had just returned. He uncovered a laptop computer sitting on the floor. Beside it was a cell phone, which was connected to it. On the screen, there were fish swimming lazily against a black background. Bolduc stared stupidly at the two devices, his head cocked.

"What's that?" asked the Longueuil cop, bending over the computer.

And he pressed the space bar on the keyboard to get rid of the screen saver. Pleau, who had already understood, yelled at him not to touch it, but it was too late. Not only did the fish vanish but the computer shut down completely with a disturbing grinding sound.

"Shit," said Bolduc angrily, rubbing his forehead. Pleau, looking like a condemned woman walking to the guillotine, connected the telephone and dialed a number.

———

"I'm no computer geek, but it isn't hard to understand. He's somewhere else, with another computer. He goes on the Internet and communicates with the computer here, which is also connected to the Internet and to his cell phone. Hamel turns on his cell phone, dials a number, and calls remotely. That's why we located the cell in Longueuil. The cell phone is here, but Hamel isn't."

Holding the receiver to his ear, Mercure nodded. He looked more weary than discouraged. Wagner was the one who was discouraged, standing off to the side rubbing his neck furiously with both hands. The other officers in the room had heard the conversation on the speakers and were silent and embarrassed. Bolduc, on the other end of the line, was also silent, waiting.

Hamel had subscribed to an Internet service somewhere. In two places, in fact, one in Longueuil, and the other . . . somewhere else. When Mercure had checked his recent credit card purchases earlier in the week, there hadn't been any transactions of that kind. Hamel must have added the two subscriptions to the Internet service he already had at home. But who was the ISP? Bell-Sympatico? No, Mercure would already have known about it from checking the calls from his cell phone. Globetrotter? Videotron? AOL?

"Who's the service provider?" asked the detective sergeant.

"We don't know. The computer shut off and we haven't been able to turn it on again," Bolduc said. "But the computer expert from the Longueuil station will be here any minute now. At any rate, Hamel had just bought the computer, the stickers from the store are still on it."

"Call back as soon as the computer is on."

He hung up. That was the signal Wagner had been waiting for to explode. He couldn't believe they'd been tricked like that! To think that they'd been searching Longueuil like idiots for the past five days! Hamel, wherever he was, must really have laughed when he thought of the look on the cops' faces when they discovered they'd been looking for him in the wrong place!

Mercure was trying to reach Sylvie Jutras to ask her what Internet service provider they used, but there was no answer. He hung up and waited silently with his arms crossed while Wagner ranted. Once again Mercure was astounded and unnerved by the detailed planning of the operation and all the precautions Hamel had taken.

Could hate give a man the power to come up with such a perfect plan?

But too much power could destroy. That was why Mercure had finally opted for something other than hate when his wife died.

But had that brought him peace?

"He could even be in the US!" shouted Wagner, whose two top shirt buttons were open.

Mercure kept on thinking, hardly noticing his superior. Hate had enabled Hamel to make such a careful plan, but hate could also make him lose control. He was in a train going three hundred kilometers an hour, and if he didn't slow down soon, he was going to crash . . . and all Mercure would be able to do would be to pick up the pieces.

He thought of the conversation he had had with Hamel earlier. About the business with the dog. Despite Hamel's bravado, Mercure had sensed that he was shaken. Had Mercure managed to slow down the runaway train—or at least to throw in some sand that in the next two days might work its way into the motor and make it grind to a halt? He hoped so, but he was far from sure.

Wagner had finished blowing off steam and finally proposed something constructive. "While we're waiting for their computer expert to call, we could start calling Internet service providers."

Just then the phone rang, and Mercure answered. It was the computer expert. Her name was Massicotte, and she had been able to turn the computer back on without any problem: the security system Hamel had used was pretty crude. She said Hamel's Internet service provider was Globetrotter, and Mercure thanked her. While Ruel called Globetrotter, Wagner rubbed his hands with satisfaction.

"So! He's not so smart after all, our doctor! He didn't think that when we found his computer, we'd trace it back to the source!"

But his satisfied mood soon gave way to doubt, and he asked Mercure, "Do you think he thought of that?"

Mercure's silence was enough to discourage Wagner.

After less than five minutes, Ruel hung up.

"Hamel did add two addresses to his Globetrotter subscription. One in Longueuil and the other in Charette. I have the full address."

They all looked at each other.

"Does anyone know where Charette is?" asked Ruel.

Cabana, who hadn't said a word up to then, went to a computer and quickly found where it was.

"It's in the Mauricie region. A tiny village about thirty kilometers from Trois-Rivières."

"There's no police force there, it's too small," Mercure said. "We'll have to find the nearest SQ detachment."

Even before he finished his sentence, Wagner had grabbed the phone.

———

The first thing Bruno did after entering the house and removing his disguise was go to the refrigerator. Just one beer! It would only be the third one of the day. That wasn't very many! He walked to the living room, forcing himself to take small sips. There, he was being reasonable. He would still be completely in control in a little while.

His gaze fell on the TV, which was still on. The TVA news was over, but there must have been a special report on his case, because a voice was saying: ". . . demonstrations not only in support of Bruno Hamel's actions, but also against them."

Standing in the middle of the living room, Bruno watched in amazement as they showed the "anti-Hamel" demonstrations in different cities.

"I can understand Bruno Hamel's reasons," explained a demonstrator, a young man of about thirty wearing a T-shirt that said "peace and love." "But I can't accept them. He's acting personally, but justice isn't personal, it's a matter for society."

Bruno clenched his teeth. It was his daughter that had been murdered, not society's! So, yes, it was his personal revenge! And he was perfectly willing to accept that!

But at the same time, those images forced him to realize that it went further; however personal his action was, it suddenly had a social impact. But he couldn't control that impact, and that was what angered him the most. If his action was to have a social impact, he wanted to explain its meaning himself, publicly; then all the people who were criticizing it would have to agree with him.

And just what was its meaning?

He gave a sigh of frustration and took a sip of beer. To hell with these sociological concerns! What had gotten into him all of a sudden, wanting to set himself up as a standard-bearer? He had never wanted that! All he wanted was to avenge his daughter's death, to free himself from the hate that was eating away at him and plunging his heart into an abyss, period!

Period!

The host of the special broadcast appeared on the TV screen with a group of seated people wearing solemn expressions.

"Now I would like to introduce my guests, who are experts in . . ."

Bruno leapt up and turned off the television. Experts now! What next? Would he become a case study in the universities? He laughed. A bitter, joyless laugh.

After a few seconds, he went to the monster's room.

He went directly to his medical bags, took out a scalpel, and, without bothering with a mask, gloves, or sterilization, went over to the table. The monster was asleep, with the intravenous tube still in his arm. When Bruno grasped his chin, he woke up with a start. For a second or two, he had the same look of a zombie, detached from reality, but when he saw the scalpel right near his face, the ritual of fear, pleas, and lamentations began again. In a strangely childlike voice, he called Bruno the Devil and said he didn't want to stay in Hell for eternity.

Unperturbed, Bruno slowly lowered the scalpel toward the monster's right eye. The monster continued pleading, moving his head frantically. For all Bruno's efforts to hold him still with his free hand, the monster had surprising energy for a man in such a pathetic state. Grimacing with the effort, Bruno managed to make a first perforation, but the head was moving too much, and the blade, instead of going in, cut the eyelid, which started to bleed.

*"Kill me! For God's sake, stop torturing me and kill me!"*

Bruno should have felt a delicious pleasure at these words, but all he could feel was disgust for the monster. But of course he was disgusting! That was why he wanted to torture him, wasn't it? So go ahead! Tear out his eyes, this piece of shit who raped and killed your little girl! Tear out his eyes and let your disgust be transformed into satisfaction! Satisfaction! *Satisfaction, dammit!*

And while he aimed for the eye again, trying as best he could to immobilize the hysterical movement of the head, the monster's shouts gradually changed to the cries of an animal . . . to the howling of a dog.

Not again! No, *not again!*

He held his scalpel high, and was about to strike at random, when a slight movement to his right made him turn his head.

He just had time to catch a glimpse of a silhouette disappearing from the doorway, a glimpse of a torn dress, a lock of hair . . . and red, too much red . . .

After a second of total stupefaction, he rushed to the door and into the living room. There was no one there. No silhouette. No dress.

With the scalpel still in his hand, he rubbed his sweat-covered forehead. The monster's cries reached him again . . . but now there were words . . . sentences . . .

*"I raped other children! I confess, I raped and killed other little girls!"*

Bruno ran back to the room. The monster, tears and blood pouring from his eyes, said between sobs, "I . . . I'm ready to confess everything . . . I'm in Hell to do penance for my sins, so I . . . I'll confess everything. I'll give you their names, I want to confess everything. But promise me . . . promise me you'll let me die in peace afterward."

Bruno was going to give him a punch to shut him up; he didn't want to know anything about him, anything about his past! But suddenly he thought of the images he had seen on TV, the demonstrations for and against him.

He went back to the living room and looked frantically for some paper and a pen. He found them on the telephone table, and took them back to the monster's room. He stood in front of the monster, paper in hand, ready to write, like a secretary waiting to take dictation. The monster seemed not to understand for a few seconds, and then a light glinted in his eye.

"You . . . you'll let me out of Hell after that?"

Bruno didn't answer, didn't even move, but looked threateningly at his prisoner. Then, in a sobbing voice, tinged with hope and fear, the monster gave the names of three little girls, the dates, and finally the names of two cities: Joliette for the first victim, and Saint-Hyacinthe for the other two. Bruno wrote quickly, gripping the pen so tightly that he nearly broke it. When he wrote each of the names, he saw the face of a little girl on the sheet of paper. Three anonymous faces, all wearing the same mask of fear and suffering, and for that reason, all resembling Jasmine.

"Will I . . . will I be able to leave Hell now?" mumbled the monster when he had finished. "I've paid now. Can I . . . can I go to Heaven? Can I . . . ?"

Bruno slowly put the notebook and pen in his pocket. He stared at the monster for a moment. Suddenly, he grabbed the scalpel and raised it high, ready to strike. The monster screamed and closed his eyes in anticipation of more torture, and his screams once again became animal . . . doglike. Bruno looked for a place to aim the scalpel, the most painful place. He hesitated with the scalpel in the air, unsure, not satisfied with the choices available. Even the eyes no longer seemed like a good idea . . . and the dog's howling was so exasperating! With a grimace of frustration, he struck completely at random and the blade landed in the left arm. He left the room immediately, leaving the scalpel stuck in the arm of the screaming monster.

He put on his disguise and left the house, hardly feeling the cold rain. He got in the car and started the motor.

He realized that it would be his second call in an hour . . . but unlike the first time, he wasn't worried. He didn't hesitate at all: it was too important this time! It was a real bombshell!

As he drove along Pioneers Road, his face showed certainty and unshakeable confidence.

———

At the other end of the line, the officer explained that he and the other guys from the SQ, the provincial police, had just arrived at the apartment in Charette and found it empty except for a portable computer, which was turned on, and a microphone.

"Would it be possible to leave two men there in case Hamel comes back? Thank you."

After hanging up, Mercure turned to Wagner.

"Hamel really planned everything. He started by creating a false trail in Longueuil . . . and he rented the apartment in Charette in case we discovered it."

"It's still a clue," Cabana said. "If he's using that apartment to call from, he can't be hiding far away."

"He could be two minutes away from Charette—or two hours!" retorted Wagner with a sigh. "How are we supposed to find him?"

Mercure, looking in his notebook, murmured,

"There's a way . . ."

Bruno stopped the car at the corner of the street. Fifty meters away stood the duplex, silhouetted against the night sky. He looked at the lighted window with his binoculars and saw the kitchen. It was still quiet, still empty. His computer was still in the same place.

Suddenly he stiffened.

The two mice were no longer chasing each other on the screen of the computer. It was black except for the blinking cursor. His screen saver wasn't on. And it was programmed to go on after twelve minutes of inactivity.

Someone had just touched his keyboard.

He slowly lowered the binoculars. A shiver went through him. He looked through the binoculars again and examined the street across from the building. There were two cars parked there, and in one of them, Bruno could make out a figure seated behind the wheel. He couldn't see the features in the dark, but he saw that the person wasn't doing anything. As if he was waiting for someone. Someone like Bruno . . .

He quickly backed his car up until he couldn't see the house. Had he been noticed? At this distance in the darkness and rain, it would be surprising. Besides, nobody had turned into the street in front of him, and nobody had followed him. He made a U-turn and continued slowly. His body was covered with sweat, and he took a couple of deep breaths.

So the police had discovered that Longueuil was a false lead and had traced him here. And all that in an hour! Good God! He'd had a close call!

But he absolutely must make that phone call tonight. It would be the last one, but he had to make it!

He saw a telephone booth in front of a store that was closed. He looked around; the street was completely deserted.

Yes, why not? It wouldn't matter if the police discovered that he had used that phone booth, now that they had already zeroed in on Charette.

He stopped the car and ran through the rain to the phone booth. He asked the operator for the number of the TVA television network in Montreal. He dialed the number, but they would not put him through to the person he wanted to talk to. When Bruno said who he was, the receptionist hesitated, perplexed, and then put him on hold. A long minute passed while he nervously watched the street, but there was still nobody there. Finally a voice on the line said tersely, "Monette here."

"I want to speak to the news director."

"You're talking to him. And you claim to be Bruno Hamel, is that right?"

"I am Bruno Hamel."

"I need proof."

The news director was trying to keep his voice even and slightly skeptical, but Bruno sensed his excitement.

"I don't have to prove anything to you, Mr. Monette. I'm calling you because my prisoner . . ."

"You're talking about Lem—"

*"Don't say his name!"* growled Bruno.

Monette didn't say anything. He must be starting to take him seriously. Bruno started again, his voice calmer.

"My prisoner made a very interesting confession. He admitted to raping and killing three other little girls. He told me their names. I can give them to you . . ."

Silence at the other end of the line.

"I thought it would make a nice story, don't you think?" continued Bruno. "You could even tell the parents of the victims and get their reactions."

"What you're telling me is serious. I must have proof that you're Hamel."

His voice was still distant, but the undertone of excitement was more and more perceptible. He *really* wanted him to be Hamel.

Bruno thought about it. A car approached and went by, but it wasn't the police.

"Perfect. Listen to me. Until today, the police were looking for me in

Longueuil. But tonight they realized I wasn't there. Now they're looking for me around Charette, in Mauricie."

"Who's to say that's true? You could be making it up."

"Call Inspector Mercure in Drummondville."

This time the silence was interrupted by a slight wet sound. Bruno imagined Monette nervously licking his lips and getting more and more excited.

"Okay, give me the names."

Bruno took out a paper and read the three names, the dates, and the two cities.

"Why are you doing this, Hamel?"

He had called him by name. He believed him. Bruno was silent for a few seconds, and then he said tersely that he had nothing more to tell him.

"Wait, one last question . . . Your prisoner . . . what condition is he in?"

Bruno discerned an emotion he found disconcerting, a kind of morbid fascination, as if . . .

He thought of the cashier at the beer store.

*I'm with you . . .*

He hung up and left the phone booth. This time, he'd have to get out of there quickly. There could already be dozens of cops combing the area.

———

Mercure, his eyes on his notebook, explained slowly, as if he was doing the calculations while he was speaking.

"My message to TVA was broadcast at 6:04. It lasted about two minutes, so it ended at 6:06. When Hamel called, it was 6:20. So his hiding place is a fourteen-minute drive from the apartment in Charette."

He tapped his lips with the pen, and then asked, "Do we have a map of the Mauricie region?"

Cabana found one and unfolded it on a table.

"Here, Charette is here."

The four men formed a circle around the table, like military strategists planning an attack.

"Look," Mercure said, pointing at the map. "Apart from the 350 and the 351, there are only winding country roads. Even if Hamel was in a hurry, he couldn't have gone more than a hundred kilometers an hour on those roads. So in fourteen minutes, he would have gone . . ."

He made a quick calculation on a sheet of paper.

"Hamel did at most twenty-three kilometers. Let's say twenty-five if he took the 350 or the 351, which are faster."

"That narrows down the search area quite a bit!" cried Ruel, pleased.

"The problem is that it could be twenty-five kilometers in any direction from Charette," Wagner pointed out. "And there are secondary roads off every main road."

"Right. Let's look at all the possibilities . . ."

They got some colored markers, figured out the area on the map, and then traced all the possibilities on the roads around the village. After a half hour, the map had a red dot at Charette with a series of branching lines all around it. It looked like a mosaic.

"There," said Mercure. "Hamel is hiding somewhere along those red lines."

"Or rather, at the ends of those red lines," Ruel said.

"Not necessarily," retorted Wagner, annoyed that his officer had failed to understand. "If he left five, six, or seven minutes after hearing the message on TV, he traveled a shorter distance. He could be twenty-five kilometers from Charette, but he could just as easily be right nearby."

Ruel scratched his head, following the red lines with his eyes.

"That means there are a lot of possibilities."

At least the area didn't extend all the way to Trois-Rivières. In fact, it only covered villages. They identified them one by one: Charette, and then Saint-Étienne-des-Grès . . . Saint-Barnabé . . . Saint-Mathieu-du-Parc . . . Saint-Élie . . . As Mercure named them, Wagner wrote the names on a sheet of paper.

"Nine!" the director sighed. "That's a lot!"

Cabana pointed out that it was still more precise than looking in Longueuil, but the joke left Wagner cold.

"And it's not just the villages we've got to search, but all the area around them!" Ruel said. "There's a lot of woods in that area! He's probably hiding in a cabin in the forest!"

"A cabin that he can get to by car and that has electricity," Mercure said. "I'd bet it's more likely a cottage that he rented under a false name and paid cash for. We'll have to ask the agencies if they've rented one in the past couple of weeks. But we mustn't overlook anything. Also ask the hotels, motels, and businesses."

Wagner agreed, won over by their optimism now that they finally had something to go on.

"Perfect!" he said to Mercure. "I'll call the guys at the SQ to ask for their cooperation. I'll send them eight of our officers."

Just then, the phone rang, and Wagner answered it. He looked surprised, and then told Mercure that somebody called Monette at TVA wanted to talk to him. The detective sergeant had a feeling of foreboding as he took the phone from Wagner. A click signaled the transfer of the call, and then Monette asked in a jovial voice, "How are you doing, Inspector?"

"To what do I owe the honor of your call, Mr. Monette?"

"Now that you know Hamel isn't in Longueuil, you'll be looking for him in the Charette area, is that right?"

Wagner had put the phone on speaker. He turned white as a sheet, which was really unusual for him. Mercure was so taken aback that he was silent for two seconds . . . two seconds that gave him away.

"It appears that I'm right," Monette said with a chuckle.

"Who gave you that information?" Mercure asked in a more emotional voice than he would have liked.

"Hamel called me almost an hour ago. I had to be sure it was really him, and you've just confirmed it. We're going to prepare our report."

"What report?"

"Watch the news. We don't have time to prepare anything much for tonight, but tomorrow we're going to have something big."

"Monette, if you don't tell me immediately what Hamel said, I'll be there in two hours breaking down the door of your office, with a court order to make you talk!"

Monette seemed to find this amusing, but he told Mercure the whole story without making him ask again. Wagner and the other police officers were astounded, and Mercure himself was speechless for a few moments. Then, in a voice that was less than convincing, he said, "I forbid you to broadcast a story on it!"

"We're not only going to broadcast it; we're planning to run a news special tomorrow at noon! And since the story won't hinder your investigation, I'd be very surprised if you succeeded in getting an injunction!"

He hung up. Mercure sighed.

"He knows we've found the apartment in Charette. When he called TVA, he must have been nearby."

Wagner smiled wryly; the guys from the SQ must have just missed him. It was really ironic!

"Three other little girls," sighed Cabana, upset. "He killed three other little girls."

The others were all silent, troubled.

"I'm starting to think like Boisvert," he added in a low voice.

"Meaning . . . ?" asked Wagner suspiciously.

But Cabana decided not to say anything more.

Mercure sat down and calmly asked the chief, "Why did Hamel go to the trouble of calling TVA to give them that information? He must know it will be on TV."

"That's what he wants."

Mercure nodded. Wagner asked if he should try to get an injunction to prevent them from reporting it.

"Monette is right. We won't find a judge who will give it to us," Mercure said after thinking for a moment.

"That's what I think," Wagner said.

He looked at Mercure for a moment and said, "You're thinking of something, aren't you?"

Mercure reflected for a few more seconds and made a vague gesture with his hand.

"At any rate," he said, changing the subject, "Hamel knows we're looking for him in the right area now. So there's no point keeping it secret. We might as well ask the local people for help."

Wagner asked him to explain. Mercure suggested that they send a press release to the major daily newspapers and TV networks in the province, explaining that Bruno Hamel was hiding in the Charette area, in Mauricie. They would name the nine villages within the perimeter and ask the residents of the area to call the provincial police if they had seen Hamel or had any clue to his whereabouts.

"There are only two days left. If we want it to be in the media tomorrow, we'll have to write the press release and send it right away."

Wagner glanced at the clock; it was almost 8:00 p.m.

"Okay," he said. "I'll get us some coffee and we'll get to work on it!"

———

At about ten thirty that night, Bruno took out one of the monster's eyes. He would have liked to remove the other one as well, but he got tired of his victim's cries, which gave him a headache. So he had put a bandage on the bloody socket and left the room.

Once again, he got no real satisfaction. He had not gone up another rung. But, unlike the day before, he didn't experience any real frustration. Tonight his mind was elsewhere. He couldn't stop thinking about his phone call to Monette; that was what had given him real satisfaction tonight. And the best was yet to come. He had watched the ten o'clock news on TVA, and of course they had hardly mentioned it. They had said only that Hamel had given the station the names of three other victims of the monster, and had ended by saying, "We will give you further details in a special report tomorrow at noon."

So the bombshell would come tomorrow. And Bruno was so eager for it that he couldn't concentrate on what he was doing. That was why tonight's torture had been disappointing.

*You keep finding reasons*, said an inner voice. *Yesterday it was alcohol, and tonight . . .*

But those reasons were true! Tomorrow, after the explosive report on TVA, he would regain his enthusiasm, he was sure. Even now, watching a silly comedy on TV with a beer in his hand, he couldn't think of anything else.

Tomorrow his story would take on greater significance, and that would give his action a kind of . . .

What, exactly?

*Why did you really tell that to the media?*

Why this question? For the bombshell, obviously! The bombshell that would explode on TV tomorrow!

He rubbed his face. Yes, tomorrow he would see. Everything would be clearer. For everyone, and for himself as well.

He tried to concentrate on the movie.

———

Mercure got home at ten fifteen, exhausted. The press release had been sent to the media. Tomorrow everyone would be talking about it.

He ate some leftover meat pie and went to bed. But as usual, he had a lot of trouble getting to sleep. It was the time of the day when the images of his wife were most persistent. There was one in particular that he hadn't been able to get out of his mind for five years: Madelaine dead with a bullet wound from a revolver in her forehead.

He tried to chase away these dark thoughts by thinking of the evening and Hamel's call to Monette. Hamel couldn't have planned that beforehand, because he hadn't had all that information about the other children. He must have learned it during the week, by torturing his prisoner. And that information had such an impact on him that he had run the risk of calling a reporter to tell it to him. Having started by wanting only to torture and kill Lemaire, he had added a new element to his plan. Why?

Hamel had gone off the rails; Mercure was convinced that that was why he had deviated from his original plan. The phone call proved it.

But how much had he deviated? Did he have a specific intention in wanting the story to go on television? The only way to find the answer was to let Monette do his report.

Suddenly, without warning, Madelaine came back into his thoughts. That led him to think of Demers. When he had seen him the day before, Mercure had really considered ending these visits. It wasn't the first time, but yesterday, the possibility seemed much stronger than before.

Strange that this would happen at the same time as the Hamel case. All week long, his thoughts about Hamel had often led him to think of Madelaine and Demers. Why was that? Of course, Mercure too had lost a loved one, as Hamel had, but it seemed to him there was more to it than that.

Sighing, he turned on the light and picked a book up from the night table, resigned to the fact that he wouldn't fall asleep quickly again tonight.

# DAY 6

THE DOG'S HOWLING WAS BECOMING UNBEARABLE, BUT BRUNO KEPT MOVING through the labyrinth. He wanted to see. And the farther he went, the more he was able to discern other sounds with the howling, dull blows that had haunted his nights since the beginning of the week.

Whimpering and blows . . . whimpering and blows . . .

Finally, he came to the end of the labyrinth. A Great Dane was lying on its side. It was Luky, or at least what was left of him. Broken and bloody, he was lying in a pool of blood and guts, but was still alive. And he was howling. A man was beating the dog with a baseball bat, and every terrible blow was followed by a horrible sound; but even more horrible were the echoes of the blows.

The man had his back to Bruno, but Bruno knew he wasn't Denis Bédard. This man's silhouette was more animal than human. Weren't those hoofs holding the bat? And those things on his head really looked like horns. It was a grotesque combination of a man and a bull . . . and Bruno decided he didn't want to know what it was. The very idea that the creature might turn around and show its face terrified him so much that he decided to retrace his steps. But a wall had appeared behind him and it was impossible to turn back. Bruno understood that he would have to look at the scene, to confront it.

All of a sudden, the bull-man stopped striking and turned around. Horrified, Bruno recognized his own features in the vaguely human face. His double stared at Bruno with mingled hatred and despair. Although the blows of the bat had stopped, the sound went on rhythmically, and the echoes grew stronger and stronger until they were louder than the blows themselves.

Paralyzed with terror, Bruno stared at his double, his head resounding with the echoes until it was unbearable, until . . .

He awoke with a start. For an instant, he thought it was evening, because the light outside the window was so dull. But his watch said ten in the morning. He got up, still feeling the heaviness, and opened the curtains. It was raining again, really hard now, and the sky looked like a storm was coming.

That dream was ridiculous. Yet just thinking of it gave him gooseflesh. That idiot Mercure. It was all his fault. He had to get rid of the memory of that dog, which really wasn't doing him any good.

He put on his filthy clothes and went to see the monster, who was in such a pitiful state that Bruno quickly put him on the intravenous again. He also changed the bandage on the empty eye socket; there was an ugly infection. The monster submitted passively, half-unconscious, his irregular breathing making an ominous whistling sound.

What if Bruno let him die? Letting him die in exhaustion and suffering would be a good torture, wouldn't it?

No, it would not be satisfying. It was too passive; Bruno wanted to be active. Satisfaction could only come through action.

He went and got two slices of toast and a glass of orange juice and fed them to the monster, who painfully swallowed what was put in his mouth. At one point, his remaining eye turned toward Bruno. He even said a few words, which Bruno had a hard time making out:

"Am I in Heaven now? Is it over . . . ?"

How could this filthy piece of rotting meat hope to go to Heaven? If such a place existed, it was Jasmine who would be there, not him! Not him! Never!

He wanted to stick his fingers in the eye, but at the last minute, he stopped himself—no more torture until this afternoon, or it would kill the monster. He settled for spitting in his face. The monster gave a feeble moan and mumbled, "I've atoned . . . I've atoned . . ."

Bruno backed up a few steps and contemplated his prisoner lying there hooked up to the intravenous tube. He no longer looked like the arrogant young man Bruno had kidnapped six days ago. In fact, he no longer looked like anything much. Coldly, Bruno made a visual assessment of his state: his body covered with welts, his two knees broken and swollen, his mangled genitals, the filthy opening in his belly, his broken nose, his right eye plucked out, and his whole body befouled with blood, pus, urine, and shit.

This was no longer a monster Bruno had in front of him, nor an unhappy, suffering human being. It was . . . nothing. Nothing at all. Yet he hated this "nothing," detested it, wanted to destroy it. But this hatred was frustrating precisely because Bruno had the impression it focused on nothing.

He left the room in ill humor and called Morin.

"I'm glad to see you made the decision that was best. For you and for me."

"Where's the money?" was all Morin said. There was resentment in his voice.

Bruno took out his notebook and explained where he would find it. Morin asked, "You're going to kill him tomorrow, right?"

"Yes," answered Bruno evenly.

"How do I know you're going to call me?"

"I don't need the money anymore, Morin. What good will it do me in prison?"

Morin didn't say anything. He was probably thinking about that argument.

"I'll call you in the morning," added Bruno.

He hung up and went to make himself some breakfast. While eating, he thought about the phone call of the night before. He was sure he would hear about it on the next news report on TV. That would give his morale a boost. It would give a new . . .

. . . *meaning?*

. . . new energy to what he was doing, would give him the encouragement he needed to climb to the top of the ladder and get the complete satisfaction that would be the culmination of this long week.

By the end of the afternoon, the monster would be a bit stronger. And then Bruno would take his feelings out on him one last time, would subject him to everything a human body can endure without dying, and would let him spend the night in agony. Tomorrow, he would get up, feast his eyes on the monster's last convulsions, and then finish him off with a bullet to the head.

After which, fully satisfied, he would call the police and surrender.

During these reflections, Sylvie didn't even cross his mind.

———

There was nobody in the quiet little street, and that suited Sylvie. She walked slowly in the rain, protected by her umbrella. Her sister had said it was crazy to go for a walk in such foul weather, but Sylvie really needed to walk in the fresh air. To search. Or at least to feel she was searching.

Because since she had come to her sister's place in Sherbrooke, avoiding all exposure to television or newspapers and keeping to herself as much as possible, she still hadn't found what she was seeking. Her mind was filled with Bruno and the madness of the last few days, preventing her from grieving as she wanted so much to. She surprised herself wondering if it was raining as hard where Bruno was hiding.

If he were with her now, things would be so simple. But that was it, he wasn't with her and he would never be with her again. So, as senseless and impossible as it might seem, she had to get him out of her thoughts and make room for Jasmine.

She got to the end of the street at the edge of the woods, the little woods Jasmine had loved. Every time they came to visit Josée, Jasmine always wanted to go for a walk there. Sylvie had often gone there with her.

On a sudden impulse, moved perhaps as much by nostalgia as by a vague hope, Sylvie went into the woods, onto the path that wound through the trees. The rustle of the rain in the leaves gave the woods a whole different atmosphere, making her want to immerse herself more deeply in her memories.

She remembered her walks with Jasmine on this path. She remembered one time a little over a year ago, when Jasmine had suggested that they leave the path and wander in the woods. They had been walking like this for a few minutes when they found a huge, splendid tree trunk lying horizontally but suspended just above the ground, and had sat down on it for a few minutes. Sylvie had taken some chocolate from her pocket. And that was the image that had suddenly come to her mind: she and her daughter sitting side by side eating the chocolate, Jasmine swinging her legs, her eyes sparkling with pleasure.

But the image remained unclear, strangely devoid of real emotion. Sylvie suddenly wanted to find that tree trunk again. She looked around her, trying to recall the point where she and Jasmine had gone off the path. But she couldn't, there was too much confusion in her head in spite of the soft whispering of the rain in the trees. For a minute, she resented Bruno, blaming him for her inability to act freely. But she pushed the thought aside; it was pointless. She brought her thoughts back to the woods, the path, the tree trunk . . . and suddenly she remembered what Jasmine had said.

"Are we going to get lost, Mommy, if we leave the path?"

The childish worry had amused Sylvie. She could have explained that it would be impossible for them to get lost in such a small woods just by leaving the path for a few minutes, but that answer was too rational, too adult. So she had gone along with Jasmine. Sylvie always kept a few hair ribbons in her pockets because Jasmine often lost them, and she had explained to the little girl that if they tied the ribbons to branches along the way, they would be able to find their way back and would not get lost.

"Like Hansel and Gretel leaving bread crumbs, only they wouldn't get eaten," Jasmine had said.

"Just like that!"

In the three minutes the great adventure in the woods had lasted, Sylvie had tied three ribbons to the trees, to Jasmine's delight. When they were walking back to the path, the little girl had asked her mother to leave the ribbons in place.

"They'll grow with the trees," she had explained with stars in her eyes. "And in two or three years, we'll come back and get them and they'll be very, very long!"

So the ribbons had remained on the branches . . . and Jasmine would never come back to see if they had grown.

Sylvie stood immobile under her umbrella in the middle of the path before starting to look for the first ribbon. While she was looking from tree to tree, she was telling herself what an idiot she was, that the wind and snow would have destroyed the ribbons. And even if they hadn't, what were her chances of finding the ribbons? The path was long and she didn't remember where she'd tied them. Nevertheless, as she walked, she kept on looking for them in the trees along her way, her step quickening as she went. She had to find the ribbons, to find the way.

Suddenly she saw the first one. A blue ribbon tied to a branch, saturated with rain. Sylvie walked over to it, incredulous, and unthinkingly walked into the woods. She remembered now. They had gone in this direction, she was almost certain. Her umbrella caught in the low branches, making it hard for her to walk. She closed it, hardly feeling the rain on her head.

She glimpsed the second ribbon, a red one. Her heart beating wildly, she went and touched it, and then continued walking into the woods. The third one must be right near here, they had walked for barely three minutes.

There it was! Bright yellow, it stood out clearly against the brown bark. Sylvie was breathing so heavily that the rain was getting in her nose and mouth. Almost running, she passed the third ribbon, now sure of the way, clearly recognizing every tree she and Jasmine had passed.

And suddenly, she saw the trunk, still in the same place, beautiful with its sheen of rain.

Sylvie stood there soaked from head to toe, her hair plastered to her face, contemplating the tree for a long time. She finally went and straddled it, and sat there very straight, swinging her legs. Then she leaned back until she was lying along the trunk. The stream of her tears mingled with the rain on the bark of the tree and fell to the ground, and sadness and happiness mingled in her sobs.

———

At noon, Bruno settled down on the couch and, very excited, turned on the television to TVA.

"We now present a special report on the latest developments in the sensational Hamel case. The story will end with either the discovery of Bruno Hamel by the police or the killing of his prisoner tomorrow, Monday, at the end of the most incredible countdown in the history of crime in Quebec."

Bruno winced at the word "crime."

The news anchor explained that Bruno Hamel had given the names of three other young victims of "his prisoner" (they were still being careful not to give his name), three more little girls who had been raped and killed in the past six years.

"We imagine that Bruno Hamel extracted this confession from his prisoner using torture."

Bruno grimaced with impatience. These details did not interest him. It was the next part that he was waiting for. The anchor added, "We went to see the parents of the three little girls, in Joliette and Saint-Hyacinthe. The mother of one of them refused to talk to us, but the parents of the two other victims gave us powerful messages."

Bruno leaned forward on the couch, clasped his hands, and rubbed them together nervously.

A couple in their forties appeared, sitting in an ordinary living room. A bit uncomfortable in front of the camera, and clearly upset, they explained that they had long ago abandoned hope of ever finding the murderer of little Sara, who had been killed six years ago in Joliette. A reporter asked what they hoped would happen now that the alleged perpetrator was in Bruno Hamel's hands. The woman hesitated briefly, as if she wasn't sure she had the right to say what she wanted to, but finally she said, "Frankly, we wouldn't really be sad if Hamel killed him tomorrow."

"We would even be glad," the husband said without a trace of irony.

Bruno relaxed his hands. There was a sparkle in his eye.

"Would you have liked to be in Bruno Hamel's place this week?" the reporter persisted.

The woman hesitated again. But there was a flash of cold hatred in the husband's eyes, fleeting, barely perceptible, but very real, as he said, "Yes, I would have liked to be there."

From the slight movement of the woman's head, Bruno understood that she agreed.

Another couple appeared, standing in front of a cute little house in Saint-Hyacinthe. Despite his sadness, the man was quite composed, but the woman was like a fury, with hate permanently rooted in her eyes. Bruno realized that it had been there for a long time, just waiting for an event like today's to explode.

"I hope he tortured him like nobody was ever tortured before!" she spat so vehemently that it made the tragedy almost seem ridiculous. "He could never suffer as much as Joëlle suffered! To think he was arrested two years ago and released for lack of proof! Some justice!"

For an instant, she gave in to sadness and her eyes filled with tears. But the hate came back immediately and she started ranting again.

"If the police want justice, they should leave Bruno Hamel alone and let him finish what he's started!"

Slowly, Bruno leaned back and sank into the couch, his face almost serene. Hardly aware that he was doing it, he took the blue ribbon out of his pocket and, with his eyes on the screen, stroked it gently with his fingers.

The reporter asked the husband if he felt the same way as his wife. The man seemed more moderate, and a little irritated by his wife's vehemence, but without hesitation, he said, "I totally approve of what Bruno Hamel is doing."

"We not only approve, but we would have liked to be with him!" added the wife, starting to cry.

Bruno made a grimace that was trying to be a smile. The anchor reappeared on the TV.

"The police have now determined the area where Hamel is hiding with his prisoner." He named nine little municipalities. Saint-Mathieu-du-Parc was one of them, but that did not worry Bruno: the police would not be searching private houses that were inhabited year-round, like Josh's.

The anchor added that if residents of these regions thought they had seen this man (and a photo of Bruno appeared in an inset), they should call the number at the bottom of the screen. When he heard the music at the end of the special report, Bruno turned off the TV and gave a deep sigh of contentment.

It was better than he'd hoped! He now had proof that what he was doing had meaning! Although the parents of the third victim had refused to speak to the media, that didn't matter; the other two couples supported him. They had even urged him to continue!

But immediately, he heard the same little inner voice as the night before.

*Is that why you called Monette yesterday? Because you suddenly need legitimacy?*

He frowned and lowered his eyes to the ribbon he was still holding. Wasn't Jasmine's death sufficient reason?

Wasn't *hate* sufficient reason?

For a second, he was shaken. Then he laughed. Of course he didn't need legitimacy! This report merely provided further evidence, external proof that he was right!

He nodded, thought for another moment, put the ribbon back in his pocket, and turned the television on again. He tried all the stations but didn't find anything interesting. He turned it off, stood up, and after a second's hesitation, walked to the little hallway. He was sure the monster wouldn't have recovered sufficiently to be tortured, but without really knowing why, he still wanted to see him.

The prisoner's one remaining eye was closed, but it opened when Bruno approached. Was it still possible to read fear in this abyss of resignation and despair? In spite of everything, he was a bit better than before. At least, he seemed more conscious, more lucid. Was he still suffering terribly? Or had his body gone completely numb?

He tried to lick his lips and said in that hoarse yet childlike voice, "I wish I could see my mother . . ."

Bruno went closer to him.

"I wish I could see . . . my mother . . ."

Bruno felt a sudden wave of nausea. Without thinking, he hit the monster hard on his broken nose. The monster moaned feebly.

At least the punch that had broken the monster's nose last night had given Bruno a few seconds of satisfaction. This time he didn't feel anything.

Of course! What he wanted was not to punch him in the nose, but to tear out his . . . break his . . .

*Kill him . . . Get this over with and kill him.*

It was the second time this ridiculous thought had come to him, and it exasperated him so much that he actually roared, startling the monster, who found the strength to give his torturer an astonished look.

Bruno rushed from the room and went into the kitchen, where he stopped, out of breath. Why such a rage? He had found the television report he had watched just a few minutes ago encouraging. Leaning against the wall, he felt his right hand trembling. Bewildered, he held it up in front of his eyes.

My God, what was happening to him?

He punched the wall and really hurt his hand, which had a calming effect on him.

He began to think in a serious and structured way. In two or three hours, he would be able to go back to his ladder and climb a couple of rungs higher.

But he had been telling himself that for two days now!

He recalled the interviews with the parents and regained some assurance. But again, the little inner voice repeated its tedious question:

*Why do you need legitimacy?*

He opened the fridge and took out a beer. He drank it in less than
two minutes, looking out the window at the rain.

———

"There's been no trace of him so far," Cabana said at the other end of the
line. "But we still have a lot of ground to cover, we've barely searched a
quarter of . . ."

"Is the SQ cooperating?" asked Wagner.

"Very well. With our guys, there are sixteen on the case."

Wagner hung up morosely and summarized the call to Mercure.
With four other officers, they were watching the end of the special report on the television set in the squad room.

Mercure listened to the hysterical mother who was sorry she couldn't
be with Hamel for the week; he looked dejected.

"I understand her," Boisvert said. "She'll feel a lot better if Hamel
kills Lemaire."

"We know what you think, Boisvert. There's no need for you to tell
us again!" Wagner said.

"I think I understand why Hamel wanted this report," Mercure murmured.

Wagner nodded as if he too understood. Mercure thought about the
idea he had had the night before about Hamel going off the rails.

"In any case," sighed Pleau, gesturing toward the TV with her chin,
"this kind of report is not going to encourage Hamel to turn himself in!"

Mercure stroked his cheek. He asked, "The journalist said the parents of one of the victims had refused to speak to reporters, didn't he?"

Wagner confirmed it. Mercure ordered Pat to call TVA and ask them
for the name of those parents. Wagner asked Mercure where he was
going with this.

"I want to meet with those parents."

"Why?"

Mercure remained silent, his eyes still riveted to the screen, although he was lost in thought and no longer saw it. He wanted to know why those parents had refused. He might be able to use the information . . . maybe.

After some ten minutes on the phone, Pat explained that there was only the mother; the father had died eight years ago. Her name was Diane Masson and she lived in Saint-Hyacinthe. Her eight-year-old daughter Charlotte had been raped and murdered four years ago.

"Do you have her phone number?"

Boisvert gave it to him, and Mercure immediately dialed it, while Wagner watched curiously. In his usual soft, hoarse voice, Mercure asked to meet the woman that afternoon. She was reluctant, but he finally got her to agree. He took down the address, thanked her, and hung up. Now Boisvert and Pleau were also looking at him curiously.

"Would you tell me why you want to meet with her?" asked the chief impatiently.

"Later . . ."

He was already heading for the door when he stopped short and went back to the telephone. He wanted to call Sylvie, Hamel's partner, to ask if she had watched the news just now. And what she thought of the report.

The phone rang for a long time and the answering machine did not pick up. He finally hung up.

"Hervé . . . ," Wagner persisted.

But Mercure was already out the door.

————

He had been watching TV for more than two hours, watching one channel for ten seconds and then changing to another channel. Since the television could only get five channels, it did not take long to go through all of them. But as the empty beer bottles accumulated at his feet, the channels changed less and less quickly. Bruno looked down and counted the number of empties: eight. Good God! It was crazy to drink so much! Getting drunk was really not a good idea. He had had proof of that two days ago.

He checked his watch, his vision a little blurry: three fifty. Maybe the monster had already regained enough strength. He'd have to go see . . . He turned off the TV, stood up, and felt dizzy for a second. He was going to head toward the hallway, but the dizziness persisted, and he went to the kitchen to throw some water on his face. He reached his hand toward the sink and saw that it was still trembling.

"Christ! Stop shaking!" he shouted.

Maybe he should wait until he sobered up . . . or else he might not feel anything, like two days ago.

Was he looking for reasons not to act?

Ridiculous! He would go immediately, right away! And he would kill him!

No, no, not kill him! Tomorrow! Not till tomorrow! Until then, he had to . . . he needed to . . . he must reach the top of the ladder, the summit of satisfaction.

He raised his eyes to the window, taking a deep breath. Outside, the rain had finally stopped, but the dark sky clearly showed that it was only a pause. Suddenly, he saw a silhouette skipping among the trees. It immediately disappeared behind a huge trunk, but he had had enough time to glimpse a familiar blue dress and a mane of chestnut hair.

He reached the door in one leap and ran outside without a coat, impervious to the cold. The sky was so overcast that it seemed like evening. The gray lake merged seamlessly with the low clouds.

"Jasmine!"

Hadn't something moved there in the woods? But Bruno wasn't sure, and the filter over his eyes made everything uniformly gray and flat. He went down the porch steps and into the forest. His shoes dragged through the dead leaves and caught on roots. He ran through the trees, ignoring the branches scratching his face, his path winding and slowed by drunkenness and by that damn heaviness that was always with him now. His crazed eyes searched for the silhouette, for his daughter. She was close by, he was sure of it, she hadn't had time to go very far.

He felt a presence behind him and turned around. He caught his breath. Jasmine was standing less than ten meters away. She was partly hidden by the branches, but he could see her tattered blue dress, her disheveled hair, her lacerated arms and legs . . . and her face, her beautiful face, covered with brownish scabs. He couldn't read her expression. Pain? Indifference? Sadness? He was convinced, however, that she was looking at him, standing straight and motionless, her skin wet with the rain from before.

No, it was not rain . . .

He started walking toward her like a sleepwalker and reached out a trembling hand.

"Jasmine!"

He thought he saw a glimmer of sadness in her eyes, a trace of disappointment on her bloodied face. And then she took two steps to the side and disappeared behind a tree.

"Jasmine!"

He ran, barely noticing that the echo of his calls was greatly amplified. He ran to the tree she had disappeared behind, his little Jasmine, his daughter, for whom he was doing all this.

There was no one behind the tree.

Stunned, Bruno looked around. His shoulders sagged as if all his strength had deserted him. He leaned his back against the tree and let himself slide to the ground. He crossed his hands over his folded knees and bent his head toward the muddy forest floor.

He was still.

———

When the detective sergeant returned from Saint-Hyacinthe, Wagner immediately joined him in his office. Mercure had an odd expression on his face, but when the chief came in, he shook himself and asked, "Any news of Hamel?"

"Nothing," Wagner said. "But they haven't searched everywhere yet. And you? Are you finally going to tell me the reason for your little visit to that woman?"

"I've convinced Diane Masson to talk to the reporters. It wasn't easy, but she agreed to do it. When she told me what she thought of this whole

Hamel business, I told her she should say it on TV, that it might help with our investigation."

"How's that? What's she going to say?"

Mercure hesitated, and his strange look came back.

"You'll soon see, on the news."

Wagner almost lost his temper, but Mercure seemed so anxious that he kept his mouth shut. The chief had a strong suspicion that the Hamel case was having an odd effect on Mercure's mind, an effect that must take him back to Madelaine's death . . .

. . . and maybe that visit to Saint-Hyacinthe had also created some strong vibrations.

Wagner knew that Mercure would talk to him about it when he was ready. So he nodded and left the office in silence.

———

The rain started again a little before six o'clock, and Bruno was still sitting against the tree, his face blank. He had been in the same position for almost two hours. He had not even been aware of the gradual coming of darkness, and it was only the first scattered drops that finally roused him from his catatonia. He looked around at the dark silhouettes of the trees and staggered to his feet. What was he doing here?

He had seen Jasmine.

He rubbed his face. He had been completely delirious.

The rain came down harder and Bruno turned around to go back. He could still feel the effects of the alcohol in his head, but the drunkenness was now only a faint intoxication.

In spite of the darkness, he found his way back to the cottage quite easily. As soon as he got there, he went to his prisoner's room. The monster had recuperated quite a lot now, and Bruno had to act. Things were really becoming urgent. But he felt so numb . . .

He looked at the time: three minutes after six. The news would be starting. Why not watch the report from noon again? It would get him in the mood, energize him, get rid of this numbness. And maybe there were new details.

Without sitting down, he tuned in to TVA, and soon they were talking about him. They explained again that he was hiding in the Charette area, and they listed the nine possible municipalities and gave the telephone number for the provincial police. Then they repeated the report from noon, and Bruno watched it again with the same sick pleasure. He had already taken a step toward the hallway, his appetite whetted, when the news reader announced that the mother of the third victim, Diane Masson, had finally agreed to talk to reporters in the afternoon, although she had refused in the morning. Interested, Bruno finally sat down.

A woman in her late thirties appeared on the screen. Not particularly beautiful or ugly, she gave an impression of strength and assurance. Sitting in her living room with five or six microphones from different radio and television stations pointed at her, she spoke in a cool, completely calm voice.

"Yes, I know Dr. Hamel is now holding the rapist and murderer of my dear Charlotte. But I do not agree with what he's doing. The murderer should be in the police's hands, not Dr. Hamel's. My husband died when my daughter was only three, but I'm sure he would have agreed with me."

Bruno's mouth slowly opened, and his eyes widened.

A journalist asked, "But after all these years of not knowing who murdered your daughter, don't you feel any satisfaction knowing that he is now suffering as much as your child and his other victims?"

An almost imperceptible grimace of pain passed over Diane Masson's face, but she recovered very quickly and answered in an even voice, "I just want to move on. And if Dr. Hamel is listening now, I want to say this to him: Don't kill that man tomorrow. Stop what you're doing and return him to the police."

Bruno's eyes were not wide open now, but almost closed—two thin incandescent slits that stared piercingly at the television screen.

"A point of view different from that of the other parents," the news anchor said. "A point of view that, in fact, is diametrically opposed . . ."

But Bruno was not listening anymore. His body straight and stiff, his muscles tensed to the breaking point, he mentally went over the woman's words. How could she be so insensitive? Didn't she care about her daughter's killer being punished?

She was a heartless woman! That was the only explanation! One of those cold mothers who had no feeling for their children!

He turned his attention back to the TV, where he once again saw groups of demonstrators, some for him, others against. The reporter's voice said, "For the first time, two opposing groups met in Drummondville about an hour ago. There was no violence, but there were heated verbal exchanges."

The screen showed dozens and dozens of men and women on the wet street, screaming insults at each other, many of them carrying signs saying either "Hamel Defender of Justice" or "Vengeance Is Wrong," depending on the camp they were in. There were a few close-ups of people explaining their positions. One of them looked straight at the camera and proclaimed, "Tomorrow will be a great day for justice!"

Bruno muted the sound, infuriated by the shouting of the demonstrators.

But he couldn't get Diane Masson out of his mind, and his rage swelled. And his hands started trembling again.

He leapt to his feet . . . He was going to go and hurt the monster. Hurt him bad, hurt him more than he had since he'd brought him here.

But he didn't go.

Was it that bitch who was making him have doubts all of a sudden? Of course not! It was just that he was too excited; if he went to the monster now, he would be carried away by rage and would surely kill him.

He took another beer. His hands were trembling so much that he couldn't unscrew the cap and he had to use a bottle opener.

Bruno spent the next half hour in complete turmoil, his mind beset by disturbing thoughts. He paced from one end of the house to the other, stopped, started again, walked decisively toward the monster's room and then froze and retraced his steps, muttered, tried to sit down and stood up again right away. He drank two beers without even realizing it, knocking over the empty bottles, which rolled across the floor.

The additional beer reawakened his drunkenness. In that mental storm, there was one constant: the words of Diane Masson. He could not get them out of his head. The other parents understood what he was doing! Why didn't she? All he had to do was forget about her, ignore her. That wasn't so complicated! Except that he wasn't able to do it. Suddenly, he wished he could talk to her and show her he was right. Yes, to have her in front of him and convince her! Convince her because . . . because . . .

Idiot, idiot, *idiot*!

And he hit the wall again, and started going around in circles again.

He stopped short, struck by an idea. He went to his bedroom and put on his false beard and wig. He came back into the living room and put on his coat. His movements were quick, but oddly jerky because of the alcohol . . . and maybe because of something else as well, a mental turmoil that threw off his whole body.

He went into the monster's room and took one of his bags. He turned toward the table and stood still for a moment. The monster was sleeping, his breath wheezing. Bruno felt the hatred rising inside him like a volcanic eruption. He had to hurt him right away. He hadn't tortured him all day. Something, anything, there were so many possibilities!

*Put out his other eye, cut off his testicles, push blades under his fingernails, stick a knife in his anus, cut out his tongue, tear the skin off his belly, puncture his eardrums, cut, tear, split, smash, pierce, poke, crush . . .*

A sudden dizziness made him stagger. He held his head in both hands and spat at the monster. Then he left the room, carrying the bag, and was soon outside.

The rain had started again, and this time the wind had come with it. Once on Pioneers Road, Bruno maintained a good speed, cutting through the wall of rain, which constantly re-formed behind him.

He was drunk, but he felt as if his senses had never been so acute, his reflexes so sharp.

What he was planning to do was absurd, he knew it. He knew that Saint-Hyacinthe was nearly two hours away. He knew, above all, that the region was crawling with cops looking for him. And yet that didn't worry him at all. In spite of all the beer he had drunk, he was driving well. When after ten minutes he came upon a police car, he didn't cringe. He didn't feel the least shiver of anxiety. They would never recognize him in the middle of the night in this weather! And the cops couldn't stop every car they met! Indeed, the police car went by without slowing down.

Although Bruno tightened his grip on the steering wheel, his hands were trembling more and more.

———

In the squad room, they were all watching the last sentences of Diane Masson's surprise appearance on TV. Boisvert was appalled; he did not understand. How could a woman whose daughter had been raped and murdered by Lemaire talk this way? Pleau gave a little sigh of irritation, and Wagner shot her an angry look, wondering how he could get her to shut up.

"Is this your doing, Hervé?" asked Boisvert, turning toward Mercure. "You went to see her this afternoon to convince her to say that, didn't you?"

Mercure, sitting on the corner of a desk, said he had met with her to find out why she had refused to talk to the media. When she explained to him, he had indeed convinced her to speak publicly.

"But those are her words, her ideas, not mine," Mercure added.

"And do you think those words will get to Hamel and make him turn himself in?" asked Bolduc.

Mercure took time to think before answering.

"I'm hoping they will push him over the top."

The other officers did not seem to understand, but Wagner was watching his inspector closely.

"Well, it wouldn't make me feel any doubts at all!" muttered Boisvert, kicking at the desk leg.

"Listen, Boisvert, if I hear another comment like that, I'll suspend you for three days!"

"He's not wrong, though," Bolduc ventured timidly.

For a second, Wagner was so enraged that he could only sputter.

When he finally got his voice back, he thundered, "I don't want to hear any more personal opinions about Hamel's actions! We're going to do everything we can to find him in the next twenty-four hours, because that's our job, dammit! Is that clear?"

The officers, daunted, were quiet. Wasn't there a story about Wagner once in one of his fits of rage biting another cop's ear? When his complexion returned more or less to normal, the chief turned to Pat, who was still at the telephone, and asked, "Any news from Mauricie?"

A stupid question, since he knew very well that the telephone had not rung for more than an hour, but he could not help asking. Pat shook his head.

Wagner turned to Mercure and said quietly, "It is incredible, though . . . that woman's detachment about what happened to her daughter, isn't it?"

"It's not really detachment, it's more complicated than that. For television, she simplified things a bit, but . . ."

He stopped. He had the same troubled look as before.

"She told you more this afternoon, huh?" asked Wagner.

"Let's say it was more . . . detailed."

But he did not elaborate. Wagner looked at him for a long time.

———

Since the rain and wind had slowed him down, it was a little after nine when Bruno stopped his car on a quiet little street in Saint-Hyacinthe. He stared hard at the house across the street. The lighted windows looked like beacons cutting through the darkness and the rain.

Since Diane Masson was a single parent, he had not had any problem finding her address in the telephone directory. Then he had taken the risk of going into a service station and buying a map of the town. The clerk, an adolescent with his nose in a used car magazine, had barely looked at his dirty, smelly, unshaven customer.

Bruno noticed that his gas tank was three-quarters empty. Would he have to fill up on the way back? He was improvising way too much all of a sudden.

He studied the house for a while. A nice beer would do him some good. He had been racked with thirst throughout the two hours on the road.

He opened his bag. First he prepared a cloth soaked in chloroform, and then a hypodermic syringe. He put the cloth in one coat pocket, the syringe in another, and examined the surroundings. The shower was helping him: there wasn't a soul in the streets. However, he saw a silhouette in one of the lighted windows of the house next door. He waited a moment. When the silhouette had disappeared, he quickly got out of the car and ran to the carport, stumbling a little. There no one could see him. He leaned against the parked automobile, took a few deep breaths, and walked to the door that led to the carport. No neighbors would see him go in or out.

At the door, he hesitated. Even if it was not locked, what would he do once he was in the house? And what if Diane Masson wasn't alone? He pinched the bridge of his nose hard, closing his eyes. The kidnapping of the monster had been planned to perfection, with nothing left to chance. And now, one day from the end, he was taking foolish risks. And for what? To convince this woman?

Shit! He should get out of here right away, before it was too late!

But he grasped the doorknob and turned it cautiously, as if he were afraid of triggering an explosion. A click. The door opened a crack. He pushed it a little and poked his head inside. A kitchen. In the sink, the remnants of a recent supper.

He stepped into the room slowly and carefully. His forehead was wet, more with sweat than with rain. A little hallway led to an open room on the left, probably the living room. From that room, he heard a voice. Diane Masson was not alone—he had to get out as quickly as possible! But then he realized that she was on the telephone. Reassured, he took a few steps down the little hallway and stopped. His back pressed against the wall, he listened, and he finally made out what the woman in the living room was saying.

"No, the inspector didn't force me to do anything! I thought about it and I agreed. It was my choice, Éric."

The inspector? Who was she talking about?

Mercure! Mercure, who had bothered him with that ridiculous story of the dog, had apparently convinced Diane Masson to talk to the media!

"No, I'd rather be alone, but thank you. These memories are too personal, do you understand? And I have to face them alone. Yes . . . I love you too."

The sound of the receiver being hung up. Bruno heard what he thought was a sigh (or a sob?) and then a rustling sound: she had stood up.

Still pressed against the wall, Bruno held his breath and took out his chloroform-soaked cloth.

And suddenly she appeared. Even before she saw him, Bruno had grabbed her with his free hand, pushed her against the wall, and pressed the cloth to her mouth and nose. A muffled scream. She struggled, but uselessly; she was small and frail. Her wide eyes, full of surprise and fear, were staring at Bruno, making him uncomfortable. He closed his eyes without releasing his grip. After several seconds, her jerking movements lost their intensity and her body went slack, and then completely inert. Bruno opened his eyes. Diane Masson was asleep.

He started breathing noisily. He stuffed the cloth in his pocket, absentmindedly wiped his mouth, and picked the woman up. He walked to the door with his burden, but then it occurred to him that he could not very well cross the street carrying a body in his arms. Someone might see him.

He thought of Diane Masson's car, in the carport, where no one could see it. And thought that it would not be dangerous to take that car, since its disappearance would not be reported until the next day, probably in the evening, and by then, it would all be over. Plus, if there was enough gas in the tank, he would not have to stop at a service station.

He found her handbag and took out the keys. He checked the blue-gray Honda Civic; the tank was half-full, which would be plenty. He put Diane Masson on the back seat of her own car and gave her an injection that would keep her asleep for close to three hours.

Two minutes later, the car backed into the street. Still nobody around. He did, however, see a silhouette in one window, the same one as before. Probably a nosy neighbor. He congratulated himself on his idea.

The car drove away. Behind the steering wheel, Bruno licked his lips. He should have looked in Masson's fridge to see if there was any beer.

———

In spite of the deluge, a dozen patrol cars, some from Drummondville, some from the provincial police, continued searching the area around Charette.

At nine twenty-three, ninety minutes before Bruno Hamel's return, a provincial police car driving along Pioneers Road passed the lane leading to Josh's cottage. But it barely slowed down, and sped up again when the driver noted that this address was not on the list of rental cabins. It was a private property. So there was no reason to check it out. How could Hamel hide in an inhabited house for a week?

All day, they had questioned the owners of motels and hotels, waiters in restaurants and merchants. At ten twenty-five, the cashier in the convenience store on the main street of Saint-Mathieu du-Parc, the one who had served Bruno Hamel two days before, was shown a photo of the doctor by a Drummondville policeman. She put on an apologetic look and replied that the face meant nothing to her, she saw so many customers every day. And as the policeman returned to his car under the rain, a little smile appeared on the woman's lips.

———

The station was practically empty. Wagner passed Mercure's office and saw the detective sergeant sitting there, his arms crossed. He went in and asked him what he was doing.

"I'm waiting."

"You're waiting!" Wagner said with humorless irony. "Is that all you can find to do?"

Mercure looked up at him. "There are a couple dozen officers searching the perimeter right now. So, at a quarter after midnight, can you tell me what else I could be doing?"

Wagner rarely saw his colleague act so cold, and he was contrite. Mercure sighed and apologized.

"We're all worn out, I think," Wagner responded.

They said nothing for a moment, and then the chief asked, "What did you really hope to get out of that interview with Diane Masson?"

Mercure put his hands behind his head and gazed into the distance.

"I have the impression . . ." He narrowed his eyes, thinking. "I have the impression that when I talked to Hamel about the dog thing yesterday, it upset him. So much so that he did something that was not planned: he called a journalist to talk about Lemaire's other victims. As if he suddenly needed to justify everything, to justify himself. I think it set off a sort of chain reaction. I wanted to add another link to the chain by asking Diane Masson to talk on TV; I knew Hamel wouldn't like it."

"That's what you meant when you spoke about him going off the rails? You think he deviated from the path he'd planned?"

"Yes, I think so."

"To the point of giving up the whole thing?"

"That's what I'm hoping."

Wagner considered this idea for a moment and looked dubious.

"But he could deviate from his path in the other direction too . . . He could finish Lemaire off sooner, even tonight."

"I know."

Mercure had said this in an even voice, but he had lowered his eyes. This time the silence was longer.

"Are you going to spend the night here?" asked Wagner.

Mercure did not answer, and the chief nodded.

"Me too, I think."

The wind briefly shook the glass in the window.

"What did Masson tell you this afternoon?"

Wagner had decided earlier to wait for Mercure to raise the subject, but this seemed like the perfect time to make an overture. With his hands still behind his neck, Mercure looked up at the chief. He gave a little smile that, though humorless, expressed real closeness. Wagner returned the smile.

"Go get yourself a coffee, and bring me one too," Mercure responded.

Bruno was standing two meters from the couch and saw her open her eyes. She seemed disoriented. She sniffed and made a face. Seeing Bruno, she sat up quickly and appeared dizzy, but quickly recovered. On the alert, she stared intently at him. She was afraid, certainly, but he admired her calm control. This was not a woman who was much given to panicking.

"What do you want with me?" asked Diane Masson a bit breathlessly. "Who are you?"

And suddenly she frowned. Her face expressed doubt, then astonishment. He knew she'd recognized him.

"My God," she said.

"It was about time you woke up," he said. "I was going to start without you."

She swallowed and asked, "Start what?"

"Taking care of the monster."

He watched her reaction. She paled a bit, but returned his gaze.

"I'm sure you'd like to hear him yelp."

"Hear what?"

"Scream, I mean."

He grimaced in annoyance. She sniffed again, nauseated.

"Lord, what's that awful smell?"

Bruno did not reply. He no longer noticed the smell in the house, and he hadn't for a long time. She looked at the mess in the house, Bruno's clothes, his face . . .

"What's happened to you?"

She looked into his eyes.

"What's *happening* to you?"

He shrugged and took a swig of beer.

"And you're drunk."

Probably a little, yes, but he was in control. His trembling hands kept trying to indicate otherwise, but he dismissed them. In fact, he had now decided to dismiss everything. He had said to hell with everybody.

Except this woman, this woman he wanted to convince, *needed* to convince.

He had a slight headache. He rubbed his forehead and paced a few steps.

"I saw what you said on television. Did Mercure make you say that?"

"Inspector Mercure didn't make me do anything. What I said is what I really think."

"You think what I'm doing is not right?"

"I think it's pointless."

Bruno licked his lips without taking his eyes off her. He said, "You must not have loved your daughter to talk that way . . ."

"I forbid you to talk that way," retorted Masson in a slightly hoarse voice. "I loved Charlotte at least as much as you loved your daughter."

"Then why don't you want her murderer dead?"

"That's not what I said."

Outside, the rain had become so violent that it felt like the whole lake was being poured onto the house.

"Why did you bring me here?"

And she looked around, as if she was trying to understand where she was. All the curtains were closed, so she could not see outside. Bruno gulped down the rest of his beer, dropped the bottle on the wood floor, and walked quickly toward the hallway, saying, "Come here."

"No, no way."

He turned toward her. She was standing in a strange position, as if she were about to enter a haunted castle. She tried to keep her expression firm, but cracks were showing.

"I know where you want to take me, and I refuse."

"Can you honestly tell me you don't want to see him!"

"That's the last thing I want!"

Bruno frowned, disconcerted by her attitude. But that was because she wasn't yet standing in front of him. Once she had the monster at her feet, she would change her mind . . .

And he wanted her to change her mind! To admit he was right! *That he was right!* And when she understood, the two of them would torture the monster together! It would be magnificent! They would be joined in vengeance and hate! And tomorrow, they would finish him off together! She had to understand! She *had to*!

"If you refuse to come see him, I'll force you!"

She remained motionless. Bruno stepped forward threateningly. She started and raised her arms. Okay, she'd do it! Satisfied, Bruno told her to go first. Walking with stiff, hesitant steps, she went into the little hallway. Bruno, behind her, told her to go into the room on the left. She stopped in the doorway for a moment to catch her breath, and went in.

When Bruno entered behind her, she was in the middle of the room with her back to him, motionless, two meters from the monster. The monster was unconscious, and he was now hanging from the two chains in the ceiling, a few centimeters from the floor, his breath wheezing. From time to time, he would move his head a little and moan feebly, but he did not open his eyes. The rain was pounding on the window, which was hidden by a curtain.

Bruno saw that Masson was covering her nose with her left hand, but he could not see her face. He tried to guess her expression. Surprise? Revulsion? Joy at seeing the monster in this condition? Anyway, she could not continue to be as detached as she claimed to be, it was impossible! He took a few steps to the right so he could see her face. With fierce joy, he recognized a flash of hate, if not of anger, in her eyes. But another emotion, bigger and more powerful, showed in her eyes, and her face and her whole body.

Distress.

Could she actually pity the monster? No, that wasn't it: the tiny flash of hatred contradicted that. The distress did not concern the monster, but seemed to . . . seemed to concern her.

Bruno was unable to react for several seconds. Then he walked to the closet, opened the door, took out the whip, and held it out to Masson. It took her several seconds to turn and look at it. Bruno waited, his face hard, the whip still in his hand. A gust of wind shook the house. The breathing of the sleeping monster filled the room. The whip trembled in Bruno's hand, but he did not even notice it.

A horrible grimace of disgust twisted Masson's mouth and she rushed from the room. After a second of surprise, Bruno dropped the whip and hurried out, sure he would find her at the door of the house. But she was in the living room, standing motionless with her back to him and her face in her hands.

"What's the matter with you?" he shouted. "You've got the murderer of your Charlotte in front of you and you're acting like a horrified little girl!"

She smothered a sob behind her hands. Bruno walked over to her, his fists clenched.

"What's the matter with you?"

Still no answer. Exasperated, Bruno grabbed the woman by the shoulders and turned her around.

"Say something, for Chrissakes!"

There was no longer horror on her face, or panic. Her calm had returned and her eyes were dry, although the pain was still there, ready to surface again at any moment.

"Do you have any idea what you've just done—done to *me*?"

He did not answer. He did not understand.

"This man no longer existed for me. I had stopped thinking about him."

"That's impossible!" retorted Bruno brutally.

"Of course it's possible! For the first three years, I wanted him dead. I had no love left for anyone, not for friends, not for lovers, not for myself. For three years, I lived in hatred. But there's no bottom to hatred, you keep sinking deeper, and I realized that as long as that man existed in my mind, I couldn't exist. Every time I thought of Charlotte, my memories would be tainted by blood and anger. And that's worse than anything."

Bruno did not move a centimeter. He would have liked to order her to be quiet, but he said nothing. Masson was speaking more and more slowly, separating each syllable. She was still looking at Bruno, but with a distant gaze. She took a deep breath and continued.

"So one year ago, I . . . I erased this man from my mind. I put the hatred behind me and I learned to live again."

"You forgot about your daughter!"

"Not my daughter, the man who killed her!" she replied harshly.

But that harshness only lasted a second, and she calmed down again.

"There's not a morning I get up without thinking about Charlotte, not a night I go to bed without feeling her arms around my neck. But I am finally open to life. Happy, I don't know, but . . . open. And especially, especially . . ."

She smiled, now serene, and Bruno was surprised to suddenly find her incredibly beautiful.

". . . when I think about my daughter, I don't see her all bloody anymore, but smiling, beautiful, and happy."

She finally seemed to really see Bruno, and her eyes darkened and filled with tears.

"And after all this time, you've . . . you've come and spoiled everything! You've brought my daughter's killer back to life! Not to hand him over to the police, no! That would have been less awful! Once arrested, he would quickly have gone out of my life again. No! You're holding him hostage, you're torturing him, you taunted me on television, and you . . . you plunged me back into darkness!"

Bruno was silent, impressed. Masson's features tensed in a desperate anger, but she wasn't crying yet.

"Inspector Mercure told me that if I said what I felt on TV, you might come to your senses! And like an idiot, I believed him! I believed him, and the worst possible thing happened: you brought me here and put me in front of *him*! Even though I didn't want it! Because I knew that if I saw him, the hatred would come back!"

This time the tears flowed, and her voice swelled with rage.

"And it came back! Do you understand what I'm saying? *It came back!*"

She gave two short, heartrending sobs, and a wave of feeling contorted her face.

"You know what I felt just now when I saw that man? I felt like my daughter had died again! And this time it's your fault! *You killed my daughter a second time!*"

Bruno was breathing noisily now. The consternation on his face gradually turned to cold anger. Diane Masson suddenly calmed down. She stopped crying, but there were still tears on her cheeks. The distress in her eyes gave way to immense pity, and she said in a faint voice, "And for the last week, with each torture you have inflicted on this man, you have killed your daughter. Again and again and again."

The punch came spontaneously. Because he had to shut her up, he had to stop her from saying such obscenities! His fist connected with Masson's jaw in a precise blow so powerful that the sound echoed off the walls, filling Bruno's skull with pain. He closed his eyes and pressed his hands over his ears, grimacing, for several seconds, until the echo finally faded and he opened his eyes again, panting. Masson was lying on the floor, unconscious.

"You have no right to say that, you bitch!" he shouted at the inert body. "You understand nothing about what I'm doing! Nothing, nothing, NOTHING!"

Still hurling insults, he walked around her. Why had she given him that sermon? Did she think she was going to change his mind? Who did she think she was dealing with? On a sudden impulse, he took from his pocket the little key that opened the rings on his prisoner's wrists, went to the door, and with the wind blowing the rain in, threw it with all his strength toward the forest. He closed the door again with a grunt of satisfaction. Even dead, the monster would rot in his chains! Bruno took a beer from the fridge and went back to Masson. He looked at her in confusion.

To hell with her! He would take care of the monster alone, that was all! He just had to give this heartless bitch a powerful sedative and she would sleep until the next day. But he knew that wouldn't work. She was supposed to join with him, not be against him! Even reduced to silence, her mere presence in the house would bother him, ruin his concentration, keep him from . . . from . . .

He gulped down the rest of the beer and threw the empty bottle against the wall, smashing it.

Dazed, he stared at Masson. She was breathing strangely. In fact, it wasn't breathing, it was . . . yes, the panting of a dog . . .

She couldn't stay there.

"Bitch, bitch, *bitch*!" he screamed.

He bent over toward her, lost his balance, and collapsed on the floor. He got to his feet again, cursing, and went and put on his coat, not bothering with his disguise. With difficulty, he put his arms under the woman and lifted her. He almost lost his balance again, and the living room started spinning. God, he was more drunk than he'd thought! But the confusion in his mind was not because of the alcohol, he knew that. It was *her*! She had to go! Her dog panting was getting louder and louder and would soon fill the whole house, echoing, it would be unbearable!

Outside, the storm was getting worse. Bruno thought he heard thunder in the distance, but he wasn't sure. The rain was so noisy, the forest was so full of activity, his mind was so confused . . .

Not very gently, he threw Masson onto the back seat of the Honda Civic. Before getting into the driver's seat, he had a moment of indecision and went back into the house. He took another beer, hesitated, and then, with a shrug, picked up the case and took it with him.

He turned the key; the engine roared and the headlights came on, lighting up the turbulent lake twenty meters from the car. A moan was audible over the din of the storm—Masson was about to wake up!

Bruno got out of the car and went back into the house again. He ran to the monster's room, but his footsteps were becoming more and more unsure and he banged his shin on the chair and cried out in pain and rage. In the room, without a glance at his unconscious prisoner, he prepared an injection, having to start over twice because his hands were trembling so much. Then he hobbled out again.

Diane Masson's eyes were open and she was half sitting up on the back seat, looking at the lake in a daze. She barely had time to recognize Bruno before he stuck the needle in her arm. Ten seconds later, she was fast asleep.

Reassured, Bruno took a deep breath and sat down behind the steering wheel. Looking out at the deluge, he hesitated. It seemed completely insane to drive in this weather. Now that Masson was asleep, he could just leave her there, couldn't he?

No. The storm was not only outside, but also in his head. And it would not subside as long as this woman remained in the house! Her last words, those horrible, insulting words, would stay in his head as long as she was here! Above all, he knew he couldn't torture the monster with her in the house. It was absurd, but that's the way it was!

In a rage, he put the car in gear and backed up the lane. He scraped a tree but made it to the road.

As the car accelerated, Bruno reached into the case and grabbed a beer.

———

Leaning against the wall, Wagner took a swallow of coffee. Mercure, behind his desk, was playing with his empty cup. For several seconds, the only sound was the wind and rain against the windowpanes. Then the chief said, "It's more detailed than what she said on TV, but . . . Why does all this upset you so much? If I know you, I'm sure you agree with her."

"That's not the question. It's just that . . . it takes me back to Madelaine's death . . . and Demers."

Wagner nodded understandingly. Mercure looked at his cup as he spoke.

"All these years, I've been trying to convince myself that my visits to Demers were a way to fight the anger. Trying to understand is better than living in hatred, isn't it?"

He looked up at Wagner. The chief did not answer. Mercure looked back down at the cup and sighed.

"Well, I'm not so sure anymore, that's just it."

He started tearing the cup into tiny pieces.

"Of everything Masson told me, you know what shook me up the most? It was that all that time that she was living with hate and anger, she was only able to see images of her daughter dead. In order to remember her alive and happy, she had to erase Lemaire. That's what she said: *erase*."

He dropped the remains of the cup and looked up at the window.

"But if I erased Demers, it seems to me that . . . that it wouldn't be fair to Madelaine."

"That may be exactly what Hamel has told himself," Wagner said softly. "If he does not kill Lemaire, it wouldn't be fair to his daughter."

Mercure grimaced, rubbed his face, and gave a long sigh. Wagner thought to himself that he had never looked so gaunt. Mercure's voice was no more than a whisper now.

"The other day, Demers told me that in visiting him, I was his worst torturer."

A sad smile.

"Have I been living in hate all these years without realizing it?"

"I think it's more complicated than that, Hervé."

Mercure nodded absently. There was a clap of thunder. Wagner turned toward the window and, with his face lit up by a flash of lightning, growled, "That's it, with the storm now . . ."

———

Bruno had been driving for about three-quarters of an hour, quite carelessly. He had met very few cars and he wouldn't have been able to say if they were police or ordinary people. Even on the highway, the traffic was very thin. He had drunk two more beers during this time, and the Honda was tending more and more to drift to the right. Twice he had felt his tires touch the shoulder and had turned back onto the pavement at the last second. But he didn't want to slow down. He wanted to get rid of this woman as quickly as possible. He could sense her behind him, and ten times he had quickly turned around, sure that she was awake and was attacking him with her accusing eyes.

He had never drunk so much in a single day, and his vision was blurring. The rain had become arrows attacking the car, the lightning nuclear explosions, and the thunder earthquakes. He suddenly had the impression that the car was no longer moving forward, but was spinning like a top.

In a moment of lucidity, he pulled over onto the shoulder. Exhausted, he leaned his forehead against the steering wheel and took deep breaths.

He felt nauseated and opened the door, sure he was going to vomit. But nothing came out. The alcohol insisted on staying inside him to rot his mind.

But there was not only alcohol, he knew.

In spite of his confusion, he tried to think. He looked at the time: one forty. He couldn't get to Saint-Hyacinthe, it was still too far, he could get himself killed.

He got out in the fury of the storm, opened the back door, and pulled Diane Masson's body out. He laid her on the grass some distance from the road and got back in the car. He drove across the median, turned into the opposite lane, and sped away.

There, she wasn't there anymore! She wasn't in his way anymore! As soon as he got back to the cottage, he could have his fun with the monster in peace!

But he couldn't get the last words she had spoken out of his mind.

He opened another beer.

He turned off the highway onto a country road. He was still driving much too fast, but he didn't care. Ahead of him was hell, a dark hell of rain, headlights, and winding roads lit by apocalyptic flashes of lightning. And those claps of thunder were becoming more and more deafening, like the blows a giant would give an animal, a . . .

Two headlights in front of him. A truck. Spinning, spinning and spinning and . . .

Bruno jerked the wheel, and barely avoided the ten-wheeler, which passed him honking furiously. Drenched in sweat, he finished his beer, laughing. He defied the trucks, as he defied the weakness and cowardice of Diane Masson! He defied the storm to kill him, to prevent him from carrying out his vengeance, his mission!

He drove on, zigzagging along the roads, which were fortunately almost deserted. Suddenly, on a curve, the car went off the road into a soggy field that soon brought it to a halt. Muttering curses, Bruno tried to back up. But the car was stuck and he was spinning his wheels. He bellowed with rage, pounding the steering wheel. He tried a series of maneuvers, going forward ten centimeters, backing up five . . . and after ten minutes, he was finally back on the road. He drove off again without slowing down.

He wanted the monster. He needed to take his feelings out on him. It was the only way to shut that woman up, to smother her terrible words.

Blinding lightning. Deafening claps of thunder, echoing endlessly . . .

At two thirty-eight in the morning, he drove past the turnoff to the cottage. He braked as hard as he could and spun around twice. He drove back to the lane and turned down it. It was too narrow for the swerving car, but there was no question of slowing down. Just when he saw the house, he ran into a tree. His forehead hit the steering wheel, but he barely felt it. He screamed insults at the tree and got out of the car. He wanted to run to the house, but he could only stagger. He slipped three times, falling in the mud and getting up again, moaning.

And the heaviness that was weighing him down mercilessly was like two giant hands pushing down with all their strength on his shoulders.

He went into the house, ignoring the television that was on but muted. As he walked toward the hallway, he struggled out of his coat. He missed the turn and bumped into the wall. He punched it, splitting the side of his hand, and continued toward his prisoner's room, wild-eyed.

The monster, still hanging by the arms, had partly regained consciousness.

This time, Bruno would climb not just one rung, but the whole ladder! He would climb to the very top, until he exploded with this final satisfaction! That was what he had wanted from the beginning, what he wanted so much!

He went and got a scalpel and staggered to the winch and released it. The chains went slack and the monster crumpled to the floor. He gave a plaintive sound, opening wide a terrified eye.

Bruno bent down beside him, holding the scalpel. Strike, anywhere! Strike, that was all, *strike*!

And he lowered the scalpel toward the monster's right thigh. But the storm outside was still in his head, the lightning and thunder continued to bombard his brain, and his vision was still full of rain and darkness.

He missed his target and the scalpel dug into the floor. The monster gave a surprised cry, frantically moving his upper body and his chained hands. Swearing, Bruno picked up the blade and struck again. This time, the scalpel sank into the thigh. More cries from the monster, who could still find the strength to express pain, but there was also a disheartened resignation in those cries, as if he was tiring of his own suffering.

Bruno pulled out the blade. Nothing! He felt nothing! He looked at the bleeding thigh, listened to the monster's moans, but he felt no joy, no satisfaction. Nothing at all!

This time, he struck on the purplish right knee. The cry was more shrill, but Bruno still felt nothing! And the thunder didn't stop! And his vision was spinning more and more! And suddenly he was nauseated, he was very close to being sick. It was too much! This time, he took aim at the intact eye. But the monster's hand intervened and the scalpel went into his palm. Under the impact, the chained hand swung back and the surgical instrument described a long arc and disappeared into a corner of the room.

With both fists, Bruno started hitting that foul face, which lolled weakly from side to side. Half of his blows missed their target, but some were so violent that blood splattered on his face. That warm blood should have excited him, given him pleasure . . .

. . . but he still felt *nothing*!

He stood up with an insane shout and gave his victim a terrible kick in the belly. The monster gave a muffled cry, and excrement spurted from the slit in his abdomen. The sight of that shit disgusted Bruno and enraged him to the point of frenzy. With hoarse cries, he administered a hysterical series of kicks. And with each impact, the monster moaned . . . a moan that was more and more animal, more and more canine. There was no question of Bruno stopping now! He would stop when he finally felt satisfaction, when his thirst for vengeance and hate was sated, not before! *Not before!* And each kick produced a sound that was more and more hollow, and each time, the black body gave its animal moan.

The black body?

It was no longer bare, bloody flesh that Bruno had in front of him, but hairy flesh . . . Hallucinating, Bruno stopped kicking and finally looked closely at his prisoner.

It was no longer the monster. It was a dog, an enormous, bloody black dog with its two front legs chained, howling in agony.

Bruno was breathing so rapidly that his lungs were on fire. The nausea had come back stronger than ever, and the thunder was still hammering his head. No, it was not thunder, it was the blows he was giving the monster, whose echoes filled the room.

At his feet, the dog was still howling, its tongue hanging out.

Bruno was gripped by a terrible fear like none he had ever felt before. He backed to the door and ran into the living room. But he stopped immediately, realizing that the echoes were following him. Moaning, he went into the bedroom and closed the door. The echoes still caught up with him, they even seemed louder. With a cry of terror, Bruno went to throw himself on the bed, but missed it and landed sprawling on the floor. Blood gushed from his nose. He crawled to the bed, pulled himself up onto it, and hid his head under the pillow.

But the echoes of the blows did not stop! Because they were in his head, Bruno now understood! And no matter if he screamed, pounded the pillow, stuck his fingers in his ears, it didn't help! The nausea became too much for him and he vomited once, twice, crying. But the echoes continued, resonating in his head and through his whole body, all his muscles, down to the tips of his fingers.

Overcome by horror and delirium, he lost consciousness lying in his own filth.

# DAY 7

DIANE MASSON HAD BEEN SITTING IN THE INTERROGATION ROOM AT A TABLE with her third coffee on it for about twenty minutes. An hour earlier, a man had spotted her on Highway 20, waving her arms in the rain, which was gradually letting up. She was shaking so much that the man had suggested he take her to the hospital in Drummondville, thirty minutes away, but she had insisted on going to the police station.

Now, she was wearing clothes that were too big for her but dry, and she had a thick gray woolen blanket pulled tightly around her. She had just told her story and was finally silent again. Her eyes, bloodshot, with dark circles under them, were staring down at her coffee. She sniffed, reached a white hand to a box of tissues, and then blew her nose, something she had done a good thirty times over the last half hour. She had a big swollen bruise on the left side of her face.

Mercure was sitting across from her. He had taken off his jacket and loosened his necktie, a sign of exhaustion. Behind him, leaning against the wall with his arms crossed, stood Wagner, barely hiding his impatience. His tie was completely undone, with the ends hanging down on either side.

The clock on the wall read four thirty-nine.

"I'm sorry," murmured Mercure.

Masson looked up at him.

"I was hoping your interview on TV would get a reaction from him, but . . . never to the point that he would kidnap you. If I'd had the slightest inkling that he would do something so incredible, I would have had your house watched."

Besides, it would have been so simple to pick him up at her house. But he kept that thought to himself.

"I'm sorry," he repeated.

"It's not your fault."

But the speed with which she averted her eyes showed that she did feel some resentment toward him. In spite of his guilt, Mercure could not help feeling a little excited.

Wagner finally said something: "You told us you were asleep when he took you to his hideout. And you were also asleep on the way back?"

"Yes."

She picked up her coffee in both hands, took a sip, and thought. Mercure was impressed by her calm, by the perfect control she managed to maintain even after such an experience.

"But I woke up for a few seconds before we left again and . . . I was confused, but I'm sure we were in my car."

Mercure asked for the make and the license number. She gave them to him, and Wagner wrote them down.

"Did you see anything during those few seconds you were awake? The outside of the house, for example?"

"No, not the house . . . As I told you, I was very dizzy, but . . . I could see water not very far away in the car's headlights . . . a lake or a river, I don't know."

"Excellent!" exclaimed Wagner, walking to the door. "I'll get a list of municipalities where they rent out cottages close to a body of water!"

"It wasn't a rented cottage," Diane Masson said.

The two police officers looked at each other, surprised. The woman took another sip of coffee, her forehead furrowed.

"A cottage you rent doesn't have any personality . . . or, at least, it takes more than a week to give it one."

Wagner and Mercure were listening and holding their breath.

"This was a real house, with nice furnishings, but it had a . . . a personality, I don't have another word for it. There was a terrible mess, but the decor, the furniture, pictures on the walls, knickknacks . . . Someone lives in that house."

She shrugged wearily.

"It's not very scientific, but that's really the impression it gave me."

"Those sorts of impressions are often the best," Mercure said approvingly, with a little smile.

"But Hamel's cottage is in the Eastern Townships, not in Mauricie," objected Wagner.

"So he's in somebody else's house," replied Mercure.

Wagner agreed, although he was caught off guard. How had Hamel done that? Had he knocked out the owner and tied him up somewhere? Or had he chosen a house whose owners were away for at least a week?

"It doesn't matter!" exclaimed Wagner, heading to the door again. "I'll go tell the guys that now they should visit all houses close to a lake or river, including private properties. And they should go in even if there's no one there!"

"That will take us a search warrant."

"Don't worry, we'll get one! I'll wake up every judge in the province if I have to!"

Mercure was left alone with Diane Masson. He told her a doctor would come and examine her shortly. She took a sip of her coffee, blew her nose again, and then asked him, "Do you believe that what I said to Hamel will make him think?"

"Well, when you said it to me yesterday afternoon, it made me think."

"About what?"

He smiled and said that it would be too complicated to explain.

"After the doctor examines you, one of my men will drive you back home if you want."

She nodded. Her gaze was suddenly distant and frightened.

"I saw him," she murmured. "I saw my daughter's murderer."

Mercure said nothing.

"It's horrible what Hamel's done to him," she added.

Mercure sighed and looked down for an instant. A shadow passed over Masson's eyes.

"When I saw him, when I realized that he was the one who had raped and killed my Charlotte, I . . . I felt something come back to life in me, something . . ."

She started to cry.

"I don't want the hate to come back! I can't go through that a second time. I can't!"

"It won't come back."

He ventured to take her hand.

"You're strong, you can fight it again. In fact, that's what you did by refusing to join Hamel. You've already won!"

She looked at him, her eyes filled with tears, and for the first time since she had come to the station, she smiled slightly.

———

There were more and more birds singing around Josh's cottage. Dawn was just breaking, but there was not a single cloud in the sky and it looked like the day was going to be beautiful.

In the bedroom, Bruno was lying on his back, covered in dried blood and vomit, with one arm hanging off the bed. His pupils were twitching under his closed eyelids, and a tic sporadically contorted his mouth. The silence in the house was complete except for the twittering from outside.

Several kilometers away, the police were about to begin searching all homes close to a lake or river.

It was five thirty-five, and Bruno's sleep was becoming more and more agitated.

———

The atmosphere in the squad room of the Drummondville station was electric. Pleau and Boisvert, who had been asked to come in early, had just arrived, still sleepy, and were being told about the latest developments. Boisvert didn't react much, but Pleau was so enthusiastic that she congratulated Mercure as if Hamel had already been found. Wagner felt obligated to set the record straight.

"Take it easy. We still have six municipalities to search. And there are lots of houses close to water in them. We might find him in half an hour—or in four hours. And in four hours, Lemaire might already be dead. We know Hamel intends to kill him today, but when exactly . . ."

"We'll just have to send more men," Pleau said.

"Just because Hamel is monopolizing our attention doesn't mean life has stopped in Drummondville. Right now, there's a store on fire downtown and I've got four guys there, so . . . As for the provincial police, they're doing what they can to help us."

"But I'm sure Hamel doesn't intend to kill Lemaire this morning."

"What do you know about it, Anne-Marie?"

She looked sheepish and did not answer. Everyone calmed down a little. Boisvert walked toward the door and Wagner asked him where he was going.

"I'm going to get some muffins. Didn't have time for breakfast this morning."

Mercure was lost in thought, leaning on a desk with his arms crossed. The chief asked him what he was thinking about.

"For him to kidnap that woman," Mercure answered, "he'd have to be really disturbed. He must be completely unhinged."

"So your plan worked. It proves that he's . . . how did you put it?"

"Gone off the rails."

"Yeah, he's gone completely off the rails . . ."

Both of them were silent. Because they were both thinking about the same thing: the unknown consequences of that. Either the train would just stop . . . or it would crash and kill all the passengers on board.

Wagner looked at the clock: five forty-four.

———

Bruno opened his eyes at seven thirty-eight.

The first thing he noticed was the smell. Then, when he tried to sit up, he couldn't help moaning: he had a splitting headache. Once he was in a sitting position, he saw the dried blood and vomit on the sheets and on his clothes. He ran his fingers through his hair, and nasty scabs fell to the mattress. He did not even have the strength to feel disgust.

For the moment, he felt nothing.

Grimacing with pain, he managed to stand up. Three hundred cannons were thundering in what felt like the remains of his skull. He considered lying down again in spite of the filth in the bed. But he couldn't sleep.

Not today.

He walked. The weight on his shoulders reminded him cruelly of its presence. After a century, he reached the hallway. He hesitated at the door to the monster's room. Would he again find a bloody, whimpering black dog? He went in. No, it was the monster, hunched on the floor like a pile of garbage with his wrists chained and his left eye closed. His breathing was labored, with the occasional disturbing rattle.

Bruno looked at him for a moment and went out again.

He walked to the living room so slowly that he barely seemed to be moving forward. He tripped over the empty bottles, saw the couch, and slumped down onto it, which set off another round of cannon fire in his head.

When he opened his eyes, he realized that the TV was still on. The morning-show host was smiling at a reporter, who was smiling at the camera and saying something.

He thought again about Diane Masson. About the monster transformed into a dog. About kicking him. And about the echoes of the blows. The echoes he still heard, that he had heard all night long in the chaos of his dreams.

Bruno no longer moved. He sat there with his mouth agape, his zombie eyes riveted on the screen that he did not see.

———

Seven forty-two.

The two men had resumed their night positions: Mercure sitting at his desk with his arms crossed, Wagner across from him, leaning against the wall with his hands behind his neck, gazing at the ceiling. There was a feeling of indescribable fatigue radiating from the two, although they had been doing practically nothing for almost two hours. Except wait. A little earlier, Mercure had tried to reach Sylvie Jutras, but in vain. If she was not home by this time, she must have left town. And he understood perfectly.

Neither had said a word for ten minutes when Mercure, his voice completely neutral, said, "I won't go see Demers anymore."

Wagner looked at him. In the same detached tone, Mercure added, "I don't regret having done it all these years, but now . . . it's enough. It's over."

With those words, he finally looked at Wagner. The chief did not say a word, but he nodded slightly.

They remained like that for three long minutes, without any discomfort.

The sudden ring of the telephone seemed out of place in such an atmosphere. Mercure was so lost in his thoughts that Wagner had to answer. It was Cabana, with a preliminary report: until now, most of the residents had been home when the police had visited (most of them had been woken up), and a few questions had been enough to dispel any suspicion. As for the empty houses, they had been searched, but in vain. There were still some cottages around Lac des Souris and Lake Eau Claire to be visited.

"It's sure taking a long time!" exclaimed the chief.

"But there's something else," continued Cabana. "The reporters know."

Mercure, who was listening on the speakerphone, stood up suddenly. Cabana explained that he had just finished visiting a house when a car pulled up—a reporter from TVA.

"He knew everything!" added Cabana. "He asked me how many houses, roughly, there were in the region that were close to a body of water!"

Wagner went to loosen his necktie, but realized it was already completely untied. He ordered Cabana not to tell the reporter anything.

"Of course not, except he's following me and I don't think he's going to give up! And a guy from the SQ told me he's had a reporter from Radio-Canada on his ass for the past ten minutes!"

"Let them follow you if they like, but don't say anything to them!" replied Wagner. "Pass the message along to everyone, understand?"

He hung up, cursing.

"In half an hour, it'll be crawling with reporters there," sighed Mercure.

"Maybe only Radio-Canada and TVA know?"

"For the time being, but like me, you know this is going to snowball."

"You think they intend to do a live report?"

"I don't know. Maybe during their morning shows, when they cover the breaking news."

Furious, Wagner paced back and forth for a few seconds. Then he made a decision: he was going to make a few phone calls and arrange things so that no TV or radio stations did any live reporting. He would argue that if the reporters alerted Hamel, it could endanger the life of the prisoner and even the lives of the police officers.

When Wagner had left the room, Mercure sat and thought for a moment, furiously rubbing his bloodshot eyes. He quickly walked to the squad room. Everyone looked at him uncomfortably—they knew about the reporters, obviously. But Mercure ignored them and turned on the TV. He flipped through the main channels. They were not talking about the search on any of them. He went back to his office, still without saying a word to anyone.

Twenty minutes later, Wagner joined him, calmer now although his face was still red.

"Okay. Not one TV or radio station is reporting it live this morning. Even so, the reporters will definitely be swarming around our guys. But they won't put anything on air before the noon news—unless we arrest him first. As soon as we have Hamel, they'll broadcast live. We don't know if Hamel watches television in the morning, but we can't take any chances."

"In fact," Mercure said finally, rubbing his cheek, "it wouldn't have changed anything at all."

Wagner didn't understand.

"What happened last night definitely sped up Hamel's change of plan," Mercure said. "I think he's made his decision. Consciously or unconsciously, he's made it. And whether or not he knows we're about to find him won't change his mind."

"And what do you think his decision is?"

Mercure opened his mouth, then closed it again and shook his head, biting his lip. Wagner walked around the desk and bent down in front of him, putting his hands on his shoulders.

"Listen, Hervé. You're right, we don't know. Besides, by this time, it could be too late, we both realize that. But let's make a deal, starting now. We act as if it is not too late. Okay? Otherwise, we'll fall apart."

Mercure looked at his superior. A little smile appeared on his lips, and he nodded and mumbled an "okay" that was both amused and sincere. Wagner agreed in turn. He stood up and quickly got serious again.

"If the reporters know, it means somebody here talked."

Mercure suddenly thought of Boisvert, who had gone out in the morning to get muffins.

He stood up and walked away from his desk. Wagner, intrigued, followed him. In the squad room, Mercure found Boisvert talking with Pleau. He said, loud enough for everyone to hear, "The reporters won't be able to broadcast live as long as we haven't arrested Hamel."

Then, directly to Boisvert, "Not too disappointed, Michel?"

Four astounded pairs of eyes turned toward Boisvert. For a good five seconds, he was as still as a statue, with his mouth open and his eyes wide. In another situation, he would have looked comical. He was acting innocent, but it was so fake that no one was fooled, and little by little, discomfort showed on all their faces.

"What, do you have any proof?" he asked, trying to defend himself but just digging himself in deeper. "One piece of evidence, just one!"

Mercure did not answer. All he did was look at Boisvert, not with blame, but with a kind of resigned sadness. Wagner glared at Boisvert, clenching his fists like a boxer waiting for the bell so he could demolish his adversary.

Boisvert finally realized that he had lost. He looked panicky and then, in self-defense, finally opted for arrogance.

"I don't regret it!"

"You goddamn idiot!" Wagner growled.

He grabbed Boisvert by the lapels and started shaking him, calling him every name in the book. Boisvert responded wildly, trying to look threatening but not daring to lash out, caught between fear and fury. Pleau and Pat stepped between the two men and urged them to calm down. They finally managed to get the chief to let go, though he kept peppering Boisvert with insults. During all this, Mercure stood apart, his face impassive.

"That's what you wanted, isn't it?" Wagner still fulminated. "You hoped the journalists would report live and that Hamel would see it on TV! So that he would hurry up and kill Lemaire!"

"Am I the only one who understands anything here?" exploded Boisvert. "If you think I'm going to just stand by while you save Lemaire's life!"

"You're a cop, Boisvert, you represent law and justice!"

"Since when does justice protect child murderers?"

"Don't you get it, you pigheaded fool? If we're trying to stop Hamel in time, it's precisely to protect him. We're not trying to protect Lemaire, we're trying to toss him in prison for twenty-five years!"

"Prison!" Boisvert laughed. "That's just what Lemaire must be hoping for now! He'll have it good in prison compared to what he's going through now! We'll be doing him a favor! The worst thing is that we'll be putting Hamel in prison too!"

"For not nearly as long—*if* we stop him in time!"

"It doesn't matter!" shouted Boisvert, shaking his head. "It's not right! Can't you see that, dammit? *It's not right!*"

They were all looking at him, shocked by this outburst. Even Wagner was quiet for a moment in spite of the rage that was swelling the veins in his neck. Alone in the middle of the circle that had formed around him, Boisvert continued to pour out his objections, but his voice trembled as if it was about to break.

"I have two kids, both under ten! Do you think . . . do you think I'd let anyone get away with doing *that* to them? Do you think I'm going to serve that kind of justice?"

"Come off it with this crap! What you're saying is purely emotional! It's not . . ."

"Yes, it's emotional!" interrupted Boisvert almost desperately, his eyes filling with tears, in contradiction with his angry expression. "Of course it's emotional! *Could it be anything else?*"

Silence. Mercure rubbed his forehead. He was tired, very, very tired. This melodramatic little scene seemed terribly banal to him. What he was seeing here was the eternal paradox of civilized man. Civilized, but always, irremediably, fatally human.

Boisvert wiped his eyes with a furtive gesture, embarrassed at being so close to tears.

"You're going to suspend me, is that it?"

"Suspend you?" exclaimed Wagner, recovering from shock. "I'll have you arrested as an accomplice! Because that's exactly what you—"

"Greg!"

It was Mercure. In a second, everyone's attention shifted to him. Wagner wondered if he should reprimand his inspector for his insolence, but he was too surprised to react. Mercure seemed to regret his tactless interruption and raised a hand in excuse. He said wearily, "Later . . ."

Now it was Wagner, suddenly drained, who rubbed his eyes. Boisvert asked with a touch of defiance, "What about me?"

Mercure glanced at him, not with contempt, but with total indifference.

"Go home. Get some rest."

Wagner did not even have the strength to protest. Boisvert hesitated for a second and finally let the fatigue and impotence show on his face. He left the station under the embarrassed gaze of the other officers.

For a long time, nobody spoke.

Suddenly, as if he had just made a firm decision, Mercure walked to the door. Wagner asked him where he was going.

"There. I want to be there when they arrest him. I want . . ."

Without stopping, he made a vague gesture.

". . . just to see him."

"It's an hour from here, Hervé!"

"I'll put on my siren and floor it."

He rushed out.

———

Officers Guy Ouellette and Karl Fulton of the provincial police were driving slowly along Pioneers Road, looking for the next house. They had just visited four houses on the shores of Lac des Souris, and according to their map, there were five or six more in the next three kilometers.

"There, just over there," Ouellette said, pointing to a little dirt lane ahead.

The car turned into the narrow, downward-sloping entrance, but it had to stop because of another vehicle partly blocking the lane, a blue-gray Honda Civic that had run into a tree. Ouellette frowned. Fulton, behind the wheel, chuckled.

"Some guy must have been pretty drunk last night."

"But why would he just leave it there? It doesn't look very badly damaged."

He asked Ouellette to check the license number of the car they were looking for. With a shrug, Fulton took out his notebook, but as he was reading the description of Diane Masson's car, his face became more sober. He raised his head to look at the license plate and double-checked it.

"Christ!" he said.

Ouellette just whistled through his teeth. Below they saw a little house partly hidden by trees.

Slowly the police car backed up and parked on Pioneers Road, and Fulton called the provincial police station.

Mercure received the call at eight forty-three. Since he had left Drum-mondville, he had been driving at breakneck speed with the siren wail-ing, and now, judging by the map unfolded on his knees, he was less than five minutes from Charette. As soon as he heard Wagner's excited voice, he knew Hamel had been found.

"Has he been arrested?" he asked, without taking his eyes off the road ahead of him.

"Not yet; we just found the house. Everything is quiet. He doesn't know he's been located. The guys are going to bust in and . . ."

"Wait, wait! Where is it exactly?"

Wagner gave the details while Mercure found Lac des Souris on the map. It was a little past Charette.

"Tell them not to do anything until I get there!" he insisted. "I'll be there in six minutes!"

"We really can't afford to wait, Hervé."

"Three minutes!"

He hung up and accelerated.

How long had he been sitting on the couch like this staring into space? Half an hour? An hour maybe? Impossible to say. The sun had gradually filled the living room and its rays now touched his face, but Bruno did not even notice.

Although his brain had not been registering the images on the tele-vision screen in front of him, one scene finally drew him out of his cata-tonia. It showed groups of demonstrators on quiet streets in the rain, fighting. Slowly he reached for the remote control and turned up the sound. The off-camera voice of a woman said, ". . . images filmed last night in the pouring rain. For the first time, the conflict between Bruno Hamel's supporters and opponents has gone from words to deeds, with altercations like the one shown here. There were a few injuries, but nothing serious. There have been scenes like this in at least three cities."

"It's incredible how big this story has gotten," said the off-camera voice of the anchor.

"Yes, and this latest wave of excitement is definitely due to the fact that today is the deadline set by Hamel. Tune in to the news at noon for more details."

Bruno looked at the images of angry people grabbing and threatening each other in the rain. One woman even tried to hit a young man with her sign, which read, "Real justice at last!" His face expressionless, Bruno closed his eyes and turned off the television with a limp hand.

Silence. Except for the echoes in his head. The echoes of the blows.

He felt a presence. Opened his eyes. Turned his head.

Jasmine was standing in the hallway.

For a few seconds, he had no reaction. Then he slowly got up and stood motionless, looking at his daughter . . . her torn blue dress, her arms and legs covered in blood, her bruised, swollen, lacerated face, her hair plastered down and dirty, and especially, especially, her eyes, so sad, so pained . . .

The silence was dizzying, as if there were no longer anything alive in the house, or outside, or anywhere else in the world.

He started to walk toward her, the weight on his shoulders making each step an ordeal. Jasmine watched him without reacting, her sad eyes riveted on him. He took her by the hand and led her to the bathroom. She followed obediently.

He undressed her. He washed her long chestnut hair until it was soft and shiny again, until its natural honey smell filled the room. With a wet towel, he cleaned her small body, wiped away all the blood, all the wounds, all the dirt. Then he attended to her face, washing her nose, mouth, cheeks, and eyelids with infinite gentleness, and the wounds disappeared under the towel. All in absolute silence. Even the running water made no sound.

There was only the echo of the blows.

Bruno finally put her blue dress, which was now clean and undamaged, back on her.

Sitting on the edge of the bathtub, he looked at his daughter in front of him. She was perfect, radiant, beautiful, and pure. As before. As she had always been. She looked at her father in silence, but the sadness had disappeared from her eyes. Bruno would have liked to hold her and hug her, but he was so dirty, so filthy, and she was so clean, so immaculate.

He took the blue ribbon out of his pocket. The cloth was clean now, with no trace of blood. He delicately tied his daughter's hair in a long, silky ponytail.

They looked at each other for a long time. Jasmine's rosy mouth turned up in a sweet, mischievous smile.

Bruno tried to smile too, but he was not able to.

The echoes prevented him.

---

When he was less than five kilometers from his destination, Mercure turned off the siren. A hundred meters away, he saw a group of some thirty people, six or seven police cars, and as many civilian cars. His heart started to beat faster and he breathed deeply.

He stopped, got out, and walked toward the police officers. They were standing and talking at the end of a little dirt road leading down into the woods. Six or seven reporters immediately surrounded him.

"Are you the officer in charge?"

"Are you going to order a surprise attack?"

"Do you think it's too late?"

"Listen," Mercure said with a patience he hadn't thought himself capable of. "I'm asking you to remain as quiet and discreet as possible until Hamel is arrested. The life of a man, perhaps even two, is at stake. If you interfere with our operation, I'll have you cleared out of here, freedom of the press notwithstanding."

His calm, authoritative tone had an effect. They all quieted down, although they looked disappointed. Mercure went over to the group of about fifteen police officers. The six from Drummondville, including Cabana, greeted him. The oldest man in the group put out his hand and introduced himself: Sergeant Normand Raîche of the SQ. He pointed to the dirt lane.

"All indications are that he doesn't know yet that we're here. It's been absolutely quiet down there. Maybe he's still asleep."

Mercure nodded and took a few steps down the lane. He could see the cottage below; it looked peaceful. So it was in that pretty little house that Hamel had been venting his fury for the past week.

He saw Diane Masson's car up against the tree, and he remembered his thought about Hamel losing it.

He returned to the group and looked around, rubbing his cheek. Not far away, the reporters were waiting, taking notes. Two of them were even speaking on camera, preparing material for a later broadcast. An ambulance from the hospital in Shawinigan was parked a little off to the side. A car passed and slowed down as the driver looked at the gathering with surprise, and then sped up again. They would have to close the road. Everybody in Saint-Mathieu-du-Parc must know what was happening by now. In ten minutes, the residents of the area would start showing up.

"This is your investigation, Mercure," Raîche said. "You're in command."

Mercure studied the police officers. They were all waiting, obviously nervous. They were with the SQ, but they were still small-town cops and they were not used to this kind of spectacular case.

But then, Mercure wasn't either.

He turned again toward the lane leading to the cottage, rubbing his cheek harder, his mind racing.

*It's over. You've done what you had to do. Now you're of no more use. What will happen, will happen.*

He bit his lip, irritated by the sun in his eyes.

"So what do we do now?" asked an officer.

———

Bruno went into the bedroom. He didn't even notice the smell of vomit anymore. He went to the desk where his revolver lay and looked at it for a few moments. The echoes in his head were not as strong, but they were still there. And he couldn't take it anymore.

He wanted those echoes to stop.

He took the revolver and left the room.

———

Mercure was deploying the officers. Three would go through the woods on the left, and three on the right. Three more, including Cabana, would go down the lane, and Mercure would go with them, with the megaphone Raîche had given him.

"We'll just approach as silently as possible, keeping hidden. We'll communicate by walkie-talkie. Nobody moves in until you get my signal. Got it?"

The officers all moved out, while the reporters looked on excitedly. Just as he was about to follow the others down the lane, Mercure saw three cars stop about fifty meters away and civilians get out. That was it, the curious onlookers were arriving.

"Hasn't the road been closed yet?"

"Closing Pioneers Road isn't that easy," Raîche explained. "It's the road that goes around the lake, and the local inhabitants . . ."

The onlookers came closer and one of them shouted, in a voice that fortunately was muffled by the distance, "Go for it, Hamel, kill the bastard!"

Mercure swore. Not another demonstration! And farther away, there were more cars arriving!

"It's imperative that you stop those people from getting close! Until we've arrested Hamel, I don't want to see or hear any of them. Is that clear?"

Raîche was already giving orders to his three remaining officers, who immediately hurried toward the onlookers.

Mercure looked toward the cottage. He saw the officers in the woods, crouching down and moving slowly toward the house.

"Let's go," he said to his three men.

And the four of them walked cautiously down the dirt lane.

Two minutes later, Mercure and his men were hiding behind Diane Masson's car. From Cabana's walkie-talkie, a low voice said, "All the men are in position. Whenever you're ready, Mercure."

Mercure gripped the megaphone with all his strength, his forehead covered in sweat. His eyes were riveted on the house. Silence. The curtains in every window were closed. Should he try to talk to Hamel? Break in? And what if it was already too late? The idea that Hamel had lost it was hammering in his head. And a thought crossed his mind again.

*There's nothing more you can do. It's all over.*

He decided to count to ten in his head and then give an order. Even though he didn't know what the order would be.

———

Bruno went into the monster's room. He was still lying on the floor, his chained arms extended in a cross on either side of his tortured body. His breathing was no more than a constant rasp, but he was conscious, because when he heard Bruno's footsteps, he tried to lift his head. Unable to do so, he just turned it a bit. When he recognized his tormentor, he gave what sounded like a sigh and closed his good eye.

Bruno stopped a few steps away from him. His expression was unusual, a strange mixture of hatred and discouragement. His head on the floor, the monster painfully opened his eye. When he saw the revolver, there was neither fear nor despair in his expression, only a kind of resigned relief. He turned his gaze and stared at something invisible, perhaps the nothingness that was gradually approaching.

Bruno was breathing a little faster. The revolver trembled slightly in his right hand. He opened his mouth and said in a harsh voice, "You killed my daughter."

The monster found the strength to recoil. He looked again at Bruno, and in spite of his exhaustion and suffering, shock contorted his mangled face. Bruno's breathing became irregular, and he gasped painfully. But he spoke again with more strength.

"You raped and killed my little Jasmine."

Then something broke inside him, as if he had been pushing against a window for too long and it had finally shattered and he had fallen. A terrible, frightening fall, but at the same time liberating, because the superhuman effort was finally over, and the body, in its fall, relaxed with a great cry.

"YOU KILLED MY DAUGHTER!"

And he burst into tears. He was sobbing so hard that he leaned both arms on his thighs and put his face down. The monster was still looking at him, his mouth open, his breath wheezing. Bruno felt something else disappearing with the tears. It was the weight on his shoulders, that terrible weight that had not let up since the coming of the darkness. It was suddenly diminishing, melting, evaporating through every pore of his skin, through every breath, every sob.

Bruno fell to his knees, crying harder and harder, more and more intensely, welcoming this new lightness.

———

They were all concealed around the cottage, waiting. Cabana, walkie-talkie in hand, was watching Mercure, waiting for him to give an order.

Just as Mercure was opening his mouth to speak, the shot rang out, causing dozens of birds in the woods to fly up into the air. All the police officers started, and one of them swore and stood up, nervously drawing his revolver. Above them on the road, there were cries of surprise. Mercure's voice, amplified by the megaphone, shouted, "Hamel, come out of the house and surrender!"

At those words, all the police officers leapt up, and a dozen revolvers were pointed toward the house. Mercure was distraught and breathing heavily behind the megaphone. Hamel had fired! It was too late! Too late!

"Hamel, I urge you to turn yourself in!" Mercure said desperately. "In twenty seconds, we are coming into the house!"

From the road above came a hysterical cacophony, in which the words "Bravo, Hamel!" were discernible.

Suddenly there was a second gunshot from inside the house, followed by absolute silence and paralysis. Even from the road above, there was no more sound. The police officers slowly lowered their weapons, resigned. Mercure turned pale and closed his eyes.

Suddenly, a creak: the door had opened.

As if they had received an electric shock, all the police officers crouched down again and raised their weapons at exactly the same moment. But immediately there was doubt. The man standing in the doorway looked like a refugee from hell—dirty, rumpled clothes, skin covered with blood and filth, thinning hair, several days' growth of beard, and a face so white, with dark rings under bloodshot eyes. For a brief moment, the police officers thought he was the victim. When they finally recognized that frightful face, all of them, including Mercure, were horrified and incredulous.

"My God," muttered Cabana, his weapon still pointed at Hamel.

Hamel took a few steps on the porch and looked grimly around him. He slowly raised his arms.

The police officers surrounded him and put him in handcuffs. Their speed and vigor contrasted sharply with the calm and resignation of their prisoner, who submitted passively without looking at anyone in particular and without uttering a sound.

Two police officers went into the cottage, including Cabana. The smell that assailed them was so horrible that they hesitated a moment, looking uneasily at the terrible disorder surrounding them. Quickly noting that the kitchen and living room were empty, they ran to the hallway, weapons still drawn, and went into the bedroom on the left.

They stopped immediately. Lemaire's body was hunched on the floor. Cabana grimaced in revulsion. The other officer put his hand over his mouth, suddenly nauseated. There was a revolver lying on the floor.

The Drummondville policeman was putting his walkie-talkie to his mouth to inform Mercure that Lemaire was dead when the body suddenly opened his good eye and feebly turned his head. His mouth hanging open, the officer slowly lowered the radio, while his colleague opened his eyes wide with horror.

Cabana noticed a detail: the two chains attached to Lemaire's wrists were broken.

———

Mercure watched the police officers escorting Hamel off the porch. Still standing by the Honda Civic, he did not move. He was no longer holding the megaphone, but instead a walkie-talkie. He was waiting, resigned.

A voice finally came from the radio.

"Lemaire isn't dead!"

Mercure blinked.

"The two shots were to break the chains on his wrists!" Cabana explained.

Mercure leaned against the car and gave a very long sigh.

"But send the paramedics in right away," Cabana continued. "He's in really bad shape!"

They must have gotten the message up on the road, because ten seconds later, the two paramedics rushed past Mercure with their stretcher and went into the house.

Mercure remained there for a few moments, leaning against the car with his left hand to his head. Finally, he turned toward the house. Hamel, in handcuffs, was accompanied by five or six police officers, all of them completely silent, awed by his nightmarish appearance and paradoxical calm. When he came within a few meters of Mercure, Hamel turned his head toward him and the two men looked at each other for the first time. Mercure knew Hamel recognized him. He smiled sadly and nodded slightly. Hamel, still walking, continued to stare at him for a moment, and then he too gave a little nod. Without smiling.

The little group had not even reached the road when the reporters came running, shouting questions, while the cameramen jostled to get as close as possible. Wearied by the idea of facing the media circus, Mercure turned his back and walked down the lane. He met the paramedics, who were hurrying back up. He had time to see Lemaire, lying on the stretcher, hooked up to an IV, with an oxygen mask over his mouth. Mercure glumly followed the stretcher with his eyes, and then continued on his way. He thought for a moment of going into the cottage, but decided against it. Later, not now. Instead, he walked down to the shore of the lake.

He looked at the sparkling expanse of water rippling with calm little waves. The thought of Madelaine crossed his mind.

He tilted his head back and, as if trying to inhale all that light, took a deep breath.

———

On the television, a special live report stated that Bruno Hamel had finally been found on the very day he was supposed to kill his hostage.

"But to everyone's surprise," announced the excited reporter, "he gave himself up without even trying to kill his victim! We can see him coming now, behind me. I'll see if I can get closer . . ."

The shaky camera managed to capture the frightening image of a ghostlike figure, handcuffed and surrounded by police.

At the Drummondville station, a dozen officers were watching the broadcast and applauding. Wagner, standing in the midst of them, nodded his head with satisfaction. He tied his necktie and sat down comfortably, sighing with contentment.

"So, Greg, it's a total victory. Right?" Bolduc said with a smile.

The chief opened his mouth to answer, but then he saw the image of Lemaire on the screen, lying on a stretcher, his face mangled, one eye missing, hooked up to an IV. He closed his mouth again, his face suddenly dark, and did not answer Bolduc.

At his house, Gaétan Morin was watching the special report as he ate his breakfast, raging inside. Goodbye to the seven thousand dollars he should have had today so he could bet it tonight at the track! His wife, sitting across from him, was also watching the images, and she was shaking her head sorrowfully.

"My God, the poor man. I can hardly imagine what a hellish week he must have gone through."

Morin chewed his toast energetically, thinking about the ninety thousand dollars he had lost in less than two weeks. He had the feeling his day would be long and depressing.

Josée Jutras was also watching the special report. When she saw her brother-in-law on the screen, she put her hand over her mouth in horror and her eyes filled with tears. She had to warn Sylvie! She stood up and went to the guest bedroom.

Sylvie was sleeping, holding the framed photo of Jasmine against her body. Josée thought to herself that this was the first night since her arrival that her sister had gone without crying, and the first morning she had slept in so late. Josée found that thought so comforting that she did not have the heart to wake Sylvie. In any case, she would know soon enough.

So she closed the door again and Sylvie continued sleeping peacefully, with Jasmine's smiling face against her breast.

———

When Bruno walked past that gaunt, weary man who looked at him so insistently, he knew right away he was Mercure. He could tell from his eyes.

So that was him. The one who had harassed him, who had been so relentless in getting into his head and undermining him. The one who, without his ever having seen him in person, had been with him all week. The one Bruno had hated so much.

He did not hate him anymore. The bitterness was gone, like the weight that had been on his shoulders. And, above all, like the echoes of the blows in his head.

But not the filter over his eyes, the filter that dulled the color of everything he saw. Bruno knew it would always be there now. It was through that filter that he saw Mercure smile sadly as he nodded.

It was through the filter that he saw the reporters rushing toward him even before they reached the road. They were holding out their microphones and pointing their cameras, asking a thousand questions at the same time. Without letting go of Bruno's arms, the police officers tried to push them back. Bruno ignored them completely.

When they reached the road, Bruno looked around. More police officers were standing to the side looking at him, some with horror, others with relief, some even with pity. Farther away, about forty people were shouting at him, either insults or approval, but all with the same rage. They wanted to get close to him, but the police kept them away, which made them furious. Bruno stared at them with a weariness bordering on contempt. Finally he looked at the ambulance and saw Lemaire being put inside. Bruno remained expressionless.

Around him, in spite of the efforts of the police, the reporters continued to bombard him with a cacophony of questions. One of them, a woman, spoke louder than the rest and Bruno was able to make out her words over those of the others.

"Bruno Hamel, you kidnapped your daughter's murderer and tortured him for a week. Do you believe this kind of action solves anything?"

Bruno turned to the reporter and looked at her for a moment, then answered flatly, "No."

Everyone was silent, waiting anxiously for him to say more. But Bruno kept looking at them gravely and added nothing.

The reporter, excited by her advantage, asked further, "So do you regret what you've done?"

Bruno appeared to think, made a face, and said in an annoyed tone, "No."

As the flurry of questions continued, the officers put him in the police car. Thirty seconds later, it drove away, pursued by the shouts of the frustrated demonstrators.

# ACKNOWLEDGMENTS

I would like to thank Dr. Valérie Bédard for her advice on medical matters.

I would like to thank Sergeant Michel Poirier and lawyer Jérôme Gagner for their advice on legal matters.

I would like to thank Bernard Rioux, Jean Mercier, and Maher Jahjah for their advice on computers and electronics.

I would like to thank René Flageole, Éric Tessier, Marc Guénette, Julie Senécal, and Camille Séguin, who read the first draft of this novel, and whose advice assisted me greatly in writing the final version.

I would like to thank Jean Pettigrew, who does not miss a single inconsistency and who continues to believe in what I am doing.

Thank you to my beloved children, Nathan and Romy, without whom this novel would surely never have been written.

Thank you to everyone at Simon & Schuster, especially Laurie Grassi, who has given me the opportunity to reach an English audience and has been a pleasure to work with.

Thank you, finally, to my sweet Sophie for her intelligent advice and her understanding of the foibles of the writer she shares her life with.

PATRICK SENÉCAL

Turn the page for a sneak peek at Patrick Senécal's next novel

# SILENT MOVE

Coming to bookstores in 2020

Translated by Howard Scott & Phyllis Aronoff

Crazy.

Such an ordinary word, used without rhyme or reason. But it's the first and only word that comes to mind at the moment. So I write it down. I don't care if it's a cliché. Originality is not what I'm concerned about now. I'm not an author. I'm a prisoner. Some will say there are similarities, but I don't have much of a head for theorizing.

Crazy, but there you have it. Frankly, I can't think of anything better. After these last three days, I have developed a deeper understanding of the word.

Three days.

It's really rather ironic. I had insisted on having something to write on, and now I have enough paper to copy out the entire Koran, but I'm completely empty. In fact, no, it's the opposite: I'm too full.

This is the first time I'm going to write about myself. I've already written some insignificant little poems, a few pseudo-intellectual short stories, but nothing really personal. Never felt the need. Until now. I need to get things off my chest and put my emotions, my fears, my questions down on paper. And my hopes, perhaps. If I ever get out of here

(God, just writing those seven words is so terrifying), I'm not at all sure I'll want anyone to read what I'm writing. I'm not writing this for anyone else.

I want to write for myself. It's my only possible escape. For now, at least. To write down events in order, that in itself will be liberating. Maybe it will help me see things more clearly.

Okay. Here we go.

It all started three days ago. Or, to be precise, on Friday, September 20, 1991. My classes at the Literature Institute were supposed to start on Monday. I had only been in Montcharles for three days, and since I didn't know this town of twenty-five thousand, I decided to take advantage of the last nice days of summer by biking around the area. At around eleven thirty, I was pedaling at a leisurely pace through the sleepy streets of the town. I made my way downtown, which was pretty but quiet, and stopped for lunch in a snack bar. It's hardly an exciting town, but since I come from Drummondville, I wasn't expecting much. In any case, I was planning to spend the weekends with Judith in Sherbrooke, only about twenty kilometers from here. So that would mean studying all week and partying all weekend. A normal schedule for any self-respecting student, right?

After lunch, I continued exploring. There were residential neighborhoods one after the other, all alike, just a series of identical, cold new houses. But I eventually found myself in an area that was a little older, and therefore more attractive, with lots of trees, no sidewalks, and not much traffic. I turned onto a street called Elm Street, which was a little isolated and had even more trees. Behind the row of houses, there was a big field. I felt a little pang of nostalgia; I had grown up near woods, and many of my happiest childhood moments were spent hanging from the branches of those trees behind my parents' house. I pedaled idly down this street, finding it more and more welcoming—widely spaced houses that were pretty, not modern, with a couple of people outside, working in their yards.

The street ended at a yellow wire mesh fence on which a sign had been hung: "END." Without getting off my bike, I leaned against the fence. On the other side, there were a few trees, then a steep gravel slope that went down about ten meters to a narrow, brownish river. On the other side of the water, wild nature reigned. No houses and no roads. I stayed there a few minutes contemplating the quiet river, before looking around. To my left, there was a wide vacant lot. The houses only started again about fifty meters on. To my right, near the fence, stood a two-storey house, a rather ordinary brown brick structure that must have been about sixty years old. It did have a certain charm, a reassuring tranquillity, maybe because it was a little isolated from the others. I turned back to the river and took a deep breath. I felt good. I was happy to be in this calm town. I thought about Judith. I would call her this evening. I would tell her I was happy. That I loved her.

I turned my bike around and headed off again.

I hadn't gone three meters when the damn cat appeared.

To think some people don't believe in luck. There is absolutely no doubt in my mind that luck exists. I almost ran it over with my bike. It came out of nowhere, a meter from my front wheel. I tried to avoid it, but you can't avoid luck. I wrenched the handlebars and I felt everything jam. My gears gave a grating groan, and a second later, I experienced the sensation of free fall for the first time.

I struggled to my feet, holding my arms and cursing. I had a scrape or two on my hands and a slightly wounded pride, but I would survive. I looked around—there was nobody on the street, and the two or three people working in their yards in the distance hadn't noticed anything. I could already feel my ego recovering. My bike had been less fortunate. The chain had come off, the handlebars were out of alignment, and the front wheel was badly twisted. Since I'm the type who breaks three fingers hammering a nail, I decided to call a taxi instead of trying to fix it.

I abandoned the remains of my ten-speed and started walking toward the big two-storey house, the one that was a little isolated from the rest. More proof that luck likes to play with us. If I had crashed a little farther away, nothing would have happened. Nothing.

This thought alone is enough to make me cry with rage.

I saw the cat disappear under the fence.

If I ever manage to get out of this nightmare, I'll offer a reward of a thousand dollars to anyone who brings me its skinned corpse. No, strike that—anyone who brings it to me alive. I'll skin it myself.

The house had three windows on the ground floor, and between the first and the second one, there was a door. The second floor also had three windows, but the first one was strangely darker than the others. Curtains? It didn't look like it.

There was a yard on the left and another door on the side. I walked up the asphalt driveway, where a car was parked. There was a taxi light on the roof of the car, an old brown Chevy. Well, well. I wouldn't turn down a little good luck.

I rang the doorbell. There was a big yard behind the house, surrounded by a high cedar hedge. Beyond that, were woods.

I checked my watch: two thirty. I rang again. The taxi convinced me to persist.

Finally, the door opened. The man must have been in his early forties and he was a little shorter than my five feet eleven. He blinked, unsure, looking surprised to see me. I explained to him what had happened, pointing to the remains of my bike in the street. The man listened to me, a bit suspicious. The little brown mustache and the mop of curly chestnut hair on his head made him look like a has-been pop singer. The typical suburbanite. He stepped outside and looked toward the street. When he saw my bike, his ridiculous mustache curled up in a wide smile and his suspicions dissolved.

"Ah, you crashed your bike!"

It seemed to reassure him. I don't know why. He looked at me, still smiling, as if I'd just told him a good joke. He even started laughing.

"Because of a cat. Ha! That's a good one! If you'd hit it you would have come out of it better. I've never trusted bicycles myself. More dangerous than cars."

I smiled in spite of myself. He had a corny sense of humor, but he seemed nice enough.

Nice.

I explained that I wanted to call a taxi.

"I'm a taxi driver myself. What luck, eh? Only I'm not on duty this afternoon and . . . I'm really busy right now."

He looked like he was actually sorry.

"No problem. Do you mind if I call one?"

He hesitated a moment, looking inside the house. He rubbed his mustache as if he were weighing the pros and cons of my request. Would it bother him that much? He was dressed in a pair of old jeans and an old T-shirt. There were stains on his clothes. He looked like he was in the middle of fixing something.

"Listen, I could go to the house next door if you're too . . ."

"No, no, of course not!" he exclaimed suddenly, smiling again. "Come in, come in."

I stepped directly into a big, strangely decorated kitchen: green wallpaper with a pattern of mauve flowers, caramel-brown cabinets, and a corn-yellow fridge. It hurt my eyes. To my left, there was a staircase to the second floor, and under the stairs was a door locked with a padlock. In front of me, near the stove, there was a wide doorway to the dining room.

The man was starting to show me where the telephone was when the front door opened and a woman entered. She stopped short and stared at me in stunned silence. She was holding a little girl by the hand.

"Maude!" The man seemed surprised. "Your walk didn't last long."

He looked annoyed, as if he was criticizing her. As for the woman, she was still staring at me. She actually looked scared.

"This young fella just crashed his bicycle, right in front of the house. Because of a cat!"

He laughed. Obviously, my accident was an inexhaustible source of amusement to him. The woman finally looked reassured. A little, at least. She was quite tall, with graying chestnut hair cut in a square hairdo, not very pretty. Her smile looked a little forced. I guessed her to be about forty-five, but her weary expression might have aged her.

"This is my wife, Maude."

I smiled politely. She blushed, averted her eyes, and said quickly in a weak voice, "I'll take Anne to her room."

The little girl, who must have been about six, was tiny and thin and had long black hair. She didn't say a word and didn't budge an inch. Really docile. She let herself be led by her mother.

Just as she was about to start up the stairs, the woman stopped abruptly and stammered to her husband, "Unless . . . it's too early . . . for me to go up?"

The man's expression changed. He suddenly looked ill at ease. In a forced voice, he asked, "Uh, no, why do you ask?"

He accompanied this false question with an icy, disapproving glare. I had no idea what was going on, but I didn't like the atmosphere. I wasn't in the mood to witness a domestic row. I just wanted to call my taxi and leave. Finally, the woman lowered her eyes, looking confused, and climbed the stairs, still holding her silent daughter's hand.

The man turned to me. He seemed to be in a good mood again. "The telephone is in the living room. You can go through the dining room. It's in the back. I'll go get your bicycle off the street and we can put it in the trunk of the taxi when it comes."

I thanked him, and he went outside. Then I noticed the little cuts on my hands were bleeding a little more than I'd realized. I went to the sink and turned on the tap. At that moment, Maude came down to the kitchen and I explained to her that I wanted to wash my hands. She looked at me for a long while in silence, almost intimidated. She had big, dark, magnificent eyes. Too bad they were so afraid. She finally said in her small voice, "You should disinfect them too."

"That's not really necessary."

"Oh yes, or else they'll get infected. There's disinfectant in the bathroom upstairs—the second door on the right."

And she lowered her eyes, as if frightened and surprised at having spoken so much. As I climbed the stairs, I saw her open a cupboard, grab a broom, and start sweeping the floor mechanically, as if she wasn't aware of what she was doing.

I climbed the steps. I imagined the kind of couple they were. He was the macho good ol' boy, master of the house. She was the submissive wife, her life dreary and sad. Some clichés are accurate.

A long, windowless hallway ran the length of the second floor. I passed the first two doors, one on the left and the other on the right. Both were closed. A few steps later I stopped in front of another door on the left and put my hand on the knob. Then I remembered that the bathroom was on the right, but I had already opened the wrong door. It was a bedroom, and it was dark. I could make out the silhouette of the little girl sitting on the bed. She turned her head toward me.

"Don't be afraid. Your mom told me I could come upstairs. I was looking for the bathroom and got the wrong door. I'm sorry."

She looked at me silently, and in spite of the dim light, I could see that she was pale, as if she were ill. Which was perhaps the case, because shouldn't she have been in school?

"You're not afraid of me, are you?"

She stared at me, still without a word. Her eyes were huge and jet-black—deep. Like the big pupils of a lifeless fish. Her long ebony hair elongated her pale face. Frankly, she intrigued me. What was she doing there, sitting all alone in the semidarkness?

"You should open your curtains. The sun is shining outside."

She didn't move, not a hair, and still said nothing as she looked at me with her big, gawking eyes. I wouldn't want to have a kid who looked like that. Definitely not.

I gently closed the door again. She must be sick. That must be it.

There were two doors left. The one at the far end was closed and the other one on the right was open, revealing the bathroom. I quickly found the disinfectant, and cleaned and dried my hands.

It was when I returned to the hallway that I heard the groan.

Not a sigh or a murmur, but a real groan. Of fatigue, of fear, or of suffering, I couldn't really say. I thought of the little girl, but a second groan told me it was coming from behind the door at the end of the hall. I walked toward it without feeling afraid yet. Why would I be afraid? I was sure everything was okay; I was starting classes in a few days, I was going to call a taxi in two minutes, and the house seemed completely normal. There was no reason for a mere moan to make me afraid. It could have been anything. When I heard the sound a third time, I simply knocked on the door and called out innocently, "Is everything okay?" At the fourth moan, I went ahead and opened the door slowly, already prepared to apologize.

What an idiot. What business was it of mine anyway?

The first thing I noticed was the walls of the room. They were bare and an atrocious sickly green color. And there were stains. When I saw them, I immediately said to myself, God, that's blood! Was that when I started being afraid? No, not really. Everything was happening too fast.

The room was totally empty, not a piece of furniture—no bed, nothing. Just a lightbulb hanging from the ceiling and someone in the corner, lying facedown on the floor, wearing a pale blue shirt and faded jeans. There was more blood on the floor under the person—too much blood.

"What . . . what the hell happened to you?"

I had absolutely no thoughts in my head. I saw someone who was moaning, lying in his own blood, and the question came out all by itself.

The guy lifted his head. In spite of his face being completely covered in blood, I could see his eyes turned toward me. His moan took the shape of words, and I made out "Help me . . ."

I was finally scared. And that fear was summed up in a shout screamed silently by my entire soul: *Get the hell out of here now!*

I turned around and hurried down the hallway. I didn't run. In spite of my fear, part of me was saying that it would be foolish to run. Running would be a confirmation that I really was in danger.

I saw the stairway at the end of the hallway, far away. Suddenly, I could hear the voice of the man downstairs.

"You let him go upstairs? Dammit, what were you thinking?"

"But . . . but you told me . . . you told me I could go upstairs! I thought . . . I said to myself that if you'd finished, that . . . nobody was up there anymore."

I heard someone quickly climbing the stairs. I started running, but the man appeared at the end of the hallway and I stopped short. We sized each other up for a brief moment. His friendly expression had given way to a mistrustful stare and he asked me where I was coming from.

"From the bathroom. Your wife told me I could come upstairs . . ."

To my surprise, my voice sounded perfectly normal. My face must have looked normal too because the man hesitated.

"Why were you running?"

"I wasn't running." This time, my voice betrayed me a bit.

The man screwed up his eyes, then his gazed moved behind me. I realized he'd seen the open door.

"You saw him, didn't you?"

"Who?"

My voice sounded like a cracked whistle. This wasn't working at all now.

He nodded gently, his face dark.

"You saw him."

Suddenly, I lost it. My voice got as shrill as a child's and I started to scream.

"What happened to that guy? Did you do that to him? Why did you do that to him? Were you trying to kill him? What's going on here? You did that to him, didn't you? Why? He's covered in blood. Why? He . . . you . . . What's the matter with him? Is it you? Is it you?"

I stopped for a second, and then I said coldly, "I'm leaving."

I started walking, convinced that nothing could stop me from leaving. When the man grabbed me by the shoulders to stop me, I was shocked and indignant. I started yelling that I wanted to get out of there immediately, squirming like a child having a temper tantrum.

I saw his fist go up, but I didn't understand why. Stupidly, I assumed he was shooing a fly or something. A second later, I was punched in the nose for the first time in my life. The effect was explosive. Everything started spinning, and my vision went blurry. As I was reeling, I admitted to myself that I was in danger. You don't just hit decent people like that, especially when they've just had a little accident—an unfair accident too, caused by a damn black cat.

The man grabbed me under my arms and dragged me with my heels trailing on the floor. I had no strength to fight back. I heard a door open. Then, I was thrown. I collapsed on something soft. A bed. I was on my back and my vision gradually cleared. Above me a face—long, white, disturbing—was staring at me shamelessly. The little girl. I was in her room. A ray of hope. In a soft, unsteady voice, I asked her to go get help.

"Anne," roared a voice, "get out of your room now!"

The little girl didn't move. I managed to reach a hand toward her. I was still having trouble speaking. I repeated, "Go . . . get . . . help."

She stared at my hand for a long time and then her eyes turned back to my face. Two big, dull eyes, empty, without surprise, pity, or fear—nothing. It was awful. I think I moaned.

I heard grumbling, half-angry, half-disgusted, and the little girl was pulled away. I closed my eyes, gathered all my strength, and finally managed to sit up, just in time to see the door close again. After a few seconds, I stood up. I was terribly dizzy, and felt like vomiting as I staggered to the door and turned the knob. Locked.

From the outside?

I pulled on the knob, pounded the door, and shouted for someone to open it. I quickly looked around the room. A child's bedroom, but soulless. Decorated, but joyless. Dolls and drawings, but sad and dusty. I walked over to the window and pulled back the curtains. The sun poured into the room, blinding me. I tried to open the window. Impossible.

I looked for something to throw, or a stick. There was a little child's chair. I grabbed it and threw it against the window. It bounced off with a strange noise, but not a single crack appeared in the window. I picked up the chair again and hit the window two, three, four times with all my strength. The window shook, but didn't break.

An unbreakable window.

I looked at the window for several seconds, completely bewildered.

I pressed my face against the glass and started yelling for help. But outside the window, there was only the vacant lot. The houses to the left were too far away for anyone to see me.

Then I heard sounds. I moved away from the window and listened. A door opened to my left. No doubt it was the door of the room at the end of the hallway, with the horrible bloodstained green walls, where the . . . the . . .

I heard heavy footsteps in the next room, the sound of someone crawling, terrified little cries. Then, a dull thud. And another. Silence. Then something—or someone—was dragged past my door. Next I heard the man's voice, out of breath and furious, shouting, "Maude, I told you your walk was too short! Go for another twenty-minute stroll with your daughter."

Ten seconds later, a door closed downstairs. The dragging sound immediately started again in the hall, moving farther away. Footsteps on the stairs, accompanied by intermittent noises, thunk . . . thunk . . . thunk. His head . . . the poor guy's head was banging on every step of the staircase.

This image propelled me against the door, and I started yelling again, begging for the door to be opened. I was in a state of total panic. I was certain the man was going to come back upstairs and give me the same treatment the other guy had received. Then I would be dragged down the hallway, it would be my head thumping on the steps . . .

I pounded the door with both fists, screaming. I finally stopped, out of breath, and listened again. Someone was coming up the stairs. I backed up a few steps, afraid, without taking my eyes off the door. Two seconds ago, I had been begging for it to be opened, but now I didn't really want it to be. The footsteps came closer, accompanied by a metallic squeaking, as if something was being rolled. The sounds went past my door. I guessed they were now in the terrible green room. I pressed my ear to the wall—muffled sounds of wet rubbing. The room was being washed. The blood was being cleaned up.

I felt like I was going to be sick.

Dizzy again, I sat down on the bed. After a few minutes, I heard the metallic squeaking again in the corridor and then it disappeared down the stairs.

The man would come back. He'd come back, open the door, and laugh and explain everything to me. Because it was a misunderstanding. Obviously. My nice bike ride couldn't end like this. It was impossible. Yes, that's the right word: impossible.

A misunderstanding.

A key in the lock. I leapt to my feet and stood in the middle of the room, my eyes riveted on the door.

It was the man. He was holding a gun at hip level. I don't know anything about firearms, but it looked like a hunting rifle, and the barrel was pointing straight at me. I never took my eyes off that weapon.

"Out," the man said.

I hesitated. What did he mean? Get out of the room? Out of the house? Leave?

I walked toward the door, and the man stepped back to let me pass. I found myself in the hallway.

"Go into the room behind you."

He meant the green room.

So it wasn't a misunderstanding after all.

I didn't move. He repeated the order with a hint of impatience in his voice. My eyes were still riveted on the barrel of the weapon. I had a feeling a snake or some other unsavory creature was going to come out of it. I started to back away. No way was I going to turn my back on that rifle. We went into the green room. There was no sign of the dying man or his blood. Total emptiness.

My back bumped against the wall. No choice but to stop. The man stood unmoving in the middle of the room for a few seconds, his weapon still pointing in my direction. I heard him sigh, then say only, "Okay."

I started crying. It was too much for me. Not loud, painful sobbing, just big tears flowing from my eyes, accompanied by weak moans. I was going to die. I knew it. He was going to kill me, and I was going to die for nothing, without ever knowing why. That idea was more horrible, more harrowing than death itself.

My legs were starting to go rubbery when I heard the man say, "What am I going to do with you now?"

Did I dare hope? I finally looked at him. He didn't look crazy or enraged. Or even dangerous, in spite of the weapon pointed at me. He just looked . . . annoyed. He had his rifle in one hand and was rubbing his mustache with the other as he looked at me with puzzlement, like someone who had to go to a boring party and was wondering how he could get out of it. His expression struck me as so incongruous that I immediately stopped crying. He laughed, as amused and jovial as he'd been before.

"You're wondering too, aren't you?" He chuckled again.

I couldn't believe it. He was threatening me with a gun and found it funny!

In a sniveling voice, I begged him not to kill me. He seemed dismayed by this and said he had no intention of killing me. Once again, tears streamed down my cheeks, but this time they were tears of relief.

"You thought I was going to kill you?" he said with a shocked expression. "What gave you that idea?"

How could I answer that? He'd hit me and was threatening me with a gun, and he wondered where I'd gotten that idea? Even if I explained it to him, I didn't think he'd understand. He simply did not seem to grasp what was happening, what was *really* happening. I considered the possibility that this man was crazy, clinically insane. But was it possible? Was it possible for a crazy person, a really crazy person, to live in a house with his family?

I thought again about the woman, and the little girl . . .

"Oh, come on, kid, I'm not going to kill you, of course not. You can put that idea right out of your head."

Now I was really sobbing. Just knowing that I was going to live unhinged me.

"It was the sight of that guy all covered in blood that got to you, huh? The guy, the blood, the rifle . . . Yeah . . . Yeah, I can understand that . . ."

Downstairs, a door opened. The man didn't even react. I finally dared to speak. My voice still trembling, I asked without even thinking, "The other guy . . . is he dead?"

He turned serious again and looked at me for a long time. I was still waiting for an answer. If he said yes, I would go into hysterics again. But what he did was worse: he totally ignored my question.

"I won't kill you, because you haven't done anything wrong. Basically, you just saw something you shouldn't have seen. That wasn't your fault, was it?"

He gave me a friendly smile, as if to show his goodwill. I've never seen someone go from one expression to another so quickly, changing emotions with such volatility. It was so unsettling that I almost forgot my fear. Almost.

"Hey, wasn't your fault, was it, kid?"

"No," I finally answered. "No, not my fault at all."

He nodded and added, more solemnly, "You have to be just. Always."

Perhaps he wasn't so out of touch with reality after all. It was as if he understood my misfortune, my innocence in this whole business. After a brief silence, he added, "Except I can't let you go . . ."

He sighed.

"You've seen things. Almost nothing, but enough to get me in trouble. When you leave here, you're going to run to the police and tell them you saw a half-dead guy in a quiet little house . . ."

I told him no, I'd never do such a thing. When I left there, I'd be so happy that I wouldn't say anything to anyone. And, when I said that, I wasn't lying. The idea of notifying the cops hadn't yet occurred to me.

"I believe you," the man said softly. "I'm sure that right now you mean what you're saying. But later, once you're home again, once you've calmed down . . . then, you'll start thinking . . ."

He tapped his forehead with his index finger, looking serious again.

"Your good citizen's conscience will tell you that you can't let a dangerous fellow like me remain at large . . . Because that's what you think, isn't it? That I'm dangerous? Because of what you've seen, you're convinced I'm a dangerous man, aren't you?"

His voice was gradually getting louder and he was clutching his weapon. Terrified by his growing anger, I assured him that I would say nothing, that I knew nothing about him, that I didn't know him . . . anything I could think of to try to convince him. But his voice got even louder, his mouth twisted, and he took two steps toward me.

"Don't bullshit me. I know people, you know. I know all of you. You see just one detail, one thing out of context, and that's it, you judge! A half-dead guy in my house, so that means I'm a criminal, right? That's what you think, all of you!"

He was shouting now, his eyes dilated with rage, the rifle shaking in his hands. I pressed myself against the wall, as if I hoped to melt into the plaster.

"You don't know," he screamed. "You don't know anything, you don't understand. You know nothing!"

He finally fell silent, out of breath. Petrified by this explosive reaction, I stared at the shaking barrel of the rifle. The man suddenly shut his eyes, grimacing, and slapped his temple with his right hand. He stood like that for several seconds, biting his lip, as if he had a huge pain in his skull and he was waiting for it to pass. During that brief respite, what struck me was the little noises coming from downstairs, from the kitchen—pots and pans, chairs being moved, the sounds you hear in a normal house. The man had gone berserk, and yet downstairs, the daily routine continued, as if . . . as if . . .

The man's features relaxed and he opened his eyes, visibly relieved. His face was still a little red, damp with sweat, but his gaze was serene. Yes, serene. He even gave me an apologetic little smile . . . the man who, ten seconds before, had looked like he was going to eat me raw.

"Anyway," he said with a vague wave of his hand, "I'm sure you understand what I mean."

There was no longer any doubt that he was crazy.

I repeated to him that I wouldn't say anything to anybody. I asked him to let me go. But he refused, said it was too risky. He explained this to me with a sad expression. Yes, sad. Shit. Was there a single human feeling that hadn't passed over that chameleon face?

I stopped crying, suddenly angry. "What are you going to do with me? If you don't kill me and you don't let me go, what are you going to do?"

He sighed and scratched his head, with the expression of someone struggling with an annoying little domestic problem. He clearly didn't realize, didn't grasp the gravity, the insanity of the situation. For the first time—and not the last—I wondered why I'd decided to turn down that street on my bike.

"I don't know . . . I really don't know."

He stroked his mustache, then announced in a decisive tone that he'd think about it. With those words, he walked toward the door, ignoring me. Before leaving the room, he gave me a reassuring smile.

The door closed, and I heard the sound of a key in the lock. I went to the door and, just going through the motions, tried to open it. Locked, of course.

Another room with a door that locked from the outside.

And that unbreakable window in the girl's bedroom . . .

This wasn't a house. It was a prison.

No more energy to shout or pound the door. No more adrenaline to struggle. I slumped down in a corner of the room and sat on the floor to wait. One sentence endlessly went through my head: *It'll be okay. It'll be okay.*

I sat still for about an hour. Then . . .

But now I have to stop for a bit. I've been writing steadily for a couple of hours and I can't feel my hand anymore. A little break for a few minutes. Afterward, I'll continue. I want to finish. Before they come back . . .